Harry

— CORAL CANYON COWBOYS —

LIZ ISAACSON

ISBN-13: 978-1-63876-380-2

The Young Family

Welcome to Coral Canyon! The Young family is BIG, and sometimes it can be hard to keep track of everyone.

<u>This is updated through Harry (Sept 3, 2024).</u>

Here's how things are right now:

Jerry and Cecily Young, 9 sons, in age-order:

1. TEX

Wife: Abigail Ingalls

His son: Bryce (30)

Children he and Abby share: Melissa (12), Carver (8), Pippa (6)

. . .

2. TRACE

    Wife: Everly Avery

    His son: Harry (26)

    Children he and Ev share: Keri (7), Clay (5), Avery (20 mo)

3. BLAZE

    Wife: Faith Cromwell

    His son: Cash (23)

    Children he and Faith share: Grace (7), Celeste (6), Tyrone (3), pregnant and due in Sept

4. OTIS

    Wife: Georgia Beck

    His daughter: Joelle (Joey / Roo, 22)

    Children he and Georgia share: OJ (Otis Judson, 10), Anaya (7)

5. MAV

    Wife: Danielle Simpson

    His daughter: Beth (18)

    Her son: Boston (21)

    Children he and Dani share: Lars (11), Emilia (7)

6. JEM

Wife: Sunny Samuelson

His kids: Cole (17), Rosie (14)

Children he and Sunny share: Ladd (7), Skye (17 mo)

7. LUKE

Wife: Sterling Boyd

His daughter: Corrine (16)

Children he and Sterling share: Ryder (7), North (5), Mattie (2)

8. MORRIS

Wife: Leighann Drummond

Children he and Leigh share: Eric (15), Rachelle (10), Skip (6), Ridge (2), Remington (Remi, 2)

9. GABRIEL (GABE)

Wife: Hilde O'Dell

His daughter: Liesl (15)

Her daughter: Lynnie (24)

Children he and Hilde share: Canyon (8), Brant, Cort, Tanner (5)

10. BRYCE

Wife: Codi Hudson

They have several dogs and horses :)

Part One:

1

Harry Young didn't exactly love the snow. But he did love sitting with Keri, Clay, and Avery cuddled around him while the flakes fell. He loved making hot chocolate for himself and the kids, and he loved watching movies while keeping the dark night and cold wind at bay.

In short, he loved being home in Coral Canyon, and since he didn't have to be in Nashville until after Valentine's Day, he'd chosen to stay in Wyoming after the holidays. It sure felt nice to have someone else looking after him. Someone making coffee in the morning, and someone filling the fridge with food.

After four months of touring, Harry was *tired*, and he didn't even want to think about having to do another album and another tour. He honestly wasn't sure how his father had done this ten times now.

With his bone-weary exhaustion plaguing him, it was no wonder he scrolled through his social media feed while a cartoon movie of a princess played in front of him and the kids.

"Holy cow," he murmured, but Keri nor Clay cared. He paused on a particular post and picture. "Sarah Endman got married."

His high school girlfriend. The only girl he'd ever confided more in than his father, than anyone. *What?* he asked himself as he stared at her beautiful face. *Did you think she was waiting around for you?*

Of course she wasn't. She'd gone to college when he'd left for Nashville. The caption on her wedding photo read, *Reid and I have been together for four years, and I'm so happy we're finally man and wife!*

Four years.

Harry shoved his phone under his leg and folded his arms, a keen sense of loneliness filling him. Sarah had been his only girlfriend in high school. He'd only dated one other person since her, and well, Harry didn't want to go into what a terrible relationship he'd had with the lead singer of a band who'd toured with him during his first album.

He let his eyes drift closed, and before he knew it, he fell asleep during the kids' movie. "Harry," Keri whispered at some point. "It's over."

"Okay," he said, opening his eyes to look at the little girl. It took a moment for her to come into focus, and she looked at him with Ev's blue eyes and Dad's dark hair. "Time for bed, little lady."

He looked over to find Clay sound asleep, his face mashed into the couch cushion. Harry had put Avery in her swing, and the baby was zonked out too. He got up and stretched, yawning as he did. He loved staying up late, and as he scooped Clay into his arms and followed Keri down the hall, a second round of energy entered his body.

He laid Clay in his bed and bent down to kiss his forehead. He covered him up and left the room to help Keri with her teeth and nightgown. Once the seven-year-old had been tucked in, with properly brushed teeth, and promises of Harry being the one to drive her to school in the morning, he left her bedroom too.

Avery didn't have her own bedroom upstairs, and she still slept in a bassinet in Harry's parents' room. He collected the baby and took her in there, wrapping her up tight so she wouldn't wake up. He'd just left that bedroom when Daddy and Ev returned home, and he met them in the kitchen.

"How'd it go?" Ev asked.

"Just fine," Harry said, indicating the mess he'd left behind in the kitchen. "I think you can see everything we did right there."

Ev took in the electric kettle, the mugs, the bowl of popcorn which only held un-popped kernels and the excess fake yellow butter Harry loved. "Mm, yes, I see."

"I'll clean it up," Harry said. He had a bedroom in the basement, but he'd been staying out at Bryce's a lot in the past couple of weeks since his cousin had gotten engaged. "I'm staying here tonight, because I promised Keri I'd drive her to school." He smiled at Ev and moved around the island and into the kitchen.

She went down the hall to assumedly check on the kids and get ready for bed, but Daddy plopped himself on a barstool and looked at Harry. That wasn't good.

"Uncle Morris said he's still negotiating a tour."

"Yeah, yep, right," Harry said. He'd told Morris, who acted as his manager, he didn't want to do a tour. He wanted to write the songs, record the songs, and have Rebel put out the album. The end.

"He also said you've asked him—well, he said you told him you didn't want another contract."

Harry turned his back on his dad as he put the half-full mugs in the sink and flipped on the faucet. "That's right," he said.

"What's your plan, then?"

A sigh moved through Harry's whole body, but his muscles felt like they'd been bound and tied. "Do I need a plan, Dad? I have like, millions of dollars in the bank. What if my plan is to sleep in the basement forever?"

"I'd say that's a terrible plan," his father said.

Harry dumped out the undrunk hot chocolate and pulled open the dishwasher. He loaded the mugs and spoons, then turned to get the bowl of popcorn. He met his father's eye, the storm inside him blowing out instantly.

"I want to write songs," Harry said. "I can do it from anywhere. You and Uncle Otis song-write. He makes good money writing songs for people who just sing them."

Daddy nodded, his dark eyes not quite all the way into Serial Killer Mode yet.

"I'm a really good songwriter," Harry said. "I can make more than the average person with one social media video than some people make in a month. With songs. With a guitar. I thought I wanted a life and a career in country music, but I don't."

Harry turned and took the bowl to the trashcan, where he dumped out the unpopped kernels. He set the bowl in the sink and let it start filling with water. He swept the trash from the hot chocolate packets and the popcorn bag off the counter and into the garbage, and still his father sat there, silent.

"Just ask it," Harry said.

"Are you going to move back here?"

Harry scrubbed the popcorn bowl, trying to find the right answer. Or at least an answer that wasn't, "I don't know."

But he didn't know.

He just wanted God to shine a light on the path he was supposed to be on. He hadn't been to church in a while, and he needed to go. He missed having a heavenly influence in his life, plain and simple.

He straightened his shoulders when he realized how slumped and folded in on himself he was. He finished rinsing the bowl and set it in the dish drainer to dry. As he faced his father, he grabbed a towel from the stove to dry his hands.

"You know what? I don't know, but I'm just going to be

bold and try to act like an adult and say, yeah. I want to move back here."

Dad's lips twitched, but he didn't smile. "Harry, you can do whatever you want."

"Daddy, you know that's not true."

"Otis writes from here."

"Otis isn't under a contract." Harry turned back to the sink and picked up the washcloth. He flipped the sink back on for the third time and started rinsing it out. "And he's proven himself. And he's awesome."

He started wiping the counter and found a carton of cream he'd left out from the hot chocolate construction. He picked it up and put it back in the fridge, and when he faced his father to wipe down the island, he paused. "I want to have music in my life, Daddy. But I don't want to be a country music star in the way I have been. I don't like touring. I like writing, and plucking through my strings, and singing, but...I just don't think the traditional path is for me."

"No one's saying it needs to be."

"Why don't you just say what you want me to do?"

"I want you to be happy."

Harry started wiping the counter. "You know what makes me happy? Babysitting the kids so you and Ev can go out." He'd really, truly been happy tonight.

"I'm hearing someone wants a wife and a family."

"Yeah." Harry didn't mean for the sigh to slip from his throat, but it did. "I can admit I'm lonely. It's insane, but even when I'm surrounded by tens of thousands of people,

I'm all alone." His chest hitched, and Harry clamped his teeth together to keep himself from saying another word. If he did, his voice would crack, and then Daddy wouldn't sleep. He'd be too worried about Harry, and that was the last thing he needed.

"Is Morris going to try to get Rebel to let you work on the album from here?"

"Yes," Harry clipped out. With the counter clean, he returned to the sink once more. He washed out the cloth and laid it out to dry before turning back to his dad. "I won't live here, and I won't live with Bryce. No matter what, Dad, I want to come back here. There's something about this place, and you're here and everyone is here."

He couldn't catch the emotion before it bled into his voice, and with his eyes locked on his daddy's, he decided he didn't have to hide anything. He wasn't "the" Harry Young here. He was just his father's son, and he could be himself.

"I miss everyone. I seriously don't know how Bryce lived away from here for so long. I miss so much, and I feel like a stranger to everyone where I live, a stranger to everyone who likes my music, and a stranger when I come home." He shook his head. "I know it doesn't make sense."

"It makes perfect sense," Daddy whispered.

"I'll get my own place," Harry said. "I can afford it, and it'll be here for me whenever I can be here too. One day." He rounded the island and sat next to his dad. "For good. Permanently. That's the goal."

Dad nodded, his chin down toward the countertop. "It's a good goal, Harry."

"Do you think I can find someone—you know—who's just...normal?"

Dad looked at him. "You mean a girl?"

"Yeah, Dad." Harry smiled at him, though the gesture felt a little tired on his face. "I mean a girl."

"All of us managed to find normal women," Dad said. "And we're big rockstars."

"True," Harry mused, but he thought it was a little different. He didn't want to call his dad old—or any of his uncles—but none of them had dated in their twenties. Daddy had been forty when he'd met Ev and started dating her. It wasn't the same as the younger culture, the younger crowd.

Maybe you'll find someone older than you, he thought, and Harry didn't hate that idea. Uncle Gabe and Aunt Hilde were quite far apart in age, and maybe it wouldn't be too big of a problem.

Especially here in Coral Canyon, where Harry wanted to be.

"Will you help me look for a place?" he asked.

"Of course I will," Dad said. "You want something big or small?"

"I'm thinking small," Harry said. "Nondescript. Normal. Average. I just want average, Daddy."

Dad chuckled. "All right. I'm sure we can find something in one of the older neighborhoods, where you'll have a little old lady bringing you banana bread every Sunday."

Harry grinned and leaned into his father's side-hug.

"Sounds perfect," he said, and he wasn't lying. Not even a little bit.

The big city life wasn't for him. The hustle and bustle of fame didn't suit him. He did have quite a bit of money, and he'd get two more disbursements from the tour, and then two more during the making of the third album.

He had money. He had savings. He had a retirement fund already. He could find a way to do what he loved and keep making money.

Now, what he needed was someone to spend it on. Someone besides himself he could focus on.

He needed to surround himself with the goodness of nature, and of his family, and of God.

And he really, really wanted to find someone to share his life with the way Bryce had, the way his daddy had, the way seemingly everyone around him had.

HARRY YOUNG ROLLED OVER IN BED, SOMEONE pounding on the door and refusing to go away. It took him a moment to remember he wasn't in his apartment in Nashville, but at home in Coral Canyon. Due to his staying-up-late-at-night habits, he wasn't surprised to find the clock on his nightstand blaring out a time of ten-twenty-four.

He was surprised that his daddy wasn't home to get the door, and as he got to his feet, he grabbed his phone and saw a text that said they'd taken the kids to Uncle Tex's for a holiday breakfast, and he should come out to the farmhouse whenever he woke up.

"Sheriff's Department," a woman yelled as Harry turned the corner and entered the hallway leading to the front door. "Is anyone home?"

"Yeah, I'm home," Harry said as he reached the door and unlocked it. He pulled it open only to receive a nasty shock of bright sunlight glinting off the snow and streaming straight into his eyes.

A blast of cold air punched him in the chest, reminding him he wasn't exactly wearing a shirt.

As he shielded his eyes and tried to contain the chatter in his teeth, the woman standing there said, "I'm Belle Graves of the Teton County Sheriff's Department. Can I ask you a few questions?"

Harry's eyes adjusted to the blinding light. Or maybe it all came from Belle and how angelic she was, standing there on the porch in black pants and a black shirt. An angel of darkness, maybe, but an angel nonetheless. She wore her dark brown hair long and down, and Harry wanted to run his fingers through it.

She'd done her makeup and while he'd never considered a Sheriff's Department vest to be a particularly sexy piece of clothing, on her, it sure was. Her dark eyes devoured him, sliding down to his bare feet and back to his face.

A flash of a smile stole across her face, and Harry had to make that happen again. Next time, for longer and aimed at him for something funny and clever he'd said to her.

"Do you live here?" she asked before he could ask her for her number.

"No," he said. "I mean, sort of."

The beautiful Belle tilted her head at him. "You *sort of* live here?"

"It's my parents' place," he said. "I'm just staying here for a while." He leaned into the doorjamb and rested his shoulder against it. "Do you want to come in? It's freezing out here."

Her eyes dropped to his bare chest. "Probably best if I do come in," she said as she squeezed up onto the step with him. "And you probably wouldn't be so cold if you had clothes on."

With that, she slipped by him and into the house, and all Harry could do was turn his head and watch her walk down the hall away from him, his heartbeat positively thrashing at him to *go with her! Answer her questions and then ask her one of your own.*

So he closed the door and followed the lovely Belle into the house, all thoughts of joining his family for a late breakfast completely and utterly gone.

2

Belle Graves took in the house, her keen eye finding and noticing details a lot of people probably wouldn't. At the sound of footsteps behind her, she turned and found the gorgeous man who'd answered the door coming into the big multi-purpose room at the back of the house.

He hadn't given his name, and Belle didn't normally just enter people's houses. Of course, men wearing only gym shorts didn't answer the door and stand there in the frigid weather in the middle of January either.

"Give me a sec," he said, and he turned left and went down the hallway, presumably back into the bedrooms. Belle reminded herself as she caught sight of the muscles in his back and shoulders—it was really just the cop in her that saw the little details—that she hadn't come here to get a date.

She had someone to find, and for all she knew, Cowboy

Cutie who'd answered the door could have Steven Bastian hidden in the basement.

"Sorry 'bout that," the man said as he returned. He had a cowboy accent, but she wasn't sure if he was from Wyoming or not. He'd said this was his parents' house, not his, and he could've been visiting from anywhere.

He now wore a dark purple shirt with four dancing potato chips on it—and they had eyes and mouths—those gray gym shorts, and a cowboy hat as he padded into the kitchen. "Coffee?" he offered in that smooth, deep voice of his.

"No, thank you," Belle said, clearing her throat and eliminating the questions about his T-shirt from her mind. She had *other* things to ask while she was here. "I'm a Missing Persons Investigator for the Teton County Sheriff's Department. I'm looking for your neighbor to the west there. Steven Bastian? Do you know him?"

"No," the man said. "Like I said, I'm just visiting my folks."

"What's your name?" she asked.

"Harry Young," he said, and he watched her for a moment.

To Belle, that sounded pretty bland, and she pulled out her notebook to write down a few things. "Who are your parents?"

"Trace and Everly Young." He pulled out the coffee pot, which already had coffee in it, and dumped it down the drain. He started to fill it with fresh water, and he looked over to her while he did. "They probably know their neighbors. Especially Ev. She runs the dance studio in town, and she knows everyone. My daddy's a bit more of a...keeps-to-himself kind of guy."

Belle scribbled something in her notebook she probably wouldn't read later. She just liked getting it down, because then she remembered it. "Have you ever seen Steven before?"

"Probably," Harry said as he measured grounds into a filter. "I lived here for several years before graduating high school."

Belle didn't even want to know, but she asked, "How long ago was that?"

"Uh, let's see."

Well, if he had to think about it, that meant it was a while ago. Belle found herself holding her breath for a reason she couldn't name. She *really* wasn't here for a date. In fact, her whole dating-men history was pot-holed at best, and she didn't need to be trying to add another reason she crashed and burned to her personal failure resume.

Remember Buck, she told herself.

Lord, it would be great if I could focus here, she thought next. But every time she blinked, she could see Harry's well-defined abs, those broad pecs, and as she'd moved by him—sure, she could admit she'd gotten in close to him—she'd gotten the slightest scent of his cologne.

"Almost six years ago now," he said.

Belle pursed her lips. "Hm." She wrote down the year, doing the math quickly, and then she wrote a 24 and circled it a few times. Was a twenty-four-year-old too young for a twenty-nine-about-to-be-thirty-year-old?

"You?" he asked.

"Excuse me?" She looked up from his age on her notepad, pure surprise coloring her thoughts.

"When did you graduate from high school?" He dipped his head into the fridge and came up with a couple of bottles of flavored cream.

Belle eyed those with extreme interest, because one of them was caramel, and she happened to have a very weak spot for cowboys with caramel cream in their big hands. "Uh, a while ago," she said. "Longer than six years ago."

"Like, a whole lot longer than six years ago, or just a few years more than six years ago?" Harry grinned at her, and Belle got the distinct impression he was flirting with her.

"Double the six," she said. "You know what? I'd love some coffee."

His smile only got brighter, and he turned to get down two mugs from the cupboard. "How long have you been a cop?"

"Eight years," she said. "I just moved into—" She cut off, because he'd completely reversed their roles here. The house felt so hot, and Belle really needed to regain control of the situation.

"How long have you been staying here?" she asked as she moved to the end of the counter. It was wintertime; that was why the house felt so stuffy and hot. It had absolutely nothing to do with Belle's traitorous pulse springing throughout her body.

"'Bout a month," Harry said.

"Wow, you don't have a job?"

He cut her a look out of the corner of his eye, his grin fading all the way to nothing. "I have a job," he said evasively.

"Work from home?"

"I'm on a break right now," he said.

Belle sensed something there, all of her cop tingles sparking at the same time. "So you might have been around to see your neighbor. He lives there alone. A little older gentleman. He's fifty-six."

"I've seen him," Harry said. "While we were shoveling snow, and when the kids wanted me to help them build a snowman."

"Yes, I saw that out front." Belle smiled at him, hoping to bring back the charm and charisma the cowboy had already shown her. But he'd shut down a little, and while his mouth tipped up, his smile certainly didn't hold the same wattage as it had before. "Your kids?" she asked, returning her attention to her notepad to madly scratch out some more items of interest about this Harry Young.

Search about him, she wrote as he said, "My daddy's. He got remarried, oh, I don't know. About eight or nine years ago. He and Ev have three kids together."

"I see, okay." She looked up, the question burning through her throat stuck there. She absolutely would not ask him if he was married or had ever been married. What would that have to do with Steven?

"Do you remember the last time you saw Steven while shoveling or building the snowman?"

"Well, it hasn't snowed in what? Four days?" Harry half-smiled, and oh, that was just as playful and sexy and bright as the full thing. "I swear, I love Coral Canyon, but when it snows, I do miss Nashville."

"Ah, Nashville," she said. "Is that where you live?"

"Sort of," he said.

"You have a lot of sort of's."

"I have a place there, yes," he said, giving her another sharp look. "But I'm buying a place here too."

He must be famous, she thought, and she knew the type who had two homes—one of which was in Nashville.

Men who thought they ruled the world because they could play a guitar. Well, Belle could do that too, thank you very much.

"So have you seen Steven in the past four days?"

"We built the snowman on Thursday afternoon," he said. "While Ev was teaching. I'm pretty sure I saw him then. He came home, and he was carrying in a couple of bags of groceries." He nodded like his memory had just kicked in. "Yeah, that's right."

"What time on Thursday?"

"I don't know. It was light. Afternoon. Keri was out of school, and she's in first grade. Four?"

"Four, okay," she said, writing it down. "And nothing since?"

"I don't think so."

"Did you notice any cars coming and going?"

Harry poured the coffee as he considered her question. He set one mug in front of her and nudged the caramel cream carton closer to her, as if he knew that was why she'd decided to change her mind and accept his offer of coffee.

"I don't recall," he said. "To be honest, I don't sleep here every night, and I was out at my cousin's on Thursday and Friday nights. I came here for the weekend, because my parents went out and I babysat, and then we went to church yesterday, and today's a holiday, so...." He trailed off then, his face suddenly blooming with the most adorable blush Belle had ever seen on a man.

Harry also had a hefty five o'clock shadow, probably because he'd shaved for church yesterday and then not again since. Belle liked the square jaw with stubble, the large, capable hands, the broad shoulders.

The potato chip T-shirt? She wasn't sure about that, but as a cop, she'd learned a long time ago not to make too many judgments too early on.

"I didn't see him on Saturday or Sunday," Harry said. "I didn't notice him at church, but I don't know if he normally goes or not."

"Because you don't live here."

"Right," he said. "And, in complete transparency, I don't really pay much attention to what's goin' on around me. My job—well, my job has trained me to focus on what's right in front of me and not much else. He may have been there, and I wouldn't have seen him."

He stirred coconut cream into his coffee, no sugar, and lifted the mug to his lips at the same time his pocket rang.

Well, his phone inside his shorts pocket rang, and he pulled it out. "It's my daddy," he said with a sigh. "I'm late for a family breakfast."

"I won't keep you," Belle said. She did splash a bit of caramel cream into her coffee, and she took a hearty gulp of it as Harry slid the call to silent. "Thanks for the coffee, and thanks for answering my questions."

She dug into her vest pocket and pulled out her card. She hated her photo on this thing, but until she ran out, she couldn't get new ones. The county didn't just replace perfectly good business cards because she'd pulled her hair up on picture day and now looked bald in the photo.

"If you see him, please call me. His daughter reported him missing, and we really need to locate him." She handed Harry the card, took another sip of her coffee, and headed for the front door.

She'd rounded the corner and entered the hall when he called, "Belle, wait," in that delicious voice. Hens and feathers, now he'd said her name, and she'd never be able to hear it in the same way again.

She turned just as he came skidding around the corner, his coffee cup still in his hand. His shoulder bumped the wall, and he grunted, and then he came to a stop in front of her. Belle raised her eyebrows as he seemed to pant in and out a couple of times.

"Yes?" she asked.

"If I wanted—I mean." He cleared his throat and pressed his eyelids closed over those dreamy, dark eyes.

"The number on this card." He held it up in the hand not holding his coffee cup. "If I call it, you'll answer?"

"Yes, sir," she said. "Day or night."

"So it's a work number."

"Yes," she said slowly. "It's my cell phone."

"Personal? Or one the Sheriff's Department issued to you?"

She cocked her head at him again, trying to get a read on him. He seemed to be putting off a very flirty vibe, but his face didn't show it, and she couldn't quite reconcile him.

"Where is the Teton County Sheriff's Department?" he asked.

"Jackson," she said. "I live there."

"Ah, I see."

"We come out to the surrounding towns as needed," she said. "It's a pretty drive, even in the winter."

"So you wouldn't be interested in maybe getting dinner with me?"

There it was, and Belle could admit that warmth seeped through her whole body. Despite the ugly, black khakis she had to wear for the job, despite the bulky vest she wore identifying herself, despite letting him steer this Q&A for a few minutes, he'd found something he liked about her.

What, she wasn't sure, but could she give him dinner to find out?

"Depends," she said.

"On what?"

"It seems to me, Mister Young," she said. "That you don't really have roots. You're here, you're there, you're in

Nashville. I'm in Jackson, and that's not here, there, or Nashville."

"It's just dinner," he said.

She shook her head, feeling a little flirty and reckless herself. "I don't date for 'justs,'" she said. She nodded to the card in his hand. "If you see Steven, please call me immediately." With that, she turned and exited the house she never should've entered in the first place.

Harry didn't call for her to wait again, and Belle gave herself an extreme amount of credit for striding down the front sidewalk to the driveway, and then back to her SUV, which she'd parked in front of the house next door, all without looking back once.

Only then did she eye the light gray house where Harry Young had answered the door. She made a few more notes, and then took out her phone to do a quick search for the man. Horror filled her with the half-sentence that came up under the first search result.

The prodigal son of country music sensation, Trace Young, Harry has taken the nation by storm with his—

"His what?" Belle asked herself, but she already knew.

Country music sensation, Trace Young.

Harry had a home in Nashville. He was "on a break" in his job.

She tapped and opened the link, the picture there making her breath catch and her pulse sprint.

Sexy, young, brilliant Harry Young on a stage, a guitar in his hand, that radiant smile blasting out to the whole world as he sang for them. He wore a pair of jeans, not gym shorts, and a T-shirt with a volcano on it that had a conversation bubble above its head that said, "I lava you."

The cowboy boots, a big shiny belt buckle, and that black cowboy hat completed Harry Young into Cowboy Perfection, not Cowboy Cutie. She quickly scanned the article about him, and he sure seemed like a superstar in his own right.

Belle looked over to the house again, but Harry wasn't there. She didn't have his number, and she would never humiliate herself by walking back to the door and telling him she'd changed her mind about going to dinner with him.

"It's *just* dinner," she said with a scoff. She'd done the casual dating scene, and it had sickened her. No, she was ready for serious, and Harry didn't even live here. Even if he did, an hour drive and fifty miles separated Coral Canyon and Jackson Hole, and Belle could barely keep up with her job, watering her plants, and feeding her cat.

She most certainly didn't have time for Harry Young.

Before she could shelve him the way she had other handsome cowboys that didn't fit into her life, her phone chimed. She pulled it out and swiped to get to the text.

This is Harry Young. My near future is a tiny bit up in the air at the moment, but I'd still love to take you to dinner. It wouldn't be JUST dinner. It would be us getting to know each other to find out if we have something.

"Something?" she wondered.

Another text came in as her eyebrows puckered.

Because I felt something between us, and I want to explore it. If you didn't, that's fine, and I will pray with everything I have that I don't see Steven so I don't have to call you and see you again, because wow, how embarrassing, right?

He'd included a smiley face, and honestly, Belle wasn't even sure how he'd typed all of that so fast. The man did have nimble fingers to be a country music star and—what had that article said?

"He's one of the best and rarest talents on the guitar," she said aloud, the words right there in her memory, as if her cop-brain knew she'd need them later and had catalogued them.

Let me know. I'm in town for at least another month.

Belle wanted to say yes, but she wasn't sure she should. What she did know was she had a debriefing meeting in seventy minutes, and she needed to make the drive back to headquarters.

She started her SUV but stalled in putting the vehicle into gear when she saw the front door of that gray house open and Harry himself jog down the front steps to the truck parked in the driveway. He launched himself behind the wheel, backed out of the driveway, and drove off.

Belle wanted to follow him. She wanted to text him back and say she'd go to dinner with him. She wanted to keep her job, which meant she had to get to her meeting.

And yet, she sat there on the side of the road, trying to decide what to do. Text Harry, follow Harry, or get on back to work?

Realistically, she couldn't sit there and she couldn't follow Harry. So, she started the drive back to Jackson and headquarters, a new dilemma in her mind now.

Go out with Harry? Or ignore his texts completely?

3

Harry finally shoved his phone in his back pocket and told himself not to look at it again. He tuned into the family party at his uncle's farmhouse, because while he'd missed the pancakes and eggs, Aunt Abby had just brought out a birthday cake.

For him.

He grinned at the flickering candles on the two-shaped and four-shaped candles as she approached. The rest of the family who'd gathered started to sing, and a squirrel of embarrassment funneled through Harry.

He shouldn't have been late. Daddy hadn't told him to set an alarm, and Harry hadn't known they'd all been waiting for him so they could sing *Happy Birthday* and shower him with gifts he didn't need.

The song ended, and cheering started. Harry grinned around at everyone, took an exaggerated breath, and blew out the two flames on the candle. The little cousins went nuts, and Harry beamed up at Aunt Abby. "Thank you," he said to her.

She half-hugged him and then said, "Uncle Tex will be serving the birthday cake, and all kids must eat on a hard floor. If you're over eighteen, you may eat your cake in the living room."

Uncle Tex cut into the cake, the deep, rich chocolate flavor evident in the dark brown color of the cake. Aunt Abby had frosted it with the classic coconut and walnut frosting for a German chocolate cake—Harry's favorite.

"For the birthday man first," Uncle Tex said as he slid an enormous piece of cake in front of Harry. He grinned like they'd all gotten up for a second Christmas morning, and Harry wouldn't deny his uncle the same smile in return.

Heck, he might be asking Uncle Tex if he could come out here and record songs. As far as Harry knew, now that Country Quad had retired, no one used the recording barn behind the farmhouse.

"This looks amazing," he said. "Thank you, Aunt Abby."

"Your momma helped," she said from where she stood next to Ev, holding the newest member of Harry's immediate family: two-month-old Avery.

"Thank you, Ev," Harry said. He loved her with his whole heart, but he'd struggled to call her momma lately. His own mother had come into his life in a bigger role, and Harry had enjoyed seeing her, getting to know her, and spending time with her.

In truth, he felt pulled in a lot of different directions

almost all the time. *This is why you should be glad Belle hasn't texted you back*, he told himself sternly. So he'd felt a flicker of attraction to the woman. That didn't mean they had to rush out to dinner that very evening.

Still, he didn't want to be rejected, and he hoped she'd tell him *no, thanks* as kindly as possible. Just to leave him hanging? She wouldn't be that cruel, would she?

Harry put the first bite of cake in his mouth, and the moist texture, the burst of chocolatey flavor, and the smooth frosting made every other thought fly out of his mouth. "My word," he moaned.

"I want cake," Keri said in her cute six-year-old voice.

"Uncle Tex is gettin' for everyone," Daddy said, his hand landing on Harry's shoulder.

"Come have some of mine, Little Miss." Harry reached for Keri in Daddy's arms, and his father slid the little girl into Harry's lap. He handed her the fork he'd just used, and she didn't care at all as she reached to get a bite of the chocolate cake.

"I have some too," Clay said, and Harry moved Keri over to his right side so Clay could climb up on his left.

"There's plenty of cake," Uncle Tex bellowed as the last piece from that platter got handed out. "No crying. Anyone crying won't get cake."

"Daddy, I didn't get any cake," Bryce said, his voice one of fake-whining.

Harry grinned at him and shook his head. Bryce picked up another plastic fork and gave it to Clay, leaning closer as he said, "Happy birthday, brother."

"Thanks," Harry said, his gaze staying on his cousin as Bryce fell back to Codi's side. He put his arm around her, and Harry couldn't help noticing the way the diamond on her left hand glinted in the bright kitchen lights at the farmhouse.

It sure did seem like everyone had what he wanted, and Harry closed his eyes and let the Young Family noise, activity, and joy seep into him. He belonged in this family, even if he didn't have a spouse or a girlfriend, or any prospects for a spouse or girlfriend.

He'd be able to show up on a dozen doorsteps, day or night, and he'd be welcomed inside, given food and a bed and love. That was what the Youngs did, and Harry let all of his negative emotions seep right out of himself.

As he took a cleansing breath, he opened his eyes. He looked at Clay, who had a wad of chocolate cake in his fist. "You want bite, Harry?" He held up his hand, and Harry smiled so he wouldn't dry heave.

"No, buddy. You have it."

Clay stuffed the cake in his mouth, and chocolate smeared all around his lips. Harry looked over to Daddy, but he'd taken the baby from Aunt Abby and patted her while she cried. Ev watched them, and Harry watched her. She'd been having some problems since Avery's birth, and Harry had watched her recede and recede into herself. Daddy had finally talked her into going to the doctor, and she'd been taking some medicine that had been helping.

Getting the dose right seemed to be taking some time, and Harry smiled at her as she looked his way. She returned the gesture and shook her head. "I'm not even sure if they're getting any cake in their mouths," she said.

"Cake!" Clay yelled. "Momma! Cake!"

Harry bounced him on his knee. "Yeah, you're eatin' cake, buddy."

Grandma came over with a rag, and she cleaned up the little boy and plucked him from Harry's lap. "Come on, you sweet boy. Let's wash you up." She bustled into the kitchen, and Harry simply basked in the energy of his family.

A COUPLE OF WEEKS LATER, HARRY DISEMBARKED FROM the plane in Nashville, his backpack on his shoulders and his stride long. He kept his eyes on the ground in front of him, because he'd learned not to make eye contact. Otherwise, he'd get stopped a dozen times between his gate and the baggage claim area.

He'd have to give out signatures and adopt his public relations smile. Harry didn't want to be rude, but he just wanted to get his bag and get back to his downtown apartment. He had a lesson with his guitar instructor tomorrow, and next week, Uncle Morris would be in town to discuss where Harry could record his next album.

Questions swarmed Harry, pressing into his mind from every direction. If he got approved to record in Coral Canyon, would Uncle Tex let him use the barn? Would he have to give up his apartment here? Should he?

Daddy had found a couple of houses for Harry to look at

in Coral Canyon, but nothing had stood out to Harry. If he got approved to record in Coral Canyon, where would he live? He couldn't stay with Daddy and Ev.

In fact, he'd been staying with Bryce for the past couple of weeks. He had a big house, and Harry helped with the horses. He liked spending time with Bryce and Codi, and Kassie and Reggie, because they never treated him like a fifth wheel.

Belle had texted to say she wasn't sure she had time to set anything up for a date, and Harry had accepted that her case load right now wasn't conducive to making dinner plans. They'd texted a little bit, and then everything had tapered into nothing.

Kassie and Reggie had postponed their wedding by a month, and Harry wondered if he should just stay down here until then. Going back and forth sounded exhausting, and Harry honestly had no idea where he'd be in a month.

He arrived at the appointed baggage claim, and the suitcases hadn't started to rotate around yet. Harry stayed out of the way, because he didn't need to stand two feet away from the carousel. When his bag showed up, he'd grab it and go.

While he waited, he called for his car, and his driver said he'd be there in ten minutes. The sound of a suitcase clunking along the metal filled the air, and Harry looked over to the belt. He edged around the end of the carousel so he could see better, but none of the few suitcases which had arrived were his.

"You're Harry Young," someone said, and a sigh pulled through his chest.

He couldn't just pretend like he hadn't heard the woman, so he glanced over to her. "Hey," he said. She couldn't be much older than him, and she stood with three other young women close to his age.

He put a smile on his face. "Are you coming home or visiting?"

"Visiting," she said. She moved closer to him, as did the people she stood with. "I can't believe I'm talking to you."

"That song about fishing with your son is one of my favorites," another woman said.

Harry nodded, his smile slipping as more people looked his way. "Thanks," he said. "I wrote that...a couple of years ago." He stepped closer to the baggage claim as he started getting surrounded.

He just needed to get his bag and go.

A woman moved right into him and extended her hand. "It's so great to meet you."

The backs of Harry's calves touched the metal of the baggage claim. He had nowhere to go, and people kept pressing toward him. And toward him. And toward him.

Harry looked past the swarm, trying to find someone to help him. His eyes landed on an airline employee, and he raised his hand. "Help," he called.

The man didn't move. The group in front of him—mostly women—got closer. Harry tried to move sideways, but an oversized suitcase had just come around the corner. It hit the back of his legs, sweeping his feet out from under him.

"Help," he yelled again, stumbling with the weight of this backpack.

Someone touched his chest; someone grabbed his arm; someone's face flashed in front of his as he fell backward onto the moving baggage claim belt. "I need help here," he called as the world went upside down.

He needed a lot of help.

4

Trace Young paced while his son's line rang. He couldn't look at Ev, and his pulse thundered through his chest at the memory of the video he'd been shown. "He's not picking up."

"It's early in Nashville still," Ev said from where she sat on the couch with their three kids.

"It's ten there," Trace said, trying hard not to growl. He wasn't upset with Ev. He wasn't upset with Harry. He just needed to know his son was okay after falling on top of luggage at a baggage carousel in the Nashville airport.

He'd been surrounded by people. They'd all been touching him. He'd called for help a couple of times.

Luke and Mav had shown up this morning with the video, and Trace hadn't been able to see the end of it. He had no idea where Harry was, if he was okay, or how he'd gotten off that moving belt with all the bags.

41

"This is Harry," his son's voice chirped, and Trace pulled the phone away from his ear to end the call. He immediately dialed again, because his nerves would not let this go.

"I might have to go to Nashville," he said to Ev.

His beautiful wife looked up and nodded at him. "We can all go," she said. "Baby, take a breath."

Trace did what she said as the line started to ring again. His chest inflated, and he held the lungful of air for a moment before releasing it.

"Daddy," Harry said.

Pure relief streamed through Trace, and the last of his air sounded like a gasp. "There you are."

Harry said nothing, and that spoke volumes. He didn't even try to do what Bryce did and say he was fine. That everything was okay. That it was nothing.

"Harry," Trace said, trying to find the right words. "Your uncles came over and showed us a video in the Nashville airport. And I just need to know you're okay." He tapped the speaker button so Ev could hear too.

His son had flown to Nashville four days ago. Four days. The incident had clearly happened upon his arrival, and Trace had heard nothing from him since.

"I don't know," Harry whispered. "I haven't left the apartment." He took a big breath, and Trace just wanted to wrap his little boy in his arms and tell him everything would be all right.

The ground had just become unstable under Trace's feet, and he sank onto a barstool. "You've got food?"

"I order everything in," Harry said. "I'm—I don't know what I am, Daddy. I'm scared."

"Tell me what happened." Trace tried to speak slowly, but his heart and mind raced. "They cut off the end of the video. Did someone come help you?"

"Two guys from the airline," he said. "They got everyone back and someone pushed the emergency stop button on the conveyor belt." Harry hardly sounded like himself, and Trace's heart broke into a million tiny pieces.

"My driver arrived, and he hauled me off the belt. We got my bag and got out of there."

"Are you hurt?"

"My shoulder was kind of hurting for a day or so," Harry said. "It's fine now. I don't know. I just feel so stupid."

"You can't travel alone anymore," Trace said.

Harry scoffed, but it wasn't in disbelief. More like angry agreement. "I feel like an idiot. Who needs a bodyguard everywhere they go?"

"You do," Trace said, watching as Ev nodded. "And it's not a bodyguard. You need an assistant. Someone who can create the buffer around you. Someone who can get your baggage for you while you wait at security. Someone to get your groceries and do all that kind of stuff."

Harry said nothing, and Trace could just imagine him shaking his head, a deep, dark fire burning in his deep, dark eyes.

"Can Ev and I come see you?"

"You don't need to do that," Harry said. "Uncle Morris will be here in a few days."

"Does he know about this?" It usually took more time for news to travel to the wilds of Coral Canyon, Wyoming, but Morris stayed pretty plugged in to whatever was happening with Harry.

"I haven't told him," Harry muttered.

"I'm going to take that as a no," Trace said, his eyes locked on Ev's. "What about your mother?"

"I haven't told anyone," Harry said. "You're the first to call me."

"Son." Trace didn't know what to say next. He didn't know what to do. God hadn't provided a manual for how to deal with his mega-celebrity son.

Be gentle came into his mind. *But be firm.*

How was he supposed to be gentle and firm at the same time?

He took a breath, pleading with the Lord for the right thing to say. When Trace opened his mouth, he said, "Ev and I are going to bring the kids for the weekend. Okay?"

"Okay," Harry said, and the fact that he didn't argue told Trace a whole lot too.

"I'm going to help you find an assistant," Trace said.

"I feel so dumb," Harry whispered.

"This is not on you," Trace said. "Those women, they...." They were everywhere, that was what. They'd cornered Harry, and he'd had nowhere to go.

"You're a big celebrity now," Trace said. "We'll get you an assistant, and everything will work out."

"Okay." Harry sniffed, and Trace had to tell himself it was

because Harry had caught a little cold, not because he was crying. He couldn't stand the thought of his boy, all alone in Nashville, crying in an apartment he hadn't left in four days.

"I think you should call your mom," he said. "Tell her about this, so she doesn't have to see it and worry."

"All right," Harry said.

"And we'll see you in a couple of days," Trace said. He had connections in Nashville, as did Morris, Otis, Luke, and Tex, and they could find someone for Harry. They absolutely could. "Would you like me to put it on the family text?"

Harry sighed, and Trace recognized the irritation mixed with exhaustion. "You know what? I will. Then I can say what I need to say."

"Okay," Trace said. He paused, not sure what his son needed to hear the most. "I love you so much," he said. "Ev and I will do anything for you. You know that, right?"

"Yeah," Harry said. "I know."

"I can't even tell you how scared I was when I saw that video," Trace said, letting his own emotion creep into his voice. He shook his head, but his throat only tightened. "Please don't put us through that again. Call us. We're here, and you don't have to be scared or embarrassed about anything in front of us."

Harry sniffed again, and this time it definitely was a sniffle. "Daddy, I'm not cut out for this."

"Come home," he said instantly. The house was too small for Harry, and they all knew it. But he could stay with

Bryce until he found his own place. Tex would move the recording studio if he had to.

"We're talking to the label next week," Harry said. "Kassie and Reggie are getting married down here. I'm gonna stay through that."

"And then?"

"I don't know yet."

Trace nodded and watched as Ev stood up with Avery, who whined and cried in her arms. She was definitely their fussiest child, and nothing about the past few months since she'd been born had been easy. Ev had some serious postpartum depression she was fighting, and Trace seemed to have forgotten how to take care of an infant.

He stood too and went to take Avery from his wife. He handed her his phone and she said, "Harry, we love you."

"Love you too, Ev."

Trace bounced Avery in his arms, tucking her blanket tighter around her. "Sh sh sh," he soothed while Ev told Harry he didn't have to be embarrassed by what had happened.

"The comments we saw were supporting you," she said. "Telling others to back off and give celebrities their space. That you're people too."

"Yeah," Harry said.

Trace watched his baby girl's eyelids drift closed only to open again. Oh, she was fighting her morning nap hard, but he'd get her to sleep, and then he'd get airplane tickets booked for him and his family to go be exactly where they needed to be.

At Harry's side.

Please, Lord, protect him until I can get there.

Trace had prayed this exact prayer over a dozen years ago, when he'd learned his ex-wife had dropped off Harry at his parents' condo. He'd gotten to Coral Canyon as quickly as he could, and he'd kept Harry under the safety of his wing since then.

He reminded himself that Harry was strong. He was a grown man now. He'd been living on his own for years.

But sometimes, a boy still needed his father, and Trace simply begged God to *please, please protect him until I can get there.*

5

Everly Young folded the young man she loved like a son into her arms the moment he opened his apartment door. "Oh, I love you," she murmured as Harry's arms came around her too. He gripped her with an urgency she couldn't name but that soared through her with the speed of hummingbird wings.

She didn't like it, because it signaled his desperation, his fear, his utter need to have a mother and a father in his life. "You made it," he finally said as he stepped back. "Where's Dad?" He looked past her, but Trace had not made it upstairs yet.

"He got a phone call right when we arrived," Ev said. "He's been texting and calling around since he spoke to you a couple of days ago." She'd left him with their baby, but Keri and Clay stood at her knee. "He'll be up in a minute with Avery."

49

She did her best to put a smile on her face, but it drooped almost instantly. "Go on, guys. Give Harry a hug." The love for her kids shone through on her face as Harry dropped into a crouch and pulled both Keri and Clay into his chest.

"Look at you guys." His smile appeared much easier than Ev's, but she knew he was hurting too. "I swear you've gotten bigger since I left."

"You've only been gone for a few days," Keri said as she giggled. She loved her older brother, because Harry was an excellent playmate. He took good care of the kids when Ev and Trace went out, and he gave them almost anything they wanted.

Ev had to tell them no sometimes, so they definitely loved Harry and never protested when date night rolled around.

Behind her, she heard Trace's voice as he came up to the second floor, and he rounded the corner with his phone still at his ear and their baby in the carrier. "I have to go," he said. "Let me know, would you?"

He wore a fierce, overprotective look in his eyes, and that only made Ev love him more. He'd been protecting and taking care of her for almost a decade now, and his Papa Bear streak extended to all four of his children—including Harry.

"Son," he said, setting the baby on the ground and moving into Harry as the younger man rose to his feet. They stood almost the same height. Harry worked out religiously, and could probably best his father in anything physical. But as Ev watched, Harry wept into his daddy's chest, and that made her weep.

Ev picked up the baby carrier and said, "Let's go in, guys. Keri, go inside the apartment." The kids did what she asked, and Ev followed them. Everything felt so heavy, and while she'd needed this getaway, it suddenly didn't feel like it would be a fun weekend in Nashville. It felt like she'd have the same problems and troubles here, but she'd be sitting on Harry's couch instead of hers.

She wanted to be happy, and Ev could pretend with smiles and scrambled eggs in the morning and getting her kids to school on time. But she just wanted to hold Avery all day long, while reruns of her favorite shows played on the TV, and she ate an entire bowl of caramel popcorn.

In fact, she'd done that several times—more times than she could actually count—in the past couple of months since her baby girl had been born. At first, she'd reasoned that it was the winter weather. The fact that it didn't get light until eight o'clock in the morning and the sun set by four-fifteen.

But as time went on, Ev knew it was more. Every thought weighed so much. Every action took so much effort. And she didn't care to do much of anything, when before, she'd run her own dance studio, put on town dances, and participated in as many of the Young Family activities and sub-families as she could.

"All right," Trace said as he and Harry entered the apartment and closed the door behind them. "Who's hungry?"

They'd been fed on the plane, and eating was just one more thing Ev had to force herself to do.

"Daddy, I want those onion rings you told me about," Clay said as he climbed up on the couch.

Trace grinned and laughed, then picked up his son. "The big giant ones?"

"That place closed," Harry said, which drew everyone's attention. He looked between Trace and Clay. "The onion rings we used to get when I'd tour with you? They were at The Fry Palace. They closed over the summer."

"Why would they close?" Trace looked truly befuddled. "Now what are we gonna do?" He glanced at Ev. "What do you feel like, sweets?"

"Anything," she said, because she didn't want to make the decision for all six of them. She didn't even want to make it for herself.

"We can order Thai," Harry said. "I know you like that, Ev."

"We're not ordering in," Trace said firmly. "It's time to go out, Harry." He set Clay on his feet. "And I've got three meetings tomorrow with possible assistants. Maybe a fourth, but I'm waiting to hear if he's available."

Trace clapped his hands together and looked around at everyone. "Does the Thai place have tables?"

"Yes," Harry said, but it was a clipped, short word, almost a bark.

"Great," Trace said easily. "We'll go there. Ev?" He turned his smile on her, and how he could be so positive and shoulder so much, she'd never understand. Just being here made her feel like shutting down, but she managed to nod.

"Daddy, what's Thai?" Clay asked, and Ev let him handle that while she got Avery out of her carseat.

"I've got to take care of Avery for a few minutes," she said. "Then we'll be ready." She loved this little girl with her whole heart, and she smiled at the infant as she prepared to change her diaper and make her a bottle.

"Can I feed her?" Keri asked.

"Of course, baby." Ev smiled at her and once Avery was changed, she gave the baby to Keri on the couch. "I'll get her bottle. Stay on the couch, remember?"

Harry had started to ask about the assistants, why he would need one, what he could have them do, and who the ones were that Trace had arranged to meet. Ev didn't pay much attention, because Trace would handle this, and Ev just wanted to be the emotional support for both Harry and her husband.

She could barely keep her head above water, but if she didn't have to handle too many details, she could link her arm through Trace's and shore him up when necessary. So she'd feed the baby, and they'd take Harry to dinner—which would be a big step for him after sequestering himself in his apartment for almost a week.

And she'd be right at his side, supporting him and loving him until he got his confidence back.

6

arry took the folder his father passed him, and he opened it and looked at the information at the top of the sheet inside. "Adam Harmon," he read. He'd be thirty years old in another couple of months, and Harry liked that he was closer in age to this potential assistant than the other two they'd seen that day.

His head pounded for a moment, and he reached for his bottle of water. Dad had set up the meetings in a conference room at Rebel Studios, something Harry hadn't even known he could do. Apparently, when a man wasn't quivering behind drawn drapes and locked doors, plenty could get done with phone calls.

And ideas.

And Harry didn't have the ideas—at least for something like this. For songs, his notebooks burst with lyrics from the past week. He'd organize them with notes and melodies if they made the cut. Sometimes the words just sat on the page for a while, without getting paired with a note. Some never made it out of the notebook.

"He assisted Cameron Junior?" Harry looked over to his father. "He hasn't been in a movie in a while."

"He moved to Portugal," Dad said like people made a Trans-Atlantic move every other day. "Adam said Cam decided he didn't need an assistant over there, because apparently, he's bought a country house in the village, and he can get his own groceries."

Embarrassment squirreled through Harry. "I can get my own groceries," Harry muttered, flipping the folder closed. He didn't want to act like a petulant child, but he folded his arms and lowered his head so it would be harder to see his eyes.

"Baby," Ev said. "This is not about what you *can* do. It's about what you *should* be doing."

Harry looked over to her, appreciating her words.

She turned toward him further, though Dad sat between them. "You know I'm not myself all the way right now." She swallowed, and Harry's ears seemed to perk up, because neither Dad nor Ev talked much about her mental state.

Dad took her hand and stroked his thumb across the back of it. Harry experienced a sense of longing, because he'd love to have someone who could comfort him—and whom he could comfort. He looked away, back to Ev.

"So I've been learning this lesson too. There are only so many hours in a day, and only so much energy I have for those hours. So there are a lot of things I *can* do, but I have to choose what's the *best thing* to do for me." She offered him a smile and wiped quickly at her right eye. "That's all you're doing."

Harry nodded. "Okay, Ev."

"Mister Young?"

Both Harry and his dad looked toward the door, where a woman had entered the room. "Mister Harmon is here."

"Yep," Dad said, and Harry simply watched the door as a tall, blond man entered the room behind her.

"Thank you, Martie," he said in a smooth voice to match his movie-star smile. He turned that on the three of them sitting at the table, and his step didn't hitch as he walked toward them. "You must be the Youngs."

Dad didn't rise as he reached out his hand. "Trace." He indicated Ev, as he'd done a couple of times now. "My wife Ev." He glanced over to Harry, who'd also shake his hand after he finished greeting Ev. "And the star of the show, Harry."

"Howdy." Harry did get to his feet, and as he shook Adam's hand, he had a really good feeling about the man. "You worked with Cam Junior?

"Sure did." Adam rocked back on his heels. "I'm sure you hear this a lot, but I really love, like *love, Small Town Girl*." He grinned and grinned. "Watching you sing it with just a guitar on that staircase?" He shook his head as in disbelief. "I showed it to the woman I was dating at the time, and we both fell in love with it."

Harry found himself grinning too. "That's great, man. That's from ages ago." He cut a look over to his father and ducked his head closer to Adam. "Before I was an adult, so we keep that on the down-low."

"Oh, sure." Adam had leaned closer, and he too straightened. "Well, I broke up with the girl—or she broke up with me—and I moved into her brother's personal assistant. Attending that wedding was a little awkward." He chuckled, and Harry really liked him.

His eyes sparkled, and while he was a little less formal than the other two men who'd come this morning, Harry liked that. He didn't just want someone to pick up his bags. He wanted a friend. He needed a buffer.

Adam pulled out a chair and sat down. "Well, I'm sure you have questions."

"I do," Dad said, and Harry would listen, but he didn't actually have any questions himself. So much of what he did happened by feel, and he had a very good feeling about Adam.

"Tell us what you did for Cam," Dad said.

Adam chuckled. "Whatever Cam wanted, and every client is different." He looked at Harry. "It's a bit of give and take in the beginning, as we each learn what Harry really wants. What he really needs from having someone like me with him. I can do the organizational things, like making sure he's where he needs to be and when—"

"Uncle Morris does that," Harry said, glancing over to his father.

"To making his appointments for personal things, to accompanying him to those to make sure no one gets too close." Adam had a briefcase with him, but he hadn't pulled anything out of it. "For Cam, I definitely acted as part personal assistant and manager, part bodyguard, and part errand boy."

"You're not an errand boy." Dad gave him a smile. "My brothers and I all needed a lot of help with all the moving pieces of our careers. Harry's just in the place where he's not traveling and playing with four of his brothers at his side. He needs someone like that."

Harry flashed a half-smile at his father. "Talk to me about the bodyguard part."

"Sure." Adam brushed his hand across his forehead to push his hair back. He hadn't overdressed for the meeting either, as he wore a pair of black khakis and a polo in pale yellow. Harry couldn't name the last time he wore a shirt with buttons outside of church, but for Adam it felt right.

"My claim to fame is I can clear an area for whoever I need to. I'm very good at reorganizing people so that someone who needs a bit of space has it."

"Like at a baggage claim," Harry said.

"You wouldn't have even been near that if I was with you," Adam said, and his smile slipped. "I'm surprised you're flying commercially, but if you want to keep doing that, okay. I just make other arrangements."

"What type of arrangements?" Dad asked.

"We always fly commercially," Harry said. "I'm not that big-time."

Adam did smile again now. "Harry, I'm not sure you understand who you are."

"I keep telling him that too," Ev said.

"You are that big, but if I need to, I'll call ahead to where we're landing, and your bags will be pulled by airline personnel. Your driver will have them, and we'll simply walk through. No stopping. No waiting." He looked over to Dad. "And I can get a security escort for that easily at all major airports, and in some cases, a completely cordoned off area so people don't get within twenty feet of you."

Harry realized his eyebrows had gone up with every word Adam said. "Sounds great," he said.

"Anything you want can be as public or as private as you want it to be," Adam said. "Restaurants, travel, a walk in the park."

"Harry does so much more than walk," Ev said. "He's at the gym for hours every day."

"And I can make sure only the people he wants to talk to him actually get to talk to him."

Harry thought of Belle, and the way Adam talked, it sounded like he could help Harry get a date with the woman. Since Harry had returned to Nashville, they'd texted a few times, just flirty things where Harry tried to learn a little more about her. Belle wasn't super forthcoming with details, but she answered him, so he took that as a positive sign.

The interview with Adam ended, and Harry got up to stretch his shoulders. "I like him," he said to his dad and Ev. "I think he's going to be the one."

"We have one more," Dad said. "And we don't have to pick one of these four at all. This is just who I was able to get in touch with quickly."

The door opened, and Martie said, "This is Michael Taylor," before Harry had even had a chance to look at the folder.

A woman walked in, and Harry balked. "No," he whispered to his father. "But I don't want a female assistant, and I *really* liked Adam."

"Her name was Michael," Dad said out of the side of his mouth. "How was I to know that was a woman's name?"

"Last one today," Ev hissed. "Let's be nice, and get through this."

"Then we'll hire Adam," Harry said just as Michael arrived, her smile far too big and far too false. No, he didn't have a good feeling about her, but he definitely wanted to get Adam back in here and offer him the job as soon as he could.

7

Harry, I need to know you're okay. Belle typed the text, the image of him toppling backward onto a moving luggage belt making her fingers fly. She didn't even care if she was overstepping.

I saw this video that concerned me, and I haven't heard from you. Please call me. Or text me back.

Harry had only called her once since they'd met last month. He definitely preferred texting over calling, Belle knew that.

She paced into her kitchen on this benign Wednesday, her day off. Her coffee still sat on the counter, along with the rest of her breakfast muffin, which she'd made for herself. She'd been eating and slowly sipping her caffeine, enjoying her sleepy day.

Then she'd seen that video of Harry. She'd recognized him instantly, though the caption had his name in it.

He hadn't texted her back, and Belle's worry climbed through her throat. She forced herself to sit down and reassess. She wasn't dating Harry. She wasn't his momma. He was a grown man, and surely he wasn't still rotating around and around with the suitcases in Nashville. She'd been meaning to update him on his neighbor for a couple of days now, and she picked up her phone and took a deep breath.

I thought you might like to know that we found Steven Bastian, your neighbor. He'd had enough of winter and gotten in the car and gone south. We found him whole and well and happy and warm in Phoenix.

She smiled thinking of that case, because she always wanted a happy ending for her missing persons cases.

Is it warm in Nashville? At least it hasn't snowed two feet in the past week, I'm sure. Belle looked up and out her dining room window, the snow piled up on her deck feet and feet deep now, in the middle of February. On days like this, in a moment when she had to bundle up in layer upon layer, she questioned her choice of where she'd bought a house.

But she loved her little red-brick house, with the wide front porch, the big back deck, the acre and a half she had for the horse she hadn't bought yet, and the dog she might get someday. Right now, all she could care for were cats, and she had three of those.

Her phone chimed, and Belle lunged for it.

Hey, Belle, Harry had said.

She waited, because surely he was typing another message. He had to be.

Thanks for texting. Sorry you had to see that video. I'm okay. My momma and daddy came this weekend, and we hired an assistant.

Belle's smile started out small, and her fingers started tapping again. *That's a great idea. Now you won't have to get your own baggage at the airport.*

Exactly. His name is Adam, and he'll do anything I want him to. Grocery shopping, errands, manage my appointments, all of it.

"So like a manager," she said aloud as she typed it.

Her phone rang, and Harry's name sat there. Her pulse blipped like it had lost its power for a moment, and then she swiped on the call. "Hey," she said.

"Ah, it's good to hear your voice." Harry wore a smile in his, and on his end of the line, a door closed. "I thought it might be easier to call. Do you have a few minutes?"

"It's my day off," she said. "So I've got all day."

"Wow, a day off," he teased. "I wonder what that's like."

"You can have any day off you want," Belle shot back at him. "You literally set your own hours every day of the week."

"I guess I can't argue with you there." He chuckled in that deep, low voice that made her shiver.

The moment sobered. "You sound good, Harry."

"I'm a lot better this week than last week," he admitted. "And Adam is kind of like a manager, and—" He sighed. "It's embarrassing to need someone to manage your life."

"No, it's not," she said. "Not when it's someone like you, Harry."

"I'm a normal person," he said, and his tone carried bite now.

Belle hesitated, because Harry Young so wasn't normal. Well, he probably was, in that he liked French fries and brisket sandwiches, and he played the guitar and wanted to own, in his words, a whole herd of horses.

But he also wasn't. His lifestyle as a mega country music star was *not* normal, and he had to know that.

"So I've got Uncle Morris managing my music career," Harry said. "And now Adam will manage my personal affairs."

"Including your finances?" Belle asked, her voice pitching up. She didn't want to lecture Harry, but she'd had so many bad experiences. "Do you know Adam? Is he a personal friend?"

"I'm still managing my finances," he said. "It's more like Adam will go get money out of an ATM for me."

"Okay," she said. "That's good."

"I sense a story here," Harry said.

Belle paused for a moment. "You're okay?"

"I'm okay," Harry said. "Adam just got here this morning, and he brought bagels and cream cheese, my favorite energy drink, and we're planning for the next few weeks."

"That's great," Belle said. "You sound happy about having an assistant."

"I am." He sighed. "I just...."

"I know how you feel," she said. She took a big breath. "I

was a tiny cog in the country music business once upon a time, and I had a manager like your Uncle Morris. Sort of. They managed everything, even my money, and I lost... everything."

Harry didn't respond instantly, and the silence pouring through the line went on and on. Finally, he said, "I'm sorry, Belle."

"It's done," she said. "I'm okay. I've recovered." She got up and wandered into her living room. Her guitar waited for her in the stand next to her electric piano. She hadn't touched it for a while. In fact, Belle didn't know the last time she'd picked up that guitar and played it.

"Have you?" Harry asked quietly.

"Maybe I'm still working on it a little bit," she said. "But I have a good job I love, and I can pay all my own bills."

"I see now why you didn't want to go out with me."

"No," Belle said quickly, turning away from her performance guitar. "It's not—you don't live here."

"That's another reason I'm calling," he said. "I've decided to, uh, I feel like I need to be here to make this album. So I'm not coming back to Coral Canyon until the album is done."

Belle nodded, the distance between them feeling so big and so small all at the same time. "I get that. You need to be in Nashville."

"I'll still come visit, of course," he said. "In fact, when my cousin gets married, will you come to the wedding with me?"

Belle ducked her head, her long dark hair hanging down

as she smiled to herself. "This is the Country Quad wedding?"

"It's Bryce," he said with a chuckle. "He's not in Country Quad."

"Tell me they won't perform there."

"I have no idea what Bryce and Codi are planning for their wedding," Harry said. "It's not until May, and maybe we won't be talking then."

"We won't?'

"I don't know," Harry said. "I hope we are, and I'd love to go to the wedding with you."

"All right," she said, going with her buzzing feelings and accepting the date. "I'd like that."

"Great," he said. "I would too."

Another bout of silence came between them, and Belle didn't mind it. "I'm glad you're okay," she said. "That video was scary."

"The experience was scary too."

"Your momma and daddy came?"

"Yeah," he said. "Yep. I feel a lot better now."

"I'm glad."

"So Steven escaped to Arizona?" The conversation moved on to something lighter, and Belle enjoyed talking to him. All too soon, he said, "Okay, I have to go talk to Adam, but I sure liked hearing your voice."

"Same," she said. "Don't be a stranger, okay?"

"I won't," he said.

The call ended, and Belle sighed into the silence now lingering in her house. She didn't mind it, and she went to refresh her coffee. With a fresh, steaming, creamed cup, she curled into her couch and put on her favorite movie. One by one, her cats joined her on the couch, and the four of them spent the rest of the morning together.

She finished her coffee and stroked Flower, the movie playing, but she didn't hear much of it. Instead, her thoughts rotated around the gorgeous Harry Young and how long it would take him to write, rehearse, and record his last album.

Belle had been in that world for a while, and the music industry certainly wasn't fast. "He won't be home for at least a year," she muttered to herself. "So don't go falling in love with him because he called you once."

8

"You stay here," Adam said as he twisted in his seat. "I just need to talk to their security to make sure we've got the right seat for you."

"Fine." Harry didn't mean to clip the word out, because he really liked Adam. But he hadn't gotten used to being driven everywhere in a black SUV with super shady windows. He wasn't used to having a personal assistant arrange where he sat at a friend's wedding, so he wouldn't be mobbed by people he didn't want to be mobbed by.

"Sorry," he murmured.

"You're fine," Adam said cheerfully. He glanced over to the driver. "Don't move from here. If someone tells you you have to, tell them you absolutely don't."

"Yes, sir," the man said, and Harry worked hard to remember his name. Kenneth. That was it. Adam got out of the SUV, and Kenneth locked the doors again the moment his closed.

"There is a lot of traffic here," Kenneth commented. "Real nice farm. These people have money."

Harry watched a couple in their Southern finest mince their way across the road and head down the decorated and marked path leading further onto the property. Kassie Goodman's parents' place, in a ritzy equine neighborhood Louisville.

"Reggie is a professional baseball player," Harry said.

"No wonder Adam has security to speak to." Kenneth wore a smile in his voice, and Harry caught the tail end of it when he glanced up to the front seat.

"Kassie's parents are pretty well-known in horseracing," he added.

"Yes, they are," Kenneth said. "The Goodmans own at least a dozen big race winners."

"Mm." Celebrity didn't impress Harry, and it never had. He'd grown up with a famous father, and he himself didn't feel any different now that people worldwide knew his name than he had when he'd been nobody in Coral Canyon. In fact, Harry craved that nobody-life in Coral Canyon, and he couldn't wait to get back to it.

He leaned his head back against the seat, a melody coming into his mind. His first instinct was to record it. Write down the notes so he could put lyrics to them later. But he'd also learned not to press himself into a corner. To let the music talk to him.

So while he waited for Adam to take care of whatever

Adam needed to take care of, Harry hummed a tune that would most likely make it onto his next album. After several minutes, he did pull out his phone and record himself singing the tune, his text message notification interrupting him for a moment.

He kept going, because Bryce just wanted to know where he was and when he'd be arriving. When he'd finished, he quickly tapped out a reply to his cousin. *I'm here, but Adam's making sure everything is set.*

I can't wait to meet Adam. Maybe I've walked by him a bunch of times and didn't know it.

Bryce had always been very good not to tease Harry about having an assistant. He said he wanted one of his own, what with Kassie's wedding being today, and Bryce and Codi's wedding coming up in only three more months.

Kassie had been living down here in Kentucky for the past month, after she'd had to postpone her wedding, and that had left Bryce short-handed on the ranch they co-owned in Wyoming. Then, she and Reggie were going on a twelve-day Mediterranean cruise, so it was still weeks before Bryce would have his cowhands back. Or horse-hands, as he didn't actually raise any cattle on his horse rescue ranch.

Tall guy, Harry said. *Black suit that looks like it cost a million bucks. Blond, clean-cut, no beard. Probably talking to the security.*

I'll look for him. This place is pretty locked down. Kassie's parents have two people checking actual invitations before letting anyone in.

I mean, can you blame them? They're high-society, and

Reggie's famous too. I'm sure the world knows about this wedding today. Harry didn't want anything like this, and he couldn't believe that an image of Belle drifted through his mind. He'd been talking to her since he'd left Coral Canyon, and she'd taken the news of his decision to stay here and record his album pretty well.

They texted; they called on the phone; Harry enjoyed talking to her. He didn't have to be *The* Harry Young with her, and she had a soothing voice that would definitely make good music. He'd tried to get more out of her about her own music career in Nashville, but she'd said she didn't want to talk about it all that much.

He'd respected that, and he'd had the tempting thought to look her up online. But he hadn't. He wouldn't want someone doing that to him, when he'd told them he wasn't ready to talk about himself, his life, whatever.

Let me know when you're in, Bryce said. *Codi and I are standing here with your momma and daddy, trying to stay out of the way, but everyone keeps coming over to meet Ev, and then you know how things go when they realize who your dad is.*

Harry's heartbeat bumped, and he yearned to be standing next to his parents too. Adam would never allow anyone to come right up to him, though, so Harry suddenly wasn't sure where he'd fit. Where he could stand. What he could and couldn't do here.

Then the back door opened, and Adam said, "We're ready for you, Mister Young." He must not be alone, because he only called Harry "Mister Young" when he stood in mixed company.

Harry turned and slid out of the oversized SUV, then reached to straighten his tie and his jacket. He hadn't even looked out this window, so he got completely caught off-guard when someone yelled, "Harry, this way."

He did automatically look that way, and no less than three cameras snapped his picture. He put a smile on his face, stood there for two breaths, and then Adam took his elbow and steered him toward the entrance to the Goodmans property.

The reporters clamored around him, but Harry kept walking. He didn't duck his head and allow his wide-brimmed cowboy hat to hide his face, so he gave them that. Then he and Adam made it past them, and he figured they could—and probably would—take photos of his back.

The lane stretched ahead of him, immaculately cared for, with emerald green grass on both sides. The Kentucky horse farm white fences welcomed everyone to a podium up ahead that had been draped with flowers as if the Good-man's had a horse who'd won the Triple Crown.

His cowboy boots—black and polished to match his deep midnight suit, jacket, and hat—scuffed along the ground as he walked, and Adam matched him stride for stride, at exactly the same pace.

They approached the gatekeepers, but Adam steered Harry around them, nodding to the two men there. One of them actually wore an earpiece, and Harry did enjoy this type of VIP treatment.

"Bryce said my parents are here," Harry said, just now realizing that Kassie was about to become his aunt. Through marriage, but still. Reggie was Ev's brother, and Harry had been calling him Uncle Reggie since Ev had come into his and his daddy's life.

He supposed Kassie was almost a decade older than him, but it still felt weird. He felt like Kassie was a friend, that they were the same age, that they'd hung out plenty of times when Harry had stayed on the ranch with Bryce. And now, with this wedding, all of that would change.

Beautiful music twinkled above them as Harry took in the huge urns of flowers, the pristine barn ahead of them, all of the doors thrown open wide, the scent of something browned and smoked and delicious.

"Yes," Adam said. "Your parents, cousin, and aunt and uncle are seated around you. I saw them when I came through before." He threw a woman a severe look as her face brightened in clear recognition of Harry. "They're holding down a private corner just through the barn." He spoke with a clip now, and his step increased.

Harry kept up with him, and he did duck his head as more people swung their attention toward him. He'd gotten used to the idea that people knew him when he didn't know them, but only intellectually. Having to actually deal with it in person was completely different.

They entered the barn, which had been set for dinner already, with beautiful linens in snowy white, glinting silver utensils, and blue flowers in the center of every table. They rose and rose and rose feet in the air, so guests could still see across the table and converse.

No expense had been spared for this wedding, clearly, and Harry wondered what his nuptials would look like. He'd do whatever he had to in order to make his bride happy, he knew that. He'd seen all of his uncles do exactly that, and he had no doubt that was all Uncle Reggie cared about.

"Harry," Adam said as they neared the other side of the barn, the doors all gaping on this side too. A nice breeze ran through the building, though it wasn't terribly warm today. The sun shone, and the sky radiated blue, so Kassie had gotten her wish for a gorgeous outdoor wedding, and Harry wouldn't be cold in his jacket.

"Mm?" Harry glanced over to Adam as his assistant slowed. He'd been doing coaching sessions with Adam, and he'd taught him to look straight ahead. *Don't look around. Don't make eye contact, then people won't feel like they can come up to you.*

So he'd been doing that, but now he slowed and stopped when Adam did. "What is it?"

"Your cousin...maybe your father—maybe both of them." He sighed and reached up and ran his hand down the side of his face. "Bryce said it was Kassie. No matter who did it, they arranged a surprise for you."

Harry blinked, searching Adam's face. "A surprise? What kind of surprise?" Was this going to draw more attention to him? He didn't want that, and he certainly didn't want anything to detract from his uncle's wedding today. He and Kassie should be the stars, not Harry.

"I've been instructed not to tell you." Adam's jaw jumped. "But I think you're still in the early stages of dealing with things in public, and you should know."

"So tell me," Harry said. "I don't care if they're mad."

"You want to know?"

"Yes." Harry tucked his hands in his pockets in an attempt to calm himself. "I can't believe my daddy and Ev thought it would be a good idea to surprise me at this wedding."

"They brought someone with them from Wyoming," he said, a frown that Harry was still learning how to read appearing between his eyes.

"Who?" As far as Harry knew, Country Quad would not be at this wedding, though Uncle Tex and Aunt Abby had come. They'd left their kids with Abby's brother and sister-in-law, as Harry expected to see his grandparents here too.

The trip had been on and off as Grandpa continued to heal from his surgery and time in the hospital last fall, but the last Harry had heard, they were coming. They wanted to support Kassie because of Bryce, and Reggie because of Ev.

"Another uncle?" he asked. He couldn't wait to see Keri and Clay, maybe even hold his new baby sister, Avery. He just wanted to be surrounded by people who knew him and loved him for who he was, not who they'd seen on stage, on an album cover, or a television program.

"It's a woman," Adam said as if women were distasteful.

"Her name is Belle Graves. She's out of Jackson Hole, and I've checked her out. She seems...."

But Adam's voice faded into white noise, because Harry's brain had caught up to his ears.

Her name is Belle Graves.

A smile covered his whole face, and he started for the big wide opening ahead of him. "How did they know?" he wondered aloud, and he didn't have to remind himself not to look around now. His focus felt laser-like, and the moment he exited the barn, the rows and rows of chairs spread before him, the altar clearly set far ahead, at the back of the yard, where a gazebo stood.

He didn't care about that at all. He wanted to see Belle.

A ringing noise sounded in his head, and Harry told himself not to be so eager. Not to play too many cards. Everyone would be watching his reaction to this "surprise," and he didn't want his parents, or Bryce and Codi, or Belle herself to see how excited he was that the Missing Person's Investigator had come from Jackson Hole to Louisville for a wedding where she knew neither the bride nor the groom.

She'd come for him, plain and simple.

"There he is," Daddy said, and Harry spun to his right. Sure enough, his father stood there, and he smiled and opened his arms to Harry. Everyone did stand in a halo of sunshine near the corner of the barn, out of the way, but clearly confident too.

"Daddy." Harry stepped into his father's arms and hugged him. He'd just seen him a few weeks ago, but pure happiness ran through him again. He pulled back and grinned at him. "Everything's ready?"

"Ev just came out," Daddy said, nodding over to Ev. Harry took a couple of steps to hug her too. "She said Kassie's dressed and ready. Her momma is just...doing something."

"She's putting on the final touches," Ev said, whatever that meant. She beamed at Harry too. "How are you, my sweet boy?" She cradled his face in her hand, and Harry felt so loved by her.

"Good," he managed to choke out. "Things are going really well, actually." He glanced over to Adam and smiled. "Adam's amazing."

"Thank you, sir," he said diplomatically. He stood with them, but out of the way as Bryce and Codi converged on him. Bryce too wore a deep, dark suit, and his tie matched Harry's bright blue one, as they were both in the wedding party. Codi wore a shiny, glittery blue dress, the same one Ev had on too.

"Brother." Bryce laughed as he put one arm around Harry and one around Codi.

"You look great," Codi said. "Bryce, you need a big hat like that."

They embraced while Harry told them it was the widest one he'd been able to find. "Well, Adam found it, but I do like it." He grinned at both of them, and he couldn't help the way his gaze darted around. He didn't see Belle, and his pulse thrashed against his ribcage like an errant whip.

"Harry!" Clay yelled as he ran toward him. Keri looked up from where she'd been crouched over the carseat, and she abandoned baby Avery in favor of Harry. He swept them both into his arms and let them squish his face and talk over one another and knock his hat to the ground.

Bryce bent to retrieve it, and as Harry swept a kiss across Keri's cheek, he spotted Belle. She didn't wear blue, but a white dress with bright pink, blue, and purple flowers all over it. She wore a flat-brimmed hat as if she'd make her way to one of the owner's boxes to watch the Derby next, and her sexy smile reached him about the time Keri said, "Look at my blue dress, Harry."

She squirmed to get down, and Harry dropped into a crouch to see it more closely. "It's sparkly," she said. "Like Momma's."

"And mine," Codi said, taking Keri's hand. She smiled down at the girl, and she smiled up at Codi. Harry marveled at how well Codi fit into the Young family, and he wondered if he'd ever be able to find someone who could do the same.

"Come on, ladies," Ev said. "The music has stopped, and that's our cue." She turned in a full circle. "You boys go sit down."

Half a second later, someone came over the speaker system and he had to be a professional voice actor as he said, "Ladies and gentlemen, the wedding of Kassandra Goodman and Reginald Avery will begin in ten minutes. Please make your way to the gazebo gardens and find your seats."

Codi, Keri, and Ev left, and Daddy swooped over to Avery and picked up her car seat. "Clay, with me," he said, extending his other hand to his son. He met Harry's eyes and then swept his gaze toward Belle. "I've got three seats for you guys."

Three? Harry thought, and then he remembered Adam. Of course. The man wouldn't leave him, Harry knew that.

He met Bryce's eyes, took his hat back, and repositioned it on his head as he asked, "How—? Why is she here?"

His cousin raised both hands in surrender. "This is the work of Kassie and Codi," he said. "I know nothing of it." He looked over to Belle too, who seemed to grow more uncomfortable with every moment Harry stayed over here while she stood half a dozen steps away. "She is pretty, though, and the women really like her." Bryce clapped him on the shoulder. "Even your mama." He grinned and then eased into step with his parents, who waved to Harry as they flowed by, plenty of other people heading into the gardens to get their seats.

Harry grinned as he faced Belle fully, glad he didn't have to do this in front of everyone. Only Adam. He raised his eyebrows and his hands as he hurried toward her. "What are you doing here?"

He wasn't sure if he could just pull her into his chest and hug her, because they hadn't even technically been on a single date. "You didn't say anything." He did wrap her up and hug her, glad when her arms came around him too. "You're stunning," he whispered in her ear. "So beautiful."

He pulled back, not wanting or needing to put on a show for anyone. He searched her face as she continued to smile at him. "You're like Prince Charming," she said, her eyes dropping to his feet. "Amazing boots. Great suit." Her gaze slid up his body. "Sexy cowboy hat."

Harry's blood burned hotly through his delicate veins. "Thank you. I seriously had no idea you'd be here. I wish I'd known. I'd have met you earlier or something."

"I believe we have a double date tomorrow night," she said as she turned toward the rows of chairs. "With Bryce and Codi."

"Ah, I see." Harry offered her his arm, and a thrill filled him when she placed her hand in the crook of his elbow. "It's amazing to see you, Belle."

And suddenly, he didn't care who saw what. Who was watching, taking pictures, or filming. He wanted to breathe in the scent of this woman's skin and find out if he could see her for breakfast and lunch before their double date dinner tomorrow night.

So he leaned closer and pressed his lips to her cheek as he inhaled deeply. "How early do I have to get up to take you to breakfast?"

"This way, Miss Graves," Adam said as Harry nearly walked right past the row where his father sat with Clay and Avery, and then a whole row of empty seats. He stared as Belle moved in front of him and said, "I'll be right here, Harry, when you get back." She nodded to Adam. "But you better go. You're in the wedding party, aren't you?"

Harry had completely forgotten, and he let Adam take him away from the beautiful Belle and over to where everyone in the wedding party had gathered while they all waited for Reggie and Kassie to come out and get this celebration started.

9

Belle had never felt more out of place and simultaneously right where she was meant to be. Dressed in her floral-patterned dress, she stood amidst a crowd of mostly strangers, all gathered on the sprawling Kentucky farm to witness the union of Kassie Goodman and Reggie Avery.

The wedding, an elegant affair set against the backdrop of the Goodman estate's horse racing legacy, buzzed with anticipation and joy. Belle's presence felt like an anomaly, a guest of neither the bride nor groom, but of Harry Young. As if he had that much power and presence.

Which he obviously did.

The ceremony unfolded like a dream painted in broad, emotional strokes of blue sky, white picket fences, and the crimson love of happily-ever-after. As Kassie walked down the aisle, radiant and full of a smile, an unexpected knot formed in Belle's throat. Perhaps it was the palpable emotions floating in the air, or maybe the realization that life offered moments of such unguarded beauty and connection.

Belle's gaze drifted to Harry, who stood as part of the wedding party, his usual reserve melting away in genuine happiness for his friends. She wondered what the weekend would hold for the two of them. She hadn't seen Harry in person in months, though his reception of her only a half-hour ago sure had brought butterflies to her ribcage. The sight of him now made her breath clog somewhere in her lungs, because he was cowboy perfection from head to toe.

She looked at Adam, the man charged with guarding Harry. She had no doubt Harry would make room for her wherever he wanted, but that didn't mean Adam would agree. Right now, he was probably checking everything about Belle, from her previous names to all of her addresses, to her credit history.

You should be glad of that, she told herself as the vows started to be exchanged. With Adam at his side, Harry didn't have to worry about falling onto a moving baggage claim as people mobbed him. Of course, he also didn't have to do his own grocery shopping anymore, and if he needed a toothbrush, Adam would simply go get him one.

Belle had no idea what that kind of life looked like. Nothing like hers, she knew that.

The throb of emotion pounding through her pinched slightly at how she and Harry sure seemed to be on different paths. Perhaps he'd spoken true months ago. When he'd said he "sort of" lived in Coral Canyon, and he didn't know what the next year held for him.

They were only half-way through that year, and Belle had no idea what tomorrow at breakfast would even look like. She and Harry hadn't actually been out on a date yet. Just because they called or texted didn't mean they were dating.

The ceremony concluded with a very baseball-like whoop, and Reggie taking Kassie into his arms and kissing her. When they turned and lifted their joined hands, Belle clued in and started clapping along with everyone else.

Kassie hugged her mom while Reggie stepped into his sister's arms—Harry's mother—and then she and Reggie started down the aisle, their faces shining with nothing but joy and happiness.

Belle wanted that. She wasn't one for big parties or large crowds, but she wanted the glow of a woman in love, and she wanted a man to look at her the way Reggie looked at Kassie. The way Bryce looked at Codi.

She sighed as the applause died and the guests started to flow after Reggie and Kassie. They had the barn set up for lunch and dancing already, and Belle honestly felt like a boulder in a raging river.

People moved around her while she stood in place, not sure how to get her legs to take that first step.

Then Harry appeared in front of her. Belle blinked. "Hey."

"Are you comin'?" he asked, offering her his arm. "Bryce said he made sure there was room for us at his table."

Belle slid her hand easily into the crook of his elbow. "Yes," she said. "Sorry, I just got lost there for a second." She hadn't even realized the whole garden had emptied. Almost. A few stragglers walked slowly toward the barn, and Belle finally got her feet to move as Harry tucked her arm close, close, close to his body.

"There's a lot going on," he said easily, taking her to the end of the row and then down the aisle toward the barn. If he noticed anyone watching them, he acted like he didn't. Belle wasn't used to having eyes on her, and she squirmed internally at the thought.

Once they entered the barn....

"So you know Codi and Bryce, huh?" Harry asked.

Belle sensed the underlying current of curiosity in his voice, and she dared to look at him. Attraction sparked through her in a powerful jolt of electricity, and it infused into her voice as she said, "Yes, a little. Codi and Kassie more than Bryce. We, uh, girls text a little bit."

"I see."

"I'm not saying anything bad about you," she said quickly. "I'll show you my texts."

Harry smiled and ducked his head. "I don't need to see them," he said quietly. "I trust you." He just said it out loud, just like that. "Now, we're getting dangerously close to the barn, and I don't know who you've met and who you haven't. My family...is...."

Belle smiled to herself and didn't offer him a way out of the sentence he'd started.

"Well, they're big," he said. "And loud. And like, not just big in numbers, but big in personality. My daddy—"

"I've met your parents," she said.

His hand dropped from his pocket, and his fingers slid between hers. "But not with me at your side." He squeezed her hand. "Not like this."

"No," she murmured. "It was a little different."

"My aunt and uncle are here," Harry said. "My grandparents."

Suddenly the pressure on her shoulders seeped down into her lungs, where it made breathing hard. The doors to the barn loomed, and Belle matched her step to Harry's, which didn't slow a bit.

They entered the magnificent barn, full of tea lights and greenery and soft, petally roses. They came in all colors, but mostly yellow, white, and pink. Not much red, and Kassie didn't seem like red-roses type of person anyway. Belle wasn't sure what type of flowers she'd have at her wedding, but she imagined light colors and fairy dust, so much like this barn.

Soft music played from overhead, and Belle came to a stop to bask in all of it. "This is so beautiful," she said.

"*You're* beautiful," Harry whispered. "Tell me where you're staying and what time to get you for breakfast."

Belle looked at him, magic flowing through her veins. She smiled, glad when Harry ducked his head and used his big ole hat to shield them from the rest of the barn. He swept his lips across her cheek and murmured, "I will get up at any hour to see you."

"Any hour?" she whispered back. Harry stayed up late and slept late, she knew that. So him saying he'd come to her at the time she said meant a great deal to her. "I think nine is early enough, don't you?"

"How long will you be in town?"

"Just until Tuesday," she said. "Bryce and Codi have a dinner planned tomorrow night."

"But you're free all day."

"Yes," Belle said. "I'm free all day."

"So nine for breakfast," he said. "Adam and I will come get you."

Belle grinned as he looked back to the barn. She found Adam standing over by a table close to the long row of seats where Kassie and Reggie would obviously sit with their families. In fact, Harry's father had just sat down in his spot, and Belle didn't see his mom.

"Does Adam come on your dates with you?"

"No," he said. "He delivers me where I need to be, and that's that. He won't sit down to pancakes with us or anything."

"Good," Belle said. "Because I don't like pancakes."

Harry blinked and swung his attention back to her. "That's very good information to know for a breakfast date."

"Come on," Belle said. "I'm staying at The Brown Hotel, along with everyone else."

Harry whistled. "Nice place."

"Of course you've stayed there."

"So I'll find us a nice place for breakfast," he said, moving again. "And then we'll go back to the hotel for lunch.

It's the origin of the Hot Brown sandwich. Did you know that?"

"I did not know that," Belle murmured as more people looked their way.

Adam met them about halfway to the table, and he nodded to both of them without saying anything. He turned and walked between Harry and everyone else, and Belle liked his subtle way of taking care of the country music star.

"Right here, sir," Adam murmured as he pulled out Harry's chair. Harry moved to the one next to him and pulled it out for Belle first.

"Everyone," he said as she sat down. "This is Belle Graves. She's...with me." He sat down and nodded across her to Codi. "You know Codi and Bryce. Then that's his momma and daddy, Abby and Tex. My grandparents over there—Cecily and Jerry. And my brother and sister." He grinned at the two kids seated at the table. "Clay and Keri."

Adam sat down beside his grandfather as Belle said, "So great to meet all of you." She smiled, and as they grinned back and Codi asked her something, Belle felt the strangest sense of...belonging.

Belle hadn't packed adequately to go on three dates with Harry in one day. She had brought a dress for dinner that night, but she'd been planning to hang out in the spa and the pool at the hotel during the day.

"So the dress will have to do for breakfast too," she

muttered to herself as she slipped it over her head. With her dark hair and features, she looked good in blues and purples. Today, she'd brought a plaid dress in the cooler colors—green, blue, purple, white.

It fell over her curves, and she tugged it to her knee. She wasn't much of a dress wearer, and she felt so out of her element in the dress. Give her a pair of black jeans and a T-shirt, and she'd be more comfortable. She'd feel more like herself.

Sighing, she stepped out of her dress and sank onto her mattress. She dialed Codi, desperation clawing at her throat.

"Heya," Codi chirped into the phone. "You're going out with Harry, right? Because Bryce and I just left, and...."

"Right, right," Belle said. "I'm going out with him. I'm just wondering...I hate the dress I brought, and I didn't account for a breakfast date." All at once, she realized she wasn't anywhere near the same size as Codi. She probably stood five inches taller than her, had a larger chest and shoulders, and it took a special blouse to cover her barrel-shaped torso.

"I don't know why I called," Belle said. "I just want to wear my travel clothes to breakfast. Would that be okay, do you think?"

"Sure," Codi said. "Wear what you want, Belle."

"It's our first date," she whispered. "I just want to be comfortable."

"They've got some cute tees in the gift shop in the lobby," Codi said. "If you've got fifteen minutes, it might be worth running down there."

Belle got to her feet and picked up the jeans she'd discarded over the recliner the first night she'd arrived here in Louisville. "I'll run and check right now," she said. "Thanks, Codi."

"Remember one thing, Belle," Codi said. "Harry's just as nervous and excited to see you as you are to see him, okay?"

Belle paused in pulling on her jeans. "I hadn't thought about it like that."

"Trust me on this," Bryce called, and Belle smiled.

"Okay," she said. "I don't have much time."

"Good luck," Codi said. "We'll pray they have the perfect shirt for you."

And because that was the kind of people Bryce and Codi were, Belle knew they would. She let them hang up as she buttoned herself into her jeans and pulled on the tee she'd worn on the plane here. Then she grabbed her thread wallet, made sure she had her room keycard, and hurried for the elevator.

"Lord," she whispered as the car descended at a painfully slow pace. "I just need one shirt I feel comfortable in. That's not too much to ask of a whole gift shop, is it?"

As the door slid open and a bell dinged, she added, "And make Harry just a little late, please. He doesn't like to get up early, and it would be fine if he overslept today." Then she hurried toward the gift shop, her prayer running through her mind the same way her pulse sprinted through her veins.

10

Harry glared at his phone, wishing the minutes would go backward instead of forward. There had been a mix-up with the car, and Adam had shown up at Harry's hotel as he'd been coming out of the elevator to let him know.

For something personal like this, Harry shouldn't have even seen Adam. The driver should've been waiting for him in the lobby, but someone had overbooked the car service, and Harry was running fifteen minutes behind.

He'd texted Belle—*mix-up with the car. Be there in a half-hour, okay?*—and she hadn't answered him yet. By all accounts, she hadn't even read the message.

Harry sighed, trying to tamp down his impatience. It was nine-fifteen in the morning, and he had plenty of hours left in the day. He'd set everything aside for today, noting with gratitude that he had a job and lifestyle that would allow him to do so.

Maybe his phone had stopped working. Or gone off the grid. He swept off a quick text to Bryce, half-hoping his cousin wouldn't get it or reply. But Bryce came right back with, *Yep, got it.*

Harry trained his eyes out the side window, imagining some of the technology from the science fiction movies his daddy liked to exist. Then he could've just stepped into a circle in his hotel, said, "The Brown Hotel," and been instantly transported there.

He said nothing to his driver, who likewise didn't speak to him. Adam had handled the tardiness at the hotel, sparing Harry, and he literally couldn't do anything about it now. Time would continue to tick forward no matter what Harry wanted, and he coached himself not to arrive for breakfast in a bad mood.

That wasn't how he wanted to spend any time with Belle, and by the time the car rolled up to the curb, Harry was already reaching for the handle. While he hadn't done so for a while, it turned out that Harry could open a door by himself.

He stood from the car as the driver hurried toward him, his face a mask of pure anxiety. "Mister Young," he said.

"I'm fine." Harry gave him the best smile he could and faced the hotel. After a moment of hesitation, he took the first step.

"I'm not to let you go inside alone," the driver said,

coming to his side. "You shouldn't even be out of the car. I can go get Miss Graves and bring her outside."

Harry met the man's eye, knowing he'd have to answer to Adam if he kept on this path of entering the hotel by himself. He looked past him to the ornate entrance, wondering how bad it could possibly be. Famous people surely went out in public sometimes. Didn't they?

The gold-rimmed doors to his right opened, and Belle herself strode out. She wore a pair of white pants and a blouse in pink, blue, and yellow stripes. Everything about her lit him up, and Harry moved toward her with the words, "She's right here. Give me two minutes with her, would you?"

"Yes, sir," the driver said, and Harry had no doubt the man would time them.

"Hey," Harry said as he met Belle. "You look fantastic." He grinned and leaned in to kiss her cheek, never happier for the Southern customs he'd had to get used to. "Mm, smell great too."

He pulled back, recognizing the pitter-patter and booming beat of his heart in subsequent seconds. He hadn't been this attracted to a woman in a long time, and his gaze dropped to Belle's smiling lips. She'd glossed them with something that gave them a darker crimson color and glinted merrily in the morning light.

"You hungry?" he asked as he took her hand in his and turned back to the car. "I can hold your hand, right?"

"Yes," she said. "To both questions." She squeezed his hand, her smile still etched in place. "I just want you to know I've never been to Louisville before. I have no idea where to go for breakfast."

Harry let the driver open the back door of the black sedan with dark privacy windows. "I've got you covered, Belle." He liked saying her name, and Harry's heart longed to be in the same physical space as her for longer than just today.

Don't wish for what you don't have, he told himself, mentally echoing something his grandfather had told him. *Be grateful for what you do have, right now, in this moment.*

And Harry had the whole day in front of him, and Belle looking at him with a sparkle in her eye, and a reservation at the best breakfast house in Louisville—according to Adam.

"I like this shirt," she said, running her hand over his chest. "You know it has mushrooms on it, right?"

Harry looked down at his dark gray t-shirt, which yes, had a variety of mushrooms on it, standing there in a row across his chest. "They're fungi," he said. "You know, it means I'm a *fun guy.*" He grinned at her, wondering if Belle had ever watched any of his online videos. He couldn't decide if he wanted her to or not. "The t-shirts...they're kind of my thing. I've been wearing these sort of funny, punny, strange tees for a while now."

"Yeah, I think I remember that now." With that, she ducked into the car and scooted over on the seat. Harry followed her, her words sinking into his ears and mind.

He pulled the door closed behind him. "So you've looked at some of my online videos." He deliberately didn't phrase it as a question.

"Only when we first met," she said. "Months ago in Coral Canyon."

"I didn't handle that too well, did I?" He took her hand again, his skin craving the touch of hers.

"You did fine," she said. "You just couldn't explain how you had a job, didn't live there, but had nothing to do for a month." She leaned her head back and smiled at him as the driver pulled away from The Brown Hotel. "Then you texted your name, and yes, I looked you up."

"Mm."

"I didn't make a habit of it."

"That's something, I guess."

"You don't want people to watch your videos? Isn't that why people post videos on social media?"

"I want people to," he said. "Not you."

"I'm a person."

Harry looked over to her, and when their eyes met, he couldn't look away even if he wanted to. "If you can stand me after today, would you go out with me again?"

Belle sobered a little bit. "How are we going to do that?" She looked away, and Harry marveled at her strength to do so. "I have to fly home tomorrow, and I've got a multi-department meeting on Wednesday." She paused for a moment and then added, "Rumor has it that we're getting split. Lots of reassignments. I might not even be an investigator later this week."

She sounded slightly down about it, and Harry's hand in hers tightened. "So let's have a phone date this weekend.

Friday night, and you can tell me all about your meetings and if you have a new job."

"A phone date?" She swung her attention back to him. "You don't strike me as a cowboy who loves talking on the phone."

He grinned at her. "You would be right. But it's not the phone. It's a video call, so I can see you and you can see me."

"So I'll get to see another funky t-shirt."

"Sure," he said. "I have a million of 'em."

"I'm sure you do." Her eyes fired at him, and he wasn't sure if she was flirting or commenting on his wealth.

"My mom buys them for me," he said. "I mean, some of them." He looked away, surprised at himself for bringing up his mother.

"She must find them online," Belle said. "Surely they don't sell stuff like this in Coral Canyon."

Harry swallowed, wanting to take his tongue with his saliva. "Uh, Ev isn't my mother," he said. "She's my step-mom."

"Oh."

"My mother lives in Europe," he said. "She's a super-model, and very connected to fashion, and she's been...." He cleared his throat and cursed himself for bringing this up. Of all the things he could've talked about, he'd chosen his mother?

Belle didn't jump in and save him. She said nothing, in fact, giving Harry plenty of room to insert his own voice. "I let her dress me for anything public I do," he said.

"Which is everything," Belle said.

Harry couldn't really argue with that, so he simply shrugged one shoulder. "I have a plethora of tees, and she designs and puts together my entire tour wardrobe." He reached up and adjusted his cowboy hat, which meant he couldn't see Belle's eyes any longer. "My relationship with her is...difficult."

"Difficult?"

"It's very much on her terms," he said. "She abandoned me at my grandparents' place in Coral Canyon when I was twelve. I didn't see her or speak to her for years." As he spoke, something healed inside Harry that he hadn't realized still wept. "But now that I'm...in country music, she finds me useful."

"Harry," Belle said quietly.

"I don't want to talk about her anymore." He cleared his throat again. "Sorry I brought her up." He looked up and into Belle's eyes again. "Tell me about your family. I mean, if you'd like."

Belle's face softened. "Sure, I mean, I don't have anything I don't want to talk about."

"Siblings?" he asked. "I've got three half-siblings. Two sisters and a brother."

"I've got an older brother," Belle said. "He branched out from our family farm in Oklahoma and works on a ranch in Texas. My younger sister is married and has two little kids. She lives a few miles from my parents, who are in Oklahoma City."

"How'd you land up in Wyoming?" he asked.

"A job," she said. "My parents didn't super love my

choice for my career, and honestly, I applied everywhere *outside* of a two-hundred-mile radius of the whole state of Oklahoma." She flashed him another sparkly smile that didn't seem to hold any past grudges. "I do miss them from time to time, but I really love my job."

"No wonder you're a little nervous about this week's meeting."

"Who said I was nervous?"

"Oh, you did, Miss Belle." He grinned at her as the car started to slow again. He glanced out the window and saw they'd arrived at Terrace Gardens. "Maybe not in those words, but I heard it."

"Maybe I did."

The car stopped, and the driver twisted toward Harry. "I'm to check on your reservation, sir."

"All right," Harry drawled, beyond doubting Adam's skills to make sure Harry was watched and cared for every step of the way. Even if he'd told the man he wanted the best breakfast date with Belle, then somewhere they could talk for a while, and then a reservation for the famed Hot Brown at The Brown Hotel for a late lunch.

They'd then meet up with Bryce and Codi for dinner that evening, and then...everyone Harry wanted to keep with him would fly back to Wyoming, and he'd make the trip to Nashville and his one-point-five-bedroom apartment.

The driver left, and a wet blanket of awkwardness descended over the back seat. "I'm sure he'll just be a moment," Harry said for a reason he couldn't fathom. In moments like this, he simply wanted to be at home with a guitar in his hand and lyrics running out of his mouth.

He fought against the apology threatening to come out, swallowing hard against it. Belle knew who he was. She knew this lifestyle, though she'd said very little about it.

"Tell me something happy," she said, and Harry looked at her again.

"Happy?"

"You fell off a cliff," she said. "I'm just trying to bring you back."

"I'm not...what?"

"Surely you felt the mood shift. It was violent." She offered him another small smile. "I don't care that the driver needs to check on your reservation."

"Yeah, well, it's...I just want to be normal."

"You are normal," she said. "This is *your* normal, and hey, we get to sit alone in a car for a few minutes."

Harry scoffed. "Yeah, scandalous." His father might actually think so, though Harry would be twenty-five-years-old this year.

"My mother would never let me park in a car with a boy," Belle said, continuing her flirt-fest with him, and Harry took a breath and relaxed.

"Have I got a story for you," Harry said.

Before he could start in on his father's constant lectures to Harry about his teenage girlfriend—all while he was sneaking around with Ev—the door opened, and the driver said, "They're ready for you, Mister Young."

Harry emerged from the car and turned back to help

Belle out. He kept his hand in hers as he then followed the driver past several people milling about on the sidewalk, as well as inside the restaurant. A waitress stood there, menus at the ready, and the driver passed Harry and Belle to her with, "This is Lauren. She's going to take good care of you for the next couple of hours."

"Thank you," Harry said, and he'd be sure to text Adam to tip this man well.

Lauren looked at Harry like he was indeed normal, and she said, "This way, Mister Young. Miss Graves," before she turned and led them through the restaurant to a private booth in the corner.

Harry slid into it so he was facing the wall, allowing Belle to sit across from him and face the restaurant. "This okay?" he asked as Lauren handed him an open menu.

"Yes," Belle said. "It's fantastic. Did you see those chandeliers?"

Harry had not, because he kept his focus lasered in on a destination, no sideways glancing allowed while out in public. But Belle shone with excitement. It practically vibrated from her, and Harry really liked that energy pouring from her.

Lauren said, "This morning, we have mimosas with pineapple juice as well as orange juice, and our chef's specials include a dukkah-spiced hardboiled egg trio over avocado toast and seasonal blackberry crepe with a honeyed crème fraiche." She leaned her knuckles on the table and smiled first at Belle, which Harry really liked, and then him. "I'll give you two a few minutes."

With that, she left, and Harry took a moment to hide behind the menu. Without looking at Belle, he said, "You never said yes or no to the phone-video date." He glanced at her over the top of the menu. "I'll order food and have it sent to your house, and I'll get dinner for myself too, and we'll eat and talk."

"Like we are now."

"Exactly."

Belle didn't cock an eyebrow at him or beat around the bush, which he also really liked. She simply said, "Sure, I'm free Friday night."

And just like that, joy burst through Harry. He'd have to rearrange some things to be free in the evening, but he'd do it. In order to see Belle, he had a feeling he'd do almost anything—and that scared him as much as it excited him.

And since he wasn't leaving his apartment for this date, he didn't even have to tell Adam about it, and that sent another jolt of blissful adrenaline through his veins.

Now, he just had to make it through the week, alone in Nashville, until a date he'd never imagined himself to be going on.

11

Belle sat down near the head of the table, one of her favorite blank notebooks in front of her. This one had a sloth on the multi-colored cover, and he rested in a hammock. It made her smile, and while Belle might take a few notes on paper, she rarely ever referenced them again.

Still, as an investigator, everyone took notes, and Belle didn't want to be left out. The man next to her clicked his pen in and then out again, in and out again. The noise grated on Belle's nerves, because the atmosphere in the conference room here at the Sheriff's Office carried more tension than ever.

Whispers of new assignments had been flying for weeks, and Belle really didn't want to be taken off missing persons. Of course, this was what they did here in Teton County. Detectives usually worked in one department for five years, and then they rotated to something else. Sex crimes. Narcotics. Homicide.

As far as assignments went, Belle had drawn a pretty sweet stick. She also hadn't been in this position for quite five years. So maybe she'd be fine.

"All right," Ben Barlow boomed as he walked into the room, his big barrel chest preceding him. He wore a houndstooth jacket that strained across his shoulders, and his tie flapped against the buttons of his bright blue shirt.

"Find a seat," he said. "We've got our cameras set up too, so please, let's raise hands to speak today, both in-person and online."

Belle glanced up to the wall, where a blue screen sat. A moment later, it blinked to life, showing five people who'd dialed in for today's meeting.

Belle only knew one of them, and even then, she only recognized Tyson Forrest's name. He'd been undercover now for what felt like a year, maybe longer, and Belle recognized the strain around his eyes as someone who didn't get enough sleep.

She saw the same look on her face sometimes.

Ben hated meetings, and he kept things moving at a crisp click. He went over advancements that had been earned, and Belle clapped alongside everyone else. Her department really was very small, and as she looked around, she realized how out of place she felt.

How out of place she was. Probably ninety percent of the people in the room were men, and everything about her very presence felt wrong.

She cleared her throat and swallowed, trying to get the self-depreciating thoughts to go too.

Ben-the-Sheriff moved on to department reassignments, and her name never got said. Relief pulled through her, though a twinge of disappointment did too. She didn't understand the warring emotions inside her.

"And now," Ben said. "We're going to hear a quick report from each of our undercover officers." He sat down, and Tyson himself moved on the screen.

He unmuted himself and gave everyone a smile. "It's good to see you guys," he said, and Belle's sympathy for the man doubled. For all of them who sacrificed everything in their lives—literally everything—all in the name of justice.

He quickly outlined the casino where he'd been implanted as an employee in the hopes of infiltrating a supposed and suspected money laundering ring. And oh, it existed. He knew about it. He contributed to it. And he'd been brought in.

"But they have women run the money," he said. "Women and children."

Disgust ran through Belle, and murmurs of the same filled the room among the officers and detectives there.

"Recommendations?" Ben asked.

"A female undercover officer," he said wearily. "It feels like moving backward, but I'm not going to be able to ever get in that van. I'm never going to know who they're handing the money to."

"Someone in Canada, I'm sure," someone in the room said.

"We know that, yes," Tyson said. "We suspect the Mazetti Family, which would be huge, of course."

An Italian crime family? Laundering money out of a casino in sleepy Wyoming? Yeah, that would be huge.

The next undercover officer gave their report and recommendation, and Ben went around to everyone. Belle had sat in these meetings before, and she looked to him to nominate officers for any new positions outside of the transfers he'd already made.

"Belle?"

"Hmm?" she answered without thinking. She blinked, coming back to herself. Had she missed something? A question meant for her? A missing persons case?

She glanced over to the men across the table from her. They stared back, sober expressions on their faces.

She threw another look to Ben. "I'm sorry," she said, going straight for the truth. "I'm not sure what you're asking me."

"I'm asking if you're ready for an undercover assignment." He nodded to the five officers on the screen behind him. "Tyson needs a woman at the Buffalo and Bison Casino."

Belle's breath left her body, and she opened her mouth to respond. But no words came. No answer.

"Take the weekend," Ben said. "Curt? I'm thinking of you for the minority training."

How he moved on so quickly stunned Belle. She was still reeling from being asked to go undercover. Or even thought of.

Images of her trio of cats ran through her mind. She'd have to get rid of those. Anything that identified her as Belle Graves would have to go.

She sucked in a breath, but no one seemed to notice.

Belle made it through the rest of the meeting, and Ben said, "Belle, I've got a folder for you to help you make your decision."

"Okay," she said, and she followed the Sheriff back to his office to get it.

"Really," he said as he handed her the thickest folder she'd ever seen in her life. "Take your time. Even if you said yes right now, it would take us weeks to get you in. Probably longer."

She nodded, her throat so narrow.

He nodded her out of the office and someone else went in as she left. She couldn't even imagine being Ben, with his revolving door of appointments, all the personnel here, any of it.

She liked her little corner of the world, and her cozy house, and her felines.

And one Harry Young.

If Belle went undercover, she'd have to cut off all contact with Harry.

Friday night found her sitting on her couch, her guitar in her arms for the third or fourth time this week. She couldn't remember when she'd played so much, but music had a special way of soothing the craggly and ragged pieces of her soul. It helped to flatten her thoughts and give her clarity to her life.

She'd called her parents and talked to her father about going undercover. They didn't want her to do it, of course. Neither her mother nor her father liked that she was in law enforcement at all.

She'd spoken to her boss in the missing person's department, and while no one would outright tell her what to do, she had gotten some good advice.

Could be good for your career, Larry had said.

You're a smart woman, Belle, her mother had said. *We trust you.*

God will guide you. Okay, so that was Belle's pastor who'd said that, a couple of weeks ago. But she believed it, and it was good advice.

Belle's fingers moved over the strings, the beautiful sounds coming from her instrument weaving through her and calming her pulse. Her Friday night online date with Harry would start in half an hour, and she'd gotten a text from him mere moments ago about how her dinner had been ordered and would be there soon.

Belle closed her eyes and opened her mouth. She had an earthy, almost grungy sound to her voice. At least that was what the music producers in Nashville had told her. Something rougher than Carrie Underwood could offer, something more authentic, something grounded.

Despite not playing for years, Belle's fingers knew right where to move. She had an instinct about where to insert her voice and when to let the guitar carry the load. Her heart-beat slowed in time with the chords, and she sang through a song she'd written for her album-that-never-came-to-be almost a decade ago now.

She'd just finished the last note and could still hear the reverberations singing through her house when the doorbell rang.

Harry had asked her for what she liked to eat, which restaurant he should order from for their video-phone date that evening, and she'd told him to "surprise me."

So her pulse picked up speed as she got to her feet, set aside her guitar, and headed for the door. She opened it to find the delivery driver already walking back to his car.

"Thank you," she called to him, and he smiled over his shoulder. Belle stepped down onto her stoop and picked up the plastic bag. It had been tied at the top, with a big red sticker for the delivery service so she'd know it hadn't been tampered with.

"Smells like Chinese," she said, a wide smile on her face as she went back inside.

Food always brought out the felines, and Belle wasn't shocked to find Flower, Mister Miles, and even Bing coming into the kitchen.

White Chinese containers indeed sat in the bag, along with a clamshell container of eggrolls and sweet and sour sauce.

Belle unloaded them all, exclaiming things like, "Oh, I love this cashew chicken," and "Mm, guys, look. it's that ham fried rice we like."

She normally didn't think herself too pathetic for talking to her cats, and she didn't tonight either. Her phone rang, and Belle's stomach swooped at the sight of Harry's name sitting there.

The Harry Young.

She almost felt like she'd fallen into a dream. Who had a famous country music star calling them for a Friday-night phone date?

Maybe another celebrity, but Belle was anything but famous. She did pick up and swipe on her phone. "Hey," she said. "I thought we were doing a video chat."

"I've joined twice," Harry said. "You're late, Miss Belle." He carried plenty of teasing in his voice, and Belle looked at the clock on her microwave.

"Oh, my goodness," she said. "I wasn't even paying attention to the time." She bustled out of the kitchen, then turned back to her cats. "You guys don't touch any of that."

Then she hurried over to the computer desk in the corner of her living room and woke the machine. "My food just got here," she said. "Sorry."

"Who were you talking to just now?" he asked, a low chuckle following. "Dogs or cats?"

"Cats," she said. "And they happen to love ham fried rice as much as I do." The real question became: How did Harry know?

"Shoot," she said next, trying to stay in the moment instead of in her mind. "I see the missed calls. Try again. I'm on now."

Harry was as technological as he was handsome, and

within five seconds, her computer rang at her. Belle knew enough to move her mouse to the green phone button and click it.

The video connected, the screen going dark for a moment, and then Harry's brilliance lighting up her corner of Wyoming. Everything inside her tensed for one awful moment, and then she sagged back into her chair at the sight of him.

"Can you hear me?" he asked, but she only heard him through her phone.

"Not on the computer," she said, once again sitting up. "Let me fiddle with my volume."

His mouth moved, and it created a weird vortex to see that but hear him through the phone, and Belle managed to get the volume up as he finished with, "...could be on my end."

"Nope," she said, getting a little reverb. "I can hear you now."

"I'm gonna hang up then." He grinned and then touched to end the call. Belle's phone went dark, but her computer made up for it.

She also had no idea what to say. She didn't want to run her job past him. She couldn't. Even if she took the under-cover job, her parents wouldn't say anything to anyone.

But she was still getting to know Harry, and as a general rule, Belle didn't trust very many people from the get-go.

"You don't have your food," he said as he chopsticked up a bite of Lo mein. "Is it there? I swear I got a notification that it was delivered."

Another bout of adrenaline shot Belle out of her chair and propelled her back to the kitchen. She seriously needed to calm down a little bit. Thankfully, her cats hadn't touched the food, and she noisily got out a plate and piled everything onto it as she said, "I got it. I just hadn't gotten it plated yet."

She had to shout from across the room, and a fine film of sweat broke out on her forehead. *Big breath*, she coached herself, and she managed to get over to the computer again with everything in one trip.

Harry gaped at her, then his smile grew and grew and grew. Belle wiped her hair out of her face. "What?"

"That was impressive," he said. "You had everything balanced on that one plate."

She whipped the fork out of her pocket where she'd stowed it. "Didn't forget this either."

"Boo," he said good-naturedly. "Didn't it come with chopsticks?"

"I try not to embarrass myself so early in a relationship," she said.

Harry sobered slightly, and then he said, "I guess we are still kind of in the early stages, aren't we?"

"I mean, I think so," she said. "We've only been out once."

"Mm, no." He took a bite and chewed quickly. His chopsticks seemed made for his hands, and Belle marveled at how he was so good at literally everything. "We had three dates on Monday alone."

"Okay, whatever," she said, grinning at him.

"And the wedding," he said. "That counts."

Belle just shook her head and tonged a piece of chicken with a cashew on it. "This is literally my favorite place in town."

"Yeah, that's what Larry said."

Belle froze and lifted her eyes to his. "You called my boss?"

"Dang it." Harry looked like he'd been hit with a taser. "I wasn't going to tell you that."

Her heart felt too big for her chest cavity. "What else did Larry say?" She didn't talk about her love life at the office. Of course, she'd never had one to talk about before either.

Still, Belle was very private.

Which is why the undercover job would be good for you, she thought. She hated that such things just popped into her mind, unbidden. At the same time, she wondered if it might be God, trying to whisper the things she should do.

Perhaps the undercover assignment was the right thing. She would have to rehome her cats, and then...walk away. She didn't have tons of close friends who would wonder where she went. Her private life made it easy for her to disappear for a while.

"Nothing much," Harry said. "I was straight to the point."

"Mm, sure," Belle said. "Someone as busy and important as you probably does."

He rolled his eyes and shook his head.

"Did you name-drop?" Belle teased.

"Is it name-dropping if it's your own name?" He cocked his eyebrows, clearly challenging her.

"Of course it is," she said, enjoying herself far more than she'd anticipated. "Did you do it?"

"I mean, I identified myself and said I was sending you dinner, and might he happen to know your favorite place in town?" He took a bite with a tree of broccoli, and she wanted to take a screenshot and send it to his momma so she knew he ate veggies sometimes.

"And he just gave it to you?"

"He asked a few questions," Harry admitted.

Belle didn't even want to know. Rather, she did, but she didn't want this date to be about this. Larry would likely tell her in the morning. Or he wouldn't. He was a low-drama boss, and he didn't get too involved in his employees' lives.

"Is that your guitar?" Harry asked next, and Belle whipped around again. Pretzels and cheese, she'd left her guitar on the couch. In plain sight.

"Yes," she said slowly.

"You said you didn't play anymore."

"I do...." She swung back toward the computer and considered him, wondering how much to tell. Then she reminded herself she was on her fifth date with this man, and it was okay to open up about some personal things. "When I'm a little stressed."

"Oh, boy." Harry gave her a soft smile. "What has you stressed, ma Belle?"

Her high school French was rusty, but she remembered what *ma belle* meant.

My beautiful.

Her throat closed, because she couldn't truly tell him about the thick file folder she'd thankfully pushed to the corner of the desk, out of sight.

"Just work," she said.

"You said you didn't get transferred."

She took another bite of chicken, chewed, and swallowed. "I didn't," she said. "But things are still moving and shaking, and I just feel...unsettled."

"I hate feeling like that," Harry said. "I'm sorry."

She took a deep breath. "It's fine. Let's talk about something better. How's the song-writing going?"

"Oh, that's not better." He raised both hands and waved them. "No work talk. There has to be something else we can talk about."

Belle searched her mind, another round of adrenaline elevating her pulse once again when nothing came forward. "I have three cats?"

Harry burst out laughing, and that made Belle giggle too. Hearing that sound...it felt like someone had tipped open her roof and poured just a little bit of magic into her life on a day when she really really needed some fairy dust.

12

Joelle Young dropped her bag as she entered her apartment, automatically turning back to the door with a sigh. She latched the chain and twisted the deadbolt, then faced the living room. The kitchen sat tucked around the corner, a...cozy space only one person could fit in at a time.

"Joey?" someone called. Her roommate, Laney.

"Yeah," she said. "It's me."

Her roommate poked her head out of her bedroom. "The timer on the—"

Shrill beeping went off, and Joey got the message. "I got it," she said.

"Good," Laney said, "Thanks. I'm washing out Paula, and that's dinner."

At least Joey wouldn't have to cook tonight, because Laney never made a meal for one. She'd moved to New York

City to go to culinary school, but Joey didn't want to cook for herself. Ever.

In fact, she'd started doubting she wanted to stay here and finish her education. *To what end?* she asked herself for at least the twentieth time. So she could go back to Coral Canyon and...make dinner for herself?

She could live with her parents again, but she didn't want to. She didn't want to go crawling back to Daddy, though no one would really see it like that. *Joey* viewed it like that, and she'd have way too many eyes on her for her to feel any different.

In the kitchen, she silenced the timer and pulled out an enormous casserole dish that smelled like fennel and sausage. She hoped it was Laney's baked pizza pasta, but it could be a breakfast casserole. With it covered with aluminum foil, Joey wouldn't know until she peeled it back.

And as a chef, she wouldn't do that right away. Food needed to rest when it came out of the oven, and she slid it onto the stovetop and tossed the potholders onto the narrow strip of counter next to the stove.

She wiped her thin, wispy, white-blonde hair off her forehead, and then scraped it all into a ponytail and secured it with a scrunchie from the bowl on the other side of the fridge.

Voices came out into the main part of the apartment, and Joey turned toward Laney and Paula. "Oh, boy," she said.

"It's just a little banana-y right now," Laney said. "It's fine. I'm going to cut it, and then we'll get the dye on." She smiled at Paula. "It's pizza pasta bake, Joey. You can eat whenever. I'll be with Paula for a little longer."

"Is Jenner coming over?"

"Later, yeah," Laney said, and Joey smiled politely at her client while Laney got the supplies she needed for the next round of styling. She didn't do hair every afternoon and evening, but she needed money to supplement her part-time job at a market near where they went to culinary school.

A tug of guilt moved through Joey, because she didn't have to work at all. Her father paid for whatever she needed to follow her dreams, and Joey wished she knew if that was still what she was doing or not.

She moved over to the couch in the living room and started texting her grandmother. *It's finally starting to get a little warmer here,* she said. *How's Coral Canyon? How's Gramps?*

Her granddad had had surgery last fall, and Joey worried over him all the time.

I wish it was getting warmer here, Grams said. *But they're predicting snow this weekend, so we're not quite out of the woods yet.*

A sense of longing and homesickness threaded through Joey, and she tapped to call her grandma. "Hey, Joey-girl," she said, her voice kind and aged and just wonderful. "How's the city?"

"Cold," Joey whispered. "Grams, I just want to come home."

Grams didn't say anything right away, which only allowed more tears to form in Joey's eyes. She didn't know what else to say. She'd called her grandmother in the past and said similar things. Her grams always seemed to know exactly what to say—and what not to say.

"Maybe you'll come home for your spring break, then," she finally said.

"Yeah." Joey sniffled and wiped her eyes. "I already have airplane tickets." But another two weeks felt impossibly far away.

"Then you'll have a whole year done," Grams said. "You'll be home for the summer, and we can try all those recipes you've collected. I can't wait to see how good you are in the kitchen now." She wore a smile in her voice, and Joey really wished she could borrow from it.

"Yeah," Joey said, drawing in a deep breath she hoped would strengthen her. "I can still live with you and Gramps?"

"Oh, I don't know, Joey-girl," Grams said with a sigh.

"There's room," she said. "You have a two-bedroom condo, and I won't take up the whole bathroom."

"There's two bathrooms," Grams said quietly. "It's just another thing you need to talk to your daddy about."

"I don't want to live with them," she said.

"Lots of college students live with their parents in the summertime," Grams said. "Look at Matthew and Lynnie. They're living with Gabe and Hilde this summer."

"Yes, but that's because they're getting married in Coral Canyon this summer," Joey said. "I could live with my mom, I guess. I just want to be closer to you guys, and I figured we could cook together, and I could help take care of Gramps, and...." She trailed off. "I could get my own place."

But she'd never lived alone before, and Joey wasn't super keen to do that. Coral Canyon was small and slow, and if she had to live alone at some point in her life, it might as well happen there. There were houses and apartments for rent, and everything would require a conversation with her daddy.

"There's room for you with your family," she said.

"I know," Joey said. "There's just so much going on with OJ now, and I don't know. I sometimes feel like I'm in the way." She whispered the last several words, almost ashamed to admit them out loud.

"Joelle," Grams said. "Your momma and daddy would be mortified to hear you say that."

"Doesn't make it less true," she said. "And it's not their fault. I'm not blaming them. I just—you know it's hard to be an island. And we act like everyone belongs in the Young family. But the truth is, there are a bunch of us that are just islands."

Grams once again didn't respond right away, but now her silence semi-irritated Joey. It meant she was trying to come up with a reason—an excuse—for how Bryce didn't need to feel like he didn't belong to his family, or why Joey shouldn't feel like that, or why Cash had no reason to doubt that his daddy loved him.

And Joey knew none of her cousins felt unloved. But that didn't mean they always felt like they belonged. Her daddy had gotten remarried, and Joey loved Georgia. She really did. One hundred percent, honestly loved her.

But they'd started a family together, and that family had stayed intact while Joey's had disintegrated. Uncle Tex and Aunt Abby had three more children, with Bryce almost twenty years older than the oldest one.

Uncle Blaze and Aunt Faith had four children—or would soon—and no, Cash wasn't fully related to any of them. Though he'd come first, he was an add-on.

That was how Joey felt. Added on. *Oh, yeah, don't forget about Roo.*

It was a hard thing to do when she was so forgettable.

"Forget I said anything," Joey said. She took in a quick breath. "It was just a hard day in the kitchen, and I need to eat." She tried to smile, glad she wasn't on a video call with Grams. For she'd have been able to see the pain pinching along her eyes and tugging her mouth into anything but a smile.

"Joey, Gramps and I would love to have you live with us this summer."

"I'll talk to Daddy," she promised, though she wasn't sure how to bring it up. Her daddy wasn't exactly intimidating, though he was tall, talented, and world-famous. Joey didn't always know how to open her mouth and speak her mind, or ask questions, or tell him the things in her heart.

He wanted to *fix* things, which Joey appreciated. She really did. But sometimes, she didn't want a fixer. She just wanted someone to listen, and then simply love her, no matter what came out of her mouth.

She let her phone fall to her lap, and she exhaled as she tipped her head back. The window in the apartment sat behind her, and Joey could feel the chill of it touch the back of her neck. "What do I want, Lord?" she asked. "Can You please help me to know what to do with my life?"

She hadn't liked college that much. So she'd left Wyoming State and come to the Culinary Institute. She'd never felt such excitement, though her daddy had stood out like a sore thumb in New York City. At the same time, he fit perfectly, because he was Otis Young, and he'd traveled the world as a guitarist and singer in the Young family band, Country Quad.

He didn't care if people looked at him, and he signed autographs and took pictures with anyone who asked. Joey didn't possess even a tenth of his charisma, and she did feel overlooked and thought about later quite often in her family.

"I know that's a me-thing," she said aloud while Laney and Paula laughed about something in the bedroom. "I know I'm only twenty, and I have a lot of life to live yet," she said. "But I don't want to waste my time. What's my next step? Go home to Coral Canyon? Stay here in the city? Keep doing culinary school?"

Joey had been considering a career in nursing lately, or perhaps she'd enjoy being a teacher. Something that got her outside her own thoughts, her own head, and allowed her to serve others. She'd only taken general education courses in Wyoming, because she hadn't known any better a couple of years ago what she wanted her life to be than she did right now.

God didn't give her any hints either, as her mind stayed stubbornly quiet and the street noise beyond the apartment glass drifted up to her from below. Joey sighed and opened her eyes. "Okay, I should eat."

She got off the couch to do that, her thoughts tumbling through her head like clothes in a dryer. If she could get them to sit still for very long, she'd call her daddy tonight and somehow, some way, find the courage to ask him to listen before she opened her heart and let him see the mess inside.

JOEY DID NOT FIND THE COURAGE TO CALL HER FATHER that night. Nor the next. She endured a brutal weekend at school, where they had to "fabricate a chicken" over and over until it was done perfectly every time.

She could now get a chicken broken down into its various parts, so the thighs, breasts, legs, and wings could be battered and fried in less than ten minutes. She knew where to insert the tip of her knife, how to lay it all out, everything.

As it turned out, Joey didn't have to find the courage to make a call. She had to find the courage to answer one from her daddy when he called on Sunday afternoon. Her heart pounded shrilly as she stared at the screen, and she swiped the call on at the last moment.

"Daddy," she said just as Laney banged a pot onto the stove. Joey got to her feet and went into the bedroom. It still smelled faintly like bleach and hair dye, but Joey only caught a whiff of it when she first entered the room. "Sorry, Laney's cooking. Just a sec." She closed the bedroom door and moved to the window between the two beds.

She didn't mind sharing a bedroom, because rent in the city was out of control, and Joey didn't want to spend more of her daddy's money.

"Hey, baby," Daddy drawled. "I'm just calling to see if you got the email about the flight change."

"Haven't seen it," Joey said. "But I'm sure I got it."

"We might need to reschedule."

"Yeah? What did they do?"

"Your flight got moved to eight a.m.," he said, his voice full of teasing. "I just don't see how you're gonna make that."

Joey smiled, partly to the city and partially to her faint reflection. "That's really early."

"I'll rebook it to something later," he said. "Could you come on Saturday instead of Sunday?"

"Yeah," Joey said. "Whatever's fine."

"Oh-ho," Daddy said with a chuckle. "We know that's not true."

Joey would've normally laughed with him and agreed. Now, she simply said, "Yeah. Hey, Daddy? Can you talk for a few minutes?"

"Sure, Roo. What's up?"

Joey swallowed, the use of her childhood nickname almost undoing her composure. "I—When I come home for the summer, I want to live with Grams and Gramps. Do you —Would you—?" She cleared her throat and turned away from the springtime hustle and bustle of the city. "I don't want you and Georgia to be upset, but I could live with them and cook with Grams and help with Gramps, and yeah."

"They are back in their place now," Daddy said thoughtfully. "They're doing well there, but I suppose they would like the company." He spoke slowly, like he was trying to figure out what Joey was really trying to say or do.

"I'm just—there's so much going on with Bryce and OJ and Bailey, and I feel—" Her throat closed, and Joey struggled to breathe. Panic built in her chest, especially when Daddy stayed silent.

"Invisible," she whispered.

"Joelle," Daddy said, and it was a rare occurrence that he used her full name.

"If I live with Grams and Gramps, I'll be useful." Joey sniffed, hating the weakness that sound leant her. "I'm okay, Daddy. I'm fine. I just—maybe I don't want to be a chef."

She hadn't intended to let that out, but now her heart felt like it had been slashed with a sharp blade. Blood poured from it, and tears leaked down her face.

"Oh," Daddy said. Nothing more.

"I feel invisible." Joey paced to the closed bedroom door and turned back to the window. "And lost. It feels like everyone around me knows exactly where they're going and how to get there, and I'm just...drifting."

She pictured the large crowds in New York City, all of them wearing their black power suits and long wool coats as they strode with purposeful steps toward their destinations. She panned back in her mind, and she spotted herself, an island in the middle of them, wearing a bright red coat.

And still, no one saw her. No one approached. No one cared about the blonde girl who didn't know what to do with her life.

I care.

The voice entered her mind but pierced right through her heart.

I see you, and I care.

Joey collapsed onto her bed then and sobbed.

"Hey, hey," Daddy said. "Talk to me, Roo. I can't stand hearing you like this."

"Can you come to the city?" she asked, not sure where that had come from. "We can just get a big hotel room that overlooks Central Park, and just—escape."

"I'll be there tomorrow," he said, his own voice a little froggy.

"I feel lost, Daddy. I'm not sure I'm a big city girl."

"I'll be there tomorrow," he said. "You'll get anchored, and we'll figure out what your next step is, okay?"

She nodded. "Okay."

"You don't need to see more than one step at a time, baby," he said gently. "You don't have to decide today if you're a chef or a, a, a marine biologist or whatever. It's okay to try one thing, then another. So don't cry, okay?"

"Okay."

"Don't feel bad. You're fine."

She pulled in a breath and reached for a tissue. She wiped her eyes and nose as she said, "Okay."

"And I'll be there tomorrow."

"I'm sorry, Daddy. I—"

"Don't apologize," Daddy said. "Feel how you feel. You're not wrong, and I'm not upset."

"I love you, Daddy."

"I love you too, Roo."

Those words had always made her feel safe and strong, and Joey smiled at her bedspread. "Tell the kids hi, and hug Georgia for me."

"She's right here," Daddy said. "Lookin' all worried."

"I'm okay," Joey said. "Just...I need you for a day is all."

"See you tomorrow."

The call ended, and Joey could only imagine the conversation in the house in Coral Canyon. Georgia would want to come too, and Joey did love her. But she quickly sent her daddy a text.

I just want you to come, Daddy. I love Georgia, and I'll see her at Spring Break, but I just want you to come.

It took him a while, and Laney had already finished dinner before he answered. *It'll just be me, Roo. See you soon.*

She finally relaxed, and later that night, as she lay in bed and closed her eyes to fall asleep, she did feel very seen. Seen by her father. Seen by her grandparents.

Seen by God, who'd told her *I see you, and I care.*

13

Bailey McAllister pulled up to the ranch house where she'd grown up, everything in Coral Canyon so green. So fresh. So new.

She felt the same way, and she took in a big breath of the Wyoming air. It felt different going down here than it did in Montana, though Bailey loved it there too. She got out of the car and opened the back to get her garment bag and the rest of her stuff. She'd be staying with her parents for the next week, with Bryce's marriage to Codi about in the middle of her trip.

"Bailey!"

She reached to close the hatch on her SUV, the sound of OJ's cheerful voice sending joy and love right into her soul. She felt like he hooked her up to an IV machine filled with only sunshine and light, and she dropped everything she'd just picked up to hug him.

"Hey, my boy," she said as he folded himself into her arms. "My goodness, you've grown so much since Christmas."

OJ definitely had gained some inches, and she felt a momentary flash of missing. So much missing. She wasn't this boy's mother, but she loved him anyway. She'd always loved him.

He stepped back and she held him by his skinny shoulders. "At least four inches." She beamed at him, and he grinned right back.

"My momma says I need all new jeans and church pants." He waved his arm. "Come on. Grandpa Graham and Grandma Laney have two new dogs, and you are going to *die*, they're so cute."

"Two new dogs?" Alarm blared through Bailey. "Like rent-a-puppies?" She quickly bent to get her things and follow OJ up the walk. He'd left the door open when he'd come out, of course, and she took the time to close it after she'd entered the house.

"Grandma Laney! She's here!" OJ ran ahead of her, and according to Bryce, the boy ran everywhere he went. Bailey and Bryce didn't have regular check-ins about anything. Sometimes he texted her things about his family, about Coral Canyon, or about their son. Most of the time, he didn't.

A dog barked, and Bailey took a little more care with her wedding clothes this time. She draped them over the back of the loveseat in the formal living room, and she set her travel bag beside it before moving down the hall and into the back of the house.

"Mom?"

The back door stood open, and she found her parents and OJ outside. And sure enough, two dogs Bailey had never seen. But as she filled the doorway and looked out, she found that they weren't puppies. Grown dogs ran around, chasing each other and a ball that OJ threw clumsily.

He laughed though, like he might be the next catcher who could throw out runners at second. Bailey smiled at him, and then her mother as she turned to face the house. "Hey, baby."

Her mom folded her into her arms, and Bailey couldn't believe she'd stayed away for almost ten years. "Hey, Mama."

"How was the drive?"

"So boring at the end," she said, though she loved coming down through Yellowstone and around the Teton Mountains. She grinned as she stepped back. "OJ is huge."

"He's grown a lot in the past six months." Her mom beamed at him. "He's always wanted more dogs."

"Where'd they come from?"

"Georgia," Mama said. "She rescues dogs, but only temporarily. I couldn't stand it when OJ came, just crying his eyes out about losing them. So we took them."

"You're insane," Bailey said.

"They're grown," Mama said, her voice a bit defensive now. "They live outside, and they'll be good friends on the ranch." She folded her arms. "Jed loves them. We love them. OJ loves them."

"How often do you have OJ now?" Bailey asked, her voice pitching up.

"About the same," Mama said. "He comes every couple of weeks."

Bailey nodded and watched her daddy and OJ play with the dogs. They looked like mutts to her, and Bailey knew animals from her job as a veterinarian in Butte.

"Mama, are we ready for Bryce to get married?" She spoke in a tiny, quiet voice, because while she'd known for years and years that she and Bryce were not meant for one another, there was still a piece of her—a very, very microscopic piece—that wasn't sure how she felt about him moving on so permanently.

Of course, she'd seen him, and he'd moved on a long time ago. He'd healed in ways she had only just started to comprehend in the past ten months or so, and Bailey actually found herself a little bit jealous of him.

"Yes," Mama said. "I think we're ready for the wedding. Lord knows that man has worked for his happiness." She threw Bailey a look, but Bailey ignored her.

She watched the dogs for another couple of minutes and then said, "I'm going to go put my stuff in my room, and then I have to take him out to Bryce."

"Yep, he'll be ready," Mama said, flashing her a smile. Then she went to rejoin them down on the grass, and Bailey turned away from the happy scene. Her emotions stormed through her as she collected her bags and took them downstairs.

Her tears filled her eyes, but they didn't fall. She couldn't believe she was back to this place, back to crying in her parents' basement. She'd been here ten years ago, and while the tears weren't for the same reason as before, it felt the same. It felt like she'd been thrown back in time, and she'd never find her way out of this deep, dark, dank basement.

"You have," she said, drawing a deep breath and wiped her eyes. "You're not the same person you were a decade ago. Not even close."

She sank down onto the bed and covered her face with her hands. "Dear God," she said aloud. "I have been working so hard here. Why does coming back here throw me for a loop every time?"

And how could she make sure it didn't again?

"Help me," she begged in a way she hadn't before. It wasn't the same kind of plea as when she'd begged for help when she'd found out she was pregnant. Or one she'd made to help her pass her finals and earn her veterinary of medicine credentials. Or one she'd done while gripping the steering wheel as she drove back into town to see OJ for the first time since she'd given him up for adoption.

This wasn't a cry for help out of desperation, but from a place of genuine longing to be helped by a loving Father in Heaven. Maybe desperate, yes, but from a different place. From her heart, and not because she was worried about what someone else would think of her. But because she wanted to be a different person, and she couldn't do it alone.

She'd been seeing a counselor for months now, and as she wept, a new kind of cleansing washed through her in a brand new way. She drew in a long, deep breath and looked up at the ceiling.

"Thank you," she whispered as everything seemed to fall back into place inside her. She hadn't started dating again, but for the first time in a decade, she felt like she might be ready to do so.

She headed down the hall to the bathroom to clean up and wash all evidence of her tears away, and then she went to get OJ and take him out to Bryce's.

"One more hard thing," she said, though she felt like perhaps she was kidding herself. She had plenty more hard things to go through, but she finally believed she could do whatever the Lord asked of her without falling apart as completely as she had in the past.

"I'll go find him," OJ said as he opened the door. He exploded from the SUV with such energy, and Bailey could only watch him go. A type of exhaustion she didn't understand weighed way down in her bones, and she'd only felt like this two other times in her life.

Right before OJ had been born. She hadn't been able to sleep for anything, and she'd been so, so tired. And once while she'd studied in her final term for her veterinary exams.

She sat in her car with the early evening streaming through her windshield, Codi's big white school bus with the cartoon dogs on the side of it off to the side of the lane that went back onto Bryce's farm.

Bailey closed her eyes and leaned her head back, searching for that center of herself she'd had an hour ago, in her basement bedroom. *It's just dinner*, she told herself. Then Codi would take OJ back to Georgia and Otis's house, and Kassie and Reggie would go home to their cute-as-apple-pie cottage just down the road, and Harry—

A sharp knock on the glass had her jerking upright and crying out. She leaned away from the window at the same time she looked that way, and it only took her a moment to recognize country music star Harry Young.

She reached to turn off her car and get out, and she swatted at Harry as he laughed. "You scared me."

"I'm sorry," he said between his chuckles. "Really, Bailey." He wrapped her in his arms and laughed again. "It's good to see you." He stepped back and looked at her. "How are you?" His eyes held a wisdom she hadn't seen in them before, and she reasoned he'd been in his mid-teens when she'd seen him last.

"I'm, uh, okay," she said, hearing the falseness of it in her own voice. "How are you? Mister Big Shot Rockstar?" She painted a smile on her face, hoping this whole night could be played behind this grin.

He smiled and shook his head. "Glad to be home for a minute."

"How long are you in town?"

"I've been here a week," he said. "I'm staying for another. Or ten days. I don't know. I, uh, have a guy who tells me what to do."

Bailey laughed, thinking he was kidding. When he didn't, she silenced herself. "Oh, you have a guy who tells you what to do."

Harry nodded. "And he told me I have a date with you tonight." He nodded to her car. "Is that why you were waitin' out here alone?" He raised his eyebrows, but Bailey wasn't going to confess all of her innermost feelings to someone she didn't know very well.

She knew Bryce and Harry were very close, and Bailey had no idea what either of them had said to the other about her. She hated this feeling, but she pushed it away and focused on the here-and-now. Harry wore no judgment on his face, and he put his hand on the small of her back and guided her around the front of her car.

"I heard my grandmother catered tonight's meal," Harry said easily. "With Joey, so we are going to eat like kings tonight." He took her up the sidewalk and right into Bryce's house without knocking. The air carried the scent of something roasted and delicious, with garlic and beef and rosemary.

Chatter echoed from the kitchen, and Bailey saw Reggie, Kassie, and Codi there, putting dishes on the table as they talked and laughed. Bailey reminded herself she had friends in Butte, and that she'd gone to dinner parties like this there too.

"Oh, hey," Kassie said, noticing them first. She abandoned her task of setting silverware on the table, and she came toward them with a handful of forks and spoons. "Harry and Bailey are here." She grinned at them and swept a kiss across Harry's cheek. "Hello, my nephew."

She wore a cheeky grin, and Bailey looked between the two of them.

"Hey, Aunt Kassie," Harry said in a deadpan. He rolled his eyes and took his cowboy hat off. He hung it on a rack next to the bookcase in Bryce's living room, and he caught her hand as he went into the kitchen.

But Bailey couldn't get past Kassie. "Hey, Bailey," she said, and she wasn't exactly cool, but she wasn't warm either.

"Hi, Kassie."

She did smile then, and she nodded her head back toward the kitchen. "Come on in. Bryce is still outside on the ranch."

"OJ went out there too," she said, suddenly worried. "I should've said something or gone with him."

"He'll be okay," Codi said, and she wore a much bigger smile as she moved around Kassie and hugged Bailey. "How was the trip? How are your parents?"

"They got two new dogs." Bailey hugged her back lightly, wondering how she could become a woman like Codi. "Some of Georgia's rescues."

Codi stepped back, surprise coloring her expression.

"You're kidding. They took Georgia's rescues? Those two big dogs?"

"Yes," Bailey said. "My mom said they'll be great on the farm."

"Well." Codi reached up and pushed her hair off her face. Today, she wasn't wearing one of her wigs, and her white hair blew around her cheek as if the simple act of the air conditioning could push it wherever it wanted. "Good for those dogs, because your parents do have a great farm." She turned and went back into the kitchen. "Come on in. We've got you by Harry and OJ, if that's okay."

"Yeah, that's fine," she said.

"Has Harry told you about his girlfriend?" Kassie asked.

"Kassie, stop using that word," Harry said in a tired voice. He'd found a spot on the couch and had his phone out, texting.

Bailey's stomach clenched. "Am I—is this going to be a problem?" She watched Harry, who didn't even look up from his device. He was probably texting his girlfriend right now.

"No," Harry said. "I don't have a girlfriend."

"You'll see her at the wedding," Kassie said. "He's bringing her as his date."

"That doesn't mean we're dating," Harry said. "It's one date. I live in Nashville. She lives in Jackson Hole." He finally looked up. "She's not my girlfriend, and everyone knows it except my *aunt* Kassie."

Before anyone could say anything else, the back door opened and the wind blew in Bryce. Tall, handsome, full-of-life-and-laughter Bryce Young. Bailey loved him on-sight, and the way he paused, took in the room, saw her, and grinned made him all the more charismatic and handsome.

"There she is," he said as if he'd been waiting all day to see her. He laughed as he came toward her, OJ behind him, and took her into his arms. "Good trip?" He stepped back and slid his arm around Codi's waist, the two of them looking at her with such hope, so much love, so much...just everything good.

Bailey felt the tears stinging in her eyes again, but she pulled them back as much as she could. She couldn't get her voice to work, so she just stood there and basked in the spirit in this house, on this ranch, with these people.

"Lord, she isn't talkin', and that's not a good sign." Bryce grinned at her. "Help us to know what to do to make her feel comfortable."

That got Bailey to shake her head, her smile more genuine than it had been since she'd arrived in town. "I had a good trip. It's good to see you guys."

She wasn't sure how the wedding would affect her in a few days, but for right now, everything had somehow been made all right. She fit here, somehow, even if her edges were rougher than the others. Even if she didn't have a partner the way Bryce had Codi and Kassie had Reggie.

She still had ties to these people, and she didn't want to sever them. She just had to figure out how to soothe the raw ends of them so she didn't have to fight tears every time she came back to Coral Canyon.

Oh, and it would be great if she could figure that all out

in the next three days, before Bryce and Codi's wedding, or she was going to be a blubbering mess.

14

Bryce Young paced in the farmhouse, his eyes automatically drifting to the big wall of windows that overlooked the deck and then the ranch. "She should be leaving soon."

"Everything is on schedule," Daddy said. "Except your tie isn't on, and heaven only knows where your cowboy hat is."

Bryce couldn't even tear his eyes from the glorious sunshine streaming through the windows. "Thank you, Lord, for good weather today."

His wedding day.

He could scarcely believe this day had come. That the sun had risen, though even in his darkest times, it always had. And today was a happy occasion, and he'd been praying and praying they'd have good weather, minimal wind, and easy travel for everyone today.

Codi's daddy and brothers and their families had been in town for a few days already. Of course, all of Bryce's uncles and their families lived in the Coral Canyon and Dog Valley area. No travel needed there.

But Harry had come in from Nashville with Adam, and his parents had a lot of friends making the drive up the apple highway to the Rising Sun Ranch for this wedding.

"I feel like I'm carrying a five-thousand-pound back-pack." He hadn't even realized he'd spoken out loud until his mom appeared in front of him. He blinked at her unsmiling face. "I'm so nervous," he admitted.

"Every cowboy is on their wedding day," Abby said diplomatically. "But you want to enjoy this, Bryce. Come on." She slid her hand down his coated arm to his hand. "Come finish getting dressed. You watchin' this farm isn't going to change anything."

His house held plenty of activity, from his grandma mixing punch in the kitchen to Uncle Trace plucking through chords on his guitar in the corner, Harry only a foot from him. Bryce was having them play the wedding march music, and they'd timed it meticulously with Kassie.

Codi was currently staged at the little red brick house where Kassie and Reggie lived, and she'd ride Dragon over to get married. Bryce was riding a pretty gray he'd named Violet, as her hair almost shone with a pale, dirty violet color, and she was sweet as pie.

He'd sell her once he and Codi returned from their honeymoon. Or maybe he wouldn't. Bryce couldn't make any decisions about anything right now.

"Bryce," Daddy said, and he looked up to find himself standing in his front living room. Harry's personal assistant sat on the couch, along with Uncle Luke, who held his baby daughter on his lap. They looked up as Bryce came to a stop.

Daddy smiled at him, and the whole world narrowed to just that. His father had been Bryce's anchor for so long, even when they weren't talking much. "Let's get your tie on." Daddy did that while Bryce lifted his chin and held very still.

He took in a long breath through his nose and as he exhaled, he forced his shoulders away from his ears. "Okay," he said as the last of the air left his lungs. "I'm calmer."

"Yeah, you spiraled there for a second." Daddy grinned at him. "The guests are almost all here. We're just waitin' on a couple of the rodeo cowboys Blaze and Jem know."

"Mm." Bryce didn't care who came to the wedding, as long as Codi showed up. Having her family there was important to her, and he wanted all of his uncles and everyone there. But rodeo cowboys Bryce probably knew but didn't interact with every day didn't matter that much to him.

"Ames Hammond hasn't arrived either," Daddy said, tugging the tie into place. "But he's on the way. He's been texting Graham."

"Bailey?" Bryce knew she'd come to town. He'd seen her a few days ago.

"She's here," Momma said. "And...your mother came, Bryce."

He jerked his attention to her. She stood at Daddy's

side, the pair of them so strong and so united. He'd looked to them for so much in the past several years, but now, he didn't quite know what to say.

"She texted me this morning," Daddy said casually, as if they were talking about the luncheon they'd have after the ceremony. "It's not a big deal, son." His hand curled up behind Bryce's head, and he guided him to look at him. "Okay? See my eyes? It's not a big deal."

"Not a big deal," Bryce said.

"She holds no power over you," Daddy said. "She's not perfect by any means, but you're her only son, and she wanted to be here."

Bryce swallowed, coming back to himself. "I did invite her."

"You sure did," Daddy said as he stepped back and dropped his hand. "Now, an alarm is going to go off on my phone in about five minutes. That's going to empty the house. We're all going to go line up and you're going to have to go out the front door with Grandma and Grandpa and get them safely to the altar." He grinned at them. "Can you do that still?"

Bryce heard the teasing quality in his daddy's voice. "Yes, Dad," he said.

"Great, because Grandpa doesn't need to be trippin' over rocks or anything." He grinned at Bryce. "I'd like to do a family prayer before the alarm goes off. You said it was okay earlier, but if you're too nervous, I—"

"No, we have to do that," Bryce said. His phone chimed

with Kassie's notification sound, and he pulled his phone out to check it. "Codi is getting in the saddle."

She wouldn't arrive for another fifteen minutes, because she was wearing her wedding dress—a garment Bryce still had not seen—and surely her hair and makeup had been done to perfection. She wanted to ride Dragon from Kassie's to wear him out so he'd behave better in front of the large crowd already staged outside.

Bryce swallowed, and then he reminded himself that if Codi could get up there in front of everyone, he certainly could. She hated the spotlight far worse than he did.

"Family prayer then," Daddy said, then he turned toward the main part of the house. "Family prayer, everyone! Let's all gather in the kitchen, please. If you're not here in sixty seconds, you're getting left out!"

"Family prayer!" OJ yelled. "Family prayer, family prayer, family prayer!"

Some of the other teens started making the words a chant, and that loosened up Bryce even more. "Fam-i-ly prayer! Fam-i-ly prayer!"

Cole clapped with every syllable, and Bryce's face heated as he got jostled to the center of the Young Family. He grabbed onto Uncle Mav, the closest man to him and said, "Thank you for being here."

"I wouldn't miss this for the whole world," Mav said. He moved back, grinning. Bryce suddenly wanted to tell every aunt how much he loved them, how amazing they all were for loving his uncles and raising his cousins.

He hugged Uncle Blaze next, his gruff, grumpy

demeanor melting away as he gathered Bryce close. "You're my hero, bud."

"Okay, okay," Daddy said. "He can't hug everyone right now. We've got less than five minutes until we all need to be headed outside." He reached up and swiped his hat from his head as kids kept coming into the house from outside.

"Hats off," Uncle Trace called, which caused more movement and more clamoring.

"Everyone here?" Daddy asked. "Dad?"

"Right here," Grandpa said, and Bryce fell back a step to stand beside his grandfather. He linked his arm through his, and they smiled at each other.

"Who's missing? Everyone check your families." Murmurs went around, and then Daddy held out a deep, dark, rich cowboy hat toward Bryce. "Your hat, son. Then you'll be ready." His whole being shone with gold, with love, with joy, and Bryce wanted to be like him so very much.

The moment lengthened, and then Daddy turned his sunshine on the rest of the family. He led them effortlessly, and Bryce could only hope to be half the father he was one day.

"All right." Daddy cleared his throat. His eyes dropped and then closed, and he pressed his cowboy hat to his thigh. "Dear Lord."

Silence draped over the house and everyone in it. Bryce settled even further into himself, into this moment right here, into his faith.

"It's been a while since we've had a wedding in this family, and this one is special for that reason alone."

Bryce fought against the emotions now spiraling through him. Surely there was activity all around outside. People still coming in to sit down. Codi's family making their way here from Kassie's house. The wind making the ribbons and flowers move and dance. The music filling the air along with the sunshine, the blue sky, and the puffy spring clouds.

None of that touched him in here, and right now, he felt himself drawing closer and closer to his father, his momma, his aunts and uncles, his nieces and nephews.

Small, slender fingers slid into his, and Bryce tipped his already ducked chin toward OJ, the little boy who'd changed everything in Bryce's life. He thought he'd known what religion and faith was before OJ.

He'd been wrong.

"Please pour out Thy spirit upon us here in Dog Valley today," Daddy said. "Bless and sanctify this ranch and all who come here today to witness the marriage of Bryce and Codi." His voice broke over both names, and Bryce only experienced an outpouring of love. Hope. Joy.

Daddy cleared his throat and said, "We love Thee, Lord, and we're grateful for Thy hand in bringing us together into this family. Bless us to get along today and always, forgive each other when necessary, and always return to Thee when we feel lost, alone, or afraid."

"Amen," Grandma whispered, and Bryce nodded along too.

"Now, it's time to get my son married, so please bless him to have a clear mind and an open heart, with his memory able to absorb as much as possible from this day. We ask these things according to Thy will, amen."

"Amen," chorused through the house in male voices, female voices, children's voices. Even a baby yelled, "-men!" after most everyone else had said their closing on the prayer, sealing it in Bryce's heart.

He opened his eyes and lifted his head, the first person he saw his uncle Luke. He grabbed onto him and held him tightly for a few seconds. "This is the best day of your life so far," he promised. "Enjoy it."

Bryce nodded and hugged Aunt Dani, then bent down and hugged OJ. "You better get outside," he said. "You're leading the whole thing."

OJ's face split into a grin. "I'll get the dogs."

Bryce chuckled as the nine-year-old headed out onto the deck. Pentagon, Codi's dog, and Lucky, Bryce's had been dressed appropriately for the wedding, with gem-studded leashes and everything, and OJ was walking them down the aisle.

That started just past the green stable, where Bryce's best horses lived while he rehabilitated them and got them ready to return to their best equine life. Tents, chairs, a gazebo, and an altar took up the space where he'd hosted the spooky Halloween walk last fall, and the wedding party would stage at the corner of the barn until Codi arrived.

He turned in a full circle, seeing people gathering their core families closer to them, giving them instructions, and straightening cowboy hats, ties, and gloves. Yes, his mother wore gloves, and Bryce couldn't leave the house without hugging Abby, the woman who'd come into his life and shown him what it meant to have a mom love him. Truly love him.

"Still nervous?" she asked as she wrapped him up.

"A little," he said. "But she's coming, so I best be ready."

"The dress is gorgeous." Abby smiled as she stepped away. "You know you're the luckiest man on the planet today, don't you?"

"One hundred percent," Bryce said. He grinned and turned toward his grandparents. They beamed at him, and his grandmother reached for his hand.

He took it easily, feeling so accepted and cherished by them. "You two ready? I need help getting to the altar. Maybe you know the way?"

"I do," Grandpa growled out as if Bryce were serious. "This way." They'd made this walk yesterday, and then he'd have to walk down the aisle flanked by his grandparents. He hadn't wanted to do so himself, and his parents were both walking in the wedding party. So Grandma and Grandpa became the obvious choices.

Once outside, Bryce breathed in the afternoon spring air here in Wyoming. The sky above him went on and on, and he said, "I'm so excited to get married."

"As you should be," Grandma said. They made their way past Codi's white bus with the cartoon dogs. Bryce had erected a semi-permanent covering over it to protect it from the elements, especially now that she didn't use it very often.

They worked around the ranch together, and she only

used the bus for a few canine clients now—Lucky and Penta included.

Uncle Trace and Harry had beaten him outside, of course, and the moment his uncle saw him, he nodded to his son. They started playing, and just like they'd worked out in their rehearsals, the classical music that had been playing stopped. Bryce wanted country music at his wedding, from the best country music band he knew.

Country Quad would perform for the dancing that would take place after dinner was served, but Bryce didn't look over to the set and waiting tables. Right now, he let his true joy shine on his face, and he paused with his grandparents between Trace and Harry while the audience got to their feet.

His phone chimed, but he didn't check it. Kassie had just told him Codi was two minutes away. They had everything timed perfectly. He'd have to wait next to the altar alone for only two more minutes, and he told himself to take the first step.

Do it, he thought. *Go. Do it now.*

Thankfully, his grandmother took that step, and Bryce had no choice but to go with her. He nodded and grinned at those in the audience he managed to see. He noted the four empty rows on either side of the extra-wide aisle that had been reserved for his enormous, loud, and amazing family.

Then he bent to kiss his grandmother, hug Granddad, and face the pastor. He shook the man's hand and took the reins from Uncle Jem, who held Violet for him. Bryce swung into the saddle, wondering how many seconds had passed since Kassie had texted.

He moved Violet into position beside the gazebo as the pastor climbed the steps to it. The whole thing really functioned as the altar, and Codi would come down the aisle on Dragon and stand next to him. They could face the pastor and a lot of the crowd from their position, something his parents had wanted.

"None of this thing where you stand with your backs to everyone," his father had said. "We want to *see* you."

And he could see all of them and right down the aisle. He took a deep breath, getting a noseful of floral, sunshine, and hope. The guests had remained standing, and now OJ stood at the other end of the aisle, the dogs waiting casually at his side, their tongues out and their eyes squinted.

Bryce couldn't stop smiling, and he wouldn't. Not now that the wedding was starting. He glanced down the aisle, and his gaze caught on Laney Whittaker, then her husband. They watched OJ like the proud grandparents they were. Everyone seemed to be looking that way instead of at Bryce.

Except Bailey.

She met Bryce's eyes, and just like she did every time he'd seen her lately, she cried. She reached up and wiped her eyes, giving him one final nod of acceptance. He hoped she could find her own happily-ever-after the way he had, and his heart pumped out an extra beat as OJ took the first step past Harry and Uncle Trace and the festivities began.

He looked down the long line of the wedding party,

hoping for a sneak peak of Codi atop her horse. But she hadn't come around the corner yet.

The procession continued, and people started peeling off left and right and standing in front of their chairs.

Bryce checked the line again, and this time, he saw his beautiful Codi. She'd opted not to wear the wig, and he grinned all the wider. He'd told her to choose for herself, and last he'd heard, she was going to wear one of her blonde, shoulder-length hairpieces.

But she hadn't, and her snowy white hair had been clipped back on the sides. She wore a radiant smile as she rode side-saddle, her skirt splayed out for all to see. She burned in the sun, so Bryce wasn't surprised to see the lacy, glimmering dress go up over her shoulders and then billow out into puffy, striking sleeves that narrowed back to hug right above her elbow.

"Dear Lord," he said right out loud. "I love her so much. Thank You for bringing Codi Hudson into my life."

Her eyes met his then, as if she'd heard his out-loud prayer, and Bryce cocked his head as if to say, *Well, you're almost mine now.*

And she ducked her head and he heard, *I think you're almost mine, cowboy.*

15

Codi Hudson had done this walk with Dragon a hundred times. Fine, maybe not that many, but it felt like it. Now that the moment was here, with at least a hundred people lining both sides of the wide aisle, her legs trembled around the horse.

Surely he'd bolt.

But Dragon remained perfectly steady, waiting for her to give him the signal to move. The faces surrounding her, staring at her, faded into a blur. All she could see was Bryce—her dashing, handsome cowboy—down by the gazebo.

She grinned with all the wattage of the stars, moon, and sun combined, and she'd seen his mouth move a few moments ago. No doubt saying something to God, the way he usually did.

The aisle in front of her waited, with everyone in the

wedding party out of the way and standing next to their chairs.

"Codi," Trace whispered, and she looked over to Bryce's uncle. He didn't look away from the crowd, and his fingers moved effortlessly over the strings of the guitar in his hand. Harry stood on her other side, matching him in skill and tone, and everything about this ranch and this family enveloped her.

"We're waitin' on you," Harry whispered now. "Are you going?"

In that moment, she realized she'd heard the same refrain three times. They really were waiting for her, and her eyes flew back to Bryce. He still wore that same smile, and Codi lifted her heels slightly to get Dragon to move.

The equine did exactly that, plodding along as smoothly as horses ever did. She bobbed with the movement, her dress making small swishing sounds she wondered if anyone else could hear.

Her eyes caught on Kassie and Reggie, and her heart grew two more sizes. Kassie had helped her so much with this wedding, and she could see herself on this ranch for a long time to come. Not only as Bryce's wife, but as Kassie's best friend.

The blue and silver ribbons waved in the Wyoming wind, and Codi smiled to go with it. Everything had come together beautifully, and her only regret was that her mama couldn't be here.

She glanced down the aisle, where she found her father stepping out from his spot in the front row. He'd be sitting with her brothers and their wives, as well as Tex and Abby and their younger children.

He'd hold the horse for her so she could get into position, her version of her daddy walking her down the aisle and giving her away on her wedding day. He wore such a huge smile, and that made Codi's eyes fill with tears.

Nothing much made her dad show any emotion at all, so that smile meant something.

Her gaze skipped over the guests, cataloguing them at the same time. Bryce's aunts and uncles, all of their children. People he'd sold horses to. Some of her long-time dog grooming clients. People she didn't know, who had to be friends of the Young family. In all honesty, they probably could've invited the entire town of Coral Canyon.

Then she saw someone she hadn't anticipated seeing today: Bryce's mother.

Corrie wore the softest smile Codi had seen on a woman's face, and before she could acknowledge the woman, a tear slipped out of her right eye. She brushed at it quickly, breaking their contact and looking up to Bryce.

He wasn't looking at his mom, and Codi wondered if he knew she'd come. They'd invited her, but she'd said she didn't know if she could make it. They'd never heard for certain one way or another.

But there she stood, and Dragon continued on, so Codi's gaze bounced to someone else. Bryce's grandmother, who actually waved at Codi. She decided she could wave back, and that got the little girls to do the same thing.

The next thing she knew, Codi was waving like a

Disney princess in a parade, and she lost the battle against her tears when she saw Abby and Tex, both of them fighting their emotions mightily.

Tex would lose against his, Codi knew that. The man stood tall and tough, dark and handsome, but he had a heart made of golden marshmallows, and he'd told Codi a bunch of times how much he loved her.

Abby had been her saving grace in everything, stepping in to be Codi's helper, friend, confidante, and wedding planner. Codi loved her so much, and while neither of them were all that great at saying the things they felt out loud, she knew Abby knew how much she was loved.

"Ready, sweet pea?"

Codi looked down at her daddy as he reached for the reins. She passed them to him, wanting to slide down into his arms and hug him tight. It had taken her and Kassie fifteen minutes to get her dress positioned just-so, with her cowgirl boots poking out, and her seat in the saddle secure. She'd never get back on Dragon once she got down.

"Yes, Daddy." She leaned down and kissed her daddy on the cheek while he did the same to her. "I love you."

"I love you too." He guided Dragon into a turn so that she could go by Bryce and into her spot for the ceremony, pausing in the precise spot she needed to be in to look her groom right in the eyes.

"I've imagined this a thousand times," he said. "And you're more beautiful than any of those." He leaned toward her, and since Codi wanted to kiss him as much as possible for the rest of her life, she touched her mouth to his.

"Hey," one of his uncles yelled. "The kissing comes after."

It sounded dangerously like Blaze, who put on a good front of being dark and dangerous, but who loved his family with a well deeper than any of the Youngs.

Codi and Bryce smiled simultaneously, which broke their kiss. Her daddy got Dragon where he needed to be, and Codi used her boot to back him up another step. Then his flank sat right against Violet's, and Codi could almost feel Bryce at her shoulder.

The heat of his body, the gentle pulse of his breath, the pure joy radiating from him and spilling out over everyone there.

Codi smiled at her brothers and sisters-in-law as the pastor climbed the stairs to the gazebo. Georgia and Dani had been on flower duty, and they'd managed to weave a bloom through every opening of the gazebo and hang bouquets of them from the tent poles as well.

The pastor opened his Bible, his gaze moving over the assembled guests before resting on Codi and Bryce. He wore such a welcoming smile, and the guitars silenced and the guests settled back into their seats in only a few seconds.

"We gather here today not only to witness the union of Bryce and Codi but to celebrate their journey together. This isn't just a joining of two people but of two hearts, bound by a love as enduring as these great mountains around us."

Codi glanced over to the Tetons in the distance, a place she and Bryce had hiked through and camped in a couple of times. *Hopefully many more times,* she thought as the sun painted glorious golds and yellows throughout the sky.

The heavenly glow cast over the gathering as the pastor read from his Bible about how a man should cleave unto his wife, and Codi's pulse began to pounce through her body. Dragon shifted his hooves, but he didn't move.

Bryce's hand slid along her lower back and around her hip, and that calmed so much inside her. She glanced at him, and he looked at her, everything turning rock-solid and steady inside her.

He was her anchor, the one person she could absolutely be herself with and he'd still want her and love her. There was nothing to be nervous about now. She'd made it down the aisle with all those eyes on her, and if Dragon could do this, so could she.

"Bryce and Codi have chosen to share their vows not on the solid ground but mounted on their horses, side by side, as equals, ready to embark on life's great adventures together." That was the pastor's cue for Codi to start her vows, which she'd labored over for too long.

Finally, it was time to just say them. She inched Dragon around so she could see Bryce better, and that put a large percentage of the crowd behind her. Even better, in her opinion.

His eyes shone—positively shone—as he gazed at her, that gorgeous smile on his face.

"Bryce," she said in the loudest voice she could. And she commanded horses—naughty horses—for a living, and she could get any dog to hold still while she bathed it and cut its hair. She could proclaim her love for Bryce in a voice that all could hear.

"You are my rock, my safe place when life is stormy and sad, and my very best friend in the whole world." She smiled at him as his eyes turned to glass. He was far better at saying how he felt, but Codi didn't do it nearly as often.

She showed her feelings by doing things. Serving others. Showing up when they needed her. Making dinner for Bryce when he'd been out on the ranch, struggling against wind and snow and darkness.

"You are so easy to love," she said, her own smile filling her whole face and sliding down deep into her soul. "And I'm so lucky that I showed up right when you were ready to be with me. I know God did that, and I know He's been with us every step of the way for the past year."

"One hundred percent He has," Bryce said, because he never hesitated to acknowledge the Lord in his life.

Codi squeezed his hands, wondering if he'd noticed her fingernails and how they had little gems glinting up near the cuticles. If he didn't now, he would. Bryce noticed everything about her.

"You are my greatest adventure, and I hope we can honor this ranch, lay in the pumpkin patch and watch the clouds, and host as many Spooky Halloween Walks as possible, for the nieces and nephews and for our own kids."

He chuckled and added, "I want that so badly."

"Then let me finish." She grinned at him as he mimed zipping his lips.

"Bryce, baby, I vow to support you, to challenge you if I

have to, to keep Lucky and Penta clean, to work with all your demon horses if you'll let me keep them, and to always, always love you, through all our days, no matter where our trails may lead us."

Bryce leaned toward her and whispered, "You can have as many horses as you want, my sunshine." He kissed her sweetly, but Codi didn't want to get teased again, so she only let him for a moment.

"It's your turn, cowboy."

He straightened and cleared his throat. "Codi, from the moment I met you—*seven* years ago now—I knew you were someone special. I may not have been ready then, but you're absolutely right when you say God orchestrated your return to Coral Canyon, to Lucky, and to me."

Her chest shook now, and she suddenly understood how hard it was to listen to someone else talk about his perspective on something she thought she understood. A shared experience, but not the same person experiencing it.

"You've become not just my forever love, but my partner, my best friend, and the person I trust the most." He glanced past her, his smile widening. "Sorry, Kassie."

The crowd behind her twittered, and Codi glanced over to his parents and her family, all sitting in the same row. Her dad had his hands clasped in his lap, but his face shone with happiness. Tex wiped his eyes, and Abby leaned into his shoulder as if holding him up while she simultaneously used him to keep herself upright.

"I promise to ride by your side, through storms and sunshine, always striving to be the man you believe I can be." His voice stayed strong yet filled with that tender emotion she'd heard before, and Codi faced him again.

"I love you," he said. "I don't know how else to say it, but I promise to say it every day for the rest of our lives. I love you, I love you, and I love you."

She couldn't stop smiling, because those words from the man she herself loved carried a massive amount of weight. They both faced the pastor, who closed his Bible and gave them a moment to settle in their saddles.

Then he said, "Codi Louise Hudson, do you pledge and promise yourself to Bryce Stephen Young, to be his legally and lawfully wedded wife, to love, honor, and cherish, for as long as you both shall live?"

"Yes," she called out. "I do."

The pastor nodded. "Bryce Stephen Young, do you pledge and promise yourself to Codi Louise Hudson, to be her legally and lawfully wedded husband, to love, honor, and cherish, for as long as you both shall live?"

"One hundred percent," he practically yelled, and that only made Codi start to laugh. He'd already said it during this ceremony, but something about his joviality and the strength of his voice tickled her.

"By the power vested in me by the state of Wyoming, I pronounce you, Codi Louise Hudson, and you, Bryce Stephen Young, husband and wife."

Codi's shoulders shook and shook with silent laughter, and she turned to Bryce full of giggles and joy.

"You're laughing," he said, his grin as big as the Tetons surrounding them.

"You...." She gasped for air, because she couldn't talk too much. "Yelled one hundred percent...at our...wedding."

He started to laugh too, and then he pulled her closer and kissed her while she kept on laughing. Dragon didn't like where he stood, and he shifted, taking Codi with him. Thankfully, her father was there, steadying him, and he gave the reins to Codi so she and Bryce could have their horseback ride into the sunset now that they were man and wife.

Around her, people cheered and applauded, and if she listened closely, she could pick out specific voices. But Bryce took her hand, expertly turned his horse, and led them away from the gazebo, away from the altar, away from the crowd.

Everything faded until it was only him and her, with sunshine, fresh air, and those glorious mountains jutting up from the ground.

He didn't take them far, only down the lane to a copse of trees that would hide them for a proper kiss. Bryce would help her out of the saddle so she didn't have to embarrass herself in front of everyone they knew and loved, and then they'd go back for dinner and dancing.

She knew the moment no one could see her, as a weight lifted from her shoulders. The world seemed to stand still around them, the only sounds the gentle rustling of new leaves and the distant laughter and chatter of their guests.

Codi met Bryce's eyes, her laughter finally subsiding all the way. "You're my favorite person in the whole world."

He slid from the saddle as he said, "I don't know why You blessed me with this woman, Lord, but I sure am thankful." He reached up to help her, and Codi finally let herself slip to the ground—right into her husband's arms.

Bryce reached out, brushing a stray lock of hair from Codi's face. "Alone at last," he murmured, his eyes reflecting all the glory of the sunset.

"Yeah," Codi replied, her voice soft, filled with wonder that her reality included Bryce Young. "It's really just us now, isn't it?"

"It's always been just us, baby. Everything else is just... scenery." Bryce pulled her close, enveloping her in his arms, and beaming love down on her. "I'm going to kiss you properly now."

She had no complaints about that, and not a laugh appeared as she kissed her husband back. She could honestly stand there and do that for a good, long while, but she couldn't. They couldn't.

Codi pulled back slightly, looking up into Bryce's eyes. "We should probably head back soon. They'll be wondering where we've escaped to."

"Trust me, Abby and every single aunt knows exactly where we are."

She laughed lightly with him, and then she turned to gather Dragon's reins. "Come on, you. You did so great, and you get the best grass tonight during the dancing."

Bryce took Violet, and together, they left the safety of the trees and faced the celebration going on without them. Yes, Abby was looking this way, and Bryce took Codi's hand as they started walking back to their own party.

"Your mom came," she said.

"Yeah," he said. "I didn't get a chance to talk to her beforehand, so."

"So we'll hug everyone, including her, and then you'll dance with me under the stars." She grinned over to him, and he gave the gesture right back to her.

"Yes, I will, baby."

"I'm surprised you didn't say 'one hundred percent,'" she teased.

He simply took it with a laugh, and Codi really did silently thank God that He'd led her back to Coral Canyon, to herself, and to Bryce Young and the entire Young family.

16

Abigail Young could stand inside the circle of her husband's arms forever and die a happy woman. She'd given her three younger children a stern lecture about acting appropriately at their older brother's wedding, and the last time she'd checked, Melissa had Carver and Pippa sitting at a table with Gabe and Hilde's children.

So she'd taken this opportunity to dance with Tex, something they didn't get to do as often as she'd like. "We should do more date nights," she said, causing him to lower his chin to get his ear closer to her mouth.

"Yeah?" he asked. "Would you go out with me?" The sexy rumble of his voice made her inside quiver, and Abby smiled against his shoulder.

"Always," she whispered, and Tex kneaded her closer. She'd watched Bryce and Codi lead everyone onto the dance floor, and the Youngs certainly knew how to throw and participate in a party. Everyone—every single one of Tex's brothers—had brought their wives out onto the floor, and Codi's brothers had done the same.

With Kassie and Reggie here, and Harry with his date-not-girlfriend, Belle, Bryce and Codi had some people their own age too.

Abby would have to give up Tex in a few minutes, as Kassie had come to say the parents' dance would be happening soon. She knew the familiar refrain to listen for—as Bryce had chosen one of Country Quad's songs for the dance.

Then Codi would dance with her daddy and Tex, and Bryce would dance with Abby...and his mother. No, he hadn't known if Corrie would come to the wedding until today, but they'd planned for him to dance with her for the whole dance if she didn't.

Abby didn't truly mind sharing Bryce with Corrie. That wound needed to heal, and she'd gladly give the two of them a chance to mend things between them if she could.

The song ended, but Tex didn't step back until he heard the first few chords of the song he'd written with Otis. Trace played this opening, as he did for a lot of Country Quad's songs, and that caused Tex to straighten and glace around. "I think...yep."

Abby squeaked as Tex spun her, relieved to find Bryce standing there waiting. He took her into his arms as easily as his daddy did, his smile wide and perfect and handsome on his newly-married face.

"Hey," he said quietly.

"Hey, yourself." She clung to him and tried to find any unrest inside him. "It's been a beautiful day."

Only she and him, and Codi and her daddy, danced now, with plenty of eyes watching them. Nerves struck Abby, and she wanted Bryce to say something.

He finally looked down at her. "Yeah," he said. "So far, things have gone great."

"So far? You worried about something?"

"I think I'm just partied out."

"You'll be okay dancing with your mom?'

"Should be." He spoke the words without a trace of emotion in his tone, but his jaw tightened, and Abby had gotten very good at reading Bryce's non-verbal cues to figure out how he really felt.

"I saw you with Bailey."

"One dance," he said. "Codi wanted to dance with OJ."

"It was sweet."

"She's doing good," Bryce said.

Abby nodded and looked over his bicep to find Tex approaching Codi. Abby's heart filled with love over and over again for the good cowboy and all those he'd brought into her life. He radiated so much goodness and love, and Abby simply liked to bask in it.

She also moved away from Bryce, but his mother hadn't come out onto the dance floor the way Tex had.

Panic reared inside Abby, and she cursed herself for acting a little prematurely. She should've stayed in Bryce's arms until Corrie had arrived.

Not only that, but Abby couldn't even see her anywhere. The faces on the sidelines blurred, and Abby couldn't quite get a full breath. Someone touched her lower back, and she nearly jumped out of her skin.

But it was just Bryce, and as she looked at him, finally seeing a face, she found him frowning mightily. "Where is she?" he asked. "I know she got the same memo as the rest of us about this dance."

Bryce stood there, also surveying the crowd at his own wedding, and Abby wanted to rage at the woman who could cut him so deeply. "Let's just—"

She cut off as Corrie pushed through the crowd, a measure of panic on her face too. "Sorry," she said loudly as she came toward Bryce in her heels and pretty, pale blue mother's dress. It glinted with gems and jewels, and she glanced at Abby. "I was having Melissa put ribbons in my hair."

She reached up to pat her dark hair where she indeed had some pink, blue, and white ribbons braided in. She wore a look of radiance, and Abby gave her the best smile she could as her adrenaline came down.

"Hey, Mom," Bryce said, and Abby headed for the sidelines. She felt every eye on her as she did, and she held her head high. A lot of Tex's brothers—fine, all of them—looked to him as a mentor. The wisest older brother who knew what to do in any situation. A source of strength.

A lot of the other wives did too, and Abby finally reached Dani and Georgia, who both took her by one arm and hugged her.

"So that's done," Georgia said, echoing how Abby felt about it. "But look at Tex."

Abby turned to watch her husband laugh at something Codi said. She loved Codi so very much, and she found herself once again thanking God that He'd led this extraordinary woman into all of their lives.

Bryce's especially, but Abby adored her too. Tex did. All the kids did. Every horse, dog, and duck Codi came in contact with adored her too.

Her mother had passed several years ago, and Abby had enjoyed the honor of planning this wedding with Codi, and she teared up at the thought of being able to watch her and Bryce build their life together now that they were married. She wondered if they'd have kids right away or not, and she prayed that no matter what they decided, that she and Tex would be able to be right there in the front row, cheering them on.

Her gaze wandered to Bryce and Corrie, who stood in a somewhat stiff way, though he easily swayed them back and forth. They did not talk, and Bryce didn't even seem to be looking at her, though his face was pointed down. Everything maternal and protective inside her wanted to march out there and rescue him, and Abby had to remind herself that Bryce was a grown man. He didn't need rescuing, at least not from this dance, and not from Corrie.

"Momma," Carver said, and Abby's attention diverted to him.

"What, baby?" She stroked his dark hair down and smiled at him. "Did you get to color Lucky?"

"I got the last one." He held the paper in his hand and lifted it to show her. "Will you hold it while I play?"

She took the line drawing of Bryce's dog that he and Codi had turned into coloring sheets for all the young cousins at this wedding and looked at her son. "Sure. When is that?"

"Reggie just came to get me and OJ," Carver said, looking back into the crowd. "So right now."

"Okay," Abby said. "Then you best go with him." She smiled her son away, grateful there were so many good men he had to look to for an example. Carver had been taking guitar lessons from Bryce for almost a year now, and Otis had been teaching OJ too.

Boston could play, as could Cash and Cole, and Harry had come up with the idea for all the younger boys who could and wanted to, to play a song for Bryce and Codi at their reception.

So she wasn't surprised to see Cash reach for Carver's hand and take it before he led him away from the party to where Reggie stood waiting with Harry, Cole and Boston.

Her mother heart squeezed again at the goodness of the children in this family. Blaze had come to Coral Canyon with a broken soul and a son he hadn't known, and they'd both been healing, growing, and providing relief for everyone since.

The song ended, and Abby started to clap along with everyone else. The festivities went back to normal, but she didn't go meet Tex on the dance floor.

Bryce and Codi came off it too, and they seemed

touched with magic. Everyone wanted to be around them, and Abby had learned from Georgia how to share her loved ones with a wide net of people. She'd seen Georgia do it over and over with OJ, though she sometimes didn't want to.

So Abby simply thanked God for people like Graham and Laney Whittaker, who stepped in and hugged both Bryce and Codi as a couple, their smiles real and genuine. All the Whittakers had come, as had the Hammonds, and Abby loved this small Wyoming town she belonged to.

The music stopped and someone said, "I need everyone's attention, please." Harry had the mic now, and as he'd been Bryce's best man, he'd already given a touching speech at the dinner.

"Yeah, right here. Spotlight me, Kassie." The spotlight shook and jiggled and jogged around the floor until it landed on Harry, who wore his rockstar smile for the crowd.

One thing about him—he had more charm and charisma than everyone in Country Quad combined, and that was one of the biggest selling points of Tex's brotherly band. They loved each other, people, and performing.

Harry did too, though he didn't love touring. "Where did the bride and groom get to?" He shaded his eyes. "They're gonna want a front-row seat for this."

"I want a front-row seat for this," Tex said as he slid his hand along Abby's waist and pulled her close. "Look how cute Carver is with that guitar."

Abby could see him, and she once again found so much right with the world. No, not everything would come up roses and not every day held sunshine and blue skies. There would be more storms in her life, in the Young Family, and with Bryce and Codi. God didn't spare anyone from the hardships, the trials, and the growth opportunities of this life.

But they had each other. Each of them knew how to forgive. And they had God. So no matter what came their way, Abby held the hope that all would be well.

"WHAT HAVE WE GOT HERE?" BRYCE CALLED TOWARD his cousin. Tex knew exactly what they had there. A male cousin guitar concert for the cousin they all loved best.

His son.

Tex had been holding onto his emotions by a thread for a week. He found himself getting emotional in the stables, feeding horses—something he'd done often with his son. Or that Bryce had done when he'd needed time to himself.

He couldn't see his other children's shoes without thinking life had gone by too fast for him and Bryce. He'd missed a lot of his son's life in the beginning, and the guilt he felt over that still cut through him powerfully sometimes.

Every day, Tex had tried to fix the mistakes he'd made earlier in life, but some things couldn't be repaired. They simply had to be acknowledged, and forgiveness had to be issued.

And his amazing son had given Tex the forgiveness he so often needed. Out of anyone, Bryce knew what it meant to truly repent, feel bad, pay a price, and reach the other side of that battle.

He laughed the loudest as OJ raised his guitar and yelled, "We're gonna play for you, Uncle Bryce!"

Uncle Bryce.

Just like Tex was Uncle Tex and not *Grandpa*.

"Oh, boy," Bryce said, still chortling from a few feet away. "Where's my dad? Look—Grandpa is out there."

Surprise ran through Tex, because while he'd known his son was going to play, he hadn't known his daddy was. He'd been through some health troubles lately, and Tex's first instinct was to jog out there and make sure Daddy had the stability and support he needed to play a guitar.

"Some of you might not know this," Harry said. "But my daddy learned to play the guitar from his daddy." He gazed over to his grandfather with love and admiration showing clearly on his face. "Gramps wasn't a professional or anything, but every evening after the work on the farm was done, he'd gather his boys around and he'd play."

Harry looked out to the crowd again. "I'm told he did it to give Grandma a few minutes of quiet in the evenings, after dinner, so she wouldn't kill them all." He laughed, as did many others.

Tex felt like bursting into tears, but he'd been keeping them dormant by laughing. His felt too loud, but he did it anyway.

"Gramps couldn't pay for guitar lessons, but I know Uncle Otis and my dad worked extra jobs to have the money they wanted for lessons. So as I was organizing this special treat for Bryce, I figured—I could get a little taste of what my daddy and uncles got as boys too."

He smiled over to his grandfather, and Abby leaned into Tex, providing some extra support for him right when he needed it. "This is great," she said.

Tex couldn't quite get his voice to work, so he just nodded. He had no idea how he'd get through good-byes tonight. Bryce and Codi were only going to Jackson Hole tonight, where they had a beautiful room at a luxury lodge before they'd continue their honeymoon in Canada.

"Take it away, Gramps," Harry said, and he seated the mic in the stand and stepped over to Reggie, who handed him his guitar too.

Daddy began to play, and Tex got transported right back to his boyhood, to the living room of the house where he now lived. He hadn't realized that Daddy had gathered the boys to give Momma a break, but it made perfect sense to him now as a parent.

Daddy had sung to them as boys, and he'd taught them loads of songs. All of Tex's musical heritage could be traced to his father, and pure gratitude streamed through him for such a gift. He'd made music his whole life, the way he'd earned a living, everything.

And he owed that all to his parents.

He didn't sing today, but he played through an old song that he'd once told his boys was the Young Family song, and Tex managed to tear his eyes from his father to see how his brothers were reacting.

Trace stood there, stoic and straight-faced, his baby in his arms. Tex knew that look, and it hid a lot. A whole lot.

Blaze had about the same reaction, though he softened as Faith said something to him and he nodded. They both looked back to the group up front, where Blaze's son Cash held a guitar expertly in his hands, watching his grandfather intently.

Morris and Gabe had linked arms, and they both smiled at their father. Mav wiped his eyes and met Tex's gaze. They nodded at one another, and Tex looked over to Jem and Luke.

They stood near each other and near their wives, and they both watched their father play with a sense of wonder accompanied by love in their expressions.

Otis wore the biggest smile of all, as he'd inherited all of his musical talent from their parents. So much song-writing ability, which seemed to have infected Harry's blood too.

Otis's free hand—the one that wasn't in his daughter's—tapped against his side, and just as Tex looked back to Daddy, he lifted the bridge of his guitar and lowered it.

All the other boys came in on the next note, and since they had pure professionals mixed with little boys like Carver, it took Tex a moment to recognize the song.

"It's the same song," he said as the crowd started to clap and cheer. He wanted to as well, but the thread keeping his emotions in check snapped.

Daddy had taught the boys in the group their family song—and they were all playing it.

His *son* was playing it.

Tex let the tears gather and burn in his eyes. He let them trickle down his face. He clapped along at the end with everyone else, and he let his smile loose when they finished.

Then he wiped his face quickly and he whistled through his teeth as he clapped for the boys with guitars.

Because he was really clapping for his family.

He was really clapping because he was so glad and so grateful to be a Young. He was really clapping for his momma and daddy, who'd taught them all so well, accepted them for who they were, and loved them unconditionally.

They'd shown him how to handle life when it got rough. They'd shown him how God would act in certain situations. They'd shown him all the best parts of himself.

So they definitely deserved the deafening applause and cheers that went on and on as the little boys ran out of the spotlight. Daddy stood and handed off his guitar while Harry did the same. Then he pulled the young man into his chest and hugged him, and Tex lost the battle against his tears all over again.

At least his wasn't the only wet face in the crowd.

17

Bailey circulated on the outskirts of Bryce and Codi's wedding, right where she wanted to be. Her cousins had formed a tight knot around her, and Stockton especially never let her get too far from him.

When she finished a drink, he took it from her and after the first alcoholic one, he'd replaced her liquid with sparkling cider. He'd danced with her in the corner, and he'd glared away anyone who looked like they might ask her to do something—anything—she didn't want to do.

That list wasn't exhaustive by any means, and all Bailey had to do was lift her hand and brush her hair away with two fingers, and Stockton would swoop in. Right now, he stood immediately next her, and she looked around.

Her parents still sat at a nearby table, along with Stockton's. "You gonna dance with anyone?" she asked.

"Not here," he said.

"If you're so salty about finding someone in Coral Canyon," she said without looking at him. "Why don't you move?"

"I like the stables here." He lifted his drink to his lips, and he still had something stronger than cider. Something he hadn't even finished yet, and they'd been celebrating with dinner and dancing for almost two hours.

Everything about it exhausted Bailey. If she ever got married, it would be a private, quiet affair at the ranch where she'd grown up. Under the open sky like Bryce and Codi, sure. But not this many people.

Of course, Bryce's family alone could fill a banquet hall, no non-blood relations needed. She spotted him with his uncle Luke, the two of them laughing over something. He exuded charm, goodness, and happiness, even from across the room, and Bailey did smile at it. At him.

"What about you?" Stockton asked. "You've been a scared rabbit all day today."

"I don't live here," she said. "I'm not interested in anyone who lives here."

Stockton took another tiny sip of his drink. "So you're not interested in coming home ever?"

Bailey's first reaction was to say, "No, not ever." But she'd learned a lot in the past decade, and one of those things was to never say never. "I don't know," she admitted. "Life is an open book, you know? A path could open up that brings me back here one day. I just don't know."

Stockton looked at her, pure surprise in his eyes. "Wow, Bay. I wasn't expecting that from you."

She nudged him with her sequined hip. "I'm not as salty as you thought, is what you mean."

He grinned and shook his head in a cowboy way of saying, *that's not what I meant, but I'm not going to argue about it.*

Bailey did like cowboys. She always had. For a while there, she'd wanted to ride the barrel racing circuit or work with horses the way Stockton did. She'd always had a keen love and soft spot for animals, and she loved her veterinary practice in Butte.

It seemed, however, that the cowboys there either left while they were young and came back broken when they were older, or they married young and settled down on ranches of their own. A severe lack of men between the ages of twenty-seven and thirty-seven—Bailey's self-imposed age range—existed, and she hadn't been out with anyone in a long time. A couple of years now.

Something inside her ached to be held by a good man again. She longed to be looked at the way Bryce looked at Codi, or the way her daddy looked at her momma.

"Oh, boy," she said, half hiding her lips behind her champagne flute. "Your daddy is coming in hot."

Stockton barely had time to react before his father arrived. Uncle Eli looked at him with a frown between his eyes, then switched his gaze to Bailey, where everything softened. "You two hidin' out over here?"

"No, sir," they recited together. She smiled, because while she was several years older than Stockton, they'd gotten along spectacularly for decades. Gotten into a lot of trouble too, but the past didn't need to be dredged up tonight.

"Bailey," Uncle Eli said. "OJ is looking for you." He swallowed a couple of times, almost like he couldn't quite get something to go down. Before he said anything else, Bailey's pulse jackhammered through her whole body.

"I know what he wants," she said quietly, barely above the din of the party.

"It's not a solo dance," Uncle Eli said. "And we've talked about it—the brothers and I—and we'll surround you two so everyone won't be staring at you."

She lifted her glass to her lips again, but found she was the one who couldn't swallow. Her feet felt swollen and huge inside her heels, and she actually started looking for the exit.

"It's not awkward," Stockton murmured. "Everyone knows about you two, and you go see him all the time now."

"I know." Bailey lowered her glass, and Uncle Eli plucked it right from her hand.

"Both of y'all need to stop loitering in this corner and go dance with someone," he said.

"I have danced with someone," Stockton said.

"Yeah, her." Uncle Eli gave him a glare that seemed a little harsh for such an occasion. "You brought that woman to this, and you've ignored her all night. It's not right."

Bailey's heartbeat somersaulted now. "You brought a date?"

Stockton had the decency to duck his head, and while the party was dark and only lit by the softest yellow lights, she could still see the flush crawling up his neck. "She knows it's not a date."

"She does *not* know that," Uncle Eli said. "She's dressed to the nines and putting on a brave face, but your mother's sitting with her, and it is not looking good. She's going to burst out crying at any moment. So either get over there and be with your date, or take her home." He made an angry noise, almost like a correction he'd give one of the horses up at the commercial stables at the lodge. "You're better than this."

With that, Uncle Eli turned on his boot heel and marched away. Bailey watched him go, shocked into stillness when she caught sight of Aunt Meg sitting with a gorgeous brunette. She indeed wore a beautiful blue dress with plenty of glinting gems, pearls around her neck and dripping from her ears, and only eyes for Stockton.

"Who is that?" Bailey asked as she looked their way.

"Darla Lyons," he said with a heavy sigh. "You weren't sure if you were coming, and I did—I *absolutely* did tell her that if you came, I wouldn't have much time for her."

"Stock." Bailey didn't know what else to say. "You didn't —you should've canceled with her." She clearly liked him, and one look at Stockton told Bailey there had been a spark for him too.

And she'd stood in the way of it.

"Go," she said in a bark. "Go right now. I'm fine. I'm going to dance with OJ." Just saying the words out loud made her lungs seize. "And I'm going to say my good-bye's." She didn't need to be here much longer. Bryce wouldn't care, and she hadn't come for him or Codi anyway.

She hadn't even come for OJ.

She'd come for herself. She'd come to prove to herself that she was ready to move on. That she could come back to Coral Canyon anytime she wanted to or needed to, and that she wouldn't be followed by nightmares, sideways glances, or gossip.

She saw the pure miracle of forgiveness and healing every time she looked at Bryce, which she did now. He stood next to OJ, bent over to hear what his biological son had to say. Then they both looked out into the crowd, and Bailey pushed Stockton in front of her.

"You go on. Get Darla and come dance by me and OJ."

"Okay," he said sheepishly, stumbling for a step or two before he evened his stride.

Bailey stepped out from underneath the edge of the tent and lifted her hand. She hated anything or anyone that called attention to her, that brought eyes to her she didn't want. But OJ was a huge part of Bryce's life, and of course he'd been a huge part of this wedding too.

"He danced with his momma," Bailey muttered to herself as Bryce caught sight of her. And Bryce hadn't spoken to his mom for years.

She could dance with OJ.

Bryce pointed to her, and their beautiful boy lit up like the Christmas tree did at Whiskey Mountain Lodge. He was so *good*, and so happy, and Bailey attributed all of that to Bryce too. In so many ways, right down to the shape of his face and his shock of dark hair, OJ was exactly like Bryce.

She'd contributed to half of his genes, and Bryce had told her all of the ways OJ was like her. He didn't like bananas, and he thought real seriously about people and things and situations. He'd been organizing a candy-and-cards initiative for the men and women who were deployed from the state of Wyoming, and his class had been sending them messages and care packages all year.

He cared about people, and he wanted to rescue every animal he came in contact with. Bryce said all of that came from her. So he looked like Bryce, but he acted like Bailey, and she let her heart fill with love with every step she took toward them.

"Hey, you," she said when she reached OJ. She pulled him into her chest for a hug. "I heard we're having a dance together." She refused to flick her gaze to Bryce to see if this was okay. She'd been slowly making her way back to center for a long time, and this was just one more tick.

Fine, it constituted about ten ticks, but repairing her relationship with Bryce and starting one with OJ wasn't the only thing she'd been working on.

"Yeah," OJ said. "Is that okay? It's not gonna be a spotlight or anything."

"We won't even announce it, Bay," Bryce said.

"Yeah, I know." She took OJ's hand and finally allowed herself to look at Bryce. He really was the most handsome cowboy in the whole world, and she wondered if she'd ever stop thinking so. She sure hoped so.

In that moment, Bailey wanted to meet someone else. Someone who would make her pulse frog around in her chest, and someone who would take care of her and their children, and someone who she could dance with in the spotlight at her own wedding—as long as there wasn't a whole bunch of other people to watch them.

Of course, her family wasn't exactly under-the-radar-flyers either, but they'd do anything for her.

Another realization hit her as quickly as the one she's just had about her love life: Her family loved her and had never stopped loving her. *She'd* been the one to withdraw from them, because her own shame and guilt had mandated it.

Not anymore.

"Hey," Bryce said. "You still here with us?" He put his hand on her elbow, and Bailey blinked back to the present.

"Yes." She cleared her throat, realizing how emotional she sounded. "Yes, I'm fine."

"Tell 'er what song you picked, bud," Bryce said. "It's coming up."

"It's one my daddy wrote," OJ said. "Well, him and Harry. It's gonna be on Harry's new album next spring."

"That's amazing," Bailey said, her smile full and real now. "What's it called?"

"The Clock on the Wall," OJ said. "I know how it starts, so when it does, we'll just go out, okay?" He looked over to her and then past her to Bryce. "Bryce taught me how to dance so I won't be steppin' on your feet or nothing."

He sounded like a miniature cowboy, and Bailey tipped

her head back and laughed. "He taught you how, huh?" She beamed down at OJ. "Did he tell you he's not that great of a dancer?"

OJ grinned right on back. "He didn't, but Uncle Tex did, and he showed me a few things too."

"Mm," Bailey said, feeling sparkly on the inside and the outside. The song keeping people on the dance floor right now ended, and another one didn't start up right away. She wondered how long she'd have to stand there with the two of them, without Codi around. All of it made her stomach clench and a line of marching ants to parade through her bloodstream.

"All right, folks," a man said, and Bailey knew Harry Young's voice. The world over knew the man's voice. "I've got a special concert for you tonight—one song from my album that I haven't even recorded yet. I wrote it with my uncle Otis, and we're gonna give you the acoustic version tonight for one of our last dances. Then, Country Quad will play a medley, and we'll wrap this shindig right on up."

He too sounded like he'd swallowed four or five cowboys to get that perfectly sexy, strong twang, and his guitar rang through the night in the next moment.

"This is it," OJ said needlessly, and he tugged on Bailey's hand.

She went with him as the floor flooded with people, her momma and daddy included. They moved right in close to Bailey and OJ, as did Uncle Eli and Aunt Meg, Uncle Andy and Aunt Becca, and Uncle Beau and his country music star wife, Aunt Lily.

They all had adult children like her, and her cousins packed the dance floor with their dates as well. Bryce and Codi found a spot, and all the Youngs came out with their wives as well.

Bailey stood a little taller than OJ still, but he'd surely shoot past her in the next couple of years as he hit puberty and became a teenager. She had a sudden urge to see all of that, be right here to witness every day, every month, every change.

At the same time, she'd given up that right a long time ago. Otis and Georgia didn't have to include her nearly as much as they did, even now. How could she ever repay them for taking her son and loving him so completely? Raising him so well, when she wouldn't have been able to?

"Who's your momma dancing with?" she asked, a horrible thought landing in her mind.

OJ looked up to her. "I don't know."

"Well, she needs someone if your daddy is playing the guitar," Bailey said. Tex and Abby swayed nearby, both of them watching her and OJ with kind smiles on their faces. Bailey didn't deserve their kindness.

Yes, you do.

The voice in her head boomed loudly, almost as if Harry had stopped playing and singing and had shouted it into the microphone. Bailey even looked around to see if anyone else had heard it.

No one seemed to, and Bailey understood it was a voice from On High, speaking directly to her.

"Maybe Grandpa," OJ said, and Bailey nodded, still

scanning for Georgia. Her heart would break if she found her on the sidelines alone while everyone else had someone special to dance with during this musical number.

A sense of love and belonging filled her, and every breath Bailey took expanded her lungs and her being until she felt like she could shoulder whatever eyes came in her direction. She could, because she was a deserving, loveable woman.

Tears filled her eyes, just as they had in her parents' basement only a few days ago. This time, though, they didn't stem from a feeling of being trapped or like she'd been thrown back in time.

This time, they came because God had just filled her with His spirit. He'd just reclaimed her from the land of the lost, and He'd just reminded her of how very loved she was.

By her parents. By Him. And by everyone at this party.

So while she'd choked back tears and smiled a plastic grin at everyone for days, and she'd just told Bryce she was fine, Bailey wasn't fine.

She was whole. Finally, finally whole again.

And that meant it was okay for her to cry.

She did, becoming the blubbering mess she'd feared she'd be at this wedding. The tears slid down her face faster than she could even lift her hand to begin wiping them, which was why she'd stationed Stockton at her side.

But with him gone, and only OJ in front of her, Bailey couldn't help her emotions.

"Are you sad or happy?" he asked in a tiny voice, and Bailey looked down at him through her tears.

She sobbed, a horrible sound she wished never to make again, but she smiled. "I'm better," she said. "It's a good better. It's...good. Happy."

He nodded and said, "Sometimes my momma cries when she's happy too." He looked to his left, and Bailey followed his gaze. Georgia stood there, and she seemed spotlighted by a string of tea lights. They made it easy to see the love for her son—as well as an underlying anxiety that only grew when she saw Bailey crying.

"You should dance with her," Bailey said, turning back to him. "I love you so much, OJ. You are the best boy in the whole world. You know that, right?"

He nodded, his eyes a little too wide. She was probably scaring him, and she quickly wiped her face as best she could. "I'm going to pass you to her, okay? Then I have to go, but we'll still go to breakfast in a couple of days, before I go back to Butte."

"Okay." He stopped dancing and wrapped his strong, skinny arms around her. She hugged him tight, tight, tight too, sealing part of him inside her to take with her no matter where she went.

She'd spent so long trying to keep him out, when what she'd needed to do was let him in. Let Bryce in. Let the Youngs in. Let her parents in.

Let God in.

Now that she had, Bailey felt like a phoenix rising from the ashes of the past decade as she turned toward Georgia and gestured her forward. She came, because Georgia was a strong, powerful, and protective mother in her own right.

She nearly collided with Bailey she hugged her so hard. "Are you okay?"

"I'm so good," she whispered. "Thank you so much for —" She didn't know how to finish. Another round of emotions cut off her vocal cords, and Bailey just stepped back, her eyes filled with tears and making Georgia blurry. "I am so good now. I feel so good."

Georgia nodded, and Bailey stepped back and indicated OJ. "He wanted to dance with his momma."

And while that person wasn't her, Bailey would always have a place in his heart. In his life. And here in Coral Canyon.

OJ grinned at Georgia, and she smiled right on back at him. They began to dance, and Bailey needed to get off this dance floor quickly. She turned, only to be met with her parents. They'd edged closer and closer, and they took her into their arms. Both of them, easily, without a word. Bailey cried silently against her mother's shoulder while her daddy's strong arms held them both up.

Someone else joined them, and Bailey would know that cologne anywhere. Bryce. Codi pressed in behind her too, and then Uncle Eli and Aunt Meg were there, padding their group hug with more arms, and more bodies, and all the acceptance in the world.

"Love you, Bailey," someone said, and she didn't even know who. Cecily and Jerry Young stood right behind her daddy, and she tried to smile at them. More aunts and more uncles arrived, Youngs and Whittakers alike, all of them insulating her, encapsulating her, hugging her.

Accepting her.

Healing her.

Rescuing her.

Murmurs of love and friendship filled the whole space, and Bailey finally found a way through her tears to the other side. The side where her emotions reigned, sure. But where she could feel them for what they truly were and not be embarrassed or upset by them.

The side where God lived and joy stood supreme.

A side where Bailey finally felt like she belonged. She'd done the work; she'd fought the fight; she'd humbled herself and repented; she'd walked through that fire.

And now, she'd come home.

18

Harry handed his guitar to his manager, Adam, everything in the world shiny and amazing. Just for this moment. Just right here on this ranch in Wyoming, with a couple hundred people.

This was the life he craved. The life he wanted more than living in his second-story apartment in Nashville, though he loved the solitude of his writing studio there. He did love the vibrancy of that city too, and he couldn't spit in God's face and tell Him he didn't want the country music career he currently had.

That life was going to pay for the next chapter for years to come. That life and the songs he wrote and the concerts he did—all the travel, the nights in hotels, the mobs of people who wanted his signature—could get him this small-town life with the people he wanted to see every day.

Adam took his guitar, just like he took care of everything else for Harry. "I'm going to go talk to people," he told him.

"Okay." Adam glanced out to the crowd, but mostly family only remained at Bryce and Codi's wedding.

Harry really just wanted to show Bailey the picture he'd managed to take while his father continued to strum, and he wanted to hug Bryce really hard, and he wanted to dance one more time with Belle, his date for tonight's wedding.

Daddy followed him down the steps from the small stage, and they rejoined their family to cheers and hugs. Harry grabbed onto Bryce and held him tight, tight, tight.

"I love you, brother," he said right in his cousin's ear.

"I love you more," Bryce said back, and as they separated, Bryce grinned hugely at him. Harry returned it, and he drew Codi into a hug too.

"You guys are such great role models," he said. "Love you, Codi."

"You'll be home soon enough," she said, and somehow that was just what Harry needed to hear.

"I will be," he said as he stepped back. He looked for Bailey, but he wasn't surprised not to see her glued to Bryce's side.

His heart leapt at the thought of her leaving before he could grab her, and he turned to scan the crowd. He caught Adam's eye, and the man simply knew Harry needed something. He came forward instantly, saying, "What is it?"

"I need to find Bailey McAllister," he said.

Adam nodded, because he knew who Bailey was. He studied photos and names of people before events like this, and Harry often relied on Adam to feed him names of the people he had to meet with, socialize with, or simply fans who'd paid VIP prices to see him.

They separated, and Harry moved to the sidelines quickly, figuring that was where Bailey would hang out. He found Graham and Laney Whittaker, her parents, and he leaned down. "Is Bailey still here?"

Laney looked up to him, surprise in her eyes for only a moment. "Yes," she said. "She went to get a drink." She pointed to the right. "Like, two minutes ago."

Harry nodded, flashing a smile. "I have something amazing to show her." He left as Graham said, "I want to see something amazing."

"I'll be back," Harry called over his shoulder, because he'd just spotted the blonde who'd charmed Bryce from the moment he'd met her.

Harry understood his cousin so much more now that he'd started something with Belle. He still wouldn't call the missing person's investigator his girlfriend. They lived in different cities and would for at least eight more months. They didn't exactly go out on dates, but Harry did call her a lot, they texted every day, and they'd had a few online dates, where he'd sent dinner to her house, gotten dinner for himself, and they'd talked via video while they ate, him in Nashville and her in Jackson Hole.

He hadn't kissed her, and the in-person encounters they'd had were two weddings: Kassie and Reggie's and now this one.

"Bailey," Harry said as he approached her. She turned toward him, her face brightening when she saw him.

"Harry." She took him into a hug. "What an amazing song. You're incredible."

"Thanks." He embraced her heartily, giving her one last squeeze before he pulled away. "I want to show you something."

She took a sip of her cider and set down the glass. "Okay."

Harry already had his phone out, and he tapped to get to the pictures. "Look." Sudden emotion overcame him, and he choked up, unable to say more. He took one last look at the pure, unadulterated love, the absolutely magic of family and anyone who felt like family coming together to surround someone who needed them.

He imagined himself in the middle of the mob of cousins, friends, aunts, uncles, parents, and grandparents, and yeah. He couldn't speak.

He turned the phone toward her and simply nodded.

Bailey watched him for an extra moment, surely cataloguing his emotion and wondering what she might find. Then she took the phone and looked at it fully. Her eyes widened, and one hand came up to cover her mouth. "Oh," she said.

Harry didn't know why this moment had been so poignant for him. He'd seen it from a unique perspective— from above, and to see that outpouring of love, of God's grace and forgiveness and Spirit...Harry had truly had a profound religious moment, and he wanted to share it with Bailey.

She looked up at him, apparently without the ability to form words too. Harry just grabbed onto her and hauled her into his chest again. "I love you," he said, his voice far rougher than it had been when he'd told Bryce the same thing. "Everyone loves you so much."

She held onto him like she might fall otherwise. "Thank you, Harry. Will you send me this?"

"In the words of Bryce, one-hundred percent." He smiled then and when he pulled back, Bailey wore a grin on her face too. She wiped at her eyes and took a big breath.

"Wow." She exhaled, part of the air forming a laugh. "Okay." She looked at his phone again. "This is just...."

"Incredible," he said. "Look at you, right there in the middle of everyone." She did indeed stand in the middle of the crowd, and they'd just piled around her, everyone extending their arms around whoever they stood beside.

"When you're inside a net this big," he said. "This strong, there's no way you can fall very far. There's no way you can get very far away. There's never a time when you don't have someone to call for help. For anything, really. Just to talk. Just if you're lonely."

He nodded to the phone. "You never get to be lonely when you're the one in the middle there where you are."

She nodded and handed his device back to him. "Is this how you feel, though you're in Nashville?"

Harry glanced around and found her parents watching

them intently. "Yeah," he said. "I'm far away, but I'm right here too." He smiled. "It's great."

"Sometimes it suffocates me." Bailey wrapped her arms around herself and looked out at the dancing still happening. "Maybe it's just me."

"It's not," Harry said. "I feel like that too. Everyone does—well, maybe not Uncle Otis or Uncle Mav or Uncle Tex...." He laughed. "But my daddy doesn't go to everything. Gabe and Luke and Morris do what works for them. We all do—but the network is there, and I'm sure glad I *know* it's there."

He put his arm around her. "That's what comforts me. They're there when I want them, and it's nice to know that."

"Yes," she agreed softly. "It is nice to know that." She looked at Harry and swept a kiss across his cheek. "Thank you, Harry. For playing your song, and taking that picture, and showing it to me, and telling me what it means to you." She smiled brilliantly at him. "Thank you for being you."

"And thank you for being you," he said right back. He tapped on his phone again. "I'll send it to you right now, because I think your momma and daddy want to see it."

"Yes, please." Bailey gave him her number, and Harry sent the pictures he'd gotten. She could choose the best one or keep them all.

That done and with Bailey walking over to her parents' table, Harry sighed and tucked his hands in his pockets.

He only had one more thing on his agenda for tonight, and that was Belle. He wanted to dance with her again, and then he'd drive her home the long hour plus twenty minutes from the Rising Sun Ranch to her house in Jackson.

He didn't see her, and he was content on the sidelines for a minute.

"What are you thinking, cowboy?"

He felt someone move to his side, and instant recognition of Belle's voice made his heart jump again. "Nothin' much," he said as coolly as he could.

She slipped her hand in his. "I know that's not true. You love being in a crowd, because it churns up your ideas for songs."

He grinned and squeezed her fingers. "I like holding your hand. That's what I'm thinking."

She laughed lightly, and Harry basked in the sound of that too. "I saw you talking to Bailey."

"Yeah," he said, glancing over to the table where she was showing her parents her phone. "I got a great picture of her while she was dancing with OJ."

"I'm sure a song will come of it."

Harry looked at her, struck by the beauty of her face. She wore plenty of makeup tonight—it was a wedding after all—but she knew how to brush it on to contour her face and enhance her lips. He couldn't help looking at them for longer than socially acceptable, and he reverted right back to being thirteen about to kiss a girl for the first time.

He reminded himself he'd done this before, and he wasn't a boy and she wasn't a girl. He was a grown man, and Belle was several years older than him. Oh, and that he stood in front of his whole family.

So he wasn't going to kiss her here. No way.

"Do you want to dance?"

"Yes." Belle let him lead her out onto the dance floor, where Harry felt instantly under the microscope. He decided he didn't care. He'd had thousands and tens of thousands of people watching him for years now. It was literally why he'd started his social media accounts—to be seen.

At least for the things he wanted known. His feelings, as complicated as they were, for Belle, he actually wanted to keep to himself.

He'd only told one person about the status of his album. Uncle Otis. Okay, fine, Uncle Morris knew too, as he managed Harry's music career, and Adam knew, because they'd celebrated together with barbecue and drinks for everyone at a small music dive that Harry loved.

It had such a great vibe, and he'd often go there just for a drink and to listen to the bands playing. The comedy sketches. He loved the people and the vibrancy, and then he could take that energy and yes, the emotion, into his song-writing.

Amazing songs, after all, were born from the purest emotions of the heart, and Harry wanted all of his to hit something inside anyone who listened to them.

"I submitted all the songs to Rebel," he whispered in Belle's ear. "I'm waiting for them to approve them, and then we'll start recording."

"Harry, that's wonderful."

His pulse thundered in his chest, because only two people knew the words teeming on his tongue now. He wasn't sure he could say them out loud, but he'd have to soon enough.

He had to talk to his daddy and Uncle Tex too.

"I asked Morris to find out if I could record here in Coral Canyon."

Belle stepped back, her eyes searching his now, pure surprise there. "Here?"

"My uncle has a professional recording studio at his farm," Harry said. "Country Quad has done a few albums from right here, with occasional trips to Nashville."

"Wow," she said.

Harry grinned at her. "I thought nothing surprised you."

She gave him a tiny push against his chest. "Obviously not. I said that one time, and it was job-related."

He eased her back into his arms. "I need to talk to everyone, so don't say anything."

"I'm gonna run right over to your father and tell him," she said dryly, her salty sense of humor something Harry really liked about her.

He danced her over to the corner of the floor, where not as many people could see them. Adam stood in the slight shadows, and Harry nodded to him.

Adam nodded back, and Harry closed his eyes, so he didn't have to see how Adam got more people away from them. He worried as he held Belle in his arms that isolating them would only draw attention to them.

But he edged up onto the grass, off the dance floor, where there was less light, and Adam had moved whoever had been there.

"You okay?" he asked Belle.

"Yes." She fit so well against him, and Harry's heart seemed to positively hammer against his ribs. With her chest pressed against his, could she feel it?

"If I move here," he whispered. "We could go out for real."

"Mm hm."

"Would you go out with me?" he asked. "Dinner, movie, standard, normal date stuff?"

She eased back and looked at him, her face a perfect mask for her emotions. Harry actually had no idea what she'd say, and his heartbeat went wild.

"I'd love to go out with you," she finally said.

A smile burst onto his face. "Perfect." He leaned closer and whispered, "I'm going to kiss you now, okay?"

"Okay," she murmured a mere moment before he touched his lips to hers. Harry would swear on his life that the lights around them surged with an enormous influx of energy, all of it coming from the two of them.

He brought her closer, one hand sliding up and into her hair as he kissed her and kissed her, his ears pricked up and ready to pull away the moment he heard Adam so much as clear his throat.

When only the music from the dance floor, which felt so far away, entered his ears, Harry did the one thing he couldn't seem to stop doing. He kept kissing Belle.

19

Belle had never been kissed with this level of precision, with this much tenderness, with so much feeling pouring from the man in front of her. Harry had claimed not to have a lot of girlfriends and not a super mega ton of experience—his words, which had made her smile—but he sure kissed as well as he sang and played the guitar.

Her skin prickled in the best of ways, and after several more strokes of his mouth against hers, she somehow remembered that she and Harry stood in the semi-shadows at his cousin's wedding. He seemed to remember it at the same time, and he pulled away and ducked his head.

Gone was his cowboy hat. As the breath in Belle's lungs returned, she pulled in a slow breath through her nose, trying to reason through what had just happened. She'd kissed Harry Young.

The Harry Young.

The country music sensation currently recording his third album—or would be soon. She thought of the file she'd taken back to the Sheriff just this past week, and it had taken a whole lot longer than a weekend to think about the undercover assignment.

The truth was Belle didn't know what to do. She'd made a pros and cons list, and they'd come out even. She'd petitioned the Lord, and He'd been frustratingly silent. In fact, the message Belle had gotten more than once was simply, *Decide, Belle, and I'll be with you.*

"Okay?" Harry asked, bringing Belle back to the present. Back to the way he held her perfectly in his arms. Back to how easily he centered her, and Belle looked up into his dark eyes.

She'd put him on both the pro and con side of her undercover assignment. The pro side was he didn't even live here, so it wasn't like she had to tell him when she disappeared. He would be very busy for the next year, recording his album and planning his studio tour. She knew his uncle and manager had gotten that approved from his record label. And Morris had started to set up the venues around Coral Canyon where Harry would play and live-stream his concerts instead of traveling from city to city and playing at stadiums and arenas.

Belle thought it was brilliant, actually, in today's day and age where everyone seemed to be attached to a device twenty-four hours a day. There would be a cover charge, but there would be no limit. No capacity to be reached. So the tickets could be cheaper, and more could attend. She couldn't wait to see how many people watched Harry Young's first live-streamed "world tour concert."

"Yeah," Belle said with a smile. "More than okay."

He looked up and out onto the dance floor, his hand sliding to take hers. She fell to his side as he stooped to pick up his cowboy hat and put it back on his head.

"I don't think I have anything to do the rest of the night," he said. "Maybe we could sneak away early."

Belle shook her head immediately. "No," she said, "I'm not taking the blame for that." She nodded over toward the tables on her right. "In fact, your father is looking straight at us, and he probably knows you're trying to plan an escape."

Sure enough, Trace Young got to his feet, never looking away from Harry and Belle, and Belle's whole face heated as she thought about his dad watching them kiss. Harry grumbled something under his breath and said, "Let me go talk to him." He walked away and met his dad halfway to where they loitered in the shadows just off the dance floor.

No, Belle would not be taking Harry from this wedding. His relationship with Bryce and Codi and everyone here in Coral Canyon meant more to him than she currently did. And while Belle could fantasize that might shift one day, in reality, it hadn't yet.

She hugged herself and looked up into the sky, where she found the beautiful pinpricks of light—the stars, God's creations.

"Help me to know what to do," she prayed.

Ben had started making plans to insert someone into the

Bison and Buffalo Casino, whether it be Belle or not, and she would need to decide in the next couple of weeks. She thought of her cats and her house, and Belle knew her fellow officers would take care of anything she needed them to so that she could pack a couple of suitcases and move into a furnished apartment in northern Wyoming and go undercover.

"Hey, so turns out we can't leave yet," Harry said as he returned. "Do you want to dance?"

"Are we really going to dance this time?" she teased.

Harry threw his head back and laughed, then said, "Yeah, we better, because my daddy said we weren't being as discreet as I thought."

He grinned at Belle, and though a measure of horror moved through her, she still let him take her hand and lead her onto the dance floor. She eased into his arms like it was the most natural thing in the world. And as they danced in Dog Valley, it didn't matter that Harry was a great big star. Right now, he was simply her small-town dance partner.

"ALL RIGHT," BELLE SAID AS SHE MUSCLED FLOWER into the cat carrier. "Now listen, you guys are going to be so happy with Jenny, okay?"

Belle could admit she shed a few tears over having to rehome her cats, but her cat sitter had told her that she'd take all three of them, and she couldn't be upset about that. It felt like a gift from God that Belle would be turning her nose up at if she did. "You guys already know her," Belle said as she put the half-full bag of cat food in a plastic bin.

She went around her house and picked up all the cat toys that had been left out. Jenny had already taken a box of those, as well as Mister Miles's scratching post and all of the cat beds. How they'd even survived here for one more night without any of their things in the spare second bedroom, Belle had no idea. Cats really could be picky and finicky. And right now, Mister Miles yowled from inside the cat carrier.

"You're fine," she told him as placatingly as possible. It was a mantra that she'd gotten used to in the past week or so since Bryce's wedding. She'd get up in the morning and go to work, and she'd tell herself she was fine.

You're fine, she told herself. *It's all going to work out.*

You're fine, she'd think as she drove to the Sheriff's office. *You just need to make a decision.*

You're fine, would stream through her mind as she put a microwave meal in for her solitary dinner at night. *The answer will come.*

Belle believed all of those things, she really did. And while she still hadn't told Ben that she wanted to accept the undercover assignment, she had started making arrangements to do so. Heck, rehoming her cats had only taken a single phone call.

She'd emailed a real estate agent about putting her house up for sale, and they would be meeting on Monday morning.

You're fine, Belle thought. *Everything will be ready when you are.*

She took the bin out to her car and started it, as the sun had been shining brighter and longer and hotter as they crept toward June. She took the cats out second, put them on the front seat, buckled the cat carrier in, and only allowed herself one sniffle as she rounded the hood of her car to get behind the driver's seat.

She drove to Jenny's house in her sundress and sandals, and she dropped her cats off with plenty of smiles and reassurances that Jenny would send loads of pictures.

If Belle went undercover, she wouldn't get any of them. She wouldn't have her same phone number anymore, or her same device. Everything would be new, everything would be changed, everything would be different.

With her cats in their new home and Belle's heart pinched against her ribs, she drove to church. She didn't always get to attend due to her work schedule and the demands on her time and energy, but she'd found herself going more and more often in the past couple of months as she contemplated the next step in her life. She sat alone as usual, in one of the side pews, and she let the music uplift her, feed her, calm her until the pastor took his place in front of the microphone.

"Who was it, brothers and sisters?" he asked. "Who left the ninety and nine to go off and find the one?"

"Jesus," someone called from the crowd, and the pastor grinned at them.

"It *was* Jesus, our Lord and Savior." He seemed to take

in the whole congregation at the same time, a unique trait of this pastor. "Do you ever feel like you're just one of the hundred sheep and your wool is the same color as everyone else's, and God really doesn't see you?"

Belle found herself nodding because yes, she felt exactly like that. Among the huge sky in Wyoming and all the beautiful stars and the millions of pine trees, how could God possibly know what *she* needed? With all the animals who needed Him, and all of his children—men, women, boys, and girls—how could He possibly know that *she* hurt and that *she* needed help?

She did often feel lost, alone, and afraid. And while she usually could take a bold step and find the light again, she had really been struggling these past couple of months.

"Jesus was about connecting with *the one*," the pastor said. "The individual. When he was with groups of people, He felt a tug on His robes, and He helped the woman with her bleeding issue. He saw *the one*."

He swung his gaze toward Belle, and it seemed as though his eyes hooked into hers. "When the woman taken in adultery was being stoned, he found her. He saw her. He helped her. Jesus Christ and Heavenly Father know each personal trial and tribulation. They know the one. He seeks after *the one* who is lost, *the one* who is hurt, *the one* who needs him most in that moment."

The pastor smiled and moved on, and Belle wondered if he'd been looking just at her or someone else. It didn't matter. His words rang with truth and peace in her heart, and she suddenly didn't feel so alone, so scared, or so invisible.

"He will bring you back to his fold," the pastor said. "If you will let him be your Shepherd. So let Him guide you. Let Him direct your steps. Let Him warn you of the pothole in the left lane, or the cliff on your right side, or the pit that has been covered with leaves just ahead, because He is the one who seeks after each of us individually."

Belle reached up and brushed at her eyes. She got into law enforcement so that she could seek after justice, so that she could provide a sense of closure and healing and peace to victims and their families. She loved her role in missing persons even though it didn't always end up right, good, or well.

She fought for the most amount of justice possible, and she wanted to keep doing that. She thought of Tyson's reports of women and children being used as money mules. And as she sat there in church and listened to the pastor's warm, honeyed voice continue to preach about the Savior, Belle had her answer.

She needed to go undercover.

20

arry reached to button his jacket as he stepped off the elevator at Rebel Records. Uncle Morris preceded him, and Adam walked at his side. Harry tossed his personal assistant a worried glance, but Adam kept his face forward, his eyes scanning left and right. Surely there would be no threat to Harry's personal safety here inside the record label, but Adam never took chances.

Harry didn't want to be here at all. He rarely met with the record label executives, and instead let Morris handle all their affairs. But Morris had proposed that Harry be able to return to Coral Canyon and record the album in the white barn studio behind his uncle Tex's house. After all, Country Quad had made three albums from there, and surely it produced a perfect sound.

Rebel had not immediately agreed. In fact, they had not told Morris yes or no but requested this meeting instead.

Harry had brainstormed with Otis, his father, and Morris for the whole weekend, and now they strode down the hall toward Lee Haskell's office.

The man who held all the power in Harry's life.

If he couldn't return to Coral Canyon to record, he'd have to be in Nashville for at least another eight months, probably longer. Harry was meticulous about his music. He would practice and practice and practice before recording. Then he would record a single song in a day, maybe two, making sure every beat, every instrument, every lyric came out perfectly.

The list of songs for the album hadn't even been approved yet. Harry's irritation and frustration with the snail's pace of making a country music album only increased the further into the building he went.

Morris didn't knock on the conference room door, and instead simply opened it, as if he were a chauffeur. Harry walked in first, with Adam only a hair's breadth behind him, and Morris came in last and closed the door.

Harry only took a couple of steps to let the men behind him enter, and then he stopped. This wasn't a meeting with simply Lee Haskell, but *seven* music producers at Rebel Records. Harry knew in that moment he would not be returning to Coral Canyon to record his last album.

"Harry," Lee said warmly as he stood. "Come in." He had to be older than Harry's father, with far less hair and a far bigger midsection.

All seven of them had taken head positions at their oval conference table. They all wore suits in black or navy blue, and Harry was eternally glad his father had counseled him to wear one as well. He and Morris wore cowboy hats, but no one else did.

Harry moved forward to start shaking hands. He hated this part of the business the most, but he was very, very good at it. He could smile. He could say things he didn't really mean, all while thinking of what he really wanted: a bowl of ice cream and his solitude in his music studio on his second-floor apartment.

No, he thought as he shook hands with a man whose name he'd already forgotten. *You don't want to be in your second-floor apartment. You want to be back in Coral Canyon.*

And he did.

No, he didn't have a place to live there. He and his parents *had* started looking at houses. Harry reasoned as he shook another hand that he could purchase a house in Coral Canyon whether he lived in it right away or not. That didn't make much sense, even for someone who had a lot of money.

"Howdy, Lee," he said, zeroing in on the man with the sharp gaze. "You called in everyone, hmm?"

"Just a little meeting, Harry," Lee said, but Harry knew it was way more than that. Once everyone had done all the formalities, Harry took the nearest seat at the table. Morris stayed on the other side, and they sat across from one another, with Adam between him and the door. Everyone took their seats, the jackets shuffling, the sounds of sighing; someone coughed.

Then Lee said, "Harry, I think you know we can't approve your request to record in Coral Canyon."

"Seems like it," Harry said.

"I'm sure your uncle has a real great studio there," Lee said. "We've heard Country Quad's albums. Real nice sound, right?"

"Right," Harry said. So what was the problem?

"We at Rebel have our own recording studios," Lee said as if Harry hadn't recorded two albums right here in this building. "They're soundproofed in a specific way. We can't send your entire band to Wyoming with you, as they have other obligations to other artists, and we have to schedule their recording time."

Harry simply nodded, deciding that no words were needed. He didn't have to affirm every single thing the man said.

"We think our sound at Rebel is real special," Lee said with a knowing smile. He glanced around at some of the other men who also nodded and smiled like they were *so* important.

Harry sometimes felt like he was important, and other times he simply knew he was a young boy with a guitar and a dream. And people who played guitars were a dime a dozen, and he wasn't all that special. He certainly wasn't curing cancer or working toward solving the world's problems.

"We'll only get the three albums from you," Lee said. "And we want them to have a consistent Rebel quality sound across all three. That means we need you to be here to record."

"I UNDERSTAND," HARRY SAID. THE ARGUMENT WAS sound; it did make sense. Harry didn't have to like it for either of those to be true.

"I wish it could be different," Lee said. "I know you're really anxious to get back to your family."

An image of the beautiful Belle Graves stole through Harry's mind. While yes, he did want to be part of the Young family, and not just in name, he also wanted to move on with his life. He was done being a country music star, but he had to fulfill his obligations before he could go live a different life.

He was trying to jump the gun and get there quicker, and Harry ducked his head as a measure of guilt and shame descended on his shoulders.

"Good news is," another man said from next to Lee. "We've approved your album list." Spike grinned and pushed a paper toward Harry. Harry made no move to try to collect the paper as the conference table was far too wide for him to do so. It got moved around from man to man until it landed in front of Harry.

"Eighteen songs." His blood started to feel like someone had poured ice crystals in it.

He looked around the table once, met Morris's gaze, and then rocked his eyes back to the man next to him. When he'd swept them all again, he stared across the table at Uncle Morris.

Eighteen songs, screamed through his head. He was contracted for twelve. Eighteen was a third more. That would take way longer to record.

"He shouldn't have submitted so many good songs then," Lee said, still grinning from ear to ear.

"If you're going to expect him to record one-third more songs for an album, his contract needs to be adjusted," Morris said evenly.

"Another third, it sounds like," Harry said.

Morris sent him a severe look, and Harry clamped his lips shut. He didn't usually get involved in negotiations. Morris handled it all, and his uncle would bring him Rebel's proposal, and Harry would agree or not agree. They would discuss, and Morris would go back to the negotiation table if he had to.

"We have drawn up an addendum to your contract," Lee said, and he nodded to the man next to Morris. By some miracle, the man's name came forward in Harry's mind.

"Well, what is it, Wayne?" Harry asked, just as Morris said, "Lay it on me, Wayne."

Wayne passed the document to Morris, who started to study it. Harry's collar felt too tight, and he told himself over and over not to reach up and adjust it. Behind them, someone knocked on the door, and everyone looked that way. A pretty woman leaned in and said, "Can I get anyone anything to drink?"

"I'll take Diet Dr. Pepper, please," Harry said.

"Same," Adam said.

"Coffee," Morris said, while all the music executives declined. Harry figured if he had to be in this room and he had to stay in Nashville, he could at least get a free soda pop from his record company.

Morris slid the document across the table to Harry and said, "The addendum is fair. They're offering you one-third more for six more songs. And it is contractually binding you to Nashville to record them."

"The online live-stream world tour is still on, right?" Harry asked. "That hasn't changed?"

"That hasn't changed," Lee said at the same time Morris shook his head.

Harry had turned in twenty-seven songs for this album. When he looked back at the list in front of him, *Long Road to Texas* still sat there. Harry really liked that song. He had tried to get it on his second album and had failed.

Big Wheel Blues, *Falling in Love in Kingston*, and *Rarin' to Go*, one of the rare rock songs that Harry had heard in his mind one morning when he'd woken up, all had made the list.

Harry did love writing music and lyrics. He did love recording songs. And he reminded himself that what he didn't love was touring, and touring was not on the menu. He carefully folded the paper and passed it to Adam, who expertly tucked it away in his inside jacket pocket.

"All right," Harry said. "Eighteen songs. I'll stay in Nashville to record them."

"Perfect," Lee said, bursting to his feet. All the other

executives did the same, almost as if they had rehearsed it. Harry stayed in his seat while Morris stood and shook hands with everyone again.

Morris put the paper in front of Harry, and Adam handed him a pen. He took a deep breath and thought, *Dear Lord, tell me right now if I shouldn't sign this.* And when God didn't throw lightning bolts into the room to stop Harry, he signed his name on the contract addendum.

Now he just had to break the bad news to everyone in Wyoming...including Belle.

LATER THAT WEEK, HARRY ANSWERED THE DOOR TO HIS apartment to find Adam standing there with the food he'd ordered for tonight's phone date.

"Thanks, brother," Harry said. "I'll see you tomorrow at ten-thirty?"

"Yep," Adam said. "For our weekend pow-wow."

The pow-wow was a meeting that Adam insisted on twice a week, once for the first few business days of the week and once as the weekend drew closer, so that both he and Harry knew what was on the young man's agenda, where he needed to be, what security needed to be arranged, what car services, what restaurants Adam needed to call— the whole nine yards.

Harry took his cheeseburger and cheese fries and went into the kitchen. His phone told him that Belle's dinner had been delivered five minutes ago, and that should have been enough time for her to talk to the cats about it, pour herself some peach lemonade, and get in front of the computer as well.

He always called her for their phone dates, which he didn't mind. He got his own food out and opened it all so that he wouldn't have to wrestle through bags and burger wrapping paper during the date.

He'd sent Belle meatloaf and mashed potatoes today from a restaurant in Jackson Hole called Edna's. When she'd confessed to him that she was one of the only kids in her fifth-grade class to choose meatloaf as her favorite food, she said she'd been teased relentlessly.

Harry had laughed and laughed and said, "I probably would have been one of the ones teasing you about it, Belle. No kid likes meatloaf." But she claimed to, and so Harry had sent her that for their date this week.

He moved over to his computer and got the call going, and Belle answered after only a couple of rings. She ran a towel through her hair, and then threw it somewhere off camera.

"Hey, Harry," she said.

Harry marveled that he'd gotten this gorgeous woman a few years older than him to pay him any attention at all, to put up with long-distance dating, to deal with a celebrity. He wasn't sure what she found interesting about him, as their date conversations were usually pretty boring—stuff about their childhoods, their siblings, and sometimes their jobs, though Belle didn't like talking about work.

He found her refreshing, a real break from what he

always had to do: think about work, write songs for work, sing songs for work, and go to guitar lessons for work. None of it felt fun anymore, but Harry had never told anyone that, not even Belle. He didn't want to complain, and he didn't want to appear ungrateful.

But he also had to get the news that he couldn't return to Coral Canyon out of his mouth and off his chest right now.

"Hey," he said. "Listen, I got to—" He trailed off, not sure how to tell her that their only contact for the next eight, ten, twelve, who knew how many months would be these phone dates. Surely she'd grow tired of him. He told himself he could take a break anytime he wanted. He had enough money to fly home to Jackson Hole whenever he wanted, even just for an evening. He could do it every weekend if he had to.

Belle simply watched him. She didn't jump in; she didn't try to ask him another question; she didn't take off on her own subject. She was beautiful and kind, she listened, she worked hard.

And though he was still getting to know her, and of course, they'd spent very little time in person together, Harry really felt like she championed him.

"I'm just going to blurt it out," he said. "Bad news. Rebel says I can't record in Coral Canyon."

"Oh, no," she said, really sounding hurt and upset. Her dark eyes shot sympathy at him, as well as multiple questions.

"I don't know how long it will take to record the album," he said. "They're having me do eighteen songs instead of twelve, so it's going to be longer. My guess is I might be done around April...of next year."

"That's ten months," she said.

"It's actually eleven." Harry's hopes fell, fell, fell. "It's not quite June yet."

"Right," she said. "Well, you know, it's okay." Everything about her brightened. "It's gonna be okay."

"Yeah," Harry picked up a fry and put it in his mouth, because he didn't know what else to say.

"We might as well get our work news out here at the beginning," Belle said.

He raised his eyes to meet hers. "You've got work news too?"

"Yeah." She looked like she might throw up, though, and so he wasn't sure if this was a promotion or if she'd lost her job. She'd never given any indication that might happen, and Harry leaned forward, suddenly tense.

"I've been offered another position in the Sheriff's Department," she said. "And I'm going to take it."

"That's great," Harry said.

"Kind of," Belle said. "Well, no, it *is* great. It's great for me. But it's not going to be so great for us."

Harry's heart pounded and pounded and pounded, and he could barely hear himself as he asked, "What do you mean?"

"I can't really tell you a lot," she said, and she looked away from the camera. "I really wish I could. You know I would, Harry. You know that, right?"

"Yeah?" he said, but it was a question. A guess.

"I've been authorized to tell you that it's an undercover position. And that means I'm selling my house. I've rehomed my cats. And I'll be getting all new devices, and I won't be able to share any of it with you." Her smile shook, and her eyes filled with tears. Her hands went round and round each other, and she dropped her eyes to them.

Harry felt like calling down thunder from heaven and demanding that she do anything else but what she just said —which was essentially, cut off all contact with him.

"Good news, though," she said. "It's an eight-month position, which means I should be done before you're finished with the album. And then maybe...." She trailed off and ducked her head. She lifted her fork and had a hunk of meatloaf and a bite of mashed potatoes on it, and that did make Harry's heart happy.

She put it in her mouth, chewed, and swallowed before she said, "Maybe we just met a year too soon. Maybe next year when you're done with the album, and I'm done with this part of my job, maybe it'll be a good time for us to meet up again."

"Maybe." It felt like the walls in his apartment had started to crumble.

"You can send letters to the Sheriff's office," she said. "My boss will read them, though, so you've got to be careful about that." She gave a light laugh. "Anything that he thinks is safe to pass on to me, he will. But Harry, I can't communicate back. I can't risk my cover that way."

"I understand," he said, and he was getting really tired

of those words. He didn't truly understand much of anything that had gone on this week.

He took a deep breath, took another bite of cheese fries, and took another look at Belle. "Promise me we'll try again when we're both back in Wyoming permanently."

She smiled at him. And if he could just freeze this one frame and look at it every day, he could stay in Nashville and record his album. He could do it without phone dates and witty texts to Belle. He absolutely could.

So he quickly navigated to the screenshot app on his phone and took a screenshot of Belle grinning at him from her computer in Wyoming to his in Nashville, as she said, "I promise."

21

Joey stepped from airplane to the jetway, dragging her carryon behind her. It fit on top of a much larger bag she'd collect from the claim in only a few minutes. Daddy followed her at her pace, though he possessed much longer legs than she did.

Everything about her felt too slow, and Joey wasn't even sure why. Maybe because she'd packed up everything she owned in New York City, put it in three suitcases, and had just arrived back in Wyoming.

Wasn't the air supposed to be fresher here? Weren't her burdens supposed to be lighter? Maybe when she got to the condo where her grandparents lived, all of those things would suddenly manifest themselves.

As it was, she and Daddy walked to the baggage claim, picked up her bags, and headed outside into the spring sunshine. She'd been home for Bryce and Codi's wedding, of course, and she'd see a lot more of them this summer, as she'd arranged to work at her cousin's ranch in the mornings. Feeding horses.

"Roo, this way," Daddy said, and she automatically turned to go with him. She had no idea where he'd parked when he'd come to the city a couple of days ago, and she let him do the heavy lifting of guiding them to his truck and putting in the suitcases. All she had to do was lay her backpack in the back seat of his truck and get in the passenger seat.

She did all of that, and Daddy filled the cab with his big personality and presence. "Ready?" He didn't look at her, because he seemed to sense that she didn't want to have his eyes on her.

"Yep." Her voice sounded far more chipper than she felt, and she relaxed further once Daddy got out of the parking lot and had them headed back to Coral Canyon. With the pure blue sky overhead, Joey finally felt some of herself returning to her mind and body.

"Okay," Daddy said. "Let's get the painful stuff out of the way on the drive there."

Joey's muscles immediately tensed up again. But she nodded and said, "Okay." She drew in a deep breath. "I know some of what you're going to ask, so I'll just start."

"Shoot," Daddy said.

"First, yes, I'm going to go see Mom. It's just not that fun anymore, and it's like she puts a timer on how much time in Dog Valley compared to Coral Canyon, and she like, has this tally for how many minutes I spend with Grams, and how she compares it to how long I do things with Grandma Sally." She huffed out her breath. "It's honestly a little easier just not to see her."

Daddy didn't say anything, but Joey saw the slight flex of his fingers on the steering wheel. "I didn't know she did that."

"I guess I never told you." Joey watched the white-capped mountains sail by on her side of the truck. They'd soon turn and drive away from the Tetons, but she sure loved being so close to them. "But it's not fun to go see her. She works from home, and I feel like I'm on top of her in that house."

"You have a bedroom there, right?"

"Yes," Joey said. "I'm going to go see her tomorrow and stay through the weekend. Then I'll be back in Coral Canyon for a bit. Grams and I are going to work through some recipes in the afternoons. I'm helping with Gramps in the evenings, because that's when she's tired, and I'm doing the morning feeding for Bryce and Codi at Rising Sun."

"That's a lot, Roo."

"I need to be busy, Daddy," she said, her voice barely filling her own ears. "I think better when I'm busy, and I'm trying to get God to tell me what to do."

"You've asked Him?"

"Why the tone of surprise?" Joey finally found the will and courage to look at her father. "Yes, I've asked Him. Many times, in fact."

"And what's He got to say?"

"He's very dodgy," she said. "He either says nothing, or

He says something like, 'Do what you'd like, Joey. I trust you.'" Familiar frustration frothed within her. "I don't know what I'd like to do. That's the problem. I just want someone to tell me what to do."

"I'm sure I can call you up at least once a day and boss you around," he said, plenty of teasing in his voice. His big, cowboy smile matched his hat, and Joey loved him so much.

He'd come before Spring Break too, just out of nowhere when she'd broken down in sobs on the phone. He'd only been there for just over twenty-four hours, but it had been enough to get her feet back on solid ground.

She'd gone ahead with her plans to live with her grandparents in Coral Canyon, and Grams had sent pictures of the bedroom Joey would have only yesterday. The curtains had been recently sewn, and Joey loved her daddy's parents so very much. Grams loved her back without conditions, and Joey felt like she had an old soul. One that connected with older people far easier than anyone her own age.

"We got you that car," Daddy said. "It's at the condo already, and Gramps has the keys."

"Thank you so much," Joey said. "Daddy, I—you know I appreciate all you've done for me, right? Paying for school and my life and everything. I really do appreciate it."

"I know you do, Roo."

"I don't think I'm going to go back to the Culinary Institute."

"When's the deadline to let them know?"

"July fifteenth," she said.

"So six weeks," he said.

"Yeah."

"There's still time then."

"Yeah," she repeated, though she wasn't sure what she needed time for. She could cook in Coral Canyon without the fancy degree from an overpriced institution. She could start her own business like Aunt Ev's brother, or she could just find a job in town. Coral Canyon had grown a bit in recent years, and while it had slowed and leveled off, there were plenty of restaurants to choose from.

She wasn't really sure what else she'd like to do, but as Daddy drove, Joey decided she was sick of feeling like a dandelion seed someone had blown off into the wind. She didn't want a current to push her around anymore, and she needed to make a decision and do something.

If it didn't work out, she'd make another one, and do something different. Eventually, she'd land on something she was supposed to do, right?

Dear Lord, that better be right.

"Living arrangements," Daddy said. "Your mother. A job. Grams and Gramps. The car. What else?"

"You tell me," Joey said.

Daddy shifted in his seat. "I want you to know that you are not invisible in our family."

"Except I kind of am," she said.

"Not to me," he said with plenty of conviction. He made the turn onto the long highway that led straight east to Coral Canyon, and he looked at her. "Not to Georgia. Absolutely not to OJ or Anaya. We see you, and we love you, even when you're not physically with us. In fact." He hit the T hard, and Joey grinned at him.

"Don't look at me like that," he grumped at her.

"You just got fired up."

"Yes, I did," he said. "Because I was going to say, in fact, when you're gone, you leave an enormous hole in all of our lives, and it's *us* who has to figure out how to live without *you*."

Joey's smile faded, and she hadn't thought about any holes she might be leaving behind when she wasn't at home. "I don't think that's true."

"Well, you're wrong," he said bluntly. "So we'll get you moved into Grams' tonight, but Georgia has a big meal planned at the house. Then you can go up to Dog Valley tomorrow like you planned, start at Bryce's, all of that."

She nodded, and when he said all the things she had going on, it did sound like a lot.

"I just have one more thing to say," he said.

"Shoot," she said, mimicking him from earlier. From the things he'd said his whole life.

"Please come see us too," he said. "Georgia has a whole box of books for you to read this summer—or however long you're here—and we miss our princess, who used to skip around with so much life, wear only pink sparkly skirts, and stay up too late reading."

Joey's eyes teared up, and she quickly brushed at them. "I miss her too."

"Maybe you could work with Georgia at the bookstore sometimes," Daddy said. "Like you did in high school. She says sometimes she just walks around the shop, thinking of you and doing things the way you would." He cleared his throat. "All right, that's all I'm gonna say about it. You're an adult, and we'll respect whatever you decide to do. Maybe it's easier not to see us too. I don't know."

"Daddy," she said, her voice a touch on the sharp side. "Of course it's not hard to see you guys."

"But maybe it is." He glanced over to her again. "I get that. Sometimes we don't go to family stuff, because it's just easier not to. Sometimes things hurt that we don't understand, or they're irritating for reasons we can't name. We get it, I promise."

Joey tugged on the sleeves of her sweatshirt. "Did you ever just not know what to do with your life?" she asked.

"I want to say yes," he said. "But the truth is, no. I've wanted to play the guitar since I was eight years old. I've been writing songs since I was ten. And Uncle Tex was older than me, and when he started talking about a band, I was seventeen years old. I would've dropped out of high school and gone with him if I thought Gramps would let me."

He chuckled. "He would've hunted me down and forced me back to the classroom." He sighed then, and Joey allowed her smile to come to her face. "It took Georgia a while to figure out how to open a book shop," she said. "Maybe I'll ask her about it."

"Talk to Bryce too," Daddy said. "He drifted for a bit, what with college, and then moving, and working at a bar, then a training facility. All that."

She nodded. "I'll talk to him about it."

"You remind me of Uncle Mav," Daddy said. "It takes a lot of courage to recognize that you're not doing what you want to do, and then do something to change that." He reached over and squeezed her hand. "I'm really proud of you, Roo."

She didn't know what to say, because she didn't think she'd done much for anyone to be proud of. With that hard conversation done, Daddy turned up the radio and simply drove, leaving Joey to her thoughts.

She simply stared, the same way she had on the airplane, and before she knew it, Daddy made the turn into her grandparents' condo complex. They had a ground unit in the corner, and Grams came outside before Daddy even had the truck in park.

Joey started to weep before she even unbuckled, because her grams had always been the epitome of someone who loved and accepted her exactly for who she was. "Grams," she said as she jogged toward her grandmother.

"Joey-girl." She opened her arms for Joey and received her right into her bosom. "You finally made it."

Joey gripped her as tightly as she dared, and then she stepped back. "Thank you for letting me do this."

"Of course. I've got a grocery list going too, and we can add to it before you get back from your mother's." She beamed at her and added, "Gramps is on his way out."

Joey turned toward the condo and went that way, her heartbeat so full of life and love. She found Gramps inside the condo, using his cane as he walked slowly toward the door. "Gramps."

She moved over to him and hugged him, his soothing voice in her ear finally making her feel absolutely welcome here. Maybe because he said, "Welcome home, Roo," or maybe because while Gramps didn't smile a whole lot, he loved hard and that meant more than anything else.

"Now, Grams says you're going to do everything I say without arguing." Joey pulled back and smiled at her grandfather. "Is that true?"

He scoffed, a familiar flash of attitude firing across his expression. "I suppose," he said.

"You're walking good with the cane." She grinned at him. "And don't tell Grams, but I'm gonna make sure you eat really well this summer."

Gramps smiled at her, and oh, that was worth the world. Joey giggled, glad she felt well enough, happy enough, to be able to do so. "I won't say a word to her."

Daddy came barreling through the door then, two of Joey's big suitcases with him. "Daddy," he bellowed as if Gramps had had surgery on his ears and not his abdomen. "You're lookin' good."

Joey knew for a fact that Daddy saw his father several times a week, but they still embraced, and as Grams came back inside the condo too with Joey's smaller bag, she suddenly had a flash of what life must've been like for her grandparents before all of their sons had started returning to town.

She couldn't even imagine them here alone, but they

had been. Only Uncle Gabe had lived within an hour of Coral Canyon, and Joey swore she saw the hand of God in that moment, standing in the small kitchen of a condominium in a fifty-five-plus community.

For God had brought back all of Grams's sons. And He'd given them all new wives, and they'd all built their families right here, where Grams and Gramps could see them, love on them, and enjoy them.

What a blessing, she thought as she took her bag from Grams and let her lead the way down the hall as if the bedroom would be hard to find. "I made up the bed," Grams said. "Abby brought new curtains. Your momma brought over your favorite pillows."

Joey stopped in the doorway and took in the room. The walls boasted white paint, but the curtains shouted with pink-and-white clouds. The bedspread boasted more pink, with a giant rainbow stretched across the middle of it.

Joy burst through Joey, especially when she took in the furry pink pillows—which were her favorite—and the billowy, pink netting that came down from the ceiling. "I love this," she whispered. "Thank you, Grams."

"Georgia came to do it," Grams said. "She, Dani, and Abby mostly put the room together. I just gave them the canvas."

Joey turned into her grandmother and hugged her. "I will thank them."

"We love you so much." Grams hugged her and then Daddy came wheeling the bags into the room.

"You're standing in the doorway, Roo. Move it or lose it."

He kept on coming, and Joey got out of the way before he ran her over with her own suitcases.

"Look at my room, Daddy." Joey gestured to it like she'd put it together herself. "Isn't it amazing?"

Daddy pushed her suitcases against the wall opposite the bed and turned in a full circle, taking everything in. "Well, this looks just like you, Roo." He grinned and slung his arm around her shoulders. "Feel good?"

"It feels great," Joey said. "Yeah, it sure does feel good to be here. To be back in Coral Canyon." She looked up at him, a lot of lines connecting into a picture of her future.

"To be home."

22

Cash Young heard the bell, lifted his spurs from the horse's sides, and took a quick moment to free his hand from the restraint on the saddle. He jumped from the bucking bronco's back, hit the dirt hard, and stumble-ran away from it.

The flanking cowboys rode in on the sides of the horse, keeping it away from Cash, who clapped his gloved hands together and looked up to the scoreboard. He'd made the time, so he'd get a score, though this was a practice session.

He'd felt good about the ride. His movements had matched the bucking of the horse, and he'd drawn a good steed. Of course, in practice, all the horses knew how to come out of the chute, and they didn't turn in tight circles, and the rides were far easier than what Cash had encountered in actual competition.

An eighty-four flashed up on the screen with his name

next to it, and Cash whooped. Clapped his hands again. Grinned as he jogged through the dirt in the arena to the fence.

"Way to go," another cowboy said, a man named Chester. "Great score."

"Thanks." Cash high-fived him when he made it to the top of the fence. He watched the next ride, expecting his trainer to come get him once all of his guys had ridden. Cash worked with a great trainer at a fantastic facility just south of Jackson Hole. He could train as much as he wanted, and he entered the amateur rodeos all over the Mountain West, including Utah, Idaho, Nevada, Wyoming, and Colorado.

Living this close to Coral Canyon allowed him to go home easily too, and Cash needed to do that soon. He hadn't been back since Bryce's wedding, and that had been a couple of months now.

His daddy and step-mom were about to have another baby too, so Cash had assumed he'd likely go when he got the text from one of his uncles that the infant had been born.

Part of him felt awkward and weird that he was twenty-two years old, and his daddy was having a baby. Of course, all of Cash's half-siblings were far younger than him. He'd been a month shy of turning sixteen when Daddy and Faith had had their first baby, a girl named Grace.

She was six now, with Celeste right behind her at five, and then a big gap until Tyrone, who'd just turned two years old last Thanksgiving. And now this new baby.

He clapped for the next cowboy, who didn't quite make the bell. The summer sun shone down on the men as they sat on the fence, most leaned forward to watch their friends ride. A lot could be learned by someone else's go-round too, and Cash had been toying with turning pro for a couple of years now.

Probably should've done it last year, he thought, not for the first time. Daddy would've had time to travel with him then, and Cash wasn't sure he could go into the PRCA alone. He'd done the traveling for the amateur circuits with his trainer and manager, and he knew how to pick up and go at the drop of a hat.

He competed in the saddle bronc riding, bull riding, and tie-down roping, and he was good. Cash knew he was good, but every night when he knelt down to pray, he thanked God for his body, his health, and his talents. He only wanted to give glory to God, and he hoped others around him would feel the spirit of the Lord and Savior Jesus Christ through Cash's treatment of them. Through his very presence in their lives.

He didn't go around preaching, but he hoped to influence people simply through how he lived his life.

No drinking. No partying. No women.

Cash's face heated at the thought of a pretty barrel racer he'd met several months ago, but Lisha Turner lived in Idaho, and he hadn't seen her in a couple of months. They were supposed to be at an upcoming event in Utah this summer together, though, so...maybe.

Cash seemed to live his whole life with the word maybe stuck in there somewhere.

Maybe he'd go home this weekend. Maybe he'd turn pro.

Maybe he'd ask Lisha out to dinner. He had her phone number, but he hadn't made a single move with the woman.

"Cash," a man called, and he turned toward Lewis, his trainer.

"Yep." He jumped down from the fence and headed toward the tall, skinny cowboy. He had to be close to Daddy's age—close to fifty—and Cash liked him a whole lot. He gave good notes on every individual ride; he praised in public; he reproved in private.

Once James and Billy had joined them, Lewis turned and led them out of the sun and into the tent. "Got some notes for each of ya." He handed out single sheets of paper, and Cash took his and looked at it.

Excellent mark out.

Great spur movement.

Keep that hand up on the downward motion. Don't lean left like you're wont to do. Balance, balance, balance.

Cash had seen all of that before. He had some parts of the saddle bronc ride down to perfection. Other parts varied with every ride he did, though he tended to lean left all the time, as noted.

His right side was his dominant side, so his left wasn't as strong. He worked out with weights—more on the left than the right. He did balance exercises to strengthen his lower back and abs, but there was always more to be done.

His sheet also said: *Great score.*

And one more thing that made Cash's breath catch in his throat.

When are you going to turn pro? I think you're ready.

Cash ripped his eyes up from the page to find Lewis's. He was going over something with James, and Cash's pulse hammered at him, almost shouting at him to interrupt. But Cash's personality wouldn't allow him to do that, and he shifted his feet left and right as he waited.

"Okay, Cash has ants in his boots," Lewis said, grinning at James. "I want you in the gym for an extra hour this week."

"Yes, sir," James said, and Lewis turned his attention to Cash.

He thrust his paper toward the trainer. "Do you mean this?"

Lewis didn't even look at the paper. He'd written it, after all. "Cash, you should've turned pro last summer."

He looked at the paper again, something settling right in his chest. "Yeah," he said. "I think I'm finally feeling ready."

"I know your daddy can help you with the application, but let me know if you need anything."

Cash met his eyes again. "You won't come with me."

Lewis grinned, but it wasn't a super happy gesture. "I train amateur cowboys, Cash."

And if Cash turned pro, he wouldn't be an amateur anymore.

"I'll get you a list of trainers for new pros," he said as he moved over to Billy to go over his notes and give him tips to improve. "Though I'm sure your daddy has some of those too."

"Yeah," Cash said, though he hadn't done what everyone assumed he had: Talk to his daddy about going pro. He turned away from the others as they started their consultation, sure his father was just waiting for Cash's phone call.

Daddy was very much like that. He didn't push Cash into corners or conversations, but he always made himself available when Cash was ready to talk.

He still had two more rides in saddle bronc today, and then he had three practice rides on bulls, but Cash jogged to the end of the fence and pulled his phone from his front pocket. Daddy's name sat right at the top of his contact list, because he talked to him the most out of any human being on the planet.

Daddy's phone only rang a couple of times before he said, "Cash, son, hey."

"Are you busy?"

"No, sir," Daddy drawled. "Jem just came over with the baby, and we're getting ready to take the kids down to the stream."

Cash could just see the slow, lazy summer afternoon in Coral Canyon. "That sounds magical."

"Where you at?" Daddy asked.

"The arena," Cash said. "I just had a great practice ride for saddle bronc."

"Yeah?"

"Yeah." Cash nodded as if his father could see him. For some reason, he didn't know how to say what he wanted to say. What had been teeming in his mind for months now. He'd never been good with talking about things, and he'd barely made it through high school. Maybe he wasn't ready for the rodeo.

He'd seen his father's videos online, and Daddy had to give interviews. He had to converse with other cowboys, trainers, lots of people. He'd have to manage a lot more than he did now if he turned pro, and so many doubts streamed through his mind.

"Say what's on your mind, son." Daddy's gentle command prompted Cash to come back to the present.

"Lewis thinks I'm ready to turn pro."

"Mm hm."

"*I* think I'm ready to turn pro," Cash amended, and that opened the dam of words stuffed down inside his throat. "And I need help with knowing what to do, and how to get the paperwork done, and which circuit you think is best." He took a quick breath. "And a new trainer, and I don't even know if I can stay here in Jackson and train."

"Okay," Daddy said. "Slow down, Cash."

He took in another breath, then another. "What do you think?"

"I think you'll be brilliant as a professional rodeo cowboy," Daddy said, quiet conviction in his voice. Of course, Cash had spoken with his father about going into the rodeo. He'd seen his father's bodily injuries, been there for the back surgeries and the subsequent recoveries. They'd talk about all of that, with mostly Daddy telling him that Cash had to be as smart and as safe as possible if he was really going to go into the rodeo.

Thus, Cash rode in the saddle bronc event, not the bareback riding. One had a saddle with more support; the other didn't.

"Thank you, Dad."

"I can get you the paperwork, and I'll poke around and see who's taking on pros in your events."

"I need a trainer, right?"

"In the beginning, you need someone who can help you navigate the pro circuit, schedule your training time, get you in the gym, yes."

Cash nodded, some part of him settling. "I've heard of some guys who have managers."

"Yes," Daddy said. "We can get you one of those too. It depends on how well you're doing, but I think you'll do great."

"You think so?" Cash didn't like how pitched-up his voice became.

"Son, you could've won the RNCFR last year. Hands down. Won it."

That was a pro rodeo circuit that included events from Idaho, Utah, and Nevada, where Cash did compete in amateur events. "Maybe," he said, to which Daddy started to laugh.

"Okay," he said among the chuckles. "Well, let's see how you do in the National Circuit Finals this year then. When do you want to file?"

"Is there a good time? A better time than others?"

"The season starts on October first," Daddy said. "We'll want to file before then, I'd guess. Then, all your events this year will earn you points on your permit that'll get you to full membership faster."

"Okay," Cash said.

"When are you coming home again?" Daddy asked.

"I was honestly going to wait until you and Faith have the baby."

"She's not due for another month and a half," Daddy said. "I can come to you." Something slammed on his end of the line, and behind him, Cash heard them call for the second-round practice rides.

He turned that way and started heading back. "I have to do another ride," he said.

"Let me talk to Momma, and I'll text you."

"Okay," Cash said. "I can honestly come this weekend."

"We'll find a time," Daddy said. "I love you, Cash. Okay? You hearing me?"

"Yes, Daddy." Cash nodded to the cowboy checking people in to their rides, and he made a check-mark on his clipboard. "I love you too."

He grinned like he'd just won a major event in the PRCA and added, "Tell the kids I love them too, and ask Faith if she'll make me some doughnuts if I come home this weekend."

Daddy laughed and said, "Son, she'll rope the world for you, you know that."

Cash's chest squeezed tight, because yes, Faith loved Cash like that. "Okay," he said. "I'm coming home this weekend, then. You don't need to check your schedule or arrange anything. It's easier for me to come to you."

"If you're sure."

"I'll see you Friday night," he said.

"I'll make sure we have all the maple flavoring and huge slabs of bacon for the doughnuts."

Cash tipped his head back and laughed, feeling lighter than he had in months. The call ended, and Cash stuffed his phone away and faced the group of cowboys also waiting for their turn in the chute.

He wasn't sure why he'd needed Lewis's permission to turn pro, but Cash felt like a huge weight had been lifted from his shoulders and his soul, and he couldn't wait to get home this weekend to see his parents and start the process of taking the next step in his career—and in his life.

Part Two: Eight months later

23

Belle checked and then double-checked for her ID and the paperwork she needed to show the judge in Tallahassee. She sighed as she sank onto the bed, because darkness still breathed over Jackson Hole, and she could imagine the biting sting the air would sink into her lungs the moment she stepped outside.

"Lord," she whispered. "Please let the Agatha at the shelter in Tallahassee be the woman I've been looking for."

It seemed fitting that her first case back in missing person's had taken her all over the place, and the latest word was that the woman she'd feared dead had actually left everything she owned—literally everything—and skipped town of her own free will. And she'd been living two thousand miles away, in Tallahassee.

How she'd even gotten there, Belle couldn't fathom.

There had to be something strong driving her, and Belle's heart hurt that Rhonda had been in such fear as to leave behind photos of her children, all of her identification, her marriage certificate though her husband had died a couple of years ago, and simply left.

Vanished.

Belle had vanished ten months ago, at least in the eyes of anyone who'd known her. Admittedly, that wasn't very many people. Probably more felines than actual human beings. The thought made her smile, and while Belle hadn't gotten any cats since her return from the casino money laundering scheme, she had returned to Jackson Hole.

Ben had asked her where she'd like to be placed, and she'd immediately chosen missing persons. She wanted to find the one who'd been lost, who'd wandered astray, who needed someone to come looking just for them.

Oh, she had *stories* about her time undercover, but Belle had lived it once, then re-lived it when she wrote her reports, and was now going through it all again for a third time as prosecutors for the Wyoming District Attorney's office prepared for the trial against Stanley Ford, Gregorio Mazetti, and the Buffalo Casino Company—which was just a front for money laundering.

The casino was closed now. The company had declared bankruptcy. The Italian mob family had hired really good lawyers. Belle had come back to Jackson, and she'd only been here for three weeks.

Her to-do list, both at work and in her personal life, was

still wildly out of control, and she dealt with the closest burning fire at all times.

"It'll be warmer in Tallahassee than here," she told herself, and that much was true. She didn't have to travel a ton for her job, and she bent down and zipped up the top of her backpack.

She thought for half a second about texting Harry Young, but then an alarm went off on her phone, and Belle reached to silence it instead. Besides, she hadn't texted with him for months now, and she could admit she'd looked at his social media from time to time.

Every post showed him in his funky T-shirts, holding his guitar, and either smiling or singing. He kept his fans up-to-date on the progress of his upcoming album, and if the public peeks into his personal life was to be believed, he was almost done.

While undercover, and to this day, she couldn't even believe she had Harry's number or could text him whenever she wanted. If only she was brave enough to let him know her undercover assignment had finished.

Part of her didn't believe he'd be interested in her. Every time she let those thoughts enter her mind, she thought of that kiss at his cousin's wedding. That had not been fake on any level, and Belle flipped her phone over and over in her palm, though she should be leaving for the airport.

Belle smiled just thinking of him, and she gave her guitar in the corner a cursory glance as she got to her feet. She put her pack over the handle of her carryon and headed outside the apartment Larry had found for her when everything had blown up at the casino and Belle had "been arrested" and brought back to Jackson Hole.

Outside, the early spring kicked against her lungs, and Belle cursed herself for not insisting on a garage. She made the drive to the airport as the sun started to lighten the land, but she still entered the building to only grays and whites in the sky. Of course, the Wyoming landscape was still waking up from the long winter. Trees had only been gray, beige, or white for months, and the leaves had just started to green up and bud in the past week.

She wasn't a big traveler, and every time she came to the Jackson airport, she had to take a moment to get her bearings. She always felt a little too bulky, though she wasn't wearing her Sherriff's Department vest today. Her hair was likewise down, and Belle told herself to blend in. Find her gate, grab some coffee, and just relax.

You're not working, she told herself as she watched a man move past her. She didn't need to notice every little detail here, and Belle put her blinders on and started walking. She knew she worked too much, but she didn't know how to cut back. Ben had told her to take a few weeks off before she dove back into her department work, but she didn't know what to do with herself all day.

So she ended up back at the office, and she'd picked up a single case out of sheer luck. Sometimes, she thought she should've taken Ben's advice and simply taken some time off. "You are," she told herself.

After she appeared before the judge and checked the

shelter, Belle was continuing to Destin, Florida for a few days of beach-relaxation time.

She'd be thirty later this year, and something about the number had her questioning everything. "Yeah," she muttered as she spotted a coffee kiosk ahead. "Probably because you have a two-bedroom rental and a guitar to show for the first three decades of your life."

Not even a cat anymore.

Oh, and that unrealized dream of plucking and crooning her way into the hearts of millions across the globe. Harry now crowded into her brain, elbowing other thoughts out of the way.

But she would not use him. She absolutely would not. She knew what that felt like, and she wouldn't knowingly do it to another human being, especially one as sweet and kind as Harry Young. He'd probably be upset she hadn't texted him the moment she could've been herself again.

Before she'd gone undercover, she'd joked about his and Adam's plain names and how they were meant for each other. He'd told her things about how he didn't like to fly, how his confidence ebbed and flowed, and how much he missed his family in Coral Canyon.

Belle had taken everything he'd told her and stuffed it into her heart. So, no, she wouldn't be asking him for contacts in the country music industry or anywhere else. Her sound was far too grunge for that anyway, and she'd stopped playing the guitar about seven years ago on top of that.

She went through the line, got her coffee, and found her

gate with plenty of time to spare. *That's another thing you've done in thirty years*, she told herself. *You're always on time.*

Like that was the top desirable trait a person could develop, or that it took three decades to perfect. She scoffed at herself, because Belle knew her life was stale, stale, stale, despite the undercover assignment.

She kept her blinders on as she stared out the window of the airport and sipped her coffee. Ever the responsible one, she stopped about halfway through so she wouldn't be too hopped up when the plane took off, and so she wouldn't have to use the bathroom four times on the way to Florida.

People moved about her, but she didn't pay attention to them. She cleared her email, answering the most important ones. She even managed to ignore the conversations around her until there were none.

In fact, everything surrounding her felt like it had disappeared. Just dropped off. The noise, the activity, all of it.

Belle's skin prickled a warning at her, and she finally looked up from her phone. Sure enough, she was the only passenger still waiting in several rows of chairs, and her heartbeat leapt up and banged in the back of her throat. "Did I miss my plane?"

Or worse, had they closed the airport, and she hadn't heard the announcement? Was there a threat?

Her pulse raced; her police training kicked in.

She looked right and saw other people down the way, most of them looking her direction. Or past her. "Strange," she murmured. Number one, Jackson Hole got a lot of celebrities, so famous-people-sightings weren't all that rare here. And she certainly wasn't anyone to look at.

She turned left and quickly flinched back when someone asked, "Are any of these seats taken, ma'am?" in a strong, Southern accent.

Belle blinked and looked up at the man in a long, black coat, black trousers, with a hint of a blue dress shirt showing through the open front of his jacket.

Oh, butterflies and biscuits. She knew that face.

Adam Harmon.

And that meant Harry Young had to be close by. Very close by.

Belle's heartbeat ran wild now, cheering as it went through her veins. She wasn't even sure why. She hadn't seen Harry in person in almost a year, and she hadn't texted with him in months. Still, she managed to say, "No, sir."

Adam rewarded her with a warm, wide smile and turned to look over his shoulder. He gestured to someone and as he stepped out of the way, the glorious sight of Harry Young filled Belle's vision.

Her tongue felt like someone had put hot glue on it, then dumped a load of sawdust. Thankfully, her eyelids still knew how to blink, and her lungs still inflated and deflated with air as she breathed in and out.

Harry glanced at Adam and said, "Thanks, brother. If you could just give me a few minutes."

"Absolutely, sir," Adam said, ever the professional, and he went back the way Harry had come. Belle looked around, realizing he'd somehow set up an entire perimeter around her—and she hadn't even noticed. Her gaze flew back to Harry's, where it locked into place.

Harry grinned at her and said, "It's really you." He indicated the seat right beside her. "Can I?"

"Yes," she choked out, sure this wasn't happening. She also couldn't look away from him. "What are you doing here?"

"Going home," he said. "Well, going back to Nashville." He reached over and took her hand in his. His skin radiated warmth, and his touch felt so welcome and so open. She almost started crying at the human, personal touch, something she hadn't had in *such* a long time.

Her fingers felt like lumps of ice compared to his, but she warmed as he continued to smile at her. "What about you?"

"Florida," grated through her throat. "I have a case there." His eyebrows went up, and Belle managed to align her fingers in his. "And—I mean, then I'm going on vacation, actually." She rolled her head to stretch her neck. "Apparently, I need to de-stress."

Harry grinned at her, and he seemed so at-ease. Questions streamed through her, but she didn't want to start throwing them at him too soon or too fast.

"Florida?" he asked. "You have a case in Florida? Did you change jobs?"

She shook her head, glad her hair was down today. "A case here has led there."

"Ah, got it." Harry looked out the window in front of them and exhaled slowly. He didn't immediately head into the next conversation topic, and Belle's mind had gone horribly blank.

After only a few seconds—which felt like an hour—he turned back to her. "I can't—can I come to Florida with you? For your vacation. Where are you going?"

"Destin," ghosted out of her mouth. It might as well have been a *yes, please come with me, Harry!*

His smile filled the whole airport with light, and Belle's gaze dropped to his mouth. She'd only gotten to kiss him that one time, and it was nowhere near enough.

"Is that a yes?" he asked, looking away from her. "I can pay my own way."

"Yeah, that's what I was worried about," Belle said dryly. She felt more like herself than she had in months, and that sure felt...nice.

Harry chuckled and squeezed her hand. "My flight's about to take off. But I really do need to hear you say, 'Yes, Harry, come to Destin, and I'll text you all the details of my vacation there,' before I ask Adam to arrange it all for me."

"No sense in making more work for the man if it's not necessary."

"Precisely." Harry looked at her again, something open and vulnerable on his face, riding in his eyes. "I'm finished with the album."

"You are?" Belle reached over and ran her fingertips down the side of his face. "Then why are you going back to Nashville?"

His smile slipped, only shining halfway on his face now. That was somehow as glorious as the full thing, and Belle had the sudden and painful realization of how deep her loneliness had become.

"Tying up loose ends," he said. "Packing the apartment. Adam and I will move up here in a couple of weeks." He sat up and pulled his hand back to his own lap. "I told myself that if it was you, that it meant something. That I shouldn't just walk on by. That I should say something."

Belle wasn't sure what that meant, so she just watched him. When he didn't continue, she said, "So say something."

He chuckled and ducked his head, that big cowboy hat covering his handsome face as he did. "Well, Miss Belle, at the risk of getting rejected in person instead of over a video date or a text, I guess I'll just say this...."

Harry looked up, that intensity in his eyes that Belle had seen in some of his videos and posts. "I'm—I want to see you. Maybe it's our year."

"Maybe."

"I can't wait to be back in Coral Canyon. Bought myself a house and everything."

"That's great, Harry," she said, and her pulse pirouetted through her body.

"I know it's not Jackson, but I'll be retired, and I have a car. And seeing you here...I'd love to go to dinner with you and start to really get to know you." He swallowed, and Belle found that the most surprising thing he'd said or done.

Not that he'd cleared the area around her without her noticing, though that had been quite the feat. Not that she'd run into him here, in a public airport. Not that he'd asked her out again, though that still astonished her greatly.

But that he seemed nervous to do it.

He was the great Harry Young, the rarest talent on the guitar in this generation, the world-famous country music star, the man with a voice of honeyed gold.

She was nobody, and that fact alone kept her from immediately agreeing to go to dinner with him.

But she did say, "I'd love it if you'd come to Destin, Harry, and I'll text you all the details of my vacation there."

24

arry could sit in the airport and talk to Belle for hours, but surely her plane would be taking off soon, and Harry knew he was late for his. He hated flying privately, and Adam arranged everything he could commercially.

Harry only carried a small backpack that he could easily slide under the seat in front of him, and Adam had his half-sized carry-on that did the same. They always flew first class, always in the second row. Adam alerted the flight attendants, pilots, airline, and anyone else he needed to that Harry would be boarding at the very last moment, that he needed to be the last passenger on the plane, and would be ducking into the second row against the window.

The end. Harry and Adam then expected not to be bothered for the duration of the flight, except for meals and drinks. Adam sat on the aisle to protect him from anything, answer any questions, and allow Harry to work or sleep the way he wanted.

Harry could admit that he'd been hesitant at first to hire a personal assistant, but now he could not imagine his life without Adam Harmon in it. He and Adam had had several powwows as Harry had prepared to leave Nashville and return to Coral Canyon, as Adam wondered if he would be needed there. Harry didn't want to let him go because he didn't know what life would be like in Coral Canyon. Yes, most people left his father and uncles alone, but Harry had been called "a horse of a different color" enough times to know that he couldn't always expect the same things that Country Quad had.

"Sir," Adam said, as he always did when they were in public. "The flight attendants are threatening to close the gate and rebook you on the next flight if you don't come right now." He glanced over to Belle. "I'm so sorry, Miss Graves."

"It's fine," Belle said in her sweet, yet somewhat rough, voice. "Go, Harry. You don't want to miss your flight."

"You'll text me?" he asked.

"I have a new phone," she said. "But I kept your number. So yeah, I'll text you."

Harry got to his feet, reassured that he would get a text from her, and he couldn't do much more than that. He'd had Adam clear the airport around her so that he could talk to her, and that seemed stalker-y enough. He quickly walked with Adam down several gates to where his plane waited and smiled at the flight attendant there.

"I'm so sorry, ma'am," he said. "Thank you for holding the plane."

She smiled in return but swallowed instead of speaking. Harry moved in front of Adam to go down the jetway to the plane. He said thank you to the flight attendants waiting right there at the front, noting that the pilot's door to the cockpit was already closed too.

He ducked down two rows, keeping his cowboy hat low so no one could see his face as he settled into the window seat and put his backpack under the seat in front of him.

With the recording done, Harry didn't have anything to work on during the flight back to Nashville. Even if he had, after seeing Belle, he was way too keyed up to do it. Adam settled beside him, sliding his carry-on smartly under the seat. They buckled, and Harry's belt had barely clicked before the plane pushed away from the gate. They really had been waiting for him, and Harry experienced a thread of guilt as it pulled against his heart and ribs.

"Something to drink, sir?" a flight attendant asked.

"Two Diet Doctor Peppers with ice," Adam said. She nodded and moved away to get their drinks.

As they hadn't taken off yet, Harry had not put his phone in airplane mode. So he heard it plainly when a notification sounded. It wasn't his father, and it wasn't Adam, as he'd assigned both of them a special notification sound so that he would know it was them when they texted.

Everyone else had the same sound, and Harry knew he didn't have to look at his phone for them if he didn't want to. But now, he brightened the screen and saw an unknown number sitting there with a Wyoming area code and the first few words that said, *This is Belle.*

His heart had never pumped so hard, not even when he ran miles in preparation for a concert tour. And this year, he didn't have to do that, as he'd be playing small venues around Coral Canyon and live-streaming his concerts for the next three months.

Rebel had paid for his band to come to Coral Canyon with him, and he had his drummer, a guitar player, a keyboard player, and his backup singers staying in a big rental house up the canyon where Uncle Blaze and Uncle Jem lived.

He actually had been praying and hoping that they wouldn't kill each other in that big house. But thankfully, when Rebel had asked him to stay there too, Harry had been able to decline. It was nowhere in his contract, and he wanted his own place in Coral Canyon.

He'd just been home for the past couple of days to sign the papers and pay for the house, and his father currently had the keys and garage code. Harry had walked around Hilde's furniture store and picked out the things he wanted, and he knew without a doubt that everything would be ready for him when he returned in a couple of weeks.

Daddy, Uncle Otis, Bryce, and Uncle Tex were making the flight to Nashville to help him pack, and then they'd all drive back together with Harry and Adam. He expected to be settled in Coral Canyon before the end of April. *That plan might change,* he told himself as he tapped to open Belle's full text.

As promised, here are the details of my vacation, she said. *I need to be in Tallahassee before a judge tomorrow, where hopefully I'll get permission to go through some homeless shelter records there for a missing persons case that I need to wrap up.*

Another text came in while he read.

Then I plan to be in Destin for five nights from Thursday to Tuesday, when I then fly back to Jackson Hole. I'll send you the link for where I'm staying.

And finally: *It is a two-bedroom condo. And if that's not too weird for you, I'm happy to have you stay in the second bedroom.*

A link to the place where she'd be staying followed that and concluded her flurry of text messages. Harry wanted nothing more but to fly there right now, cover every square foot of that condo in rose petals and candles and all of her favorite foods—from cashew chicken to meatloaf to pepperoni pizza with Alfredo sauce—and be waiting for her in the kitchen when she arrived on Thursday. His thumbs flew as the plane continued to taxi down the jetway.

Thanks so much, Belle. It really was so great to see you. I've got a few things to do and tie up with Adam, and I'll let you know when I can make it to Florida. He'd no sooner hit send on that text before Adam said, "What are you smiling about, cowboy?"

Harry looked over to him as if he needed an explanation.

He'd had Adam clear the entire area where Belle had been sitting simply so Harry could go talk to her, for crying out loud.

"Belle texted," he said, and he handed Adam his phone.

Adam read the short messages quickly and said, "You're going to Destin, Florida?" with plenty of incredulity in his voice.

Harry leaned back and closed his eyes. "Yes," he said. "I want to go to Destin, Florida, with Belle on her vacation." She had been undercover for months, and he hadn't heard from her. He'd thought about her every single day, though. He'd written her several times and mailed those letters to the Sheriff's office. He'd never once gotten a reply. He wondered if Belle had really gotten the messages the way she'd said her boss would pass them along.

He had not dated anyone else in the past ten months. He didn't need anyone while he recorded his album, because no one was Belle. He wasn't interested in anyone other than her, and he didn't need the experience of asking out women and going on first dates.

Adam sighed heavily, telling Harry that he was being maybe a little irrational, plenty insufferable, and probably demanding. But Harry had talked about Belle plenty of times, so many that Adam surely knew how he felt about her still.

As the plane picked up speed, Harry relived his kiss with Belle during Bryce's wedding for probably the hundredth time.

"Can you do it?" Harry asked. "What's my schedule like?"

"Of course we can do it," Adam said quietly, handing Harry his phone. He opened his eyes to take it and swiped and tapped to put it in airplane mode before he tucked it into the pocket in the seat in front of him. "Destin from Nashville is probably an hour," Adam said. "And it's a really popular vacation spot in Florida. We should have no trouble getting a flight."

"In first class, in the second row?" Harry asked.

"Heck, you could probably drive it," Adam said. "Then you'd have a car. You could leave whenever you want."

The flight attendant didn't return with their drinks, which made sense as the plane was literally taking off right now. Harry wished he had something to distract himself from this conversation.

"Are you planning to go the whole time?" Adam asked. "Maybe just Friday and Saturday? What are you thinking?"

Harry was thinking he wanted to see Belle as much as possible, hear all of her stories—or at least any that she could tell him—and share all of his with her from the past ten months.

Sometimes he couldn't believe that ten months had passed without her, and other days had been agonizingly slow, or he'd been in a bad mood—angry, irritable, and near tears—that he hadn't been able to see her or talk to her. He wondered if she felt the same, and he needed to find out.

"I'd like to go on Thursday," he said. "It's only Monday.

That gives me Tuesday and Wednesday to do whatever I need to do."

"What you need to do, Harry," Adam said. "Is continue coordinating with Morris about your upcoming live-stream concerts and go through your apartment. I imagine you can take a few days off from both of those to go to Destin."

"I'd imagine so," Harry agreed.

Adam said nothing more, though Harry knew he'd just caused a mountain of work for the man. Arranging travel for Harry was no small feat, and Adam usually handled it weeks or months in advance, so that he'd be able to speak to the proper authorities and make sure that Harry had the security clearance and privacy that he required.

"What do you think I should do?" Harry asked.

"Do, sir?" Adam asked.

"Stay with her?" Harry wondered out loud. "Or get my own place nearby?"

"Well," Adam said. "It's the first week of April and probably a very popular time in Destin. We should see if there are any places available at all before you make that decision."

"Hmm, true," Harry said. "Will you look into that for me?"

"Yes," Adam said. "You don't think you want to stay with her?"

"I think *she* might not want me to stay with her," Harry said. "It might not be about what I want. And I need to look at the floor plan of that place to see if it's even big enough for two of us."

Secretly, Harry wanted to be right at Belle's side. He knew he'd acted a little overeager by holding her hand within the first ten seconds of sitting down—and then inviting himself on her vacation with her?

An overeager beaver, he was.

This trip to Destin was probably the first vacation she'd taken in years. Coming to his uncle's wedding surely hadn't been a vacation, though they had gone out. Harry suddenly realized he had so much more to learn about Belle. She'd obviously gone back to the missing persons unit with the Teton County Sheriff's Department, and he wondered if that's where she wanted to be.

She'd had to give up her cats, and he wanted to know if she'd gotten them back.

She'd sold her house, and Harry knew that because he'd seriously considered buying it for her and holding on to it until she returned from her undercover assignment. In the end, he decided that would be irrational and coming on way too strong for where they were in their relationship. And he'd watched the house go to someone else.

Harry didn't doze, but after he drank his Diet Dr. Pepper and the flight attendant had cleared away the cup, he closed his eyes again, reclined the seat, and let his fantasies about Belle run wild. Now that he'd seen her again, talked to her, even if it was only for ten minutes, his appetite for her had been whetted, and he needed to have her in his life.

Jackson Hole sat an hour away from Coral Canyon, and Harry couldn't help wondering if Belle could make the move to the small Wyoming town that he loved so much, where all of his family lived and where they could start to build a life together.

You're not going to ask her on this vacation, he told himself sternly. *You're going to use it to get to know her again, get caught up, and then hopefully pick up where you left off at Bryce's wedding.*

They'd had a couple of phone dates after that, and then he'd buried himself in making his third album, and Belle had simply gone off the grid. She hadn't told him when or where, as that was the whole nature of going undercover. But as he flew back to Nashville from Coral Canyon for hopefully the last time, Harry's heart expanded and grew and ballooned with hope upon hope upon hope that the timing for him and Belle was finally right.

25

T he car where Belle rode in the backseat pulled up to a four-story condo building that seemed to be radiating the Florida sunshine. "Thank you," she said to the driver. She stuffed her purse in her backpack and reached for the door handle.

He got out to get her big suitcase, and Belle slid her backpack over the handle of it and pulled out her phone so that she could pay the driver for the ride. He drove off before she finished that, but she got the job done and then tapped over to her vacation reservation email to get the code for the door. She'd looked at it ten times that morning already, and she knew the unit sat on the ground floor with easy beach access right out the back.

She wheeled her suitcase to the door and typed in the code to enter. One long hallway stretched in front of her, down to the living, kitchen, and dining room at the back of the house. Sunlight streamed in back there as windows stood sentinel from floor to ceiling and wall to wall, and a screened-in sun porch also offered another place to eat breakfast, lunch, or dinner, as well as lounge while reading a book.

Immediately to her left, in a little alcove in the hall, stood a stackable washer and dryer and then the doorway to the master suite. Belle wheeled her backpack and suitcase in there, noting the big king bed that she'd probably need a step to climb up into, a beautiful bureau with a television on it, and around the corner to the right, the bathroom.

She sighed to be here in this condo, because it was so unlike anything she'd ever done in her life. She didn't need bells and whistles. She didn't pay for extravagant, expensive vacations. Heck, she didn't even take regular vacations. Most of what she'd done in the past seven or eight years since leaving Nashville and landing in Wyoming was hike in the Tetons or visit Yellowstone to watch Old Faithful go off. Those were things she could do in a day on her day off from work that would reset her, recenter her, and remind her that God existed and good people lived in the world.

In a job like hers, it was easy to think everyone had something to hide, had done terrible things or wanted to do them, or committed crimes. She left her things in the bedroom and went down the hall again.

Also on her right, another bedroom appeared, this one with a double bed and a twin, a tiny TV mounted to the wall, and a nightstand between the two beds. No dresser, but it did connect to the main bathroom, which also had a hall entrance.

She glanced around for a moment, because this would be where Harry would stay. She had a stackable washer and dryer unit, a bathroom, and a solid, strong wall separating her bed from his.

Her heartbeat pumped out several extra thumps simply thinking about him being in this space with her. They hadn't had a lot of in-person interaction, but they'd exchanged hundreds of texts in the past couple of days, and he'd called her on Monday night, Tuesday night, and last night, in his words, "just to hear the sound of your voice."

He sure seemed to like her as much as he had last year. And while that baffled Belle as much as it ever had, it also caused a smile to come to her face. She continued down the hall another few steps, where she found a galley kitchen with a big, long island in the middle. She could go toward the kitchen sink and then turn and step down into the living room or continue straight and step down to the same space.

A giant dining room table for eight stood there, all the chairs waiting for guests. Two big recliners faced a full-sized couch with the television between them. And then she reached the wall of windows. The door slid open from the corner, going about halfway across the condo, so that she could step outside to the screened porch, which she did. She took in a deep breath of the sunshine, the sound of the sea, the shrieking of seagulls, and the sea breeze.

Two loungers sat out in the sun porch, as well as a small table with four chairs. With screens everywhere, including a door, she stepped through that, and ten feet down a narrow sidewalk with grass on both sides, she met the sand. The beach stretched in front of her and to her right; to her left, in front of the next building over, a giant swimming pool where splashing, laughing families called to one another.

Cabanas and umbrellas had been set up in the sand in front of her, with loungers that had clearly been moved around according to individual needs.

She could see herself lying there, spraying herself with plenty of sunscreen since she'd just survived another winter in Wyoming—this one undercover, no less—and reading, eating frozen grapes, and basking in the warmth of the sun and the knowledge that she was free.

Not living another life anymore, with a name that wasn't her own.

Not watching her back.

Not weighing and reweighing every word she said.

Not trying to quiet her pulse during every conversation, every work shift, every time she drove the van.

She pushed those memories out of her head as she walked across the hot, white sand to a vacant lounger under a blue umbrella. She sighed as she sat down and stretched her legs in front of her and reached her arms up over her head. Everything relaxed as she exhaled and she closed her eyes and thought, *Thank you, Lord, for creating beautiful places like this for weary people like me.*

She'd felt more and more seen since taking the undercover assignment, and her testimony of her Lord and Savior, Jesus Christ, had grown and was stronger than ever. She knew He saw her. She knew He cared. She knew she could go to Him for anything, and He would help her, even if that help came in the form of silence. Even if that help came from someone she didn't know. Even if that came in the form of having Harry Young stay with her for the next few days as they rekindled their romance.

She'd left her phone inside, and that needled at her, because Harry said that he was landing about the time that she could check-in, and she timed her arrival here at this beachside condo for the moment that she could enter.

She stayed outside for another few minutes, and then the need to know if he'd texted nagged at her too much to stay outside. She went back to the master bedroom and got her phone out of her backpack to check it.

Sure enough, Harry had called and texted, and his message read, *Landed safely, and I'm on the way. I should be there in thirty minutes. I know what unit number we're in, and I could just knock on the door, or you can give me the code and I'll just come in.*

He'd sent one more message: *Are you there yet? I don't want to get there before you. You should see it first.*

She wasn't sure why that mattered, but she smiled as she texted him back. *I'm here, and you can come in with the code 42475. I might be out on the beach, so come find me if I'm not in the condo.*

With that, Belle set aside her phone and quickly changed into her swimsuit. A cute romper that was bright blue with pink, peach, yellow, and white flowers splashed across it. She swung her suitcase up onto her bed and opened it to get out the sunscreen, her hat, and a swimming suit cover-up. Armed with those things, as well as her phone so she could read, Belle left the condo again in favor of the lounger in the shade. Another one sat on the other side of the umbrella pole, and she figured Harry could ease himself into that as easily as he'd reentered her life.

They'd need to go to the grocery store later, because he'd confessed that he liked having a fridge full of soda pop, and she wanted to stock it with bottled water and fruit. He'd looked up places and restaurants around town where they could eat. When he'd told her that, Belle had asked, "Is Adam coming?"

"No," Harry had said. "And I'm actually pretty nervous about it. I haven't flown anywhere without Adam in over a year. I don't go anywhere without him. But Destin is a ritzy, high-end place, and I imagine they have celebrities there often. He's made reservations for us at several places, and he's told them that I'm a VIP who wants privacy. So I think it will be okay."

She hadn't rented a car, but Harry had, and she teased him relentlessly about his driving ability, seeing as how he got driven everywhere he went.

"I can do it," he'd said. "And I can't wait to prove it to you."

She'd laughed, and she had really enjoyed the past couple of days of texting and talking to Harry. He'd sent her the listing of the house he'd just bought, and she'd been surprised to see how normal and average it was.

He told her, "That was my goal. I don't need a great big

mansion. It's just me. It's small-town Coral Canyon, and I just want to write songs and live my life."

That was that.

That was what he was going to do now: be a country music songwriter. But he wasn't going to perform anything he wrote. He wasn't going to make any of the albums himself. He said he could if he wanted to, and he could release them independently and probably make far more than he did with Rebel, as his uncle had a recording studio behind his farmhouse on the eastern edge of Coral Canyon.

That intrigued Belle, and she wanted to know more about that. Her country music dreams had died a horrible, shattering death, but the more she talked to Harry, the more she realized that social media was not the same as it had been a decade ago.

She could probably do the same thing he had by getting herself a nice tripod, a ring light, and setting herself up on a set of stairs with a guitar and a song she'd written. She might be able to be as popular as him. She might be able to monetize her social media accounts and make money.

And if he knew how to record songs from a barn in Coral Canyon and release them independently, surely she could learn too.

"Is that what you want?" she asked herself as she settled onto the lounger and started to spray herself with the 70 SPF sunscreen so that her wickedly white skin wouldn't burn on the first day. "Do you want to try your hand at country music again?"

The idea sounded ridiculous in her own voice, and yet it

sat there in her heart and mind and wouldn't go away. Because of that, Belle also had to question her current career choice. The more coveted positions, like being a supervisor over missing persons, could have been hers if she'd wanted it. But she'd taken her old job as an investigator and called it good. She still sought justice for those who had been hurt, but she'd seen so many ugly things in the past ten months.

As Belle truly thought about it, she stared out over the water, which always came ashore, lapping, waving, splashing, roaring. It never stopped. And that was how Belle felt about crime. It was never going to go away. They would never eradicate it. And she felt weary right down to her very bones because of that.

"Maybe you do need a change," she whispered to herself, and she settled her sun hat on her head and leaned back as another relaxing sigh left her mouth.

All kinds of ideas had been swimming in her head since Harry had sat down next to her in the Jackson Hole airport. She lived in a rental apartment right now that her boss at the Sheriff's department had found for her. It wasn't a permanent housing solution, but she didn't want to buy in Jackson Hole again.

No, even while she'd prepared for her court date and then to visit the shelter, both of which she'd done successfully—and she had located Rhonda; that case was now closed—she'd been searching real estate listings in Coral Canyon.

It was a small town that had experienced a boom of growth a few years ago, but the market had evened out again. The market was lower, and she'd found a dozen things that fit her budget. "Yeah," she told herself. "Your budget if you have a job."

She'd also flipped through the pictures of Harry's house multiple times. And while it wasn't a large mansion with all the newest, nicest things like in-floor heating, marble countertops, and decks that extended over lakes, it was plenty big enough for him, a wife, and their kids.

Five bedrooms, as well as a dedicated office space where he'd be writing his songs. He'd live in one of the bedrooms, which left four more for children or guests. *Four bedrooms,* she thought.

She'd known Harry to be a planner, and the house he'd bought definitely testified to that, so maybe she didn't need to buy a house at all. "Well, you're not going to move in with him while you're dating," she muttered.

Just because they were sharing this condo for the next few nights didn't mean that she could start renting a bedroom down the hall from him, in his new house, in Coral Canyon. She scoffed out loud at the very idea, but she wasn't sure if it was the idea of living with him in Coral Canyon or simply living in Coral Canyon at all. She tried to project out, future cast, and see where she should be.

What was the scene when she woke up in the morning? What did she see out her front window? Where did she need to go each day? Was it to the Sheriff's Department for her next case?

Did she see a parking lot outside her apartment building when she opened her front window, or did she see the glorious sight of the Tetons rising in the distance, piercing the sky with their snow-capped pinnacles?

She hadn't gotten that far as Belle loved looking at real estate listings, and that had consumed her—along with solving her latest case—for the past couple of days. Belle didn't do anything very fast, and she needed to tell Harry that, so that he wasn't expecting them to go from nothing to something amazing in only a few days.

At the same time, Belle's whole life had been shaken up and put in a blender on high, and perhaps she *would* fall in love with Harry in only a few days, and they'd start planning their life together in Coral Canyon before she flew home from this vacation. Being in close quarters with someone like that really helped a person get to know them quickly. Belle knew that from her time undercover, but she could barely believe that she'd agreed that Harry could come on this vacation with her.

She set everything aside and told herself, "You're on vacation. You need to enjoy it."

"Do you think you're not going to enjoy it?"

She startled and sat up as she looked over to where Harry Young himself stood. He had not changed into his swim trunks and brought out a hat and sunscreen, but he was gloriously handsome in the Florida sunshine, wearing a pair of khaki shorts and a T-shirt that had an upside-down astronaut on it that said, *The gravity of this situation is dire.*

Belle started to get up, and he said, "No, don't. Stay there. I'll go get changed. Do you need anything?"

"We don't have anything," she said. "We've got to go to the grocery store."

"Sure, but I can order something," he said.

Belle thought, *Of course he can.* Harry was a pro at ordering in, and he had all of the food delivery apps on his phone. Surely they worked in Destin just as they did in Nashville.

"I'm gonna get an ice cream or a soda," he said. "It's hot here."

"Both of those sound good," she said.

He grinned and looked at her with such fondness that Belle could barely believe he meant it for her. "Great," he said. "I'll be back in a few minutes, and you can tell me how you're planning to enjoy the next five days here on the beach with me." With that, he walked away, his sexy grin in place and Belle's heart pumping faster than it ever had before.

Half the things she thought about Harry she couldn't say out loud, including all of the things that she had been fantasizing about: moving to Coral Canyon to be closer to him, moving into his house with him to be his wife and the mother of his children, and a great many other things that the cowboy country music star could probably give her as he rescued her from this boring life she'd lived for the past thirty-one years.

26

Harry changed and prepared to leave the beach condo, completely self-conscious about walking out to the umbrella where Belle lay in her cute swimsuit, without wearing a shirt. But he didn't wear a shirt at the beach, and he told himself over and over that he'd be there for the next five days with this woman, and he better get over any body issues he had if he wanted to have a real relationship with her.

So he exited, the screen door slamming closed behind him, and he cringed at the resulting smack of metal on metal. He kept going, his towel draped over his arm and a bottle of sunscreen in his hand, as he approached the empty lounger on the other half of the shade where Belle lay.

"Will you help me with my back?" he asked.

Belle looked up at him, her sunglasses covering a large portion of her face and concealing her eyes from him.

"Sure," she said, as if she regularly rubbed down men as they sat together on the beach. Harry knew she didn't, and while his heart throbbed in his throat, he told himself that hers probably was too.

"Oh, you have the cream kind," she said as she took the bottle from him. Harry sat on the end of her lounger, and she pulled her legs back to make room for him. He swallowed as she squeezed some of the white cream into her hands and then handed him the bottle again.

He did the same and said, "Yeah, my mom thinks this works way better than the spray." He got his own healthy dose of snowy white cream, rubbed his hands together, and started spreading it down his arms and across his chest. "I gotta say, I don't spend much time outside, so I need all the protection I can get."

"You're at least tan," she said, and her hands landed on his shoulders, sending pure male desire down his spine. "You look like you've been working out a lot, too."

He smiled to himself as he nodded. "Yeah, I guess it's become part of my routine."

"Do you still go at night?" Her hands moved steadily down his lats and toward the waistband of his swim trunks. She reached for the bottle again, and he passed it to her.

"Yeah," he said. "Feels like I do everything in the afternoon and evening. I'm up till two in the morning. I sleep till nine or ten. I get a real slow start in the morning, catch up on everything going on with Adam. Admin work is what I call it."

And he sighed like he didn't like it. "Then, I'm ready to

play the guitar, do my lessons, work on songs, work out, and record in the afternoon and evening."

"So that hasn't changed."

"Nope." He took the sunscreen back to get more. "Tell me something about you that hasn't changed."

"Oh, uh, let's see," Belle said. "I had to rehome my cats, and I haven't gotten any new ones." She sighed as she rubbed up his sides. Harry spread sunscreen across his abs and then moved his hand to cover hers. He twined his fingers with hers right against his ribcage and squeezed before letting go.

"And I want to get another cat," she said as she removed her hands from his body. "So that hasn't changed."

"I think you'll get one," he said.

"Yeah, the apartment I'm in right now doesn't allow pets," she said. "So when I get a new place...."

So many questions streamed through his mind, and he wanted to let them all out at once—a tornado of words that he could just throw at her and hope that she could put them all in order and give him the answers he wanted.

"Are you going to buy somewhere in Jackson?" he asked, trying to make his voice casual—and failing.

"Someone's interested in where I live?" Belle teased.

He squirted more sunscreen on his hands and rubbed up into his ears and hair, across his forehead, and down his nose. He didn't have to say he was interested in where Belle lived for her to know he was interested in where she lived.

So he just asked, "Well?"

"I don't know," Belle said. "There are a lot of balls up in the air right now."

"Is that so?" he asked. "Tell me which ones."

She finished with his back, and Harry moved over to his own lounger, so he could do his legs and feet. He met her eyes, and Belle pushed her sunglasses into place before he could see her expression.

He'd seen this tactic before, actually, and he'd worked hard to break down the barriers Belle tried to put up. He knew if he simply waited, the more she would tell him. The more he got to know her, the more comfortable she would be with him. He reminded himself that they hadn't spoken in ten months, and a person could change a lot in that amount of time. His attraction to her hadn't, and he sure was glad of that.

"Where I'm going to live for one," she said. "What I'm going to do for a job, for another." She looked away, studying the undulating water in the Gulf of Mexico in front of them.

Harry waited a few seconds, finished up his calf, and asked, "You don't like your job?"

"I do." She let out a long breath. "But I feel like I need to change. There's something you should probably know about me, Mister Young." He liked that her voice had gone back to teasing.

"Well, you better tell me then, Miss Belle." Two could play her game, and Harry found flirting with her extremely easy and exceptionally rewarding at the same time.

"I kind of have a gypsy soul," she said. "I'm really passionate about something for a little while until it...well, until it isn't all that exciting anymore. I kind of outgrow it, I guess, and then I move on to something else. And I'm starting to feel like I might be at the end of my law enforcement career."

Harry wasn't sure he liked that explanation, but he nodded. "How long have you been doing it?"

"Nine years," she said.

"And you were in country music before that, right?"

"Yep," she said. "Just for a few years right out of high school."

"Do you have a gypsy soul when it comes to your boyfriends?" he asked, keeping his head down. He cursed himself for leaving his cowboy hat inside, as Belle wore a cute sun hat that shielded her face, plus those sunglasses so he couldn't see anything telling anyway.

"I don't know," Belle said. "Haven't had a lot of boyfriends, remember?"

"Yes, I do remember that," Harry said. "Made me really happy inside." He kicked a grin over to her, and Belle rewarded him with a laugh.

"So you're moving back to Coral Canyon?" she asked.

"Yeah. In two weeks," he said. "My daddy and a couple of my uncles are coming, as well as my cousin Bryce. Adam, of course, will be there to help me. We're going to get my apartment all cleaned out, loaded up on the truck, and I'll be off."

"You driving back?" she asked. "Or are you having one of those big trucking companies come move you?"

"I'm doing it myself," he said.

"You have the money to pay for someone else to do it."

"Yeah, I sure do," he said. "Well, kind of. I just bought a house in Coral Canyon."

"Yes, I know," Belle said as he reached over and took her hand in his. "You sent me the link, remember?"

"Oh right," Harry said. "You never did say what you thought of it."

Belle looked over to him, and he wanted to lean across the distance and kiss her. He couldn't see her eyes, but he sure liked the way her lips tipped up into a smile and revealed her white teeth and that sunny personality she tried to keep hidden from others. She hadn't succeeded with him, another thing he was exceptionally glad about.

"You really want to know what I think of the house you bought in Coral Canyon?"

"Yes, absolutely I do." Harry took his turn to watch the waves because he wasn't sure he could kiss Belle right now, and he didn't want to move too fast with her.

They'd exchanged a lot of texts and phone calls over the past few days. She hadn't protested to any of those.

When he told her he'd meet her here on Thursday afternoon at check-in and he'd fly back to Nashville when she went back to Jackson Hole on Tuesday morning, she hadn't argued with him about that either.

She'd been out on the beach when he'd arrived here at the condo, and that had given him a few moments to take in the space and how they would be separated. He had his own bathroom. She had hers. He had his own bedroom. She had hers. They'd share the living room, dining room. And Harry really wanted to hold her on that couch tonight while they watched a movie, the beautiful Gulf Coast sun sinking into the water beyond the screened-in porch.

"I think, Mister Young," Belle said as she too faced the water. "That you bought that house with a future in mind. That's what it looked like to me."

Harry couldn't argue with her, so he said nothing.

"Seemed to be enough for a wife and family," she continued. "Somewhere you could be long term. Somewhere where you're around all your aunts and uncles and cousins. Just like you want to be."

His voice scratched on the way out as he said, "Yep, that's why I bought it." Harry had tried leaving Coral Canyon for a dream that he'd thought he wanted. He'd worked hard. He'd achieved it. And it turned out that that was not the lifestyle he wanted long term. And now he was fighting for a different reality, a different future, a different way of living that was still great and still amazing and still worthy.

His thoughts ran rampant through his head, and Harry decided maybe he could just get a couple of them out. "I just want to ask you something," he said. "You can pass on answering if you want."

"You have always been gracious with allowing me to pass if there's something I don't want to answer." She ran her thumb along the side of his, and Harry told himself that this woman liked him as much as he liked her.

"If you don't have a house in Jackson Hole," he said slowly, trying to get his thoughts to line up and make sense.

"And you're thinking about a career change, and now there's me—us—I guess...." He stuttered over the words. "Would you consider coming to Coral Canyon and maybe finding somewhere there to live?"

He looked at her, but it took her several long seconds before she returned the favor. "Can you take off your sunglasses so I can see your beautiful eyes?" He gave her a smile, but he really wanted to judge her reaction to his question.

"It's really bright out here," Belle said. "I'm surprised you can see without sunglasses."

"I have them inside," he said. "I just forgot to grab them." Part of him wanted to run away right now, go get his sunglasses, and then come back. So he released her hand and started to stand.

"Where are you going?" she asked, seemingly surprised.

"To get my sunglasses," he said. "Give you a minute to think about what I just said, what I just asked. And again, you can pass if you want." He couldn't stand to be there for another second, his overeagerness choking him as he walked away.

The moment he slid the door closed behind him, he muttered, "Stupid, stupid, stupid, stupid, Harry. Why did you ask her that?" He continued through the living room, up the step, and past the kitchen into his bedroom.

He sat down on the double bed, pure frustration boiling through him. Maybe he could just text her that he wanted her to pass. He quickly pulled his phone out of his pocket and sent her a quick message. *I don't want you to answer that question I just asked, okay? I'm going to pull a pass card for you.*

Then he threw his phone on the bed and stared toward the ceiling. "Lord," he whispered, taking a page out of Bryce's book and uttering his prayer aloud. "I like this woman a lot. I've always known I've liked her a lot. And now, with so many doors open in front of me, it seems cruel that we wouldn't be able to walk through one of them together. What do You think?"

Harry's pulse slowed, but he pushed all other distractions out of his life and out of his mind and tried to listen to God. He wasn't always successful, and God wasn't always so loud. Sometimes He took His sweet time answering Harry's prayers. And today, his phone chimed again. Not with Belle's assigned sound, so he picked it up and saw that Bryce had texted.

Hey, brother, he'd said. *Codi and I want to make the trip to Nashville together. Is it okay if she comes?*

Of course, Harry tapped out without even thinking about it. *What are you guys going to do with your ranch while you're gone?*

Oh, Kassie and Reggie are going to take care of it, Bryce said. *Uncle Jem and Uncle Blaze come out too when I'm gone. Uncle Luke sometimes stays at the house with his little boys. It'll be fine.*

Harry's throat narrowed at how many uncles Bryce had just named to come help him on his ranch whenever he and Codi wanted to leave. Harry wanted that kind of support too. He wanted all the aunts and uncles surrounding him, and he knew they would. They already had.

Hilde had sent him picture after picture of the furniture he'd picked out for his new house as it had been arriving, and she staged it for him. He wanted to be with all the younger cousins and all of his older ones too, as Joey had just moved back to Coral Canyon as well. Cash had just turned pro, and Harry told himself he needed to text Boston and find out what the young man was doing as well.

Harry: *I can't wait to be in Coral Canyon with everybody.*

Bryce: *How's it going in Destin? Are you there yet? Wait, is that tomorrow?*

I just got here, Harry sent back to him. *And I've already made a fool of myself with Belle.*

And because Bryce was Bryce, and Harry was Harry, he expected his phone to ring and his cousin to be on the other end of the line. And exactly that happened.

"What do you mean you made a fool of yourself already?" Bryce asked when Harry answered, without even saying hello.

"Well." Harry sighed. "I asked her if she would consider moving to Coral Canyon. She doesn't have a permanent place in Jackson Hole, you know? She's just living in an apartment that doesn't even allow pets. And she wants a cat. And she's thinking about changing jobs. And it just spewed out of my mouth that she should move to Coral Canyon."

"And this." Harry stood up and paced away from the door and toward the window. "Is after she told me that I bought a house thinking of the future with a wife and children. It's just all a mess." He sighed again, and he was eternally grateful to Bryce who didn't jump right in and say something immediately to reassure Harry that he hadn't messed up.

"There's a lot to unpack there," Bryce said with a chuckle.

"Yeah, no joke," Harry said.

"I don't think you've messed up with her though," Bryce said. "Who wouldn't want to be asked by a famous country music star to move closer to them so that he can date them?" Bryce laughed and added, "Codi just raised her eyebrows and said, 'If he asked me to move to Coral Canyon to be closer to him, I'd pack my bags right now.'"

Harry laughed too because he knew Codi loved Bryce unconditionally and would never leave him.

"Oh, she's taking the phone," Bryce yelled as scuffling came through the line.

Codi said, "Harry."

"Yeah," he said. He did like Codi a lot. She was very, very good for Bryce, a hard worker, and one of the kindest people Harry had ever met.

"I don't think you can mess up with Belle too badly," she said.

"You don't think so?" Harry said. "She's a strong-willed woman, Codi. She's smart. She's beautiful. She's talented, and I'm rushing her only *weeks* after she's finished her undercover assignment. That's the very definition of messing up with Belle Graves."

"Well, here's what I know," Codi said. "She doesn't have my number anymore, and she doesn't have Bryce's, and she doesn't have Kassie's. And do you know why?"

He looked out the window at the branches of the palm trees waving in the breeze. "No," he muttered. "I don't know why."

"Because she gave up everything to go undercover," Codi said. "She gave up her phone, her devices, and all of her contacts. But do you know whose number she kept? And I suspect that it's the *only* number she kept."

Harry swallowed, seeing where Codi was driving. "I don't know what you mean."

"Did she ask you for your number when you ran into her in the airport a few days ago?" Codi asked, her voice even— not accusatory and not teasing.

"No," he said.

"No," Codi agreed. "And she texted you within five minutes of you walking away and getting on your plane. She had *your* number in her *new phone*, Harry. She kept your number. You're *the one thing* she kept from her life before she went undercover. She didn't keep her cats. She didn't keep her home. She had a brand new job, and she knew no one. But she kept your number."

Harry ducked his head, realizing the weight of what Codi had said. "You're right," he said. "Maybe I haven't messed up too badly."

"What did she say?"

"I ran away like a fool," he said. "Told her I needed to

come get my sunglasses. And then I just texted her and told her I didn't want her to answer the question."

Codi hummed. "What do you think, Bryce? What should he do?"

"Well, he should get his sunglasses and get his butt back out on the beach," Bryce said. "He's not there for a five-day vacation to get a suntan. He's there to make Belle fall in love with him."

Harry grinned because that wasn't the *sole* reason he'd come to Florida. *But it's definitely one of them*, his mind whispered at him.

And Codi said, "One-hundred percent," which caused all three of them to laugh.

"All right," Harry said. "Let me get back out there and see if I've messed up too badly. Love you guys."

Bryce and Codi both chorused they loved him, and Harry tapped to end the call. He took a big breath, lifted his thoroughly sunscreened shoulders, and blew it out before he turned and...found Belle standing in the doorway.

She held up her phone, her dark eyes free from sunglasses and burning dark liquid fire in his direction. "You haven't messed up too badly. And I don't want to be a liar and say that I haven't thought about moving to Coral Canyon. I have."

Harry's heart grew wings of hope, and he took quick steps toward her. "You have?" He wasn't sure he could just gather her up in his arms, but he did anyway, and she eased right into his chest, her breath wafting softly against his bare skin.

"Yes, of course I have."

He wasn't sure why she'd included "of course" in there, but he sure liked hearing it. He pulled back a little bit, which drew her away from him too. As he looked at her, he decided that his sole goal for coming to Destin for the next five days maybe *should* be to make Belle fall in love with him.

And to do that, he better tell the truth.

So he said, "Belle, I have missed you beyond measure every day for the past ten months, two weeks, and two days. Any day I can't hear your voice is a bad day for me. So I apologize if I'm coming on too strong. Or if you're not ready for everything you get when you get me. I can be patient. I can wait. But I really like you, and I want to be close to you. And I want to see you every day and hold you and fall in love with you."

He swallowed, the lyrics to a new song emerging in his mind as he waited for Belle to say something or do something. Several seconds ticked by, and then she finally said, "I can't get my words to line up the way you do. But I can do this."

And she stretched up and kissed him.

Harry had not been anticipating that, but he was here for it. He wrapped her in his arms and pulled her closer and kissed her back, and kissed her back, and kissed her back.

27

"Road trip," Bryce yelled as he came into the farmhouse kitchen, where he lived with his wife and two dogs.

Codi worked at the counter, her back to him, as she fed their dogs their special breakfast. When she turned to look over her shoulder at him, she said, "We've been on a road trip before. You don't need to be so loud."

Bryce grinned at his wife of the past eleven months and drew her away from scooping green beans out of a can and into a dog food bowl. "We've never flown anywhere before," he said. "Besides our honeymoon." He grinned down at her and kissed her gently.

Codi was not a morning person, and Bryce loved everything about a new day, including the way the sun rose and painted the mountains behind the mountains and hills to the east in golds and oranges, and the Tetons to the west in blue and white.

"Plus, we get a few days off the ranch together," he said, as he moved away from her to set his toast for breakfast.

No sooner had he pushed the lever down when Codi said, "Can I say our prayer today?"

"One-hundred percent," he said, and he put his arm around her waist and bowed his head. He prayed every morning while his toast browned, the habit becoming something he and Codi had done together since the day she'd moved into the farmhouse after becoming his wife.

"Dear Lord," Codi said. "Bless us with safe travel to Jackson today, that the roads will be clear and other drivers will be mindful of us. Bless the pilots and those working on the plane to have clear minds and that all will go well. May we be able to arrive in Nashville with willing hands and helpful hearts, ready to help Harry and Adam make their move from Nashville to Coral Canyon." She paused and swallowed, and Bryce thought she might not be able to say much more before his toast popped up. That was the beauty of the toaster prayer. He couldn't go on and on, and he saved his nighttime prayer for that, where he knelt down by his bed and poured out his heart to the Lord.

"Bless Bryce that he won't start crying when I tell him that we're going to have a baby before Thanksgiving. Amen."

"Amen," Bryce bellowed. And then everything Codi had just said caught up to him. He sucked in a breath and turned toward his wife. She was already crying.

"Bless Bryce that he won't start crying," he echoed. His hands moved to her belly, which was still flat as ever. "You're gonna have a baby." Wonder and awe overcame him as well as another wave of pure love from God.

Codi nodded and sniffled. She wiped her eyes and pushed her pure white hair back and said, "*We're* going to have a baby, Bryce."

Bryce didn't start crying. Instead, he pumped both fists into the air as he whooped and hollered. He grabbed onto Codi and held her tight, spinning her around right there in their kitchen.

"This is so amazing." As he calmed and the adrenaline bled out of his body and his pulse quieted, yes, the tears came. Bryce had shed a lot of tears over babies in the past, some of them happy but most of them not. But this morning, when he and Codi would only be doing their morning feeding and then loading their already packed suitcases into his truck and heading for the airport, Bryce cried some of the happiest tears of his life.

WHEN HE AND CODI DISEMBARKED FROM THE PLANE IN Nashville, she said, "I mean it now, baby, you're not to say a word to anyone. It's too soon for them to know."

"But you think you're due in November," he said.

"I haven't been to the doctor yet," she said, something she'd told him a half-dozen times since the toaster prayer that morning. They talked about names, and if they wanted a boy or a girl, and which bedroom they would use in the farmhouse for a nursery.

His daddy, Uncle Otis, and Uncle Trace had taken an earlier flight and should already be here. So Bryce hadn't had to keep his voice down so that his father wouldn't overhear about the pregnancy.

"Yes," Codi said, "I think I'm due in November. My period is a little weird, Bryce, remember? But I took a pregnancy test yesterday morning and again this morning, and they were both positive. I haven't had my period since February, so I *think* November." She gave him a look as they approached baggage claim. "I'm maybe six or eight weeks along. It's too soon to tell people."

"Okay," he said. "I got it." She threw him another severe look and then stood there and waited while he went to get their bags. Bryce had such fond memories of everyone who had come to help him move from Louisville to Coral Canyon when he'd made his triumphant return, and he'd wanted to be there when Harry did the same.

Not that Harry had run away because he'd gotten his college girlfriend pregnant and couldn't face the family. But it still felt like a significant, faith-filled move to leave behind an enormous country music career in favor of a small-town Wyoming life.

Codi had called a ride, and they arrived at Harry's downtown apartment only half an hour later. When they climbed to the second floor and turned the corner, the door stood open to Harry's apartment, and laughter came barreling out of it.

Bryce's heart warmed and his smile ticked up. He hurried toward the apartment, where he found his uncles and his father, Harry and Adam, and a whole heap of boxes, takeout containers, and guitars propped against the couch in the living room.

He let Codi enter the apartment first while he stood in the doorway and watched them all welcome her to their fold. His daddy gave her a hug, and Uncle Otis put his arm around her shoulders.

Bryce's tears pricked at his eyeballs again. He pushed them away, because his father would know instantly that something was wrong. And while having a baby this time wasn't something bad or wrong, Bryce still couldn't give it away by crying over it.

He thought of that morning's toaster prayer, and he doubled down on it as he entered the apartment and hugged Uncle Otis. "You guys look like you're having a jam session instead of a packing session."

"Well, Harry got hit with some inspiration right in the middle of cleaning out the kitchen cupboard," Uncle Otis said. "Then Trace said he was hungry, so we had to order food. And you know how things kind of spiral from there." He laughed, and Bryce did too, as he moved over to Uncle Trace.

He hugged him and pounded him on the back. "Are we going to survive this move?"

"I think this will be our easiest one yet," Uncle Trace drawled.

"That's because we have Adam arranging every single

little detail," Bryce said. He grinned at Harry's assistant from over his father's shoulder and then stepped over to hug Adam too.

Harry's assistant always tried to shake his hand first, but Bryce did that and pulled him straight into a shoulder-to-shoulder hug. "I'm so glad you're moving to Coral Canyon with him, brother."

"I am too," Adam said, and he sounded a little bit surprised. "I mean, I don't know what I'm going to do there, but I'm excited about something new."

"You're going to do the exact same thing you do now," Harry said.

"But you might not need someone to go pick up sour cream in small-town Coral Canyon," Adam said, and it sounded like a discussion they had had many times before. They probably had.

Adam said nothing more, and Harry pressed his mouth into a tight line. When Bryce came face to face with him, he played the grumpy cat while Bryce salivated and smiled like the golden retriever.

"Hey, brother," Bryce said, pulling Harry into a hug. "Did you get me anything to eat?"

"It's my dad," Harry mumbled into his shoulder. He pulled back, and his grumpy smile came onto his face. "Of course we ordered something for you and Codi, and some for Abby and Georgia and all the cousins who are over the age of fifteen back home. There's enough for all of them."

Bryce tipped his head back and laughed, releasing some of the tension in the apartment, in his chest, maybe way down deep in his soul. Then he moved over to Codi, who stood in the kitchen with Uncle Otis as they chatted. "Looks like there's enough for everyone," he said. "What do you want, baby?"

"I want some of that spicy chicken," she said, pointing to a half-empty container of brightly sauced chicken. "And the noodles with lots of sauce, and as many mushrooms as they have in there."

"I picked out all my mushrooms and tossed them back," Uncle Otis said. "So there should be plenty."

"I told him not to do it," Daddy said as he joined Bryce in the kitchen. "But I guess it's good for something." He gave Codi another squeeze. "How are you, my dear?"

Codi shot Bryce a look and said, "Doing just fine, sir."

"How was your flight, Dad?"

"Oh, you know, it was a flight." Daddy grinned at her and then at Bryce. He didn't seem to notice anything was off about either of them. His momma would have, and Bryce silently thanked the Lord that she had stayed in Coral Canyon with the little kids instead of joining Daddy to help Harry move home.

Bryce dished up the food that Codi wanted and put the plate in front of her and then got his own. He sat at the bar too, while conversations went on and Harry led everyone into his music studio to show them what he needed help boxing up.

Just the two of them now, Bryce leaned over to Codi. "When we tell everyone about the baby, can we have a party at our house instead of just using the family text?"

She looked at him, her blue eyes blazing. "You told me we wouldn't have to have a party for everything."

"We won't," he said. "But this is a really big deal to me." He stayed sober as he said it, and Codi searched his face. She had to understand much more of what he wasn't saying than what he was, as she had in other important conversations.

Relief pounded through him when she nodded knowingly, smiled, and stretched up to kiss his cheek. "Of course, we'll have the best party in the world," she said. "When we tell everyone that we're going to have a baby that we get to keep and raise."

He grinned and nodded and said, "Thank you, Codi." And in his mind, he added, *Thank you, dear Lord*, as well.

28

elle pulled up to the address she'd been given and looked at Harry's house. He had a three-car garage with a flat cement pad out front that extended around the side of the house as well. For maybe a boat, or motorhome, or anything else Harry wanted to park there.

It was a single-story house with loft windows, but she knew he had a basement as well. Five bedrooms, four bathrooms, two living areas, and a dedicated office with a half-acre fenced backyard.

Harry had been talking about getting a dog since their beach vacation, and he'd even said any cats that she adopted would be welcome to use one of the bedrooms for their cat scratching posts, beds, and overall feline palace.

Belle could admit the five days she'd spent with Harry in Destin had been some of the best days of her life, and that she had absolutely started falling in love with him all over again. She'd talked to Larry and Ben at the Teton County Sheriff's Department, and she had not taken on another case.

She hadn't put in her two weeks' notice yet, because she was waiting to see how she felt when Harry became a permanent resident of Coral Canyon, Wyoming, while she still lived somewhere else.

Deep down inside, she knew already that it would really bother her and that she would likely be making the move an hour east of Jackson Hole to be closer to her boyfriend. She'd been looking at rentals, as well as cats that she could adopt from the animal shelter, and making plans for her own version of her Coral Canyon future.

Her phone chimed and Harry's text flashed up on the screen in her car. *Ten minutes!*

She expected to see his aunts' and uncles' cars in the driveway or parked up and down the street, but the curb sat clear.

She parked on the street in front of his house, so he could have full access to the driveway. Perhaps they'd all be arriving any minute, and she'd have to meet them all alone. Belle told herself she'd done many more, much harder things than meeting her boyfriend's family. Images of using her own body to protect a child on the floor of the van where they'd been moving a quarter of a million dollars flashed through her mind.

It struck and left the way lightning did, and Belle was glad for that. She didn't want these memories to stay forever.

She didn't want to dwell on them. She didn't want them to define her.

She got out of the SUV and headed for the house. Harry had given her the code to the garage, and she typed it in. The big white door squealed and protested, but it lifted. Belle walked into his empty garage and then up the few steps to the cement pad landing to the garage entrance to the house.

She hesitated for a moment, remembered the things that she brought to put in his house to welcome him home, and hurried back to her SUV to collect them from the back. Her pulse ran high now, her adrenaline kicking at her to *hurry up and get this done*.

She thought of how expertly Harry had held her on the couch every evening in Destin as they watched movies together after a long day of splashing in the water, soaking up the sun, talking about their lives, and playing board games.

Inside, she found a gorgeous brown microfiber couch that she and Harry would fit on easily and comfortably. She couldn't wait to cuddle with him there, whatever he chose on the screen in front of them, but neither of them paying attention to it. He'd run his fingers through her hair and ask her a question, which would reveal more of her life to him. She'd do the same to him and then he'd kiss her until she felt sure she was all the way in love with the cowboy rock star.

Inside, she quickly assembled the cupcake tower and lifted the lid on the pink box that held all the cupcakes she'd purchased that morning. She set them out, and in the very top one, she pinned a flag that said, "Welcome Home!"

She didn't want to explore his house too much without him there because he'd promised her a tour when he arrived. Confusion ran through her when she realized that he had to be only a minute away and not another single person in the Young family had arrived.

She'd been expecting a massive welcome home party for Harry as he'd told her how they'd all gathered at Bryce's farmhouse when he and Kassie had made the move from Louisville to Dog Valley.

So where were they?

Belle moved out of the kitchen and living area in the back of the house and went down the hall toward the office, which held a front window. She startled when she saw a big black truck parked in the driveway.

He was here.

But she didn't see Harry himself, and as she watched, the truck backed out of the driveway and left. Maybe someone had simply come the wrong way and had used this driveway to turn around and head back the way they came.

Then behind her, the door opened and Harry called, "Belle?"

"I'm here," she called back, and she hurried down the hall into the kitchen. She found him standing in front of the cupcake tower, a broad smile on his face.

And she knew in that moment that she needed to move here.

With feelings running up and around and through her,

she launched herself into his arms, laughing as she said, "You're here."

"I'm here," he said back. He held her, gazed at her, and grinned. "Someone's happy I'm here."

Belle was, and she had nothing to protest as Harry lowered his head and kissed her. Yes, she definitely needed to find an apartment quickly and make the move to be closer to Harry.

He didn't kiss her for too long before he turned his attention to the cupcakes. "These are incredible."

"I bought them," she said. "Full disclosure." She glanced to the garage door behind him. "Where's everyone else?"

"I just sent Adam down the road to create a blockade," he said as he picked up a chocolate cupcake with diamond-snow frosting and a bright blue star poking out of that. "I told them they have to give me a half-hour with you alone, and then they can all come."

"You're telling me your aunts and uncles are waiting down the street right now? Behind a blockade?"

Harry laughed and shook his head. "No, I told the aunts and uncles that I would be here around four."

Belle knew what time it was, but she still glanced over to the clock on the microwave. "It's two-forty-five."

"Exactly." He peeled back the paper on the cupcake and extended it to her.

Belle took it, Harry's sweetness almost overwhelming her. "So we're delaying your dad, your uncle Otis, and your uncle Tex," she said. "And Bryce and Codi."

"Bryce is in on it." Harry picked up another cupcake

and started to unwrap it. "He's going to pull over and say he has a flat tire and get everyone to stop and help him."

Belle grinned at him as he took the first bite of his welcome-home treat. "And what do we need an hour and fifteen minutes for, Mister Young?"

His eyes dropped to her mouth, and he lowered his head as he said, "I can think of a few things," just before he kissed her again with a smidge of chocolate still on his lips.

BELLE RAISED HER HEAD FROM HARRY'S CHEST WHEN the garage door opened behind her again. "They're here," she said, and she sat up quickly, so that it wouldn't be his father who walked in on them cuddling on the couch.

She got to her feet as Harry groaned as he sat up too. "Here we go." He took her hand, and she expected to meet dozens of people all with his last name today. She told herself that she'd met most of them already. First at Kassie and Reggie's wedding over a year ago, and then at Bryce and Codi's just under a year ago.

Sure enough, his dad walked in first, and he'd obviously stopped by his house to get his wife and children, because they all clamored inside, the little kids who could talk yelling, "Harry, Harry, Harry, we're here, Harry!"

Harry laughed and left her side so that he could scoop Keri and Clay into his arms and hug them. "You're here, you're here," he said, mimicking them. "And now I'm here too. You guys want to stay over at my place tonight?"

"Do they have beds?" Trace asked as the kids cheered and started asking if they could sleepover, and he smiled at Belle and stepped in to hug her. "Oh, it's so good to see you again, Belle."

"You too, Mister Young," she said, really sinking into the hug. She'd been so starved of human touch while undercover, and Belle wondered if she'd ever feel completely human again.

"It's just Trace," he said as he stepped back. Everly took his place, and she took Belle's face in both of her hands. She studied her for a moment, such kindness streaming through her expression, and Belle had no idea what Harry had told his parents about their relationship or about her disappearance. She had no idea if they knew she'd been undercover or not.

Ev smiled at her warmly, everything about her twinkling with such love as she said, "We have prayed for you every day, and we are *so* glad you are back."

"Mom," Harry said quickly, and Ev dropped her hands and stepped back.

"What?" she said.

"I told you not to embarrass me," he grumbled.

"You're not embarrassing," Belle said quickly, and she smiled at Ev while simultaneously sliding her hand into Harry's. "Thank you for praying for me. I needed it, and I'm sure it made a difference."

Ev nodded, her eyes still stuck on Harry, and the door opened again. This time from the garage and from the front. More voices entered, more people spilled into the back of the house. Harry's uncle Tex and his son Bryce, and his wife Codi. From the front came Abby and their three younger kids, and they all carried food.

"Right here," Abby said, and she directed everyone into the kitchen where they started laying things out. "Georgia was right behind us, and she has all the drinks."

Belle hugged Codi, tears pressing into her eyes hard and fast. "I need your number again."

"Yes, you do," Codi said. "We have a girl's luncheon that we need to have. And I know Kassie will make her grandmother's buttermilk biscuits and pimento pinwheels, and we can all share everything that's happened in the last year." She pulled back and smiled at Belle. "I'm so glad you're here, Belle."

"I am too."

"Are you going to move to Coral Canyon?"

Harry growled, his fingers once again seeking Belle's. "Codi. I told you not to ask her that."

"It's fine," Belle said, giving his hand a squeeze. She liked that he'd been talking about her openly with his family, that he wanted to protect her from all their prying eyes and maybe-difficult questions.

"I actually am going to move here." She looked at Harry, and he stared back at her, his mouth falling open a little bit.

"You are?" he said at the same time as Bryce. "Well, I'm glad someone told me," Harry added in his grumbly, growly voice.

Bryce only laughed, and more Youngs arrived at the

house, sweeping Harry away from Belle before she could explain more.

More men and women and all of their kids. Luke and Sterling and their three little children and one teenager. Jem and Sunny and their four kids. Blaze and Faith with their baby who was only seven months old, who immediately got passed to Ev to take care of while the other three kids swarmed Harry.

Everyone seemed to want a piece of him, and when they came over to him, they all told Belle how much they'd missed her and how glad they were that she was back. She didn't get a chance to talk to Harry again before his aunt Hilde arrived in all of her five-foot-ten sophistication.

She wore a pair of black slacks and a black short-sleeved blouse with billowy sleeves, and it was Ev who finally got on a chair and raised her hands high above her head. "Everyone, Hilde would like to give Harry a tour of his house with all of the furniture pieces that have been provided by her store."

"He bought them," Hilde said loudly, giving Ev a look that spoke volumes. "Harry *bought* the furniture, everyone."

A few titters moved through the crowd, and then Ev said, "If you want to go with Hilde and Harry, group up over here. Everyone else, come on over and get some food. We can spill out onto the back patio as well."

Harry seemed a little shell-shocked. Belle grinned at him and said, "Hey, you're the one who wanted to move back here to be closer to your family."

He laughed, which became such music to her ears.

Harry usually played the serious and stoic part and didn't do a whole lot of laughing.

He kept a tight hold of her hand as they went with Hilde. Bryce and Codi came with them, and so did Adam and some of the older teenagers. None of the aunts or uncles seemed that keen on taking the tour, probably because they'd already seen it all as Hilde had brought in the furniture and staged it all for Harry.

"Did your house come with any of this?" Belle asked as Hilde led them into the first room off the living room—a full bathroom.

"Not a single thing," Harry said. "And I replaced all the carpet too."

"We have a wonderful selection of carpets," Hilde said smoothly. "Harry chose a beautiful line in The Mastercraft series."

As if Belle would know what any of that meant. Still, she grinned at Harry, who grinned back at her, and they continued down the hall. She saw bedroom upon bedroom, all of which had been set up with beds.

"Why did you buy all the beds?" Belle asked.

"For the cousins," he said. "Or my brother and sister. They like to come stay with me, and I've gotta have somewhere for them to sleep. Can't just throw them on the floor." He grinned at her and pressed a kiss to her temple.

"Oh no, you certainly can't," Belle said with a grin.

Everywhere she looked, she saw money. She chastised herself because *of course* Harry Young had money. He was a mega music star with three albums out and eight million social media followers. He could put up a video and have a million likes and thousands upon tens of thousands of comments within an hour.

When the tour concluded, Belle found herself in the kitchen, loading up her plate with fettuccine, one scoop of Alfredo sauce and one scoop of meat sauce from the pasta bar. She took two meatballs, half an Italian sausage, a slice of garlic bread, and a big cup of peach punch before she turned to try to find somewhere to sit.

She came face to face with Harry, who had just come through the line with her. "Where are you looking to move to around Coral Canyon?"

"I don't know," she said. "I've just been casually browsing online rentals."

"So you don't want to buy?" he asked.

Belle lifted her eyebrows at him, questions and surprise streaming through her. "Why would I need to buy? So I can sell it when you and I decide we're going to get married?"

"You guys are talking about marriage already?" Abby said, suddenly appearing at Belle's side.

"No," Harry barked out. "And Abby, don't you dare say a word."

He met Belle's eyes again, plenty of smoke and fire in his dark eyes, and turned away from her. "There's a couple of seats over here," he said in his gruff voice.

Belle went with him, something giddy and something glad inside her. She hadn't exactly said, *I'm going to marry you, Harry Young, and move into this house with you,* but she really didn't understand why she needed to buy a house when he had a perfectly good one that he'd purposely bought with a future family in mind.

Maybe he's not working toward that, she thought, and then she remembered what he'd said to her in the condo in Destin.

He wanted her here so they could date. So they could fall in love. So he could have a wife and family. He'd made it very clear that he'd quit country music so that he could come back here to find exactly those things.

So she wasn't going to be embarrassed about what she'd said. And no, she didn't want Abby spreading it around the family that she and Harry had talked about getting married only three weeks into their new relationship—because they hadn't.

She also wasn't going to be sorry for saying she'd been looking at rentals, not houses for sale. She hadn't quite had the chance to explain, but when she and Harry could find a few minutes alone, she'd open her heart and tell him more.

I'm looking to rent, Harry, she thought. *Because the next house I live in that I own will be with my husband.*

There.

As she settled at the table beside him, Belle allowed herself to hope and pray that the man who'd become her husband would be one Harry Young.

29

Harry sat in the recliner across from his desk, in his home office in Coral Canyon. Though he'd been living in his house for a week now, he still experienced bouts of disbelief that this had become his life.

He'd imagined it for a couple of years now. He'd planned it. He'd looked at a dozen houses before buying this one.

But it still felt a bit surreal to him sometimes. This was one of those times, as he listened to Uncle Morris finish his outline for the following week's concerts.

Three. Harry had to do three of them, and the total travel miles came out to less than twenty-five—and that included getting there and getting back to his house.

His time wouldn't be wasted in travel. He wouldn't have to go through security lines. The record label wouldn't be paying for first-class flights or huge teams of people to put on a massive stadium show.

No, Harry would have his band—which would barely fit on some of the stages in the restaurants, coffee shops, and venues around Coral Canyon and Jackson Hole where Adam and Morris had arranged for Harry's live-streamed world tour—his guitar, and himself.

The set list included half new songs from the third album, which was simply titled *Legacy*, and half bestselling and well-loved songs from his first two albums.

His father usually played a few songs with him, as did Uncle Otis, and with all the members of Country Quad only minutes away now, Harry had added three of their best songs to his set list.

Five shows would include them. His father would perform at all of them, as would Bryce, and as Morris looked up, his eyebrows reaching for his hairline, Harry had one more thing he wanted to add to the setlist.

Him and Belle.

"How does it look?" Morris asked. "We'll kick things off on Tuesday night at Devil's Tower. They have a great stage, and it might all be downhill from there."

Harry grinned, because the Youngs had filled Daily Grind for a New Year's family talent show, and that stage would barely fit him and his guitar. "You're probably right."

They were playing the coffee shop on Friday morning, which would allow for different time zones around the world to tune into the live-stream. No, Harry wasn't a morning person, but he could be up and ready by nine a.m. when he was getting paid a lot of money to do so.

And Saturday night, Harry and his band would be at The Branding Iron. Big places—hot spots—around Coral Canyon, and Harry had a one-sheet for each of them as well. He'd work in the venue and why he loved it, how it contributed to the fabric of small-town Coral Canyon and thus, himself, throughout the concert.

The film crew had tested their cameras and angles at all three locations already this week, and Harry's fingers tightened around his phone. "I'm working on one more thing," he said, drawing his daddy's attention as well as Uncle Morris's.

Adam too relaxed in the office, his ankle resting on his knee. He looked up with only his eyes, his own tablet laying in his lap, now being ignored.

Harry met his gaze, swallowed, and faced his manager. "Belle used to be in country music." His voice scratched across his vocal cords and the back of his tongue, and he cleared it to make it smooth again. "I want to ask her to play and sing a single song with me."

Silence pressed down into the office. Daddy finally broke it with, "Will Rebel allow that?"

Harry looked at Morris, who'd taken a seat behind the professional desk where Harry hoped to write a lot of music. "I don't know. They don't have a problem with me singing Country Quad songs or including you and Bryce."

His phone buzzed against his thigh, but he didn't look at it. Belle had found an apartment near the cute, quaint downtown street that housed the post office, Aunt Georgia's bookshop, clothing boutiques, and the Boot Barn where Harry had once bought his back-to-school cowboy boots with Ev, back when she was still his father's girlfriend.

She could move in anytime, and that day was tomorrow. Harry couldn't believe how much his life had changed in a single month, and he quickly closed his eyes and thought, *Thank you, God, for hearing me.*

"You've asked her?" Morris asked.

"I plan to this weekend," Harry said coolly. "She won't have to do every show. She could join the tour when we go to Jackson in a few weeks. She has friends and co-workers there."

Well, sort of. She'd confessed to him that she didn't have many friends, and she'd put in her two weeks' notice on Monday.

When Harry had asked her what she'd do for work here in Coral Canyon, she'd said. "I'm still working through that," with a smile.

"Let me step out and call Don," Morris said. Donald Summers approved anything relating to Harry's tour, and he'd been lax and casual about the setlist in the past. Harry could only pray he'd be that way again.

"Perhaps you should ask her right now," Daddy said. "Things between you two seem serious already."

"I mean, sure," Harry said. "I've been interested in her forever, Dad. It's not like I only met her a few weeks ago."

Daddy's frown didn't budge, and Harry worked hard

not to roll his eyes. "Maybe the timing is right now," he said. "And I really like her."

"So you're serious."

"Of course," Harry said. "I've never dated if it wasn't serious."

"Oh-ho," Daddy chortled, tossing a look to Adam. "What about Iriana? When you broke up with her, you told us it was never anything serious. That you knew that from the beginning."

Harry did roll his eyes now. "Right, I knew that. Just like I know this relationship *is* serious—and has been since the beginning." He watched his father. "What? You think I don't know how I feel? You don't trust me to make this kind of decision?"

His daddy's face softened, and he ducked behind his cowboy hat. "Of course I trust you."

"You think I'm too young, then."

"I think you're still finding your feet, yeah," Daddy said. "Not that you're too young, but that you're very...hungry, Harry. You're *starving* for this life, and I don't want you to snatch up the first woman that comes along simply because she's there."

Harry's first instinct was to argue back, but instead, he sat still with his daddy's words. After several long seconds, where Morris's muted voice filtered back to them from further inside the house, Harry finally nodded. "Okay," he whispered. "I hear you."

Daddy nodded, his throat working as he swallowed too.

"Perhaps singing and working with her will show you a

different side of her," Adam said, giving his input. He rarely did, so Harry perked up and listened. "Allow you to truly get to know her in a unique way."

"That's a good point," Harry said slowly. Belle didn't volunteer a ton of information, and Harry did allow her to pass whenever he asked her something she didn't want to talk about.

She paid him the same favor, but sitting in his office, thinking of her and talking about his relationship with her, he absolutely wanted to know everything about her. He wanted to get to a point where neither one of them had to pass, because they'd talked through everything that mattered to both of them.

"Should I text her?" he asked. "She's moving here tomorrow."

"Does she need help?" Daddy asked.

Harry shook his head. "She says she doesn't own much, and Bryce and Reggie are coming. With the four of us, we should be fine."

"Momma is making dinner," Daddy said. "We'll come see the place about five-thirty."

Harry's pulse leapfrogged, but he nodded. "I'll let her know."

"Your mother has already texted her," Daddy said. "That's how I know it's happening."

Harry looked up from his phone, where he'd been about to text Belle the far easier message about his momma bringing her food tomorrow night. "She texted Belle?"

"Apparently."

"How'd she get her phone number?"

"I suppose she asked her," Daddy said, a guard in his voice now.

Harry wasn't sure why, but that sent irritation spiraling through him. He glanced over to Adam. "Do you have her number?"

"No, sir," Adam said.

Harry indicated his assistant. "If Adam doesn't have it, then Momma doesn't need it."

"You'll need to talk to her about that," Daddy said.

"Daddy." Harry reached up and rubbed his eyes.

"Or Belle," Daddy said. "Last time I checked, she was a grown adult—five years older than you, in fact—and could make her own decisions about who she gives her phone number to."

"He's not wrong," Adam said.

"Adam."

"You're not either, Harry," he said. "If you don't like it, you should talk to Belle."

Harry shook his head and started a message to his girlfriend.

Morris and I are putting the final touches on my livestream world tour, and I'd love to perform with you. Can we talk about that tonight when I come to help you finish packing?

"All right," Morris said as he re-entered the office. "Don's on-board with it, as long as it's not one of the new songs from the album."

Joy pierced Harry's heart, and he nodded. "Okay, no

problem. I'm asking her now, and I'll talk to her about it tonight."

"It shouldn't be hard to add one song to the setlist," Morris said. "We'll have two mics and stools for Bryce anyway, and he can just walk out and she can walk in."

"That's what I was thinking," Harry said as he tapped to send the message he'd already typed out. "We have one more thing, don't we?"

Harry glanced over to Adam, who once again looked away from his tablet.

"We do?" Daddy asked.

"I'm also unaware of another item," Morris said.

"It's Boston," Adam said, and he reached into his briefcase bag and extracted two identical folders. "Harry would like him to be the tour physical facilities manager starting in Week 2, and we'd like your eyes on this contract before Harry approaches Boston and Maverik."

Daddy had his homicidal-cowboy look down pat as he took the folder Adam handed him without looking away from Harry. "You want to hire your cousin?"

Harry didn't hesitate as he said, "I sure do. He's home from college for the summer, and I know no one else sees it, but he's not happy to be living at home." He nodded to the two-page document in the folder. "That actually offers him a place to live, right here in my basement."

"Harry," Daddy said in his warning tone.

"He's twenty, almost twenty-one years old," Harry said. "An adult." He looked down at his phone, wishing Belle had already responded with an enthusiastic *Of course! I'd love to play for you and with you during your live-stream concerts!*

She hadn't.

"And I know exactly how he feels." He looked up at his family members. "How Joey feels, and Cash, and Bryce, and...and all the 'extra' kids in this family."

"There are no 'extra kids' in this family," Daddy said. "You all belong right where you are."

"I know that's how *you* see it," Harry said. "How all the uncles see it. But the truth is...we don't always feel like that, and Boston has it worse, because he's not actually a Young at all. He feels even more like an add-on, an extra, someone who could just as easily be discarded as included."

"This is a great contract," Morris said, his voice somber and quiet. "Have you spoken to him about this at all?"

"Have you mentioned it to Mav?" Daddy asked, finally flipping open the folder.

Harry shook his head. "I've said nothing to either of them. I simply *saw* Boston at my welcome home party, and I've been texting him this week."

"We think he'll be thrilled and say yes," Adam said. "Simply based on the conversations Harry has had with him."

"Don't you need a job?" Daddy asked Adam.

Adam simply smiled at him with all the professionalism in the world. Adam too had found an apartment in Coral Canyon, as Harry didn't need or want live-in help. "I'm still plenty busy, sir, especially arranging travel and security for Harry during the next three months of the online tour."

"He's helping with the coordination of the band's travel too," Morris said.

Adam nodded at him too, but Harry did wonder where Adam would fit once the tour ended. He didn't have to know right now, and Adam had said he was a grown man and could figure out his own employment, whether he stayed with Harry or not.

"When are you going to talk to Boston and Mav?" Daddy asked.

"If you think the contract looks good," Harry said, and he had a feeling the contract was generous and amazing and Boston would snap it up and sign it immediately. "Then I'll text him and Mav and invite them to breakfast with me and Adam tomorrow morning. Then, we'll help Belle move into her place, and apparently, we're having dinner with y'all."

He still wasn't happy about that, and he felt like he needed to make a list of all the things he needed to talk to Belle about.

"I think it's an amazingly generous contract," Daddy said.

"Great," Harry said, and he nodded over to Adam. "Will you please text Boston and Mav and set up breakfast?"

"Perhaps Sunday, sir?" Adam asked, already swiping on his phone. "Belle is planning to be in Coral Canyon by nine, and a breakfast before that will require you to be...awake at an hour when you're usually not."

Harry just wanted it all done, but he supposed one more day wouldn't matter. "Sunday is fine," he said. "You could send them the contract in advance, so they can review it before we meet."

"I'll get it done." Adam stood and left the office, presumably to collect his laptop, where he liked to conduct his business.

Harry's phone buzzed, and he glanced at it to find Belle's name there. "Oh, she's responded," he said.

We can talk about it, she said. *But I'll tell you right now, I'm not sure I'd be comfortable doing that.*

Which part? he asked. *Playing with me on the tour, or playing one of your songs for me?*

Both, she said. *Harry, I left that life behind a long time ago.*

But you still play, he said. Playing, singing, songwriting, and music meant a great deal to him, and it had to her at one time in her life too. He wanted to share that with her.

He *craved* it, and Harry reminded himself that music was very personal. He didn't share everything with everyone, because it would expose a deep part of himself he was still exploring.

Think about it, he said. *And tell me what you want for dinner tonight, and I'll get it before I come help you pack.*

She didn't answer right away, and Harry looked up to find Morris packing away everything he'd gotten out to show Harry how the first week of the tour would go. He jumped to his feet and rounded the desk to hug his uncle. "Thank you, Uncle Morris. I would be lost without you."

"You're welcome, son." Uncle Morris gripped him back and grinned at him as he stepped away.

Harry met his daddy's eyes as he stood, and he said, "I'll talk to Ev about what she's texting Belle, okay?"

Harry nodded, and then he hugged his father too. "I really like her," he whispered. "I promise I'm not going to lose my head with her, okay?"

"Mm." Daddy hugged him and then pulled back, taking Harry by both shoulders. "But falling in love is a little bit crazy, and it's okay to let yourself feel all of those things too, okay?"

"Does it make you crazy?" Harry asked. "Because I feel kind of crazy when it comes to Belle."

Morris chuckled and said, "Love absolutely makes you crazy," right before he left the office and then the house.

Daddy gave Harry one of his rare grins and echoed something Adam had said earlier in the meeting. "He's not wrong." He dropped his hands and fell back a step to pick up his phone and stuff it in his back pocket. "And it's kind of fun to go a little crazy for someone you're falling in love with," he added. "So try to enjoy it—if that's what this is."

Harry nodded, and he managed to walk his father to the front door too. It closed, and Harry stood there facing it, wondering if he'd started falling in love with Belle yet.

"Of course you have," he muttered to himself. And it had only been spurred forward by her saying she wasn't going to buy a house here, because he had one, and if they got married....

Harry had the fantasy of a wife and family right there, almost within his grasp, and he'd thought plenty about it.

Now, he just needed more time, more experiences, and his feelings to be more solid and certain to know if his future was Harry and Belle Forever.

30

Belle glared at her guitar as the clock clicked closer and closer to six. Harry wouldn't be a moment late, she knew that. Not in the evening.

Not only that, but he'd texted almost two hours ago to say he was leaving Coral Canyon, and he might actually be early.

She didn't mind that, because she'd only worked half the day today, and she'd stopped by the grocery store to get some boxes on her way home.

She'd already filled them, so she wasn't sure how Harry was going to help her with the packing tonight, though she still had one cupboard in her bathroom to box up, as well as all of her dishes in the kitchen.

"You just need more boxes," she told herself as she paced away from the guitar in its stand beside the window and moved toward the front door of the apartment.

She hadn't kept everything from her time before she'd gone undercover. She'd rented a small ten-by-twenty-foot storage unit for her couch, her grandmother's dining room table and chairs, her bed, and her guitar.

She wasn't an overly complicated woman who owned gowns or closets full of clothing. She only had a handful of pairs of shoes, and Belle had her whole bedroom packed. She had a change of clothes for tomorrow, and a suitcase for the weekend so she'd have time to get everything unpacked at her new place in Coral Canyon.

The move should be easy, Belle thought. Being closer to Harry was what she wanted.

Then, he'd complicated things by asking her to play with him.

"*For* him," she growled to the peephole that still showed her an empty hallway in front of her apartment.

Truth be told, she wasn't sure which was worse. Playing for him privately or agreeing to be live-streamed at his side for the world to see. To judge. To leave comments on her technique, the sound of her voice, the way she held her guitar.

Some people could be ruthless, everyone had an opinion, and social media wasn't all rainbows, cupcakes, and unicorns.

Plus, she'd already failed in country music. Would Harry find her sound outdated? Her voice too grunge? Her songs totally antiquated?

She paced back toward the window just as someone knocked on the door. Her heart flew to the top of her skull and clattered against the hard bone there, leaving her stunned for a few moments.

"It's me, Belle," Harry called.

She practically ran to the door now and whipped it open to find her handsome cowboy boyfriend standing there. He wore dark-wash jeans, one of his tamer tees with the Teton Mountain range on it without any words or funny sayings, and cowboy boots. A matching cowboy hat sat on his head, and he carried an oversized brown bag with the Wild Wyoming logo on the front of it.

"Hey, my Belle." Harry eased into the apartment, and Belle looked out and down the second-floor landing and hallway. She didn't see anyone there, and she wasn't sneaking her boyfriend into her apartment against his mother's wishes besides.

Harry moved into the kitchen as Belle closed and locked the door, then turned to face him. He didn't seem nervous or worried about anything as he lifted out a recyclable container and said, "This is the baby wedge salad, no blue cheese."

Belle told herself to get over there and greet him, and her legs managed to start walking. "Hey," she said as she arrived at his side.

He paused in getting out the food and turned toward her. "You're nervous."

"A little."

"Too nervous to kiss me hello?" He offered her a small smile, with plenty of softness in his eyes.

"No," she murmured, and she tipped her head back and

let her eyes drift closed. She wasn't going to kiss him hello; he'd have to kiss her, which he did. Harry had big, capable hands, and he moved one up her back and into her hair, which she'd left down and added a wave to for tonight's date.

He kissed her softly, sweetly, for a few seconds, and then his next stroke intensified, driving a bolt of passion through her.

She liked kissing him both ways, and she simply let him carry on as long as he wanted. When he finally pulled away, he breathed in harshly and then blew all that air out. "You— I really like kissing you," he said.

She liked kissing him too, but she didn't know how to make her voice work the way his did. "It means a lot to me that you drive so far and pick up exactly what I want for dinner," she said. "Just to be with me."

"I'm happy to do it," he whispered, the paper bag rustling again as he plunged both hands into it. "I got the steak frittes, because they looked amazing, and I got you the chicken pot pie you wanted."

He lifted both containers out, and Belle turned to get down plates. Most of her dates with Harry revolved around food, and she wanted something a little different for their first outing together in Coral Canyon.

"So, I had an idea," she said.

Harry lifted his eyebrows. "Lay it on me, Miss Belle."

"Would you go out with me on Monday?" she asked. "In the afternoon. I want to go to the animal shelter and find a cat to adopt."

"Sounds like a good time," he said. "I'd love to do that with you."

Belle grinned at him, finally relaxing a little bit. "You could look for a dog, maybe."

"Sure," Harry said easily, and while he had a grumpy, serious side, he could be sweet and personable too. He'd claimed to have taken classes to deal with fans, and Belle had told him she didn't want him using any of those skills on her. That he should simply get to be himself.

He'd promised, and she'd never felt like he'd been putting on a show for her since they'd run into each other in the airport almost a month ago now.

"What kind of cat are you gonna get?" he asked as he plated her food and pushed it closer to her.

"I'm not sure," she said. "I looked online, and they have a few options, but cats get adopted all the time, and we're not going until after the weekend." She shrugged. "Maybe they'll all be gone after a weekend adoption frenzy."

Harry chuckled, and Belle liked the very presence of him in her apartment, in her life—and she realized that meant so much more than just having him over for dinner.

He finished up with his food and slid the baby wedge onto a third plate. Then he picked up both plates and headed for Belle's small table on the other side of the peninsula.

She joined him, set down her plate, and returned to the kitchen to get the drinks she'd also picked up on the way home from work. Diet Dr. Pepper for Harry—his favorite soda pop—and Glacier Ice Gatorade for her.

He beamed up at her as she put the one-liter bottle down beside his plate. "Thank you, sweetheart." He watched her open her Gatorade and take a drink before she sat down.

She picked up her fork and broke off a piece of puff pastry to take a bite of her chicken pot pie. "I might not be good enough to play with you, Harry."

"I don't believe that for a second," he said, zero hesitation from her statement to his.

"I haven't played in a while," she said.

"You kept your guitar," he said quietly. "All these years, even after you had a terrible experience, even when you got rid of so much of who you are to go undercover." He looked at her with those dark, serious eyes, something dancing and fiery in them. "Just like you kept my phone number, you kept that guitar."

She nodded, tears pricking her eyes. "What if you hate how I sing? Hate the songs I labored over and loved?"

"What if I love them?"

Belle took the bite of her pot pie, but it was very hard to chew and swallow. "This is very hard for me, Harry."

"I hear you," he said.

"I had a manager who fed me lies," she told him. "Instead of just telling me I wasn't good enough, and I should just write for someone else."

"That's all I want to do," he said.

"Yes, but the difference is you're good enough to sing your own songs too."

"*Good enough* is subjective."

She pinned him with one of her police officer looks, and he blinked rapidly a couple of times. "I need you to promise me something."

"Lay it out."

"If I play for you, you have to promise me that if I'm not good, you'll just say so."

"I promise," he said.

"If you hate the way my voice sounds, you'll just tell me. I don't need your pity. I don't want to embarrass myself on your live-stream—or tank it—just because I'm your girlfriend."

She swallowed, but she had more to say. "And I'm terrified that if I'm not good enough for you on the guitar, that I won't be good enough for you, period."

"Belle."

She looked down at her food, unable to maintain eye contact with someone as strong and powerful as Harry. "So if that's a deal-breaker for you, I'd rather just not play for you at all." She looked up and into the gorgeous depths of his eyes. He wasn't shuttering anything off right now, and Belle felt like she could see into his soul.

"If it's a deal-breaker, you have to promise not to break-up with me right away, so that I won't know it. You can do it later, for any other reason you want, even if it's because I'm not up to your caliber as a musician."

Harry gazed at her, and then lifted his hand to cradle her face in one of those amazing palms. "I'm interested in you for far more than your musical ability," he said, and that was one of the best compliments Belle had ever received. "You've got something you can play for me tonight?"

Belle moved away from his hand, and he dropped it so she could take another bite of her dinner. "Yes," she practically choked out. "If you can make all those promises and mean them."

"I promise to tell you what I really think of your voice, your ability, and I promise I won't break-up with you over any of it."

She nodded and picked up her knife so she could cut into the wedge salad. "Okay," she said.

"Did you write all your songs for the album-that-never-was?"

She nodded. "Yes, sir."

"Then I can't wait to hear even just one song," he said. "I feel like I'm going to learn so much about you." He smiled, but the gesture didn't stay for long. "Songs are so personal, right?"

"Usually," she said.

"So moving day tomorrow," he said, moving on to something else. "My daddy and Morris thought the contract for Boston was amazing, and I'm meeting with him and Mav on Sunday morning for breakfast." He grinned as he speared some steak and French fries. "And then we have a date at the animal shelter on Monday night."

"Life is good," Belle murmured, to which Harry practically yelled, "Amen."

An hour later, Belle's fingers tingled, and she shook her hands out as her nerves assaulted her on all sides.

She told herself she always felt like this before playing and performing, even when it was just her trio of cats in the house to hear her. The moment she started playing, she'd fall into the music, and she'd relax into something she knew as intimately as she knew herself.

"Ready?" she asked, and Harry nodded from behind his phone. He held it up in front of his face to record her, claiming he wanted to be able to go over it more than once before giving her his true opinion. He'd promised not to post it anywhere online, though Belle had thought about asking him how to get the right angle, set up the ring lights just right, and which mic to buy so she could record videos the way he did.

She hadn't brought it up in the week or two since she'd thought it, and she marveled that Harry had come to her with the idea to play for him.

She ducked her head and looked at her fingers on the strings of her old guitar. She'd been through so much with this instrument, and it wouldn't fail her. She knew that.

She let the air flow out of her lungs as she heard the opening notes of the song she'd written just for herself, and when she breathed in again, she started to play. Her fingertips pressed easily against the strings, and her pick moved precisely where it needed to go.

She looked up and smiled, not even seeing the camera anymore, and when she opened her mouth to sing, she hit the note exactly in tune. Her lower voice didn't always impress people, and the slow vibrato and gravelly quality of it had been passed over more times than she could count.

I walk these empty halls where memories still linger,
Echoes of laughter warm like the touch of your fingers.
The porch swing's creakin', but it brings me comfort,
Every corner of this house whispers love's sweet presence.

She knew the just-right place to let the guitar sing while she breathed, and then she started into the chorus.

I come home to shadows, where your love still holds me tight,
The stars above are shining, guiding me through the night.

I whisper to the sunrise, Love will light my way,
Embraced by your strong presence, every single day.

She sang through the second verse, then the bridge, and back to the chorus again. She finished by holding out that last note in her higher register, and then let her fingers walk along the strings and pluck out that last, satisfying chord before she opened her eyes and let the echo of the song ring through the small apartment.

Embraced by your strong presence, every single day.

She looked over to Harry to find him staring openly at her. His phone sat on the couch beside him, and he didn't even blink.

Belle cleared her throat and lowered her guitar to balance against the sofa. "Well?"

Please be honest, she thought. She didn't want to think of Harry as a liar, and her chest and all her most vital organs buzzed with fear, adrenaline, and satisfaction. She'd played as well as she could, and Belle loved that song.

No matter who else did, she did, and she told herself the

same thing she had been for the past eight years. *Even if you're the only person who ever hears and enjoys that song, that's enough. You're enough.*

Harry finally blinked, as if coming back into his body. "That was incredible."

Belle blinked, her mind going blank. "You're just saying that."

"I absolutely am not," he said, his voice hoarse. "I've never heard anyone sing like that before." He dropped to his knees and walked on them until he met where she sat on the couch. He pushed her knees to the side as he gathered her in his arms.

"It was beautiful, my Belle. What an amazing story." He brushed her bangs out of her face. "What an absolutely stunning voice you have."

He smiled softly at her, and Belle couldn't duck her head and avoid him, not as close as he'd gotten. In that moment, she realized how far she'd let him in, and she didn't care if he saw the tears in her eyes.

They filled, and a tear slipped down her cheek. Harry wiped it away, everything about him kind and wonderful. "Will you lend me the sheet music so I can learn it too? I would absolutely *love* to play that with you during my world tour." He pressed a chaste kiss to her cheek and then just below her ear. "Incredible. You're absolutely incredible."

Belle wrapped her arms around him and held on tight, because she hadn't felt incredible for such a long time, and here he was reinventing everything she thought about herself, showing her what her life could truly be, and reigniting her love for something she'd thought she'd have to give up permanently.

She had kept her guitar all these years, not quite able to walk away yet. She'd done the same thing with Harry's number, and as they breathed in together, Belle fell a tiny bit in love with him.

And it felt good, and right, and peaceful—the opposite of what her life had been for the past year, so she really knew the difference.

"Do you have a contract for me to look at?" she asked, and Harry pulled back.

She swiped at her eyes and met his, as serious as ever. "I've been burned before, and while I don't think you'll take my song and claim it as yours, I'm going to need to see a contract before I give you any sheet music."

"Of course." Harry got to his feet and retrieved his phone. "I'll text Morris right now."

She stood and crowded into his side so she could see his message too. "Did you record the whole song?"

"Only about half," he said. "I was just so mesmerized that I forgot to hold the phone up." He grinned at her and finished texting. "I can send it to Morris, so he can get it approved by our tour manager at Rebel." His eyebrows went up, and then he lowered his phone.

"If you want, Belle. That song...I can tell it means a lot to you, and if you'd rather not share it with the world through my live-stream, I understand. I will honor that. Maybe you have something else."

"I have other songs," Belle said, considering her options

as well as what he'd said. She truly would be sharing a very intimate piece of her heart and soul if she let Harry learn that song, if they performed it together for the online world to see and listen to.

"But that's my best one, and I think I should lead with my very best."

Harry nodded, took her face in his hands, and kissed her with trembling lips. "I'm falling in love with you," he whispered. "And I feel wild and crazy about it, but that song...it comforted me. It soothed me and reminded me that love can be soft and beautiful and wonderful and so, so strong." He smiled at her with only his lips, no teeth showing. No mega-rockstar wattage. "Thank you, baby. Thank you so much for sharing that with me."

Tears threatened to run down her face again, but she managed to nod without crying. "Thank you for asking me."

He stepped out of her arms and picked up her guitar. She thought he might play it, but he simply put it back in the stand. "Now, can I hold you on the couch while we watch a movie? Or have we done that to death and you'll think I'm boring?"

Belle wanted nothing more than that, so she gathered her remotes and handed them to him. "Okay, but you still have to help me pack up the kitchen tonight, and I'm out of boxes."

His mega-watt grin appeared then, and he said, "No problem, baby. I'll order some right now, and we'll get the work done after the movie."

As Belle lay in his arms while he flipped through the

streaming apps she had to find a movie, she listened to the comforting beat of his heart and inhaled the sexy, woodsy scent of his cologne—and let herself fall wildly and crazily in love with him.

Wildly and crazily in love, she thought, and for the first time since she'd left country music almost a decade ago, brand-new song lyrics ran through her head.

What a blessing, what a gift, she thought, the lyrics becoming a prayer she'd be able to sing, exactly like the song she'd just performed for Harry.

31

J oey tied an apron around her waist and smiled at the other girls working in the back of the bakery.

She'd now quit college twice, and Joey had to work hard most days to hold her head up high and go about her day. She didn't want her grandparents or her daddy to think she was lazy, so she'd gotten an afternoon position at Cake Bites to complement her early-morning job at Daily Grind.

Harry would be playing one of his live-stream concerts next week, and Joey had made sure she'd been scheduled.

She loved her cousin with her whole heart, as Harry had already started texting all the older cousins about having dinner and dessert and movie night at his house now that he'd returned to Coral Canyon.

His online world tour ran through May, June, and July, with three or four venues each week, most of them in Coral

Canyon, though Harry was playing three weeks out of Jackson Hole.

"I need you on pick-up orders today, Joelle," Miriam said, and Joey nodded and reached back to tighten her ponytail.

"Yes, ma'am," she said. "Let me put on the skates, and I'll check the clipboard."

"We have over a dozen pickups tonight," she said. "Lots of parties this weekend, apparently."

Joey actually liked the pickup shift, because she could rollerskate out to the line, get names, and come back to get the orders. Miriam had worked out a system that kept the pick-up line separate from those coming in with new orders or simply for a sweet treat on the way home from work, and Joey had to skate across the parking lot to a designated lane at the back. In the evening, it was shaded, and she'd gotten this job after demonstrating both her skills in the kitchen and on roller skates.

She plucked her pair from the overhead cubbies and sat on the bench to switch out her shoes for the skates.

Then she rollered over to the tiny to-go office in the back corner of the bakery. They had racks and racks stationed there, many of them full of boxes already. Cupcakes ready to be picked up, and Joey grabbed the clipboard that hung by a rope outside the office.

Sure enough, over twenty orders sat there, and Joey had a feeling her four-hour shift was going to be very busy. A trickle of sweat already ran down her back, as the air conditioning didn't quite reach this remote corner of the shop, and the bell signaling tires had rolled into the cupcake pick-up lane sounded overhead.

Joey unhooked the clipboard, made sure she had a pen over her ear, and pushed out the door to the asphalt beyond. She boogied toward the white sedan there, where a woman rolled down her window. "Can I get your name?" she asked, noting another truck pulling into the pick-up lane.

"Amanda Barber," she said. "I should have three dozen cupcakes ready."

Joey found her name and made a check beside it. "You sure do. Give me a minute."

She moved to the truck behind Amanda and repeated the process. Bethany Farmer had five dozen cupcakes for a band party, and while Joey didn't need to know the details of what the treats were for, a lot of people said so when they picked up.

Joey could only carry two dozen cupcakes at a time, as per the bakery's policy, so she had four trips in front of her as she skated back to the door in the corner.

She rehung the clipboard and located Amanda's first two dozen cupcakes. Back and forth she went, and by the time she'd delivered those eight boxes, three more vehicles had lined up for pick-ups.

Another skater joined her, and together, Belinda and Joey worked on getting the cupcakes to those who'd ordered and paid for them.

She took a moment to get a drink though she had two orders to deliver, and when Joey finally felt hydrated and cool enough to go back outside, two dozen cupcakes in her arms, she found Scott Olds standing next to his driver's door, his arms folded.

Joey's heartbeat throbbed as she approached. "Sorry for that wait, Mister Olds," she said in the brightest voice she could muster after being on skates for two hours.

"That other girl went in and out twice while I waited," he grumped at her.

She didn't have to explain to him that even she deserved a water break and the chance to cool off. And it wasn't even all that hot in town yet. So she said nothing as she slowed to a stop in front of him. "I, uh, have your cupcakes here."

"I want to speak to your manager about your laziness."

Joey felt like she'd been struck in the throat, and she opened her mouth to respond, but nothing came out. Scott grabbed the cupcakes from her so fast that she got thrown off-balance. She rolled toward him though she tried to stop, and then she did that too abruptly. Her ankle buckled, and Joey started to fall.

She yelped as she flailed her arms, trying to find something to grab onto. Her hands only met air, and pain rippled up her leg. Her daddy had often teased her about her skinny legs, and how he wondered how they held up her body.

And right now, they weren't.

The man who'd grabbed the cupcakes opened his back door as Joey's knee hit the ground, and she had a brief moment to worry about her head hitting the door before a pair of strong arms encircled her.

"I got you," a man said in a rich, rumbling tenor.

Pain smarted through the knee that had hit the asphalt,

which happened to be the same side as her aching ankle. Her long, white-blonde hair felt plastered to her face, and she just wanted to go inside, find a corner, and cry for a minute.

"You owe this young woman an apology," the man said as he righted Joey. She just wanted to disappear, but the man kept his arm around her. "You knocked her down."

"Oh, please," Scott-the-customer said. "She took ten minutes to bring out my cupcakes, and I still don't even have them all yet."

Humiliation filled Joey, and she just wanted to skate away. Down the row of cars, Belinda delivered a couple of boxes of cupcakes and glanced her way.

And then she looked at the man who'd come to her rescue.

Buttermilk pancakes, she swore in her head. "Adam?" she asked.

The man looked at her, and sure enough, it was Adam Harmon. Harry's assistant. He wasn't wearing his usual slacks, white shirt and tie, and crisp suit jacket, but a pair of jeans and a sweatshirt with a huge wolf head on it.

It was at least two sizes too big, and Joey blinked, trying to get the images she'd seen of Adam online to mesh with this dressed-down casual, almost sloppy version of him.

"I'm sorry," he said smoothly. He threw Scott a death glare. "See how easy that was?"

"I'm not apologizing to her. She should be fired."

"You're ridiculous." Adam turned and marched away

from the line, from Scott, from Joey. "What's the name? I'll get your cupcakes myself."

"Scott Olds," he called after Adam, and Joey wasn't sure if she should stay there or not. Of course she shouldn't, and she turned expertly and skated away slowly, testing out the strength of her ankle as she moved gingerly.

"Adam," she called after him. "I can get the cupcakes." She caught him fairly easily and slowed to skate at his walking pace. "You don't know who I am, do you?"

Adam looked at her fully. "I'm guessing you know Harry."

"He's my cousin." Joey smiled at Adam, her pulse doing more than it should if she wanted Adam as a friend. She immediately rebelled against the idea of trying to get him to ask for her number.

One, he had to be at least a decade older than her. Two, he worked with Harry. Both of those were strikes, and yet, Joey couldn't help smiling at him with every ounce of flirt she possessed.

"I can get the cupcakes," she said. "Did you have some?"

"Yes," Adam said. "For Harry to take to Belle to celebrate her move to town."

"Oh, of course," Joey said, though no one had brought her a dozen cupcakes when she'd moved back. Not true, she reminded herself. Grams and Gramps had welcomed her with open arms; some of the aunts had set up her room in her grandparent's condo, and Joey had no right to have her heart pinching through the narrow space between two ribs.

And yet, it still did. She didn't know how to stop it, and she wished her shift was over.

"Are you coming over to Belle's after you get off?" Adam asked as Joey approached the door.

"I don't know," she said.

"I believe both Harry and Trace invited the whole family on the group text," he said.

"Oh, I hardly ever check that thing," Joey said. Then she didn't have to get her feelings hurt, and it sure seemed like everything lately made her throat tighten. She let him pull open the door, and she handed him the last two boxes for Scott, and then she selected the two she saw with Adam's name on them.

"How many do you have?" she asked. He hadn't immediately turned to go back to Scott, and the man yelled from across the parking lot.

"Six," Adam said. "I'll come get the last two."

Belinda skated up as Joey pushed out of the doorway. "You okay, Joey?" she asked.

"Yeah," she said.

"Your knee is bleeding."

Joey didn't look down at it, though her knee now stung more than before. "I'll come back and clean it up."

"I'll ask Miriam to give us someone else," Belinda said. "You need to get that bandaged."

Joey let Adam handle Scott, feeling shakier and shakier by the moment. She took the pink boxes of cupcakes to Adam's SUV and put them in the backseat before her vision started to swim.

She wasn't sure how long she stood there, one hand on the headrest of the driver's seat, while she breathed in and out in long strokes of air, trying to get her body to cooperate with her. She accidentally looked down at her leg and saw the blood, and oh, that so wasn't okay.

She wasn't okay, and she pressed her eyes closed to get the sight of her bloody knee and shin out of her sight. But the damage had been done, and her stomach swooped and knotted, and she was for-sure going to pass out now.

"Hey, hey, hey," Adam said, plenty of concern in his voice as he came up beside her. He practically threw the four dozen cupcakes into the backseat, and then his warm, delicious hands landed on her body again. "Are you okay?"

Embarrassment only heated Joey's face and head further. "No," she managed to say. "I think I'm going to pass out."

"Sit down," Adam commanded, but Joey couldn't move her legs.

He turned her so she faced him, and she sagged against Adam's chest, whose solid, strong body held her up easily. She opened her eyes and met his, and Joey tried to smile at him. Surely she looked like a deranged clown, and she had no idea what she was thinking when she said, "You smell really good."

Adam frowned at her.

The world around her swayed, and she said, "I'd go out with you if you asked," just before she blacked out.

32

Adam Harmon had no idea what to do with the gorgeous blonde in his arms. He knew she was far too young for him, as well as a Young, which made her completely off-limits. He couldn't even *imagine* telling Harry he was going out with one of his cousins. The very idea was laughable—and fire-able.

He'd been toying with leaving behind celebrity assisting and finding something else to do to earn money. Truth be told, Adam could quit assisting Harry and live off his savings for several years, especially if he stayed here in small-town Coral Canyon.

And Adam was tired. He held himself to a high standard, and he'd enjoyed over a decade in the entertainment and celebrity world. He'd immediately taken to the slower pace of Coral Canyon, and he'd been as eager to move here as Harry had been.

"Help," he called as someone rolled down their window. "She passed out."

The woman—someone much closer to his age—jumped out of her car and hurried toward him. "Oh, dear," she said. "I'll call nine-one-one."

Adam was sure Joey would not like that, but he didn't have another solution. He did his best to push the cupcakes out of the way, and he cringed as one of the boxes fell onto the floor on the passenger side of his SUV. But he couldn't hold Joey's dead weight for much longer. Not that she was a big woman. Quite the opposite, and Adam searched his memories for her age.

Too young, he thought. Too young, too young, too young. He finally got her into the backseat, and he got the seat to recline as much as it would while the woman a few feet from him told the EMTs where they were.

In the car, Joey made a terrible moaning sound, and Adam returned his attention to her. "Hey," he said. "You're okay. You just passed out, but I caught you." He tried not to feel too proud of himself. He couldn't believe he'd gotten out of his SUV in the first place, but he couldn't stand to see someone get mistreated.

Joey moaned again, and this time her eyes fluttered open.

"She's waking up," he said to the woman, and she relayed the information to the dispatcher.

"Adam?" Joey asked, and Adam leaned into his vehicle, right over here.

"I'm right here, Joey," he said. "You're okay."

"I don't—I saw my own blood." Her face had gone about as white as the paint on his SUV.

"Here's a first aid kit, Mister Harmon," the other skater said, and Adam backed out of his SUV to take it from her. He didn't have time to ask her how she'd known his name before she rollered away to deliver the two dozen cupcakes in her arms.

"They want to know if we need an ambulance," the woman said.

"No," Joey practically yelled, and she sat up. "I'm okay. I just don't like the sight of my own blood." She looked from her to Adam. "Would you help me get it cleaned up?"

"Of course," he said diplomatically.

"Is everything okay?" another woman asked, and Adam turned to welcome her to the fray.

"I'm okay, Miriam," Joey said as she wiped her hair off her forehead. "I just stumbled and skinned my knee, and I accidentally saw it."

Miriam crowded into the open doorway of the SUV and looked at Joey's knee. "okay, but if you can't stay on deliveries, I'll move you to the counter."

"She passed out," Adam said, his overprotective streak rising up. Why he wanted to protect this woman, he didn't know. "She needs to get cleaned up and go home."

Joey didn't argue with him, and Miriam likewise blinked at him.

"I'm going to get her knee cleaned up and then I'll take her home," he said. "I work for her cousin."

"I know who you are," Miriam said. "And Joey can decide for herself."

"Of course she can," Adam said smoothly, and then he clicked open the first aid kit. "Joey, can you put your leg out of the car?"

She did, and Adam ripped open an antiseptic wipe. He cleaned up the blood quickly, and said, "It's just a scrape," though it looked decently bad. He covered it with a couple of bandages and added, "Good as new."

Joey's face had pinked up again, and she gave him a smile. "Thank you, Adam."

"Of course." He closed the first aid kit and checked over his shoulder. Miriam had left, as had the other women on rollerskates. When he faced Joey again, she'd started to stand from the back of his car. "What would you like to do? Miriam said you could get a different assignment or go home."

"I'll go talk to my boss."

Adam held out his hand, letting it hover only a few inches from Joey as she found her balance on her skates. "Okay," he said. "Do you want me to wait and make sure you're okay?"

Their eyes met, and something powerful and charged shot between them. Adam had not dated for a few years now, as being on-call for a megastar didn't leave much personal time. He'd lost girlfriends because of his job, as he had to up and leave whatever he was doing when his bosses needed something.

"I'd like to check up on you later," Adam said, working

hard not to clear his throat. "Should I have Harry text you?" He hated how much of a coward he was for not asking her directly for her number. He coughed as a gust of wind kicked up, and he took a look at the scattered cupcake boxes.

When he looked at her again, he'd found some unknown reserve of bravery. "Or, if you give me your number, I can simply contact you directly."

He hated how formal his request had been, and Adam pressed his eyes closed in a long blink. Joey still hadn't said anything, and he just wanted to leave. "I should get these cupcakes over to Belle's new apartment." He backed up a step, and then started around the SUV to the other side, as he'd pushed the cupcakes over there to make room for Joey.

"Maybe I'll see you there," he said, and he smiled and waved to her, clearly dismissing her.

She gave him a kind smile—surely her way of letting him down easy—and then limp-skated back toward the door in the corner of the bakery.

Adam righted all 6 dozen cupcakes, noting that ten or twelve of them had definitely been jostled enough to notice. Heaven knew there'd be so much food at Belle's that a few slightly smooshed cupcakes wouldn't be noticed or needed.

With everything set, Adam got behind the wheel of his SUV and tossed a look toward the bakery. Joey hadn't come back out, and he told himself to get out of there before he did something twice as foolish as he already had.

"How obvious can I be?" he wondered as he made the drive from the bakery to Belle's almost-downtown apartment, something that only took six minutes.

When he walked in with half of the cupcakes, Harry looked over from where he'd just watered one of Belle's potted plants. Seeing him do something like that made Adam smile, because Harry had been so unhappy for such a long time.

"There you are," Harry said. "What took you so long?" He came forward and took the boxes from Adam, plain curiosity in his expression.

Adam's face heated, and he turned to leave again. "I have three more boxes to bring in." He retreated back to his SUV and collected the last of the desserts, and he put them with the others on the slip of Belle's countertop.

Harry gave him a look that said he'd ask Adam again about what had happened at the bakery, and he glanced around the part of the apartment he could see. This place had two bedrooms and two bathrooms, with a spacious living room, dining room, and kitchen, and if Adam hadn't found a pretty perfect house rental of his own, he'd consider these apartments.

"Where's Belle?" Adam asked, the knot in his throat so tight and so big.

"She called her mom," Harry said. "She's in the bedroom talking to her."

Adam nodded and cleared his throat, which made his boss and best friend perk up again.

"Just spit it out," Harry said, his tone somewhat grumpy. He didn't like secrets, and he didn't like prolonged conversations. He'd been down-to-earth and kind, and Harry Young was Adam's favorite client out of anyone he'd ever worked with.

"How old is your cousin Joey?" Adam asked.

Harry stopped fiddling with whatever was in the box on the dining room table—a family heirloom of Belle's, Adam had been informed. "My...cousin...Joey?" He spoke like he didn't understand those words in that order.

"She works at the bakery where we ordered cupcakes," Adam said, glancing over to the pastry boxes. "Someone was harassing her, and I helped her a little."

"Okay," Harry said slowly. "And now you want to know how old she is? Why?"

Adam shrugged, his face burning. He hated feeling like this, and it hardly ever happened to him. He usually exuded confidence, and he knew all the details of every situation inside and out. He knew who to call at every establishment, and he could explain himself and what he needed for Harry in two tight sentences.

"Are you telling me you're interested in asking her out?" Harry asked.

"I didn't say that."

"Your face is bright red," Harry said with a chuckle. "And I hate to say it, brother, but she's far too young for you."

"Yeah," Adam mumbled. "What? She's twenty-two or so?"

"Twenty-two, yeah," Harry said. "And you know you're thirty-two, right?"

"I'm only thirty-one, actually," Adam said.

Harry grinned at him and started to laugh. "I can't wait for you to explain it like that to my uncle Otis." He laughed, and laughed, and laughed.

Adam finally rolled his eyes and said, "All right, I got it. She's off-limits."

"I mean, if you want to keep your teeth," Harry said, still chortling. He hadn't said he had a problem with it, and Adam had met Otis Young several times. He worked with Harry a lot on the songwriting, and he'd come to help them both move a few weeks ago.

Adam had known intellectually about Joey, but he hadn't spent too much time thinking of her. Now, though, he sincerely hoped she'd finish up her shift at Cake Bites and decide to drop by Belle's to welcome her to town.

Then he'd get to see her again, talk to her and make sure she was okay, and maybe, just maybe, get that elusive phone number for himself.

33

oston Simpson stood with his arms folded as he watched the cameraman do a test shot of where Harry would be standing once the concert started. He shifted his feet back and forth and lifted his thumbnail to his teeth, though he'd never been much of a nail biter before. Of course, he'd never been a physical facilities coordinator before either, and he had no idea what Harry saw in him that had prompted him to offer him such a position.

"How does it look?" the man called to where Boston stood with the main cameraman, the one who had the frontal shot of the stage. The drum set had already been set up, along with two mics, two stools, keyboards off to the side, and an additional guitar. Sometimes Harry played and sang acoustically, and that second stool wouldn't always be there, as Bryce only played a few songs with Harry.

Boston, dressed head to toe in black—black slacks, black

dress shoes, black polo—would don a headset and stand out of the way until it was time to bring out what Bryce needed to perform with Harry. His pulse positively pounded. He couldn't believe this was where he stood, and this was his life for the next three months.

He'd lived in Coral Canyon since the age of seven and had grown up with Harry and Bryce. They'd always included him, but he was a decade younger than Bryce and five years younger than Harry. He hadn't truly thought they'd seen him as they'd been off living their own lives for the past several years while he finished up high school and tried to figure out what he wanted to do with his life.

Boston had no idea in that department, but he'd gone to school for a year, taken a lot of general studies and some engineering classes—enough to know he didn't want to do engineering—and come back. He hadn't wanted to move back into his mom and dad's place, but he didn't have anywhere else. He'd been helping Bryce and Kassie at the Rising Sun Ranch until two days ago, when a text from Adam Harmon had blown up his whole world. A contract had come in. He'd had breakfast with Harry and Adam, and he'd signed on as Harry's physical facilities coordinator that very morning.

Harry managed all of his own social media, and he'd posted that morning about tonight's first live stream for the online concert tour. He'd given everyone a discount code if they hadn't gotten their access ticket yet, and sales had been through the roof. All of that was part of Boston's job. He was supposed to monitor how many people watched live, how many logged in later with their ticket, and how many overall tickets had been sold.

Rebel Records had dedicated tech support for anyone who couldn't get in. Boston had spoken to them yesterday at length to make sure he understood the procedure and could help as well.

His laptop waited on a small two-top table that didn't have a great view of the stage. When he wasn't helping Harry get his guitars and guiding Bryce on the stage, he'd sit over there watching online to make sure everything went the way it was supposed to.

The camera crew had a manager doing the same thing, and he gave a thumbs-up to the man doing the crowd visuals. Harry was here somewhere as the concert started in another ninety minutes, and Boston forced his hand away from his mouth and tried to infuse some measure of comfort and calmness into himself. This would be his life for the next three months, and he'd never been more excited.

Harry, of course, had toured for both of his previous albums, and walking out onto a small stage in one of the most popular restaurants in Coral Canyon would be nothing like taking the stage in a football stadium that could hold sixty thousand people.

No, Boston wasn't worried about Harry at all. He'd seen his cousin's videos on social media already, and Harry could set up on the landing of a staircase, sing a song, and get millions of views and likes. That was free, though, and they were expecting people to pay for this experience.

There was no opening band and no break for Harry. It

would be him for one-hundred-twenty minutes, charming the crowd who'd managed to get reservations at Devil's Tower, as well as anyone tuning in through their computer screen with a mic and his guitar.

Please, please, let the technology work, Boston prayed. He wanted this to be a success. He'd want this to be a success for Harry, whether he was on his team or not. He figured a prayer couldn't hurt.

His phone buzzed, and Boston held it in his hand so he could easily lift it up and look at it.

After party tonight at the band's house, Shane had texted. *Starting about ten-thirty, and it'll run until one. You don't need to bring anything. Rebel has ordered food and drinks, and we can't wait to celebrate Harry's first online concert!*

Boston swallowed because he'd literally been in this job for forty-eight hours. Adam had given him a folder of all the people playing with Harry, as Harry didn't really have a band.

Rebel had assigned them to him, and they'd recorded Harry's album with him. They'd rented a house in the gated community for the next three months where they would live and work with Harry as he did his online concert tour.

Boston had studied them yesterday morning as well as again today, and he knew them by face and name. But that didn't mean he *knew* them. He wasn't friends with them, and they probably hadn't been given a sheet with his name, picture, and facts about him.

He'd never been the greatest at making friends, and as

each individual bandmate confirmed, as well as Harry and Adam, Boston wondered if he could simply skip the after-party.

The camera crew continued to call back and forth to each other, and Boston paid attention so that he knew what they were looking for and could be aware of it at other venues. They'd play The Branding Iron and Daily Grind this week, and the coffee shop would present a massive challenge.

Aunt Michelle owned it, and the Youngs had had their New Year talent show there a couple of years ago. It had barely fit all of them, and there had been no cameras. No angles that needed to be met. No acoustics that really mattered. Boston had already been in contact with her, and he planned to visit Daily Grind tomorrow morning, about the same time Harry would be performing on Friday.

That evening, he'd go to The Branding Iron and do the same thing. Harry had said that Boston didn't need to start until next week, but he didn't see the point in saddling horses and mucking out stalls when he could dive right into this new responsibility.

He'd much rather be doing this, and Boston wondered what that meant for his future.

"You haven't confirmed for the after-party."

He startled and looked over to Adam, who wore a knowing expression. "Yeah, I don't know if I'll go."

"You're part of the team," Adam said. "The camera crew will be there, the band, me, Harry, and anyone contributing to the tour." Adam didn't look at him as he spoke, and

Boston wondered if he'd be a good assistant to celebrities and the rich and famous the way Adam was.

He didn't even know how to get into that business, but he had someone right beside him to ask. Still, he kept the questions buried, because Adam wasn't going anywhere, and Boston had plenty to learn for what he'd already been tasked to do.

"Even Bryce said he was coming," Adam said with a chuckle.

"All right," Boston said, giving in. "I'll be there."

"You can drive separately," Adam said. "So that you don't have to stay the whole time if you don't want to. You know the code to the garage."

"Yep." Boston really appreciated that Adam didn't say "Harry's garage," though it absolutely was Harry's garage. He'd moved in yesterday because he'd barely unpacked after returning home from college, so all he'd had to do was a load of laundry, pack up his clothes, make his bed in his momma's basement, and move into Harry's. He'd only been there for a single day, and he was already far happier than he'd been living with his parents.

And Boston loved his parents. He did. He loved Maverik Young, who'd raised him and taken care of him the way a daddy was supposed to. It was nothing against them.

He just didn't enjoy being the odd man out in his own family. Beth, Mav's daughter, who was only a year younger than him, had not returned home for the summer. She'd opted to stay in Jackson Hole with her mother. Her mom had gotten remarried too, but she had not had any more children.

Boston's mom and Mav had had two more, and it often felt like he and Beth were islands floating out in the middle of The Great Young Sea, forgotten specks that people wondered about every once in a while, but didn't truly care to visit.

He thought he'd been alone in feeling that way until Beth had brought it up a few years ago. She said Joey felt the same way, but none of them knew what to do about it.

Harry had been texting all of the older cousins, and that included Boston, Joey, Beth, Bryce, Cash, Corinne, Rosie, and Cole. Lynnie too, though she didn't have the Young last name either. She and Matthew had been married last year, and they had jobs in Seattle. Aunt Hilde and Uncle Gabe put things about them—their accomplishments, how amazing they were, the wonderful lives they lived—on the family text.

His mom and dad never put anything about him because he wasn't special. He didn't do anything noteworthy.

Even as he thought it, the Lord chastised him. *You and Harry got a million texts on Sunday*, Boston thought. That had more to do with Harry than him, because his cousin had sent a picture of him and Boston grinning from ear to ear while Boston held up the contract, and Harry explained that he'd just hired Boston to be on his tour team. There had been hundreds of texts that day, lots of congratulations, and

Boston could admit that he'd felt loved. He'd felt part of the Young family.

He finally felt like he belonged.

"How are we doing here?" the manager at Devil's Tower asked as she approached Adam and Boston.

"Good," Boston said as he stepped forward and shook Sally's hand. "I think they're set with the cameras."

"Our diners are here," she said. "We'd like to seat them in this area and get their orders, so that when the concert starts, we won't have waitstaff in the way."

"Absolutely," Boston said, glancing over to the cameraman. "You guys are set, right, Jake?"

"All set," Jake said, and he got down off the step stool he used when he filmed. "This is going to be here, but it's off. We're not recording right now."

Sally smiled and clapped her hands. "I'm so excited about this." She checked over her shoulder, and Boston saw the line of people waiting to get in too. "We're bringing in our diners now. Everyone will be served and have their drinks and dessert before Harry comes out."

"Harry wants to do a few minutes with everyone before the cameras start streaming," Boston said. "He'll come out about six-fifty and just chat with people at the tables, if that's all right."

Adam cut a look over to Boston, and he'd forgotten something. His mind blitzed, and he searched for what he needed to also ask. Adam waited patiently, and Boston loved him for it.

Thankfully, his mind kicked in, and he remembered.

"Oh, as you seat people, would you have your waitstaff talk to the diners and ask if it's okay if Harry talks to them right before the concert starts?"

"It won't be on the live stream," Boston added quickly, cutting a glance over to Adam, who nodded almost imperceptibly. "But Harry wants me to do a little bit of filming for his social media. We'll set it to music, so it doesn't matter what the patrons say. We just want to show Harry interacting with people before the concert starts, and he wants to thank people for coming to be here in person because it is much easier to play for a crowd than for a camera."

"Absolutely," Sally said. "I'll instruct our hostesses to ask, and I'll give you a list of any tables that don't want to talk to him." She trilled out a light laugh. "I can't believe anyone wouldn't want to. They purchased tickets to eat here, for crying out loud, just to see him."

"Well, I'm sure your reservation docket is full," Adam said.

"Oh, it is," she said. "But we'll make sure that this section is cleared for him before he begins."

"That's great," Boston said. "Thank you so much, Sally." And he reached out and shook the woman's hand. Harry had said that he could get Boston into some online PR classes, and Boston had taken him up on that offer. He'd done one last night, and one simple thing he'd learned: use someone's name.

Everyone wanted to be recognized by their name, and Sally beamed at him as she shook his hand and said, "We're going to start seating people now."

"Sounds great," Boston and Adam said together, and then Boston looked at Adam and said, "I'm going to go see what else Harry needs."

Adam smiled and nodded and said, "I'm going to order a tower of onion rings."

Boston chuckled as he walked away, but he entered the private dining room in the back corner of the restaurant straight-faced. Gratitude overcame him the moment he looked at his cousin, who plucked over his guitar strings with a pair of headphones on. He paused and simply watched him, overcome with the goodness of God.

Harry had *seen him*, but Boston knew that it was the Lord who had inspired him, who had opened his eyes, and who had prompted Harry to bring Boston back into the Young fold.

<h1 style="text-align:center">34</h1>

arry was used to having dozens of people surrounding him before a concert—loads of security, the stage manager, staff coordinating lights, timing, announcements, all of it. He wouldn't be running out onto a national stage with tens of thousands of people screaming his name, who'd been waiting for him for an hour through another band.

But the pressure settled on his shoulders all the same.

He had to be personable. He had to *glow* with happiness to be playing a guitar and singing. He had to ooze charm and charisma. And since he hadn't wanted to do this tour at all from the very beginning, conjuring up all of those things felt like a monumental task that Harry would fail at.

Boston and Adam had both been in the private dining room for the past half-hour. All of the band members had arrived, the camera crew had gotten food, and the general tension in the air felt like it could snap Harry's neck at any moment.

"It's six-forty-five, sir," Boston said, and Harry wanted to tell his cousin he didn't have to call him *sir*. At the same time, his very best friend in the whole world still called him *sir* in public, and Harry reminded himself that both Boston and Adam, while friends and family members, were employees as well.

"Thank you, Boston," he said, because if Harry had learned one thing from his father as a country music star, it was that gratitude and kindness would always win.

"You have a list of tables I can visit?" Harry asked.

"All of them," Boston said. "There wasn't anyone who didn't agree to be filmed."

"Okay." Harry had forgotten how many tables they'd set up in the main concert area. It didn't really matter. He would go around to all of them, say hello, thank people for coming, possibly get some shots that they could put on their social media to try to sell more tickets, and sign album covers, posters, or whatever else someone asked him to.

No, he didn't particularly want to do this concert, but he would put in a good faith effort to make it successful. Rebel Records had been good to him. They'd paid him a lot, and then allowed him to do this concert his way instead of traveling all over.

"Has anyone seen Belle?" he asked.

Though she wasn't playing with him that evening, he'd gotten a contract for her. She was playing ten shows in Jackson Hole—and would be paid a lot for them.

"I saw her on my way in," Bryce said as he came to Harry's side. "You ready to do this?" He hugged Harry, and getting a hug from Bryce was like hugging the Lord Himself.

"I'm ready," Harry said.

"All right," Bryce said. "I think they're waiting for us in the dining room."

"Dessert has just been served," Boston confirmed. "Everyone has their cheesecake and drinks for the duration of the concert now."

Harry's nerves boiled at him, just as they had every other time he'd had to perform. He told himself he'd done this many times before. He knew his songs inside and out. He had memorized everything about Devil's Tower. All he had to do now was get out there and do it.

"Do I have two minutes?" Harry asked.

"You have ninety seconds," Boston said, his eyebrows going up.

"All right." He grinned at Bryce and put his arm around him. "It's time for one of your toaster prayers, brother."

He grinned at his cousin and then raised his hand. "Everyone who wants to have prayer before we go out, over here."

His team immediately dropped what they were doing, stopped their conversations, their pre-concert rituals, all of it. They circled up around him, and he nodded to Bryce, his heart already full. "You're down to sixty seconds."

"Well, we better not be wasting any more time then," Bryce said, his personality as bright as the moon and the sun put together. "Dear Lord," he said, not even removing his cowboy hat. "We're real grateful that Harry's able to do his concerts from right here in Coral Canyon and Jackson Hole this year. Having somewhere to call home is such a blessing. And we're really grateful that within this room, we can be home when we're with each other. Bless every voice and hand and finger tonight as they sing and play that they will land in exactly the right spots, and that we can bring Thee glory through music and performing. Bless anyone who needs to hear a special message in one of the songs or through the lyrics, that their hearts will be open and their ears will be able to hear the messages that Thou has for them."

He paused, and Bryce had already prayed longer than they had time for, but Harry didn't rush him, and no one cleared their throat. Then Bryce simply said, "Amen," and their prayer circle broke up.

"Amen," Harry muttered to himself while others said it much louder than he did.

"Ten minutes, guys," Boston said. "Harry, let's go." He led the way out of the private dining room. Harry went second, with Bryce behind him and Adam following them all. As he approached the stage area and the section of the restaurant that had been cordoned off, Harry quickly counted the tables—twelve. They'd paid a premium price to be in that section, and Harry wanted to make it worthwhile.

"We need to give more time before the concert," he said to Boston. "There's twelve tables here—that's not even a minute per table."

"I'll check with The Branding Iron," Boston said. "See

how many they've got. Michelle won't have tables at the Daily Grind."

Harry sure did like how his cousin knew all of this in only a couple of short days. He knew Boston had just needed a chance to step into the spotlight.

"It'll be standing room only there, with coffee or decaf at the door."

Harry stuffed away his emotion, though it would bleed through in the songs, and he could use all he could get. "Three minutes per table, Boston. People might want to get something signed. And we don't have much time for that here."

"Yes, sir," Boston said.

Slightly frustrated, Harry stepped past everyone protecting him and entered the dining area. The first people who saw him gasped and started to clap. Harry waved them off, but the damage had been done, and soon enough the entire restaurant applauded. He grinned and met the woman's eyes who started it all.

"Pretty sure I failed your biology class," he said. "You don't need to be clapping for me."

This got some laughter, and Mrs. Hoffman grabbed onto him and hugged him. He embraced her back, taking precious moments to do so.

Harry moved quickly to say hello to those people in the reserved dining area. Adam had taught him to have tunnel vision, to keep his head down, focus on one thing, and don't make eye contact. But this was the opposite of that.

Harry tried to give everyone the time they wanted, to

say hello and thank them for coming. He scrawled his name on the cover of his third album several times, he laughed, he made expert small talk—and he knew when the main cameraman got up on his stool.

That meant he had one minute to be on stage. He still had four tables to go, and he looked at Bryce. They had not rehearsed anything, and Harry didn't want Bryce opening his first online world concert.

So he got up on stage, picked up the mic, and said, "We're going to be starting here in about a minute. I apologize to those of you who I didn't get to speak to yet. If you have something for me to sign or want to chat, I'm willing to stay after for as long as it takes." He grinned at his parents in a booth off to the side. Of course, they wouldn't take a table away from someone else, but he sure was glad to see them there.

He didn't see Belle either, and for half a second, he thought about saying her name into the microphone, just so that she would raise her hand, and he'd be able to see her. At the same time, Harry knew that would mortify her, so he simply scanned the restaurant.

When he met Adam's eyes, his assistant's eyebrows went up, clearly asking, *What are you looking for?*

Harry stood in front of a live mic, and Boston gestured him off the stage to come get his guitar. He wasn't supposed to start the live stream on the stage, and Harry got down as quick as he could.

"Where's Belle?" he muttered to Adam.

"She's got a table right on the other side of the wall here, sir," Adam said.

Harry wanted to go say hello, give her a kiss, and ground himself. Instead, his cameraman called out, "Five seconds," and added, "five...four...three...." and then only gestured, two—one—with his fingers before making a fist.

Zero.

It was time.

Harry transformed into the country music star he'd been for the past few years. They'd recorded a voiceover introduction already at Rebel Records, and Boston had donned a headset and proceeded to send out the drummer and then keyboard player, Harry's bassist, and their backup singers, all in time with that voiceover.

Boston put his palm on Harry's chest and watched the stage as people clapped and welcomed the band to Devil's Tower. The energy in the restaurant had spiked, but it wasn't full of tension, more like apprehension and excitement. When Boston lowered his fist, he placed his palm on Harry's back and said, "Go, go, go."

Harry jogged out into view of the camera. He wasn't Uncle Luke, and he didn't rip off his shirt and do backflips, but he raised both hands high above his head as the crowd in front of him got to their feet again.

Thirty people in the vicinity of the camera, and probably a hundred fifty in the whole restaurant, clapped for him. Harry brought his hands together in a praying gesture and bowed before he stepped up onto the stage, adjusted the mic, and said, "Welcome to the greatest small town in the world, Coral Canyon, Wyoming!"

HOURS LATER, HARRY SIMPLY WANTED TO TAKE BELLE back to her apartment and lay down on her cushy couch while they put something on TV. That had become his favorite thing, and he hadn't even known he needed it in his life.

But he liked being with her, and he liked that they sometimes talked and sometimes didn't. He liked how the world became very small while he lay on the couch with his girlfriend in his arms.

INSTEAD OF DOING ANY OF THAT, HE PULLED UP TO A big mansion in the gated community, having gone by Uncle Blaze's house on the right several houses back. Plenty of cars sat out front, and Harry peered at all the lit windows throwing light out onto the lawn and driveway.

"Here we go," he said.

"I should have driven myself," Belle said. "You're going to be here all night."

He was late to his own after-party because he'd stayed at Devil's Tower to greet people, talk to them, and sign albums and posters.

"We'll stay an hour," he said. "I do whatever I want."

She grinned over at him and said, "Of course, you do," with a slight laugh.

"I mean, I don't do *whatever* I want," he said.

"Yeah," she said. "Because if it was *whatever* you want, we'd go home."

"Is that what you want, my Belle?" he asked.

"Well, it's almost midnight," she said. "And I'm not exactly what you'd call a party animal."

Harry laughed because no, Belle did not have the party animal personality.

"It's the first concert," he murmured. "It went really well. We have to go in."

"Yeah, over fifty thousand tickets sold," she said. "For an *online* concert."

Harry couldn't help grinning. "Get as many as that in Atlanta."

"Okay, Mister Arrogant."

He looked over to her and grinned. "And bonus, I didn't have to fly there."

She leaned toward him and kissed him, and Harry really just wanted to do that for the rest of the night. Instead, he pulled away, got out, and came to help her down from the truck. The garage door stood up, and Harry went in that way instead of going to the front door. The country music bopped through the closed door as he approached. It faded into silence as he climbed a few steps to the cement pad and then opened the door, Belle's hand in his behind him.

Inside the house, he entered a mudroom, which provided a calm before the storm. Further in the house, he heard voices talking and laughing, but no one had put more music on yet.

"It looks like people are taking off their shoes here," Belle said, but Harry wasn't going to do that. He hated taking his shoes off in public. It felt demeaning, and he left her on a bench while she started to unlace her sandals to remove them.

"I'll be right back," he said. "You want something to drink?"

"Yes," she said. "Ginger ale or Coke Zero."

"You got it." He hovered in the doorway and peered out into the kitchen. Two of his backup singers stood at the island, nursing appetizers and drinks.

"I can't wait to meet his girlfriend," one of them said, a woman named Mariah who had a high soprano voice as clear as a bird.

"I don't care if I meet her," the other one—CeCe—said. "It's *Belle Graves*." She sneered out the name in a way that made Harry's ribs close in around his vital organs, ready to protect them violently.

"So?" Mariah said. "Do you know her?"

Harry's heart pounded. CeCe leaned in closer and said in a mock whisper, "She couldn't hack it in country music several years ago. She's a complete failure." She glanced into the living room, but not over her shoulder, toward the mudroom where Harry stood. "No wonder she's been buttering up to Harry. She probably thinks he can get her into the industry again."

. . .

"WELL, I STILL WANT TO MEET HER," MARIAH SAID, and she tossed her strawberry blonde hair over her shoulder and lifted her drink to her lips.

Harry wasn't sure what to do, and he became aware of Belle moving past him and toward the women. She said, "Hey, CeCe, what are you drinking?"

The other woman shrieked and said, "Oh my goodness, Belle, it's *so* great to see you again," in one of the fakest voices Harry had ever heard.

He scoffed right out loud, and that brought all three women's attention to him. Something dangerous and dark swirled within him, rose from his fingertips as they curled into fists, and moved up his arms and into his shoulders, and then his chest.

And Harry knew he was about to explode.

35

"Harry," Belle said, and she took a step toward him. "Don't." She refused to look at CeCe Holmes, for the woman didn't deserve her attention.

Harry actually growled at her, and oh, Belle didn't think she could stop this tornado. Maybe it was a tsunami, a hurricane, or both. He glared at her and then at the two women. "Belle is not my girlfriend just so she can get back into country music," he said in a plain, monotone, crisp voice. "You need to apologize to her right now."

Pure humiliation filled Belle, and she honestly should have expected this. The country music world was big and yet also really small, as evidenced by having CeCe Holmes here. She'd been a backup singer in Nashville for the past decade, and Belle had gotten to know her there in her last year of trying to make it with a record label.

"I didn't say that," Mariah said. "I said I was very excited to meet you, Belle." She smiled at her and said, "I'm Mariah Barry. It's nice to meet you."

Belle forced a smile. "Belle Graves."

She looked at CeCe, everything in her telling her to get out of there right now. Just run away. She hated that she had to put her sandals back on to leave the house. She hated that her raw emotions teemed just beneath her tongue. Tears gathered in her eyes, and she looked away, scanning down the bar to find something to drink.

"Come on, Harry," she said. "There's plenty of Diet Doctor Pepper here."

"No," Harry said. "CeCe needs to apologize, or CeCe will be finding herself another job."

"I'm sorry, Belle," CeCe said quickly. "Really."

BELLE TURNED FROM FURTHER DOWN THE COUNTER and watched as CeCe looked between Harry and then her. "Really, I'm sorry."

"It's fine," Belle said. "It's nothing."

Harry glared at CeCe as he moved past her and came to take Belle's hand in his.

"You don't have to do that," she whispered at him.

"Well, you're not my girlfriend just because I can get you into country music," he said loudly.

"Of course not," she hissed. "But she's not worth it, and you embarrassed me."

Harry towed her toward the living room, where several

of his bandmates waited, as well as Boston and Adam. They both watched him, clearly sensing something off, and Belle just wanted everything to be normal.

"Let's talk about this later," she said quietly, and then she pulled her hand away from Harry and went to congratulate Boston on his first successful online concert.

Harry interacted with his friends and crew, but he never lightened up. The storm inside him brewed, boiled, and blew. Belle didn't mind his grumpy attitude, and in fact, she found him downright attractive because of it—but not when it put her in the spotlight like it had tonight.

"You better take him home," Adam said about an hour later. "He doesn't look like he's having any fun at all."

He grinned at Harry, who simply rolled his eyes. "Yeah, I'm done for today." He got up from the couch where he'd been sitting and called around, "Thank you everyone for a great concert. Thank you. Thank you so much. Call time on Friday?" He looked at Boston, clearly expecting him to know the details he didn't.

Boston scrambled to his feet and set aside his can of Coke Zero. "Call time on Friday morning is seven a.m. at Daily Grind. Call time on Saturday, three p.m. at The Branding Iron. If you need anything, don't hesitate to contact me."

"Thank you," Harry said again, smiling now as he left the living room. "Really, thank you all."

Belle had done her best to talk to people, something she was quite good at. Nobody really scared her, as she'd had to interview plenty of people as a police officer. She didn't like being in the spotlight much, but all eyes came to her as Harry drew her to his side and placed a kiss on her temple.

"We'll see everyone in a couple of days," he said, and then he turned her toward the mudroom. Harry hadn't taken off his boots, but he waited for her while she re-laced her sandals on her feet. He then went outside to his truck and helped her in. They didn't speak on the way back to her apartment either. Belle wasn't sure what to say, and Harry clearly had too many words inside him.

As he pulled into the parking lot at her apartment building, he said, "I didn't mean to embarrass you."

"I know that," she said.

"I still want to fire CeCe."

"I wouldn't," Belle said. "She apologized, and you'll have to give a reason. And what are you going to say? She wasn't nice to my girlfriend?"

"Yes," Harry said. "That's exactly what I'm going to say. It's *my* concert tour. She doesn't have to be here."

Belle just shook her head. "It won't do any good. I'm sure she's not the only person who feels that way."

"Why would they?" Harry said. "You've never *once* asked me to introduce you to anyone. You didn't ask to be on this tour. You didn't ask to play for me. You *never* gave me a song." He pulled into a spot and jammed his truck into park.

Belle looked at him, wondering if he really didn't understand how most normal people thought. "But *they* don't know that, Harry. For all they know, I *did* do all those things."

She swallowed, the truth straining to come out. "And

besides," she said. "I did think about asking you for some tips on how to set up cameras and lights, so that I could play my songs on social media the way you do."

He blinked at her. "I can show you how to do that," he said.

"But is that me using you?" she asked.

"Social media is a really great place for musicians these days," he said. "It wouldn't matter if we were dating or not. You could totally do what I did. Hundreds and thousands of people do. You're not using me."

"Okay." She reached over and took his hand. "Are you going to be mad forever?"

"No," he said, but he still sounded totally mad.

"Is it too late for you to come in and lay on my couch with me?" Belle gave him a small smile, another sentence pressing against her vocal cords. "I think I need you to promise me one more thing."

"All right," he said. "What is it?"

"If you ever do feel like I'm using you, you have to tell me," she said. "Because the very last thing I want—when I met you last year, I didn't know who Harry Young was. When you texted me your name, I looked you up, and that's when I learned you were a country music star. And in fact, it was a strike against you."

"It was a strike against me?" he asked, incredulous. "How is having a good job a strike against me?"

"It was." She looked at his hand, their fingers inter-twined, and she played with his thumb. "Remember, I don't like country music. I didn't like the industry. I felt used and abused, and I never, *never* want you to feel like that. Not because of me."

"Okay," he said. "If you don't want to play in Jackson, you don't have to."

"I've already signed the contract. I thought long and hard about it. I prayed about it, and I can play in Jackson." She looked up at him, wishing she could just peel back the layers of her mind and let him see them. Let him see how important it was to her that he know her intentions were and always had been innocent and pure.

"People might fall in love with you," he said with a small smile. "They might think you're better than me. Rebel loved the twenty-second sample I sent them, and they've asked lots of questions about you already."

"I'm not going into country music," Belle said as she looked out the windshield and then through her side window. "I do like writing songs, though."

"Maybe we'll become a famous songwriting duo," he whispered.

Belle took a few seconds to really imagine what that would be like. She couldn't quite see it, because so many things in her life had not turned out the way she'd fantasized.

Her mind held so many memories of bad things, rough situations, terrifying emotions.

Then she turned to face Harry again, and all the purity and innocence he possessed filtered into her heart, giving her courage. "I asked your mom for a recommendation for a counselor."

Harry pulled in a breath and searched her face with those dark eyes. At least they didn't accuse her of anything.

"I know you don't like me talking to her too much," Belle said. "I swear I'm not—"

"You can talk to her as much as you want." Harry ducked his head, showing her the top of his cowboy hat. "I just want you to talk to me too."

"I *am* talking to you too," she said. "I feel like I need to talk to someone about my time undercover." She didn't speak very loud, almost like if she did, something black and ugly would come out and stain them both.

"The Sheriff's Department will pay for it. I've already filed the paperwork with Larry. They said anyone I pick here will be approved."

"All right," Harry said. "There's no problem with getting the help you need."

She reached over and cradled his face in her hand, causing him to lift his head and look at her. "Your mom said you saw a counselor when you were a teenager. For a little bit."

"Yep," he said. "I was really struggling with my mother's abandonment. My dad put me in counseling. It helped."

Belle nodded, somewhat surprised he hadn't gone into Grumpy Cat mode over his mom telling her something he hadn't divulged yet.

"I'm going to miss the show at Souper Salad next week," she said. "I've been called to Jackson to record testimony for the District Attorney."

"Okay," Harry said. "Do you want me to go with you?"

Belle nodded and pressed her lips together as they started to shake. "Yes, I want you to go with me," she said. "But you have a concert that night."

"It's at night," he said. "We'll be back in time."

"But what if we're not?" Belle asked.

"Then I'll call a car and head back here. You can drive my truck back and rush in last-minute to see my brilliant performance." He grinned at her, and she marveled at how he could turn any situation into something that made her smile.

"I want to go with you," he said. "When is it?"

"Wednesday," she said.

"Wednesday. I'll have Adam put it on my calendar."

A snake struck inside Belle's stomach, and she had to get the words out before they poisoned her. "Is there any part of your life you manage yourself?"

Harry once again blinked, blinked, blinked at her.

"I don't want Adam to know," she said. "I like him. He's a nice guy, and I know he's your best friend, and you trust him with everything. But isn't there anything that can just be...you? Stuff that just we know about?"

"This is just us right now," he said, a measure of frustration in his voice.

A new day had started an hour ago, and Belle simply wanted to head inside and go to bed. So she leaned toward Harry and kissed him gently before she said, "I'm just going to go to bed, okay? I'll see you tomorrow."

"All right," Harry whispered, but he didn't sound happy about it. "Can I bring lunch by?"

"Yeah," Belle said. "I'm just going to be looking for jobs online and finishing up paperwork for the Department. My last day is on Friday."

"I know." He tucked her hair behind her ear in such a sweet gesture that Belle wanted to stay in the car with him, or she wanted to invite him in to lay on the couch the way he wanted.

At the same time, they'd both had a very busy evening filled with a lot of ups and downs and roller-coaster-emotions. Belle wanted to figure out why what CeCe said had bothered him so much, and why him being unable to manage even one of his own appointments bothered her so much.

"See you tomorrow." She got out of his truck by herself. She didn't look back as she walked toward her apartment and started up the steps. "You knew who you were getting when you went out with him," she told herself. "It's unfair to now be upset that he acts like a celebrity when you *knew* he was a celebrity."

That was true, and yet Belle didn't want Adam to manage Harry's personal affairs. If he couldn't keep track of what day she needed to be in Jackson for her deposition, then she didn't want him to come.

Her phone sounded as she keyed her way into her apartment. She glanced at it, knowing it was Harry. *Sweet dreams, my Belle.*

Another text came in that said, *Can we lay on your couch tomorrow afternoon? It's my favorite thing to do.*

She smiled softly, closed the door behind her, and

locked it before she texted him back. *Why is that your favorite thing to do?*

She really didn't need a multitude of compliments, but she did want to know why Harry liked that so much. He didn't seem like a lazy man, as she'd seen him work harder than anyone Belle had ever met.

Because when it's me and you on the couch, he said. *It's just me and you. I feel strong and capable, and I can manage my own life when it's just me and you.*

"Me and you." Belle sighed out the words, because they too sounded like a song title for something she'd very much like to write.

Tell me what time we need to go to Jackson on Wednesday, and I'll put it on my calendar. And I'll be there. Adam won't be involved.

Belle sank onto her couch, relief running through her. *Thank you, Harry.* And then she typed out, *Yes, we can lay on the couch tomorrow afternoon—but only after we stop by the animal shelter again. I still want a cat.*

36

Harry walked along the aisle of crates, Belle's hand in his. "They have way more cats here today."

"They do," Belle replied. "It's amazing what a difference two days makes. I read online that they restock midweek in preparation for weekend adoptions."

She stopped in front of a crate holding a gray, white, and black cat. "Look how cute this one is."

For all the strength Belle possessed in her demeanor, her attitude, her personality, even her arms and shoulders, Harry did like the softer side of her. She hardly ever raised her voice. While she had an intense personality and believed deeply in things, she was quiet and more reserved.

She reminded him a little bit of Codi, though her coloring was the exact opposite. A swell of gratitude rose through him that his life included the small-town animal shelter, a good woman like Belle, and a slow Wednesday afternoon.

She motioned to the volunteer who'd been helping them. "I want to see this one."

She had taken a couple of other cats out of their crates. One of them had not settled into her arms at all, and Belle wanted a cuddly cat. Harry wasn't sure those two words went together in the same sentence, but Belle claimed they did. All of the cats he knew acted like queens and princes, their tails held mightily in the air as they stalked the earth looking for their next kingdom to rule. Or maybe that was just Aunt Georgia's cats, Onyx and Obsidian.

Harry smiled to himself as the volunteer unlocked the crate and gathered the cat into her arms. She passed it to Belle, who giggled and said, "Oh, he's chunky."

"He's one of our bigger shorthairs," the volunteer said. "His name is Simba. We got him yesterday. The vets already checked him, and he's in good health, ready to take home."

Belle met Harry's eyes, and he knew she'd be taking that cat home today. "Do you keep their names?" he asked the volunteer.

The woman blinked at him, and Harry had seen this look before. She recognized him. He labeled it *starstruck* because she somehow expected him to act differently than normal people. Uncle Luke had told him that would wear off over time, and Harry sincerely hoped so.

Maybe not during the concert tour, he thought, as he made a splash around town, disrupted regular dining time, and put on performances. His first four concerts had gone really well. Diners, bistros, restaurants, and pizza joints—heck, even a clothing boutique—had contacted him and asked if Harry would be willing to add more stops to his online tour.

But Harry was not willing to add more stops to his online tour. Even if he wanted to, Rebel would have to approve any dates and venues. They'd have to pay for the camera crew and the band, and more nights in that big mansion up the canyon. He didn't want any of it.

The online concert tour was thirty-six performances, three per week for twelve weeks. He'd done a full week and one concert this week, with two more to go. People would have plenty of opportunities to see him, and he figured the allure of crooning out country songs in a coffee shop would wear off pretty quickly.

Belle took Simba over to the play area and sat down with him. He looked up at her immediately, and Harry could admit the cat was super cute, with his all-white paws from the ankle down, his long tail in a darker gray with black stripes, and his white front chest. The shelter had bathed and cleaned him up, and he looked really amazing.

Belle crouched down and tossed a tiny play mouse a few feet away. Simba looked at it for a few long seconds and then pounced. Belle's laughter filled the room, and Harry felt himself slipping and sliding toward the edge of a cliff.

He still had plenty of questions about her time undercover. Or maybe he didn't. Maybe he simply needed to get to know her as she was now. He'd known her before too, and the core elements of her were the same. She loved Wyoming. She loved God. She loved cats.

And all he could do was hope that she could love him too.

She straightened and reached for his hand. Harry gladly gave it to her and helped her stand as she said, "I want this one."

"Just gonna get one, sweetheart?" He leaned over and pressed his lips to her temple.

"Yeah," she said. "I'm just going to get one for now."

She wouldn't have a job with the Sheriff's Department after Friday. They'd start rehearsing together for her concerts in Jackson, which started in three weeks. In fact, they'd practice a little bit later this afternoon.

As the volunteer went to start the adoption paperwork for Simba, Harry knelt down to play with the cat. "You never answered about cousin movie night." He kept his head ducked and his cowboy hat covering his eyes.

"I'm not a Young cousin."

"You're with me," he said. "Codi's gonna be there."

Belle did like Codi, and Harry knew they texted and talked, and he knew Codi wanted to have girls' luncheons with Belle and Kassie. As far as Harry knew, nothing like that had happened yet. Belle had only been in Coral Canyon for a week and a half, and she'd been unpacking, settling in, quitting her job, looking for another one, and now adopting a feline.

"You don't think your other cousins will care?" she asked.

"I think the other cousins would like to meet you," he said. "Without five thousand babies around."

The weight of her gaze made his neck bend even further. He finally looked up when he couldn't stand it anymore. "I guess that sounded a little bitter."

"Just a little," she agreed.

"Joey and Boston are coming," he said, wondering if he needed to go see a counselor about his feelings of…he wasn't even sure what he felt. Left out, maybe. He knew he wasn't the only one, that a lot of the older kids in the family—the ones from their daddy's first marriages—felt the way he did.

Added on. Extras. Leftovers, though they'd come first.

"Bryce and Codi, Reggie and Kassie, me and you."

"So do you think Joey and Boston will feel like it's a couple's night?" she asked.

"No," he said quickly. "Corinne is going to get Liesl and Rosie, so there'll be plenty of single people there."

His eyes burned into hers. "We're single."

"But we're a couple, Harry," she said, and he liked how easily the words came out of her mouth.

"Beth's in Jackson and won't come," he said. "Cash is training in Montana this week. He can't make it."

"Don't you have a couple of younger cousins?" she asked.

"Liesl and Eric, yep," he said. "Rosie said she talked to Liesl, but I haven't heard from her. And Eric…." Harry trailed off because Eric was also in a unique position within the Young family.

He was one of the older kids, yes. He did come from a

first marriage, yes. But that first marriage happened to be the same as his parents' second marriage.

All of his siblings were his full siblings, as Uncle Morris and Aunt Leigh had gotten remarried when Eric was only four years old. So the age gap wasn't quite as big as, say, between Harry and his younger sister, or Bryce and his.

Harry shook his head because he was determined to invite anyone fourteen years and older, and that included Eric. Thus, he'd invited him.

"It's pizza and ice cream sundaes and the movie *Twilight*," he said with a grin. "It's not serious."

Belle smiled back at him and tossed out a ribbon for Simba to try to catch this time. She pulled it away from him, though he caught it with his claws and it shredded a little bit.

"Let me see if I have this afternoon and evening mapped out for you," she said, and Harry liked this game.

He simply nodded and smiled. "Go on."

"We're gonna get this cat," she said, glancing over to Simba. "You're going to take me to the pet store so that I can get him a bed and some food and a few toys. Maybe a cat sweater or something."

She grinned, and oh, Harry liked the sight of those curled lips on her face.

"And then, we're going to go back to my apartment and we're going to practice for the concert."

Harry hadn't realized he needed to stop by the pet store, but otherwise, she had nailed the things on his agenda.

"At some point," she said. "We're going to put on a

movie, and you're going to hold me on the couch before we have to get over to your house, where your cousins will come over, you'll order pizza, and make ice cream sundaes, and we'll all watch *Twilight*."

"Technically," Harry said. "Reggie and Kassie are my aunt and uncle. But otherwise, that sounds about like the perfect afternoon and evening to me."

Belle tipped forward, and Harry knew that look on her face. He quickly slipped his cowboy hat off and pressed it to her back as he kissed her.

"Sounds about perfect to me too, cowboy," she said.

"Well then, let's get this cat and hit the pet store," Harry whispered.

She nodded, and they did exactly that.

When they arrived at her apartment, he helped her unload the cat toys while she clipped the price tag off the cat bed and situated it in the corner.

"Look, Simba," she said, only a slight coo to her voice now. "This is where you can sleep."

She showed the cat around to all the rooms, put out his food and water bowls, gave him both, and then turned, beaming to Harry. He'd removed all the price tags and product tags from the toys, and he nodded to them in the basket.

"Is this where you want these?"

"Yep," she said, and she came closer.

"This cat's made you real happy," he said, and Belle sobered.

"Yeah," she said. "I don't like coming home alone. And my other cats always greeted me."

"So they acted like dogs," he said.

She swatted his chest, and he fell back a mock step. "Cats can be nice."

"If you say so." He grinned at her and opened the drawer to put her scissors away.

"You didn't even look at dogs at the shelter. I know you didn't see any over the weekend you'd like, but surely they had new ones today."

"Surely," he agreed. Harry had toyed with the idea of getting a dog, but he didn't want to do it until the concert tour ended.

"What's on your mind?" she asked when he didn't say anything for several long seconds.

He glanced over to her, not really sure if this was what he wanted to add to today's agenda. "I was just wondering," he said anyway. "If you got an appointment with the counselor."

"Yep," she said. "I'm seeing Doctor Frederickson next week. Thursday."

"Mm, okay." He nodded at her while she took the cat toy basket over to the spot next to Simba's bed. "You don't have to tell me about it or anything." He turned to her fully and gazed across the room at her.

"You're so beautiful." He smiled, glad when she returned the gesture. "But I'd be willing to listen to anything you wanted to tell me about your time undercover."

All of a sudden, he realized why this had been gnawing at him. He wanted her to know that *he* was a safe place for her, that *he* would take anything she wanted to give him and hold it for her. *He* would bear it. *He* would carry it, so she didn't have to.

"I don't *need* to know. But if you wanted to, I'm here. I'm willing to listen, and I won't judge you."

Belle looked away, a slight wobble in her chin.

"Thank you, Harry," she said. "I've told my boss and the prosecutors, obviously." She moved over to her sliding glass door that went out onto a tiny balcony and simply looked out at the summer day. "It's not that I think you'll judge me or that I'm ashamed of any of it. It's just...."

Her shoulders lifted as she breathed, and everything in her sagged as she exhaled. "It's just a lot, and you already have a lot going on. And I don't know...."

He gave her another couple of seconds, and then he asked, "Will you look at me, please?"

She did instantly. No fear there, and Harry hoped all he broadcasted toward her was love and acceptance and kindness.

"Like I said, you don't have to tell me. I'm fine not knowing. But I don't want you to not tell me because you think I can't handle it or I'm too busy."

"I know you can handle it," she said.

"Then I'm too busy?"

"It's not that exactly," she said. "It's just, I don't want this to be what we talk about every time we're together."

"Sure," he said. "We used to talk about work at the

beginning of our video dates, and then move on to other things."

She offered him another small smile. "You're very good at compartmentalizing."

He laughed and said, "You're the queen of that, Belle."

She grinned too and turned to pick up her guitar. "Can we just play?" She looped the strap over her shoulder and looked at him. "I'm ready to play."

"I'm always ready to play with you." He moved out of her kitchen and over to the dining room table, where he'd put his guitar. He opened the case and pulled it out, and they started to warm up together—getting their fingers moving, tightening and loosening the strings on their guitars, and casting shy glances at one another.

Playing and singing with another person was an extremely intimate experience, and Harry's pulse quickened.

"I started working on some of our back and forth," he said. "That we'll do when you first come out on stage."

"Okay," she said. "I didn't know you had to write that out."

"I don't *have* to," he said. "We don't need to stick to the script every time, but it's nice to have an idea of what we might say to each other and how long it takes. And I always like to have something that segues right into the song."

"I can help you with something about the venues," she said.

"Exactly. Stuff like that. I'll have Uncle Morris send you a list of them."

She nodded, and then she moved easily into the opening notes of her song. Harry could sit with Belle and play the guitar forever, and as she sang the opening verse and he came in on the chorus, he couldn't help thinking that they worked really well together.

Their voices wove together and produced a sound that was neither his nor hers, but uniquely theirs. And the thoughts in his head moved into feelings in his heart that told him he could write songs with this woman for years, and he could love her, and they could raise a family together.

As they played through her song, hardly any mistakes from either one of them, he finally felt like the pieces of his life that he'd been laboring over for so long were finally coming together into a bigger picture—and that picture would not be complete without Belle Graves in it.

37

Kassie Avery glanced around the remodeled living room at Harry's house. She'd been here before, of course. She'd come to welcome him home and had stopped by with a bag of her sugar cookies after his first concert last week.

Now, she took in the boxes and boxes of pizza—far too many for the eleven people who had gathered here tonight. Of course, Cole, who was seventeen, had a hollow leg for a stomach. And Boston, Bryce, and Reggie were no lightweights either, not when it came to meat lovers pizza.

Kassie caught her husband's eye, her emotions immediately soaring toward the stratosphere. But this wasn't her party, nor her house, and she wasn't sure if Harry wanted to do any announcements or welcome speeches.

The doorbell rang, and he jogged toward it, saying,

"That'll be the ice cream," while everyone else stayed in the back of the house, talking and laughing.

Kassie wanted to join them, but her skin felt stitched on wrong. She wasn't sure why, other than large groups of people made her nervous, especially the Youngs—which also didn't make sense, as she'd been an honorary member of the Young family for many years now.

She attended everything with Bryce. In the eight years since they bought the Rising Sun Ranch and lived in Dog Valley with his family nearby, his grandmother brought her food, as did his mom and aunt. And whenever they needed help on the ranch, all of his uncles came right over, ready to step in.

Kassie loved them all, but they also reminded her that her family was not like this. *So you'll create one that is*, she thought as Harry returned to the kitchen with at least a gallon of ice cream for every person.

"My word," Codi said in that dry tone she had, and which Kassie loved. "How many people did you think were coming tonight?"

"I like ice cream," Harry said with a grin, obviously determined to be joyful tonight. "Plenty of leftovers."

She wondered if his door was as open as Bryce's and if his family just walked through it all the time. Probably, as he lived in town, much closer to everyone than Bryce did. Kassie loved her and Reggie's little red brick cottage out of the way. No one ever came there who didn't mean to, and she always knew when someone was coming.

"All right," Harry said after he'd heaved the gallons and

gallons of ice cream onto his dining room table. "Welcome to our first cousin movie night." He grinned, his enthusiasm for this event contagious.

"In the Young family," he said. "We usually start with some announcements. And I don't know if anyone has anything they want to tell us all tonight just for this crowd. I want you to know that whatever we do here is just between us, for this middle generation of Youngs." He gave a half smile, as if he'd just come up with the label for their group. "I think my only announcement is that I'm obviously an over-buyer. So eat as much pizza and ice cream as you can while you're here."

Everyone laughed, and they all looked around at one another. Kassie was the oldest one there besides Reggie, who had a couple of years on her. The group ranged from the fourteen-year-olds like Rosie and Liesl, all the way to her and Reggie—who was nearing forty.

She understood what Harry was trying to do: take the cousins from all of their daddy's first marriages and make them feel important, make sure they didn't get lost or over-looked, make sure they felt like Youngs too.

Bryce had often felt left out, like he didn't belong, like he was an add-on, like his daddy had started a second family and left him behind. Kassie understood feeling like a second-class citizen inside her own family, and she wouldn't wish it on anyone.

But teenagers and twenty-somethings didn't usually make "announcements" at any of the family parties. So she wasn't surprised to hear only silence streaming through Harry's house.

Then she raised her hand halfway and said, "Reggie and I have something."

Her throat closed, but she swallowed hard against the knot forming there. She'd already called and told her mom, and the next step would be to tell Bryce and Codi, who stood right in front of her.

She could tell Reggie's sister too, and then the news would go out to the entire Young family. She cleared her throat. "I'm going to have a baby in December."

A beat of silence filled the house, and then Harry whooped. He started to clap, his smile as wide as she'd ever seen it on the stages around America. "That's so great." He came over to her and hugged her tight. "Way to go, Aunt Kassie."

He loved teasing her that she was his aunt, and Kassie always returned the favor. She hugged him back, gave Belle a light hug, and then faced Bryce and Codi. They drew her into their arms at the same time, and she wept happy tears against her best friend's shoulder.

She and Bryce still worked incredibly well together at the Rising Sun Ranch, but their relationship had definitely changed. It had to, because she was married to her best friend now, as was Bryce. They still needed each other. Their relationship was still special and one-of-a-kind, but it wasn't the same as it had been when they'd bought the ranch and moved here together.

Sometimes Kassie mourned it, and other times she

thanked the good Lord above that she'd been able to transition. Some of the things she used to tell Bryce and rely on Bryce for, she'd now take to Reggie. He wanted that just as much as he'd wanted to be a father.

While it hadn't been easy for her to get pregnant, and God might only give them this one baby, Kassie was determined to devote everything she had to her husband. She stepped out of Bryce and Codi's arms and moved right to Reggie's side. They hugged him next, and no one else had anything to announce, so Harry said, "Let's load up with pizza and ice cream and get this movie started."

"I'll come babysit for you," Rosie said, coming to Kassie's side. "I'm a real good babysitter."

"I've heard that," Kassie said. She smiled at the teenager who possessed so much spunk and spirit. "I'd love to have you come babysit for us."

Rosie grinned. "I hope you have a girl. Girls are the best." She immediately joined the fray to get food, because she never seemed to get enough to eat either.

Kassie grinned at her, though part of her feared having a baby girl. Or rather, a teenage one she couldn't just carve a pumpkin with and then send home.

She told herself she had a long time before she'd have to deal with a teenager as she got in line and picked up a couple of pieces of pizza. She enjoyed seeing Rosie, Liesl, and Corinne be so close, and she noted that Boston and Cole didn't get too far from Harry. From Cole to Boston to Harry spanned almost a decade, but the three of them got along great.

"You want meat lovers or supreme?" Reggie asked.

Kassie's stomach swooped. "I don't know if I can eat any pizza," she said, looking at one of the boxes that held the all-meat pie. "It's so greasy."

"Ice cream then?" Reggie said. "It looks like he got about fifty kinds. I know what you like." He grinned and went to get her dessert for dinner.

She watched him go and then turned back to Codi and Bryce. She caught Codi wiping her eyes quickly, and an alarm sounded inside her. But then Belle joined them and said, "Congratulations, Kassie."

"Thank you." She nodded toward the fridge. "I heard you say that pizza looks greasy, and I know Harry has some baked potato soup in his fridge. Would you like me to heat that up for you?"

Kassie's first instinct was to say no. She didn't typically like people fawning over her. And she was still getting to know Belle, so she definitely didn't want to make her do anything. As she opened her mouth to say no, she was fine, Bryce said, "Yeah, she'd love that, Belle."

Kassie glared at him.

"What?" He took her empty paper plate from her. "You love baked potato soup. It's my grandma's, and you were just complaining yesterday that you'd eaten yours too fast."

"Okay, I'll heat it up," Belle said, and she glanced at Kassie and then Codi and Bryce as she walked away.

"You're holding up the pizza line," Bryce said with a grin, and Kassie fell back a step to let him by.

"The movie's starting!" Harry called. He had two full-size couches, as well as beanbags in his living room, so there'd be plenty of places to sit.

"Here you go, baby," Bryce said, handing Codi a plate laden with pizza. That had to be for both of them, and Kassie wondered why he didn't just take a whole box over to the couch. Either she'd imagined Codi's brief appearance of tears, or Bryce really was just that chipper. He *was* one of the more positive people Kassie had ever met and known, something she really liked about him.

"Pralines and caramel, sweetheart," Reggie said, handing her a bowl. "I'm going to claim a place on the couch for us, okay?"

"Okay," she said, and she let him lead her over to it before he went to get his own dinner.

Belle brought her a bowl of soup, and everyone found a place so that they could watch about teenage vampires in Washington State. Kassie was nearing the end of her first trimester. The baked potato soup went down so much easier than a piece of pizza would have, and she prayed that she'd start feeling better soon.

But she knew that no matter what, no matter if she threw up every day, no sacrifice would be too great to bring Reggie's baby into the world.

38

Belle paced like a caged tiger in the appointed backstage room at the ritzy restaurant where she'd be playing her first concert gig in over ten years.

The Globe in Jackson Hole required reservations, and men had to wear jackets. Women couldn't wear shorts. Everything about this moment felt wrong, like she'd been dropped into someone else's life and couldn't get out.

"Belle," Boston said.

When she turned to face him, the world narrowed to just his handsome features, his wide eyes, and that headset he wore.

"You're on in five," he said. "Harry only has one more song, and then we'll be introducing you."

She nodded, her teeth clenched together. She wanted to run out the back door of this restaurant and vomit. Then she'd get in her car and just drive as far and as fast as she could. She knew the way to northern Wyoming, and she could go even further into Montana, up through Canada, and never have to be seen again.

It was a strange thought for someone who had worried so much about being seen and heard. Boston didn't turn and leave because his job was to make sure she got delivered to the stage with her guitar ready to go.

Harry had wanted her to wear a funky T-shirt the way he did, but Belle had flatly refused. People already thought she was using him for her advantage, and the last thing she wanted to do was copy his T-shirts. So she wore what Belle felt most comfortable in: a pair of blue jeans, a pair of cowgirl boots with a really pointy toe, and a sleeveless blouse made of the lightest fabric she could find.

She knew she looked good in lavender and blue, and she'd found this blouse just down the street at one of the high-end boutiques. It billowed in a pale purple with blue and navy flowers splashed across it.

Belle had loved it on sight, and it fit great as well. She'd spent too much money on it, but Harry said the concert tour had a budget and that he could pay for her wardrobe. She'd taken him up on that, and she prayed with everything she had as she left the corner of the room to collect her guitar that no one would find out about the clothes he'd bought for her.

"All right," she said. "I'm ready."

"You're warmed up and everything?" Boston asked.

She nodded in tight bursts as she looped the strap of her guitar around her neck. "I'm ready," she said again. She'd been back in this room, warming up, singing, strumming her guitar, and pacing for the past hour since Harry's live stream had started.

As she left the room behind Boston, she coached herself with every step to just take one more. *Please be with me*, she prayed. *I don't have to be perfect, but please don't let me make a fool of myself.*

Belle hadn't performed live for a long time, but she knew that *live* meant *no do-overs*. They couldn't stop and go back to the beginning the way she and Harry had just yesterday when she'd made a mistake.

For all the times that Belle had wanted to be seen, she couldn't believe that she didn't want that now. In fact, she didn't want any eyes on her at all.

Boston brought her to the edge of the camera range where she'd stood when Harry had come out to greet everyone at the Globe. He'd taken forty-five minutes before the concert even started to go around and talk to patrons and guests, sign albums and posters and T-shirts and cards, and then he'd jogged out from this very spot, taken his guitar from the bassist, and welcomed everyone to Jackson Hole.

It was his first concert tour here, and he'd already played with Bryce, which meant his cousin sat out in the audience. As Belle watched, he casually lifted a glass of soda to his lips and took a drink. Codi sat with him, at a table for four alongside Kassie and Reggie. Belle really didn't want to perform now, because none of them had heard her sing before.

"No one has," she whispered.

"What was that?" Boston asked, leaning closer.

She shook her head. "Nothing."

Harry finished the song he was playing, and he grinned out into the crowd as they clapped and whooped and cheered for him. Then he twisted his guitar around to his back and leaned into the mic.

"You come out when he says your name," Boston hissed, and he didn't wait for Belle to confirm before he took off. He carried a stool in his hand and went right up on the stage, placing it next to where Harry stood. Then he jogged back toward her and picked up the next one.

"My next number is one that I didn't even write," Harry said. "It comes with a very special guest who's only performing with me for the next ten shows, right here in Jackson Hole, Wyoming."

"We chose Jackson Hole for her to perform with me, because she lived and worked here for several years, and she loves this small mountain town and all its restaurants and shops and tourists as much as I love Coral Canyon."

He looked over to her, his smile absolutely radiant, and Belle once again felt like she might throw up. She couldn't return the smile, but Harry acted like she had.

"She's a gorgeous singer and a talented songwriter, and she also happens to be my girlfriend."

He threw his hand toward her and said, "Please, welcome to the stage here at the Globe in Jackson Hole: Belle Graves."

The crowd clapped appropriately for someone they'd never heard of before, but who obviously excited Harry. Belle forced herself to take the first step out of the shadows. She did, instantly feeling the weight and zoom of the cameras as they landed on her. She walked toward the stage, her smile suddenly there, and she took the two steps up and right into Harry's arms.

Harry had left his mic to greet her. He paused, hugged her, swept a kiss along her cheek, and whispered, "We've got this," in her ear. Before he turned to face the restaurant crowd and cameras again, he took her hand and led her back toward the mics, where he stopped at hers and said, "Isn't she amazing?"

Bryce, Codi, Reggie, and Kassie all cheered louder than the others, yee-hawing and whooping, and that made Belle grin all the wider as she shook her head at them. Harry settled himself onto his stool, getting his guitar into position, and Belle did the same. Her mic was too high, and Boston adjusted it for her.

"Thank you, Harry," she said. "You're too kind."

"I'm just glad she said yes, folks," Harry said, and that caused laughter to go through the restaurant. Harry chuckled too and asked, "In all seriousness, how long was it until our real first date?"

Belle knew this script, but he sounded so natural, and she hoped she could be as well. "I met Harry when I was looking for someone who had been reported missing," she said, gazing out into the crowd. She looked straight into the camera, imagining that she was at lunch with her best friend. "I had no idea who he was, and he was real cagey about what he did for a living. Wouldn't tell me where he lived, told me he had a job, but he 'just wasn't working right now,' that kind of stuff."

Harry laughed right out loud. "I did totally do all that, and this was after I answered the door without wearing a shirt."

Belle laughed too, and the sound of it made her marvel. She sounded truly happy, and Belle wanted nothing more than to be happy. As she looked at Harry under the bright lights that had been set up specifically for this concert in this restaurant, Belle had the distinct thought and feeling and confirmation that she was where she was supposed to be. She reached over and threaded her fingers through Harry's.

"He asked me out pretty much right away," she said. "But I wouldn't commit because he didn't live here. In fact, I'm pretty sure I said something like, 'I live in Jackson, and you live here, there, or Nashville, and that's nowhere near Jackson.'"

She grinned and said, "We had a few phone dates before life blew up. And then somehow, miraculously, God brought us back together in the airport, of all places."

Harry wore a soft grin and so many feelings in his expression. "Finally, airports are good for something," he said, and that caused more laughter.

"This song is called 'These Empty Halls,'" Belle said, sticking to the script, though part of her wanted to derail everything. "I wrote it a while ago in my own failed attempt to become a country music singer. It's for anyone who's ever loved someone or something so deep that you can still feel them after they're gone."

She nodded over to Harry, who said, "'These Empty Halls,' ladies and gentlemen."

She started to strum, and just like always, whenever she played this song, her fingers knew their spots on the strings, and every movement felt effortless. A constant prayer moved through her mind as she plucked closer and closer to the first word she'd need to sing all by herself.

"I walk these empty halls where memories still linger."

Harry joined her then, his guitar adding body and fullness to hers. He was such an expert at what he did that he made no mistakes, and Belle sank into the song. When his voice joined hers on the chorus, "I come home to shadows where your love still holds me tight," Belle had to dig down deep to hold her tears back and keep her voice strong.

She played until the end, Harry adding the riff that he'd written just for his guitar to finish out the piece. She looked over to him, pure joy bursting through her. He grinned back at her. Finally, they played the last note, and they let their guitars reverberate through the space.

Everyone in the restaurant seemed to be holding their breath, wondering if that was really the end of the song or not. Finally, Belle took her hands off her guitar. Harry did too, and the restaurant erupted.

They had a planned outro too, because Belle was only playing this one song with him. With the talking and the playing, she only had to be on stage for seven minutes. Never had they rehearsed Harry getting up and yelling, "Isn't she incredible?" before he drew her into a big cowboy bear hug.

But he did do that, and Belle had to bow several times as the applause went on and on before she could get away from the stage and breathe.

And she instantly wanted to get back out there and perform again.

EVERY CELL IN BELLE'S BODY STILL VIBRATED AS HARRY followed her into her hotel room that night. They'd be living and staying in Jackson for the next month, and he had a suite up a few floors and down the other hall.

"I just can't believe it," Belle said, her eyes glued to her phone. "These comments are actually nice."

Harry chuckled behind her and closed the door. "I told you it would be amazing."

He had, but still. "Boston put up a twenty-second clip of the song," she said. "Forty-nine minutes ago." She turned toward him, her eyes as big as she'd ever made them. "It has three million likes and just over a million comments already."

She held up her phone, pure disbelief pouring through her. "And they're all nice."

Her portion of the concert had been finished for less than two hours. Boston had recorded the song with Harry's phone, and then posted a shortened clip with the words, *Debut performance by country music sensation Belle Graves, only in Jackson with me for the next nine shows.*

That was the whole caption on Harry's social media,

and then of course the hashtags that Harry and Boston and Uncle Morris had chosen for this tour. Then there was Belle's name: #BelleGraves, #TheseEmptyHalls, her self-titled song.

The one she couldn't get a record label in Nashville to pick up and produce.

"It's just unbelievable."

"You've gone viral, baby," he said, his arm snaking around her. "Are you too big-time to lay with me on the couch?"

Belle couldn't tease back with him right now, because she'd never been viral. She wasn't the type of woman to go viral, and she didn't know how to deal with viral eyes.

"This is scary for me," she whispered, and she laid her head against Harry's chest so she could listen to the steady thrum of his heart and try to find strength and courage from it.

"It's scary, all right," he whispered. "Because you're gonna have fifteen hundred people from Nashville calling you after this."

"Don't say that," Belle said.

"Well, you're not going to go to Nashville, are you?"

"No," she said.

"You won't even consider it?" he pressed.

Belle sighed as she pushed out of his arms. She'd told him about her experience in Nashville and how she'd had a manager who'd stolen from her and ruined everything. She paced away from him and over to the window.

"You don't have to decide right now," he said as he came

up behind her. He slid one hand along her arm. The strength of his chest behind her back felt so comforting and so warm.

"Come lay down."

She let him lead her to the couch, but it wasn't very comfortable at all. He groaned as he sat back up. "This is terrible," he said. "Maybe the couch in my room will be better." He looked over to her. "You want to try it?"

She looked twenty feet over to the bed, but she wasn't sure if she could suggest that they lay there, even if they didn't do anything but hold each other and talk about the incredible concert Harry had just finished and her tiny, seven-minute part in it. He must have seen her looking, because he looked that way too. Then he got up without a word, took her hand, and led her over to the bed.

He kicked off his boots and climbed on first, and Belle eased into his arms, both of them lying on top of the comforter.

"Yeah, this is way nicer," he murmured.

"Tell me how it's just me and you," she said. "Tell me how small the world is right now."

She couldn't even imagine all those people online listening to her song, even if it was only twenty seconds. Boston had, of course, posted a snippet where both Harry and Belle were playing and singing together, as it was Harry's social media and Harry's concert tour.

"The world is so small," Harry whispered. "It's just this room. Just this bed. It's just you in my arms, and me at your side."

He started to take a breath, and Belle mimicked him. She held hers while he did, and then she exhaled, letting everything go—the enormity of the sky, the vastness of the universe—until everything narrowed down to just Wyoming, then Jackson Hole, then this hotel, then just her room, then just her and Harry lying on the bed together.

"You're safe with me, Belle," he whispered, and that made tears come to her eyes. She leaned her head back and looked at this dark, beautiful, handsome cowboy.

"I'm falling in love with you, Harry," she said.

He didn't grin or beam or put on any of his celebrity persona. He simply growled out, "Good," and kissed her.

39

Harry raised his hand when the waiter said, "Ribeye, medium rare, no onions," and the man put his food in front of him.

He had to admit that this leg of the tour in Jackson felt more like what he'd done for the past two albums. Living out of hotel rooms, eating at restaurants with the band and crew after every show, laughing, smiling, making friends and bonds and memories.

"Crispy chicken sandwich," the waiter said next, and Belle raised her hand.

Harry grinned over at her plate of food because, in this high-end restaurant, their meal for tonight looked amazing.

"That looks good," Harry said, taking in the golden, crispy onion rings. Belle loved onion rings.

"Sure does," she said. She leaned closer and hugged his bicep. "Can I have some of your French fries?"

She'd ordered onion rings with the expectation that they could split and share, so he'd get half fries, and she'd get half onion rings.

"Sure thing," he said, and he pushed his plate a little closer to hers.

She only had two more shows with him in Jackson, and then they'd go back to Coral Canyon for the last month of the tour. She'd been getting daily solicitations from managers, talent scouts, agents, and record producers in Nashville since the first show had aired a few weeks ago. She told him about all of them. Every. Single. One.

Harry had listened to her read every email, all the excitement in Belle's voice, and he tried to be the best supportive boyfriend he could. But deep down, Harry did not want her to go to Nashville. In fact, late at night, after he finally finished everything for the day, in the deepest, darkest part of the evening, fear crept in—fear that she would leave Coral Canyon, fear that he was not a strong enough force hold to keep her there, fear that, once again, the timing of their relationship wasn't right.

Harry pushed hard against that fear as it crowded into his throat right there at the dinner table. The clanking of silverware against plates, his friends talking, and all the delicious scents of the food couldn't drive away the fact that the country music industry hadn't been ready for Belle ten years ago, but they certainly were now.

She had told him a couple of times that it sure was nice to have her talent recognized. And while she hadn't been seeing a counselor since the tour started, Harry had seen her come alive on the stage in a way she hadn't been before.

Some people were simply meant to perform. His dad, Uncle Tex, Uncle Luke, Uncle Otis, Bryce—they all had talent and charm and charisma in spades, and Belle did too. They bantered back and forth for a few minutes before they played her song. The script was long gone because, while she looked like a frightened field mouse in the very moment before she stepped on stage, the second her foot hit those planks, she switched on.

She was still his Belle. He could still see her there, all the very best parts of her on display for everyone else to see too.

"You're not eating," she said, and he jolted a little bit because he'd once again lost himself in his thoughts—his worrisome thoughts about losing Belle before he'd really had a chance to have her—because he loved laying on the couch with her.

And since they'd been in Jackson, he got to hold her in a bed, and he could admit that he'd spoiled himself, and he'd started thinking of them as husband and wife laying in their own bed in his house in Coral Canyon. It was quiet and slow, and everything that Harry needed in his life after eight years in the country music industry.

But Belle had had that quiet and slow life during those eight years. As he dipped his head and gave her the best smile he could, which wasn't a smile at all, he prayed, *Please, dear Lord, please don't let me lose her. Please don't take her from me. Please, please, please.*

"Yeah, just admiring my steak," he said. "They got a perfect sear on this thing."

"It's incredible," Jordy, his bassist, said from down the table. "Man, Wyoming's the place to come if you want a good steak."

Harry grinned at him and cut off one of the perfectly browned, crispy corners of his steak. "You want some, sweetheart?"

Belle was a food sharer, which Harry didn't mind at all, and she did take a couple of pieces of his steak and sample two of the steak sauces that had been brought out.

"I don't like that raspberry one," she said. "Too sweet." She wiped her mouth with her napkin, and Harry grinned at her.

"I think that *beet soup* got you all confused," he said. "This sauce is not sweet." He swiped his steak through it because the saltiness and richness of the meat cut through the sweetness of the raspberry steak sauce perfectly. "It's incredible." He put the bite in his mouth and groaned in an over-exaggerated way.

Belle laughed, and some of Harry's fears faded into the night.

He always took Belle back to her room at the end of the night, and they stayed there for a little while together, shrinking the world, calming the noise, and talking intimately. It was his favorite part of Jackson Hole, and one he wanted permanently in his life. Tonight, as he kicked his boots off and climbed on her bed, he said, "I love listening to you laugh, sweetheart."

She grinned at him and flopped down on the bed next to him, her arm sliding across his waist to his back. "This tour has been way more fun than I thought it would be."

"Yeah?" He brushed her hair back, enjoying the silky, soft quality of it. "You thought you wouldn't like it?"

"I thought I'd hate it," she admitted.

"Your opinion of country music has changed," he said, and it wasn't a question.

"Yeah, you could say that."

Oh, he'd said it all right. "How many emails did you get today?" he asked.

"Just two," she said with a sigh.

"Phone calls?"

"Only one of those."

Frustration frothed in Harry's veins. She told him about the emails and calls, and she'd even gotten some direct messages on social media as hers had blown up with every additional concert where she performed.

She didn't have a professional account for her songwriting or her music, but simply a personal username that people had tracked down. And she'd never, ever told him what she was going to do with all the emails, the solicitations, the phone calls.

And he had to know.

"Can we talk about something serious?" he asked.

"We can talk about anything you want."

"I need to know what you're thinking about...." He paused for a minute, because he wasn't sure what to put in the blank. Country music? Nashville? Songwriting?

"—about the emails and phone calls," he said. "Are you... going to answer any of them? And what are you going to say?"

"I suppose I should answer them, shouldn't I?" she asked in a quiet, serious voice.

The Belle he'd first met, the one who had called concerned when she'd seen the video of him falling on the baggage carousel, the one who took a few minutes to warm up on their video dates, the one who told him she was going to go undercover.

"I mean, you should probably answer them, yes," he said. "And that's what I want to know too. I want to know what the answer is to their questions, their interest."

Belle threaded her fingers through one of his belt loops on his side. "I know what the answer is." She cleared her throat and settled further into his arms. "Sort of."

"Sort of?"

"I don't want to be what you are, Harry."

Relief like he'd never know flowed through him, but he sensed a really big "but" in there.

"I can't command a stage for two hours," she said. "I do okay for seven minutes, and I love singing and playing with you."

"I really like it too," he said.

"Do you know how many songs I've written since I moved to Coral Canyon?" she asked.

"Oh," he said with a slight chuckle. "Someone's been holding out on me."

She giggled into his chest and said, "I've told you."

"No, Miss Belle, you have *not* told me that you've been writing songs," he said. "Not a single word of that has met my ears."

Belle giggled again, the sound sweet and pure and tapering quickly. "Four," she said. "I've written four songs in less than two months. I didn't even do that when I was in Nashville. It's just like the words are there, the inspiration is there. It's like Coral Canyon has this magic conduit that my creativity has tapped into."

"It's a pretty special place," he said, pushing her hair back and running his fingers along the top of her ear and down her neck.

"So I want to tell all the music producers that, no, I'm not going to come to Nashville and be a country music artist, but I want their connections," she said. "They're the people that we're going to be selling songs to, and I don't want to rely on you to sell my songs."

"You're not using me, baby," he said, something she'd been very concerned about.

"So I've been toying with emailing them back," she said. "And letting them know that I write all my own music, and I'm happy to talk to them about that music and maybe suggesting artists that would be good fit for it, but that I don't actually want to be an artist myself." She lifted her head, and Harry met her eyes. "Is that a good idea?"

"I think it's a brilliant idea," he said. "There's nothing wrong with networking, and *they're* coming to *you*."

"Yeah, that's what I thought." She smiled at him, but it didn't stay long and it didn't reach her eyes.

Those held nothing but worry and anxiety, and he cradled her face in his hand and said, "Tell me what else is bothering you."

"I think it's just the enormity of this," she said. "You've been living it for a while, so I think you're more used to it. But every day I feel like I wake up in a dream. It's not my life; it's someone else's."

"All that matters," Harry said. "Is that it's a life you want to live. So I guess that's the question that you have to answer: Is the life you're living right now the one you want to keep living?"

Harry really wanted her to say yes or something like, *Only if we get married, Harry,* and then kiss him. She didn't do either, but her eyes stayed round as moons, wide and worried, and she didn't say anything, which only sent Harry's round of anxiety and adrenaline to that deep, dark place where all of his hidden fears lived.

40

"It goes over there, baby," Everly said to Clay, who bobbed under the weight of the speaker.

This year, for the Fourth of July celebration in the park, Everly had organized a children's dance-off to take place in the early evening, right before the food trucks and booths shut down for the concert and subsequent fireworks. The clock ticked closer and closer to four when her event would start, and sweat ran down her neck and forehead from the July heat.

Trace had filled a wheelbarrow with ice, fruit-flavored sodas, and various flavors of lemonade, and he currently stood with all the kids while Everly finished her preparations for the dance. He manned the stroller with Avery in it, their little girl who was about twenty months old now.

Those past twenty months had really taken their toll on Everly, even if she didn't want to admit it. She had not had quite the postpartum depression with Keri and Clay that she'd dealt with with Avery, and she thanked the good Lord above that she'd started to feel more like herself this year.

She couldn't quite describe what it felt like to live each day without color. She was awake. She was alive. There was just nothing to it. The sky wasn't blue. The birds didn't chirp. Nothing brought happiness or joy. Everything simply existed in shades of gray. She fed her kids. She worried over Harry. She cried more than ever.

Trace had been steady and strong by her side, and she'd seen a counselor and gotten on medication that had introduced a blip of color in her life. But really, it made her numb.

And she didn't want that either.

But for months, she existed in numb grayness. In the end, she decided that wasn't working for her either. She did not want to miss Clay's first day of first grade, or Avery's first step, or the day when Keri got her ears pierced when she turned eight.

She wanted to live and breathe joy, to experience life in bold strokes and bright color. So she'd gone off the medication, stayed with the counselor, and started working through anything she could.

An alarm went off on her phone, and Everly reached to silence it as she connected the cable from the stereo system to her phone. She turned and faced Trace and all the kids, a smile on her face that felt real for the first time in months.

"All right," she said as she danced over to the kids. "Who's ready for this?"

The kids all jumped and squealed, and one of the things Everly had done to introduce more vibrancy in her life was to return to her studio. She'd never sold it, but she had hired teachers so that she could raise her kids and be there for them after school instead of in the studio.

But in January, she had taken back a tiny tots ballet class and the teen hip-hop class. It took two hours of her week, and Trace didn't have a job. He could be with the kids in the afternoon just fine—every afternoon if she wanted him to— and she had started to feel more like herself.

"All right, all soda cans have to go in this bucket," Trace said, and he held up a huge garbage can. "Soda cans here. Make sure they're empty. Dump them out on the grass over there."

She loved watching her tall, dark, cowboy husband interact with children, because it showed the opposite side of who he pretended to be in Country Quad.

"Come on out onto the dance floor," she said, indicating the area that she had roped off with burlap ribbon. "You're going to need a few feet around you, so spread out."

She had come up with a simple routine to teach the kids —a twenty-four-beat dance—and then they would do a dance-off. Everyone would go home with a prize and hopefully a smile, including Everly.

All three of her kids attended, though Avery was barely big enough to bounce up and down in her diaper and her red, white, and blue striped romper. She made Everly laugh more than once, and by the time the class finished, it felt like she had climbed Mount Everest.

Trace and the kids helped her clean up, putting every-thing in one big bin that her husband lifted with his strong muscles and put in the wheelbarrow.

"Let's go, kids," he said, and they made the trek from the boutique and food truck area to the three red umbrellas that Cecily set up every year. Those umbrellas were a beacon, a homing call for all the Youngs, the Whitakers, and the Hammonds. Because Everly had done the dance, she, Trace, and their family approached a large group of people who'd already set up and already started to eat whatever Trace's momma had brought.

When Otis spotted them, he jumped to his feet and went to help Trace by taking the tote off the top of the wheelbarrow. "How'd it go?" he asked.

"We've got loads of soda and lemonade left," Trace yelled, parking the wheelbarrow next to the table where Cecily had spread out the food. "Come on, kids. Come get something to drink."

Everly loved Cecily and Jerry with her whole heart, and she leaned down to hug the older woman who'd become her mother figure in the past decade.

"How'd it go?" she asked, patting Ev's shoulder.

"Real good," Ev said. "Felt good to be out there again."

Cecily sandwiched one of her hands between two of her papery, weathered ones. "I'm sure it did, dear. There's plenty of food, and I saved you one of the peach tarts since I know you don't like cooked apples."

Ev grinned at her, her heart filled with so much love. "Thank you, Cecily." She hugged Jerry and gave him a quick kiss before she moved over to the table to help her kids get dinner.

How Cecily had so many different family recipes that could feed a crowd, Ev would never understand. But this year, she saw that Shawn had brought all the sides, and Cecily had simply made huge trays of sweet and sour meatballs. The rolls and buns she recognized from Pork and Beans as well.

She glanced around to find her brother sitting with Reggie and Kassie, who held Shawn and Enid's youngest, a four-month-old boy they'd named Isaac. Everly loved that the Youngs included her family as if they'd always belonged to them, and she nodded over to them.

"Can we sit over there this year?" she asked Trace.

"Fine with me," he said, and he took the chairs that they had set out earlier and moved them over by Ev's brother.

The kids all sat on blankets, some of the older ones playing cards while the younger ones had toys and coloring books to keep them entertained until the fireworks started. Ev nodded to Graham and Laney Whitaker, who sat next to Bryce and Codi, as she went by. While she could name every single man, woman, and child there tonight, she just wanted to be surrounded by her brothers and husband.

She sat down next to Shawn, and he reached over and squeezed her hand. "How'd it go?"

"It was great." She flashed him a smile. She sighed as she looked up into the sky that would darken and then have pops of bright white, red, and blue light flying through it soon enough.

She thought, *Mama, it's a day of celebration.*

Everly used to talk to her mom all the time, but she only did in rare circumstances these days.

I'm doing so much better, she thought. *I recognize myself when I look in the mirror now. But I don't think you'd recognize me. My life is so different—and so, so good.*

She opened her eyes and looked around, and the thoughts in her head weren't just for her mom anymore, but for her too.

She did have an amazing life, with a beautiful family, though she'd lost her parents too early.

And it felt so good to acknowledge that, and to really, truly *feel* it.

41

Bryce's heartbeat pounded and hammered, speeding the closer he got to Rising Sun Ranch. He loved his acreage in Wyoming with his whole soul, especially now that Codi lived there and ran the ranch with him. He didn't have to carry so much pressure with her at his side; his mistakes were easily forgiven. And she had a keen mind that helped him see through problems and come up with solutions.

It was just nice to not be alone.

He glanced over to his daddy, who drove toward the T-junction where he'd turn and continue up to Dog Valley. Abby rode in the passenger seat in front of him, but all of Bryce's siblings were already at the farm.

Codi had recruited everyone ages five to twenty-five, to come help her decorate their house for the party they were hosting that night. Harry wasn't finished with his online concert tour yet, but when he was, they would have a big party at his house too.

Bryce had deliberately left Harry, Belle, Kassie, and Reggie off the decorating crew. His stomach buzzed with live wasps because he wasn't sure how they would take this news.

"Oh, they're going to be fine," he grumbled to himself. This was good news.

He and Codi were going to be parents, and he was going to get to keep this baby, love it, and raise it. But he was incredibly close with Kassie still, despite them both being married for the past year or so. He and Harry were best friends. Bryce had been playing every show with him, and it had been incredibly difficult to keep this secret from him in the past several weeks.

Luckily, Harry had a master planner in Adam, and Bryce and Codi had met with him and asked for his help in planning this party and keeping it secret from those they didn't want to know until they arrived. Bryce cleared his throat and said, "Dad, if Uncle Morris wants to quit managing the band, I know who you can hire."

His daddy looked at him in the rearview mirror. "Oh yeah? Who's that?"

"Adam," Bryce said instantly.

"Harry's Adam?" Dad asked.

"Yeah," Bryce said.

"I suppose he won't need to work for Harry for very much longer," Daddy mused.

"What's he going to do for him? Buy his milk here in

Coral Canyon?" He grinned and shook his head because he knew his cousin hated having an assistant, though it had definitely been helpful for him, and he loved Adam like a brother. Everyone in the Young family did.

"I'm sure he's going to be looking for another job," Bryce said.

"That is not a bad idea," Abby said.

Uncle Morris and Aunt Leigh had five children now, and they'd been building their new house for over a year. They still hadn't moved in, because they'd encountered some water problems after they'd poured the foundation, and the whole thing had to be ripped out and started over.

"There shouldn't be too much," Dad said. "We're retired."

"There's still a ton and you know it," Abby said. "Morris still works a full-time job while the rest of you sleep in and enjoy your families full-time."

He scoffed as he looked over to Abby. "I don't know about that."

"Ask Leigh," Abby shot back.

Bryce grinned at their banter, though he knew they absolutely loved each other too.

Dad reached the T-junction and made the right turn that would take them further north and a little bit further west to Dog Valley. They'd be at Rising Sun Ranch in ten minutes, and Bryce pulled his phone out and texted his wife as much.

We're ready, she said.

Do you want me to get an ETA on everyone else? Bryce texted her.

I'll put it on the family text, she said. A few seconds later, he navigated over to that and found that she had just messaged, *We're ready for everyone! Let us know how far out you are.*

Messages came in, and most people were five to fifteen minutes out. That only fueled Bryce's nerves. In no more than fifteen minutes, everyone would know that he was going to be a father again. He still couldn't believe it most nights when he knelt down to pray and thank God for His blessings, for the opportunity to have OJ in his life, and for the trust God had given him to try again.

You'll need to tell the Whittakers, he thought. *And Bailey.* Bryce's mind and world slowed enough for him to think of her. She still lived in Butte, but she'd been in consistent contact with OJ and her parents since his wedding last year.

"What are we having for dinner?" Daddy asked.

"Oh, Codi asked how far out we are," Abby said. "I'm going to tell her we're about five minutes."

"It's a pizza party," Bryce said. "That's the easiest way to feed a million people."

Daddy chuckled. While there weren't quite a *million* people in the Young family, it sure felt like it sometimes. They'd invited everyone tonight—Wade and Cheryl, all of the Averys, Denzel and Michelle, Sunny's brother and sister and their spouses, Georgia's parents, and of course, Grams and Gramps. Dad made the turn that took them off the highway and down the lane that led to the ranch, but he stopped much sooner than Bryce expected.

"They're lined up here," Daddy said.

Bryce leaned over and looked out the windshield between his parents. "I see," he said. "Let me go see what's going on."

He got out of the truck before his dad could protest, though he already knew exactly why Codi had staged a traffic jam. He jogged past Uncle Luke in his giant SUV, because he refused to drive a minivan, then Morris in exactly that vehicle, Trace and Ev in their truck, and to Gramps and Grams, who had arrived first.

Someone had put up some sawhorses to block the driveway, probably OJ, and Bryce's heart pumped double-time.

Bryce gazed at the farmhouse he'd fallen in love with the moment he'd stepped inside. Maybe from the moment he'd seen it from the curb. Either way, he'd known this was his home from the beginning.

From here, he couldn't see any of the balloons or streamers or signs proclaiming that Codi was going to have a baby. But he could only imagine what it would look like inside. He'd seen all the decorations; they'd been sitting on his kitchen table for two weeks now, and he and Codi had barely been able to cram themselves there to eat.

Grams rolled down her window and said, "Codi says she wants everyone to come around to the back deck before she'll let us into the house."

"Sure," Bryce said.

"She said when you got here, you'd move the sawhorses so we could park," Gramps said.

Bryce nodded and said, "Okay," in the most cheerful voice he could muster. He pulled out his phone and checked the family text as well, not that he thought Grams would be lying. He saw Codi's message, and he hastened to move the sawhorses.

Then he started motioning people into the driveway and along the dirt road that led past the house and further back onto the farm so they could park. He'd hosted everyone at his house before for spooky Halloween walks, OJ's birthday last year, and other events, and he had plenty of parking. They'd celebrated the Fourth of July last week, and he didn't want his grandparents to be out in the heat for long, but the temperatures weren't too bad today.

When his dad pulled in to where Bryce indicated, he motioned for him to roll down the window. "Can you please go ahead and make sure that no one goes into the house until Codi says it's okay?"

"What's going on?" Daddy asked.

"She said she wants us to stay on the back deck," Abby said.

"She's probably doing something with the kids," Bryce said, which wasn't exactly a lie.

Daddy parked and said, "I'll handle it." As he got out, Bryce heard him yelling to his brothers as he continued to direct the parking. He had to actually count on his fingers to make sure everyone had arrived, and when they had, Bryce pulled out his phone and texted Codi.

We're all here. I'm coming in the front door.

He did that quickly, pulling it closed behind him and locking it so no one could follow him. The living room held balloons in a variety of pastel colors—pink, blue, yellow, green, violet, pale peach, and white. They'd been blown up with a helium tank, with matching strings hanging down from them.

"Wow," Bryce said as he dodged through all the strings and into the kitchen. He didn't see Codi or any of the kids, and he had no idea where they could possibly be. Plenty of people stood on the back deck, and he knew they wouldn't have patience for very long. These were the Youngs, after all.

To his right, down the hall, he heard, "Are you ready?" and then a huge cheer lifted through the house. Codi had staged them all back there. He got out of the way as she came toward him.

"This place looks great," he said. "I had Boston go outside and look into the windows to make sure we couldn't see the banner."

She'd hung a huge *Congratulations!* banner from the ceiling between the living room and the kitchen, with baby rattles, cartoon babies, and rocking horses on it.

"Do you think they'll get the message when they walk in?"

"One hundred percent," Bryce said, grinning at her. He put his arm around her and brought her to his side, because they'd planned to stand beneath the banner.

"Congratulations, Bryce," Rosie said as she led the

cousins down the hallway. "I'm so excited we're getting so many new babies in the family."

He held out his fist for her to bump. "You'll babysit for us before anyone else, right?"

Rosie glowed under the praise, and Bryce couldn't stop smiling.

"All right, guys," the fourteen-year-old said, starting to boss everyone around—one of her superpowers. "Remember what we rehearsed?"

"Yes," came from the group of Young children, their voices not quite lining up.

"What day is Codi due?" Rosie yelled.

"November twenty-sixth!" they chorused back to them.

"The day before Thanksgiving," Bryce whispered to himself, another swell of gratitude, love, and joy filling him.

Rosie looked over to OJ, who looked at her very seriously.

"I think they're ready," he said as he turned back to the group. "Everyone pile in closer. We want our mommas and daddies to see all of us."

Once all the kids surrounded them, Codi said, "All right, OJ. You can let them in."

OJ half-walked, half-skipped to the sliding glass door and pulled it open. "All right, now everyone settle down." It took a few seconds for that to actually happen, as he still had a little boy voice that didn't carry very far.

"Everyone is going to come in," he yelled to the adults. "And you're going to line up and face us all. We have something to tell you." He held up both hands. "Do I need to repeat that for those of you in the back?"

Bryce burst out laughing because it was so OJ and so his family to have to have things repeated for those in the back. "You're gonna come in!" OJ yelled. "And line up facing us!" He spoke slower this time, and he was so stinking cute. "We have something to tell you!"

Codi giggled against his chest as Bryce quieted. OJ turned around and said, "I did my best with this family."

"You killed it, bud," Bryce said as OJ hurried to his spot on the end.

Daddy came in first, as he'd been holding everyone back. He'd only taken one step before he came to a complete stop, blocking everyone else's entrance to the house. His eyes fixated on the banner above Bryce and Codi and all the kids. "Dear God," he said in a tone filled with reverence and awe.

"Don't just stop right there," Abby griped at him, and she squeezed past him. She, too, came to a complete stop as she took in the scene before her, then sucked in a breath and covered her mouth with both of her hands.

Half a squeal made it out of her mouth before OJ said, "Aunt Abby, you're supposed to come in and face us."

"You're blocking everyone, Momma," Bryce said.

Her eyes came to his, wide and dark and filled with hope. He'd been kidding himself if he thought he'd be able to do this with dry eyes, because he was a sympathy crier. If someone else started to tear up, he did too.

And right now, Abby had tears streaming down her face. She moved out of the way, and more people came in. Their voices grew louder and louder, because the surprise was out of the bag.

OJ once again stepped forward and said, "Everyone quiet down now," as he held up both hands.

Once the family had listened to him, he turned around and said, "Ready? Three, two, one." He even held up three fingers and lowered them one by one.

Then he swept his arm toward the kids, the go-signal he'd come up with while Bryce had gathered the eggs OJ should've gotten.

It took a couple of seconds to get all of the kids' voices to work as one, but when they did, they said, "Bryce and Codi are going to welcome our baby to their family," in a near-chant.

OJ turned around and waved as if he was trying to get the crowd pumped up. That got everybody to whoop and holler. They could do all the shrieking they wanted now. OJ cut them off as if he was a grand maestro and turned back around and said, "When are they going to have the baby?"

And all of the kids yelled, "Nov-em-ber twent-y-sixth!"

OJ turned around and called, "It's a Thanksgiving *babyyyyyyy!*" holding on to the last sound in the word "baby" for too long. Classic OJ.

The cheers and applause started again. This time, the kids broke ranks and gathered around Bryce and Codi, making them the nucleus of the celebration. Their parents did the same, coming forward to congratulate them on the addition that would soon come to their family.

Bryce hugged his cousins, aunts, and uncles, smiling big

as his tears mostly stayed dormant until he came face to face with Uncle Otis.

Uncle Otis grinned and said, "I guess you're not going to be giving me this one."

Bryce shook his head as Uncle Otis pulled him into a hug and held on tight. "I sure do love you, son," Otis said. "You're going to be the best daddy in the whole world."

He stepped back and then to the side, and Bryce came face to face with his momma and daddy. He opened his arms for both of them. They stepped in to hug him, and all he could think was, *God is a God of miracles. He is so kind. He is so good. He is so forgiving.*

God is a God of miracles.

42

Belle broke her kiss with Harry and rolled away from him when she heard voices coming from the front of his house.

Definitely his father. "Your parents are here," she whispered, starting to sit up.

Harry's arms around her tightened like vices, holding her against his chest. "If we're quiet, maybe they'll go away," he whispered.

Disbelief tore through Belle. He didn't believe that, did he?

A couple of inches separated them, and she found his eyes twinkling with mischief.

"They're going to catch us," she whispered.

His father's voice came closer. She could make out words now, and she heard Trace say, "My son knows better than to do something he doesn't want me to walk in on."

"I'm just saying, baby," Everly said. "Belle's car is out in the driveway."

"Then he should have locked his door," Trace practically yelled. "Or gone over to her place."

Harry's chest started to shake as he laughed. An alarm sounded in Belle's head. "This is why you're always coming to my apartment, isn't it?" she asked, pressing into his bicep with one of her knuckles.

Harry nodded, his laughter getting louder. He wouldn't be able to hide from his daddy now, and Belle currently *lay on top of him.*

"Let me go," she said, trying to stuff away her embarrassment and stop herself from laughing at the same time.

"They're not here," Everly said. "Let's go, Trace."

"Oh, he's here," Trace said, and his voice landed practically on top of Belle. They did lay on the couch right on the edge of the living room, and Trace would have to look straight down to see them, which he did in the next moment.

"Hey, Daddy," Harry said as if he wasn't doing anything wrong. He wasn't embarrassed one iota, but Belle's face burned with humiliation.

"I knew you were here," Trace said in his homicidal cowboy voice. "We still going to dinner?"

"Yes," Belle said, her stomach growling on cue. "If you could get your son to let go of me."

"Let go of the woman, Harry," Trace growled.

Harry burst out laughing now. His arms did loosen around Belle, and she managed to sit up, brush her hair out of her face, and then get to her feet, pure humiliation sliding through her like slippery oil.

"Howdy, Trace," she said, extending her hand across where Harry lay on the couch to shake his father's hand, who stood right behind it.

Everly gave her a kind smile and then looked down at Harry. "You're lucky she doesn't break up with you."

"Oh, she's not gonna break up with me," Harry said with another laugh. "But maybe you guys could knock or use the doorbell."

"Like I said," Trace said. "You can lock the door or go to her place."

They had spent an extraordinary amount of time at Belle's house, laying on her couch and watching her TV, kissing, and talking. She just hadn't put two and two together until now of why Harry came there all the time though he had a much bigger and nicer home.

"If I lock my door." Harry too sat up, and he ran his hands through his hair as it had been mussed a bit. "Then all I have is a bunch of fists banging on it, and that's no fun."

"At least you won't get caught making out with your girlfriend," Trace said, shooting Belle a look. "Not that I blame you, Belle."

"Oh, of course not," Harry said as he got to his feet. "Don't blame *Belle*. She doesn't kiss me back or anything." He grinned at her, kissed her right there in front of his parents, and went around the couch to hug his father. "Can we please not go anywhere that's gonna make us sit outside? It's too hot."

"You'd think your blood would've warmed from your time in Nashville," his father said as he clapped him on the back.

"Yeah, well, it didn't," Harry said. "I'm tired of being hot and sweaty while sitting in a restaurant."

"That's just from the stage lights," his dad said. "And plus, you only have seven more shows."

"Seven more shows," Harry said wearily as he stepped out of his daddy's arms.

They bore such a striking resemblance to each other, and Belle realized that she'd never seen a picture of his mother. He told her that she was a supermodel, tall and dark, which was why he was an impressive six-foot-four with the deepest, darkest eyes, hair to match, and skin that tanned immaculately. When he wore all black…Belle shivered just thinking about him.

"I heard you had some business stuff you wanted to talk about tonight," Trace said as he turned his attention back to Belle.

She swallowed and looked over to Harry, who had suddenly sobered. She'd gotten a lot of interest from producers, talent scouts, and agents in the country music industry, and she'd been working on an email response to them. She had phone numbers she could call too, and she simply wanted to get everything organized before she did anything.

"Yes," she said. "Is Otis going to meet us there?"

"Yep, he and Georgia are on the way already," Trace said. "So we better head out."

She nodded and ran her hands through her hair to

smooth it enough to pull into a ponytail. As she approached Everly, she reached up and held out a barrette. "Keri made this for you."

Belle's heart warmed instantly, and she took the barrette from Harry's mom. "Oh, it's adorable." She abandoned the idea of a ponytail and let her hair fall down again. She then clipped it up on the left side and grinned at Ev. "Good?"

"Can I take a picture for Keri? She'll be thrilled."

"She thinks she's going to make enough for a bicycle by selling barrettes," Trace said darkly. "I'm pretty sure we've spent more on the supplies than she's made."

Ev ignored the venom in her husband's voice and snapped the picture. She smiled fondly at it while Harry went to put on his cowboy boots.

After he'd left, Ev leaned close to say, "That boy is in love with you."

Belle smiled and looked down at the ground. "You really think so?"

"Absolutely, I do," Ev said. "I've known Harry a long time. He can be intense about things he's really passionate about. You're brave to bring up business in front of him."

Belle looked up and into Everly's eyes. "I want his opinion," she said. "He's a smart businessman."

"Who's a smart businessman?" Harry asked as he came back. "Are you poisoning her?" He glared at his momma with an edge of distrust in his eyes.

"Of course not," Ev said, and she held Harry too.

"You *are* a smart businessman," Belle said. "Don't worry.

I'm not saying anything bad." She grinned at him, and they followed his parents outside.

Belle let Harry and his dad and mom chit-chat on the way to the restaurant, and she lost herself inside her own head. The things that she wanted to talk to Trace and Harry and Otis about swirled through her mind, making her toes curl and her stomach whirl.

She made it through pleasantries with Otis and Georgia, hugging and kissing them both before the six of them sat down in a big round booth in the corner of a restaurant where Harry had not played in Coral Canyon.

Two waiters approached, both male, and one of them said, "Howdy, Young family," as he put down coasters for their drinks. "I've got Colby shadowing me tonight. He's brand new at the restaurant, and in fact, he's freaking out that we're over here talking to a couple of country music stars." The waiter laughed, and Trace simply smiled. Otis did too, as did Harry. Belle saw the charm just ooze out of them, and no wonder they were so loved.

"So I told him we don't ask for autographs. But if y'all want to sign something for him, he's probably not going to protest." He laughed and said, "Tell me what you'll have to drink."

"I want this apple cider mimosa," Everly said, pointing to the menu.

"Diet Doctor Pepper," Harry said.

"Diet Coke," Trace said.

"I want a virgin mojito, please," Belle said.

"Diet Mountain Dew," Otis said, and Georgia opted for water with lemon.

"We'll be right back," he said. It took Colby another second to tear his eyes away from the table and follow his shadow. That was when Belle realized that he'd been looking at *her*—not Trace or Otis or Harry, but her.

She swallowed and said, "I'm gonna die if I don't say it."

Otis laughed, his chuckles making her heart warm, because he wasn't laughing at her. More like he sympathized with her. "All right, spit it out. We can order after."

Belle took Harry's hand under the table and squeezed hard. "I haven't even told Harry this yet, and I don't know if it's a good idea or not." She took a deep breath and blew it out. She shouldn't have started before she had her drink, because she had nothing to hide behind.

"I've had a lot of producers and scouts and agents and others email or call me since they saw me play with Harry." She pressed her lips together, finding them so dry, and she started to dig in her purse for a tube of Chapstick.

"I had this wild idea that I should host a meet-and-greet." She cleared her throat because she had a couple more things to say, and they were the worst ones.

She looked around the table, noting how open and unassuming Otis was, but Georgia watched her with a hint of wariness in her expression. Harry had his head down, his cowboy hat hiding his face. Everly watched her with wide eyes, and Trace played the grumpy, dark cowboy in their pair, the one watching her with plenty of hesitation and apprehension.

"In Nashville," she said, and Harry jerked his head up.

"In Nashville," he echoed.

"It's a one-time trip," she said. "A meet-and-greet somewhere there. I don't know where. I was kind of...." She trailed off and decided she'd come this far, and she couldn't stop now. "I was hoping you could help me figure out where, or I could ask Adam to help me coordinate it. He's really good at that kind of stuff."

"Hmm. Yes, he is," Trace said.

"And I'll go there, and I can play some of my songs for everyone. Or not. Could it just be a meet-and-greet? Meet the songwriter." She looked at Harry and bent down to really see his eyes under the brim of his hat. "Not the artist. The songwriter."

That was it. That was her whole pitch. That was her idea. She had been going through her songs and organizing them. She'd written four new ones now and currently had a fifth going strong. And of course, she had almost two dozen from her previous life in country music.

"I have an email drafted," she said. "I would love to have any of you look at it who will and help me with it."

She glanced around, having a hard time making judgments from expressions now, something she'd once been so good at. "If you don't want to, that's fine too," she added quickly. "I don't want to put anyone out."

No one said anything, and as Belle surveyed them, she realized that everyone watched Harry, clearly waiting for him to take the lead.

"All right, here are those drinks," the waiter said as he

returned. Their sodas and mocktails got passed out, and then he said, "You guys need a few more minutes to look at the menu?" He met Belle's eyes and added, "I can see you do. Come on, Colby. We'll be back in a few minutes," and he walked away.

Belle picked up her menu and started studying it. She was new to Coral Canyon and hadn't been here before. She tipped the menu toward Harry, effectively cutting off Trace's and Everly's view of them on her right.

"Have you frequented this establishment before?" she asked in a low voice that brought his eyes to hers, and they practically teemed with emotion.

"Yes," he growled.

"What's good?" She leaned her head into his shoulder and looked at the menu. "The meet-and-greet is a bad idea."

"I don't think it's a bad idea," he grumbled. "I just don't like it."

"Why not?"

"If y'all are going to talk," Georgia said. "Say it out loud for all of us to hear. Maybe we'll agree or disagree."

Belle lowered her menu, and Harry sent his aunt one of his icy glares. But, oh, Georgia simply gave it back to him. "Whispering in a crowd is rude."

"I said, I don't think it's a bad idea," he said in a loud enough voice for everyone at the table to hear. "I just don't like it."

"And I asked him why he didn't like it," Belle said. "But I think I know already."

"Yes, me too," Everly said. "Harry thinks he's going to lose you to Nashville."

Harry growled, but Belle locked her eyes on him. "Is that true?" she asked. "You think you're going to lose me to Nashville?"

He shook his head. "No, of course not."

"I've told you a million times, I don't want to live in Nashville. I don't want to be a country music artist."

"Then why would you go to Nashville?"

"Because that's where you sell songs," Otis said, and Belle gestured to him with her palm.

"You said networking wasn't a bad thing," she said. "And in fact, I want you to come with me. Can you imagine who we can get there if it's a meet-and-greet with *the* Harry Young?"

"Don't call me that," he growled, and he went back to his menu.

Belle looked down the table to Trace, and to her surprise, he gave her a smile and shook his head as if Harry was being stubborn about going out to find Easter eggs.

"Don't mind Harry," he said. "He's obviously in a bad mood after getting caught making out."

"Making out?" Georgia asked, plenty of interest in her voice.

Harry sighed and slapped his menu down on the table. "Me sitting in the middle of this booth was a real bad idea."

Everyone laughed except for him. Belle once again slid her hand into his under the table and squeezed. "That's the idea. I don't want to talk about it anymore tonight, but maybe y'all can think about it and let me know what you think. And if you would like to see the email, I'm happy to share it."

She swallowed and said, "Just one more thing."

"Go on, then," Harry said. "You won't be able to eat until you spit it out."

And she wouldn't. She was thrilled that he knew she wouldn't.

"I'm going to ask Adam to help," she said. "If I decide to do it, because he's really good at coordinating things like this. And I'm going pay him. Is it in his contract that he can't help someone else while he's working for you?"

"No," Harry said.

"Actually, he does have an NDA," Trace said. "Not to disclose who he's working with, but I guess that doesn't really matter here."

"Doesn't matter at all, Daddy," Harry said. "But thanks for bringing it up." He rolled his eyes and lifted his menu so that it was only four inches from his face and no one else could see him.

Belle sighed inwardly and looked over to Trace and Everly, worry streaming through her. Everly gave her a kind smile and nodded, which gave Belle confidence and courage that her idea was good. Even Harry had said it was good. He just didn't like it. He'd never told her he was afraid that he'd lose her to Nashville, and she'd have to talk to him about that later.

Belle looked over to Georgia and Otis, so many questions streaming from her. She didn't want to wait for feedback, and Otis seemed to know it. "I think it's a phenomenal idea, Belle. I know a lot of people in Nashville who I've sold songs to, and I'd be happy to send them an invitation if you do a meet-and-greet there."

She nodded and said, "Thank you so much, Otis. If it makes it to that step, I'll let you know."

"Would you stop saying 'if'?" Harry asked, his voice right back to Super-Grump. "You're gonna do this meet and greet, and it's gonna be amazing, and you're gonna get fifty billion people who want to buy your songs."

Tense silence settled over the booth, expanded into the corner of the restaurant, and seemed to flow through the whole building, cutting off all the chatter and the clattering of silverware against plates and the sound of the kitchen beyond.

"Well," Belle said, her voice trembling in her throat but solid as it came out of her mouth, "I think *fifty billion* is an exaggeration."

"Yeah, and don't sound so happy about your girlfriend having a *great idea* and finding a way to make a living," Everly said. "This could help you too, you know."

Harry opened his mouth and then promptly shut it.

"It's okay," Belle said in a bright voice, because it was. "Harry won't want to use me this way, I know." She turned and looked at him again, but he wouldn't quite meet her eyes. "We don't like to feel like we're using one another to get ahead."

"I told you it was a good idea," Harry said.

"He'll come around," Trace said. "Give him a few days.

And since he never stopped talking about that trip to Florida with you, I'm pretty sure you'll be making this trip to Nash-ville too."

"Daddy," Harry said.

"What are you trying to hide from her?" Trace asked. "Because I'm looking at the two of you, and she's not hiding anything, Harry. She wants you in her life. She's claimed you right in front of all of us. Who cares if she knows you talked about that trip to Florida like it was the greatest thing that ever happened to you?"

Belle grinned and turned toward him again. "The trip to Florida was the greatest thing that ever happened to you?"

"See?" Harry grumbled. "See? *This* is why I don't want you to say stuff like that."

Trace laughed, and when he did, it lit up the entire world. Belle joined him, and she leaned in close to Harry and said, "The trip to Florida was the greatest thing that ever happened to me too, Harry."

Now she just had to keep working on her idea for this meet-and-greet-the-songwriter-in-Nashville, and she could only pray that Harry would see her vision and know that her heart belonged to him and Coral Canyon and no one and nowhere else.

43

Harry pushed his way into Belle's apartment, calling out, "It's just me, baby."

"Come on back," she yelled.

Harry turned to close the door and then paused to pat Simba, who had just jumped up onto the back of the couch. "How you doing, cat?" he asked, admitting to himself that it was nice to have another living thing greet him when he came home.

Of course, this wasn't his home. He walked along the back of the couch through the living room and turned left to go down the hall. In Belle's second bedroom, she had set up two six-foot tables where she had started to lay out her plans for the meet-and-greet in Nashville.

Harry had just finished his world concert tour last night with one of the huge Young family parties that morning, complete with plenty of waffles, maple syrup, bacon, sausage, and the biggest vat of scrambled eggs he'd ever seen in his life.

They'd celebrated at Uncle Morris's house, and Harry had now completed all of his contractual obligations to Rebel Records in Nashville. As he went into the bedroom, he felt like God Himself had lifted an enormous weight from his shoulders, and he could breathe in a way he never had before.

When Belle straightened and turned to look at him, a glorious smile on her face, Harry saw everything he wanted in his life in her.

"Hey there," she said pleasantly, walking toward him with a skip to her step before landing in his arms. She kissed him for only a quick moment and then turned back to the table. "Come look at this guest list. Otis gave me a bunch of names. I've listed everyone who's contacted me, and I've got your people at Rebel and King Country. Adam added a few names, and we want to make sure it's comprehensive." She glanced over to him. "How was your call with your mom?"

"It was a call with my mom," he said, hoping that would stitch it all up and she wouldn't ask him anything else.

"So you'll tell me later." She turned her attention to the three sheets of paper laid out on the far end of the table.

"We're going to design an announcement," Adam said. "That we can mail to some people and email to others."

"Have you chosen a date yet?" Harry asked, trying to clear the cobwebs, anger, and grumpiness from his voice. This should be a good thing. Belle deserved to make a career for herself as a country music songwriter. He certainly didn't want to stand in the way of that. He also just didn't want to go back to Nashville.

Simba pressed up against his leg, rubbing against him, which helped ease some additional tension from Harry's muscles.

"I'm thinking the week after Labor Day," Belle said, and she had the next three months of calendars taped on the wall behind the table. August loomed only a few days away, and Harry couldn't believe that the past four months with her had flown by so quickly.

"I'm done with my record," he said.

Belle grinned at him. "You're done with Rebel," she said, and that made him smile too.

"I'm done with Rebel." He pressed his lips to hers and kissed her until Adam cleared his throat and said, "I think September twelfth is a great day," in a very loud voice.

Belle giggled and ducked her head. She pointed to the calendar. "If we mail the invitations this week, that will give people five weeks to put it on their calendar. Do you think that's enough time?"

"In country music, sometimes they move at the speed of a sloth," Harry said. "And sometimes you have to be right there to catch the lightning in a bottle. If they can't make it in five weeks, that's their loss."

"That's right," Adam said. "It's their loss."

"Okay," Belle said. "I'll send this list with you." She gathered up the papers, folded them in half, and left them on the table. "I want you to help me with the venue next."

Adam shuffled down the table, as did Harry and Belle, and she had three pictures laid out.

"Adam has worked his magic," she said, indicating the first picture. Harry recognized it, as he'd been there several times.

The Motown building.

"And we can have the meet-and-greet in the ground floor lobby here, which has a bar and restaurant that will serve drinks and appetizers."

"The Motown building," Harry said. "Wow. A couple of record studios are housed in that building."

"Right," Belle said. "King Country said that we could use their conference room and space, but we'd have to bring in all of our own food."

"I'm going to veto that," Harry said. "I like the Motown building far more."

"I do too," Adam said.

"The third option." She cleared her throat and looked over to Adam. "Is your old apartment."

"What?" Harry looked down at the picture there. "My old apartment? Why would we ever go there?"

"Nostalgia," she said. "The place where Harry Young wrote three albums, practiced them to the point where he could record them perfectly when he walked into the studio." She nudged him with her hip. "It's available right now, and Adam contacted the landlord and asked how much it would be for us to rent it for a week."

"A week?" Harry's eyebrows went up. He did not want

to go back to Nashville, back to his old apartment, for a week.

"Yeah," she said. "I figured we could stay there too. It kills a whole bunch of birds with one stone."

"Does it?" He looked at her, incredulous that she believed for even a moment that he'd want to go back there. Kind of like how his mother still didn't understand why Harry had quit his country music career.

"Belle, honey, it's not a furnished apartment. There's one bedroom and a half-room that I used as a studio. The living room is tiny. This is not a good idea."

She searched his face, and Harry wasn't sure what she saw, but he couldn't hide anything from her fast enough, and then he realized he didn't want to. "I don't want to go back to my old apartment."

"Okay," she said plainly. "I think the Motown building is the best choice."

"The Motown building is definitely it," Adam said, and he flipped over the other two pictures and slid them underneath the one of the Motown building. It was dressed up in Nashville with over a dozen stories, and the lobby did have an open bar with a casual restaurant.

"It's going to cost a lot," she said. "I have a little bit of money left from the sale of my house, and I'm going to use that."

"I can help," Harry said quietly.

"No," she said quickly. "I told you I'm not taking any money from you on this."

He turned his back on Adam and took Belle into his

arms. "Baby, we're in this together, remember?" He leaned closer and took in a deep breath of the scent of her skin, her hair. Everything about her intoxicated him.

"I'm going with you. I'm going to be at the meet-and-greet too. I want to sell songs for a living too. I can pay for the food."

She looked down to where she twisted her hands in his collar. "I know you can."

"Will you let me?" He bent his head and skated his lips along the soft skin of her neck.

He was used to doing a lot of personal things in front of Adam and telling him extremely intimate details of his life. He had not told anyone how he felt about Belle, but he knew his parents could see it, and his aunts and uncles, his grandparents, Bryce and Codi, anyone who looked at them, could see how he felt about Belle.

Adam surely knew already. With his lips catching against her earlobe, he said, "When you turned and looked at me when I just walked in...."

"Yeah?" she asked.

"I thought, 'I love her.'" He cleared his throat quietly and kept his face buried in the softness of neck. "I'm in love with you."

He backed up and looked at her. "So I can pay for the food. I just need you to let me."

Tears filled her eyes, and she pressed her lips together and nodded quickly. "Okay."

"Okay," he said, then he released her and bounced back to Adam's side.

"Excuse me," she said, and she hurried out of the room.

Harry sighed and peered down at the table at what Adam had glued his gaze to. "Is this the menu?"

"You're remarkably composed," Adam said. "For a man who just told the woman he loved that he loved her, and she didn't say it back."

"She will," Harry said with as much confidence as he could. "I know she will. She's been really nervous about this meet-and-greet."

"She wants you to be so happy," Adam said.

"I know that," Harry said. "I'm working on it."

"A trip to Nashville doesn't mean you're going back permanently, sir," Adam said, and Harry hated the reversion to 'sir' instead of his name. He cleared his throat then and said, "I've got to be real honest. I don't think you or Belle is going to need me in the current capacity in which I work now that the tour is done."

"Maybe not," Harry murmured though he didn't want to admit it.

"I'm going to work on this meet-and-greet with Belle for the next several weeks," he said. "And I'm thinking about setting up some appointments in Nashville while I'm there."

"No way," Harry said.

"No way?" Adam asked, turning toward him in his crisp polo and his khakis, his eyebrows raised toward the ceiling.

"No way. I don't want you to go," Harry said, his chest suddenly vibrating and about to collapse in on itself. "You're my best friend."

"Your daddy is your best friend. Bryce, Kassie, Reggie,

and now Belle." Adam searched Harry's face, his dark blue eyes so intense. "You can let me go, sir."

"But I don't want to," Harry said. "You're going to fall madly in love with Joey, and you're going to marry her. And you're going to live here in Coral Canyon. You're going to be part of the family. Just like you have been for the past year."

Something inside Harry really wanted that. He craved it. But even as Adam shook his head, Harry knew he couldn't keep the man in Coral Canyon.

"You said it yourself," Adam said in a crisp voice as he turned back to the next item on the table. "I'm too old for Joey."

"You haven't even tried," Harry said.

"No," Adam said. "And I'm not going to." He cut Harry a look. "Just because you think someone is beautiful doesn't mean you're going to marry them. Doesn't make it right."

"Aunt Hilde and Uncle Gabe are really far apart," Harry said. "Heck, my daddy and Everly are eight or nine years apart."

"The difference is," Adam said, "Everly was not twenty when she met your daddy."

"Well, Joey's twenty-two."

"Harry." He sighed extensively. "I don't want your uncle to kill me."

Harry opened his mouth to argue again, and Adam cut him a look that silenced him. "I don't want to talk about this anymore, sir. Please."

"All right," Belle said as she walked back into the room, and Harry turned toward her.

He met her halfway and took her into his arms again. "I'm sorry I'm such a grump," he whispered, his mouth right at her ear.

"You're fine," she said. "I know this is hard for you to talk about."

"Yeah," he said. "Like I know you didn't tell me you loved me too. But you will when it's easier for you to say." He raised his eyebrows at her, and Belle simply nodded. That was good enough for Harry for now.

Then he too returned his attention to the tables to go over the last of the details for the event so that they could get the invitations out in the next week.

He couldn't help being a little grumpy about going to Nashville, even if he did get to go with the woman he loved. He felt like he'd gained so much, but that only meant he had a lot to lose now too.

Starting with Adam, he thought, and his heart wailed, and he willed God to slow down time so Harry could keep his assistant and best friend for as long as possible.

44

"So you'll call me the moment you touch down in Oklahoma City," Harry said, taking Belle's face into both of his warm, capable hands. Belle smiled at him, feeling so loved and cherished as she stood outside the Jackson Hole airport.

"Yes," she said, "I'll call you the moment I touch down in Oklahoma City." She swallowed, and she couldn't hide that movement—that tell of her nerves—from Harry. He felt it, and his eyebrows went up, even as he lowered his head to kiss her.

They had talked about him going with her to visit her parents before she went on to Nashville for the meet-and-greet. In the end, Belle hadn't been home in over a year, and she decided she wanted to visit her folks alone and that she'd meet him and Adam in Nashville.

"I wish I was going with you," he said as he pulled away. "Are you nervous?"

She nodded because she'd told Harry that her parents didn't really agree with her career choices and never had.

"They'll be happy to see you," he said. "I mean, I know they know you're safe, but they'll still be happy to see you." He grinned at her. "It's always better to see you in person than to not."

Belle smiled up at him because she liked how he felt about her. It showed on his face and exuded from every pore of his body. Belle wanted to echo the things he'd said to her for the past month, about how much he cared about her, how much he loved her. She hadn't found a way to do that yet. She felt like she'd gotten on a mechanical bucking bull, and she had to hold on with both hands as it thrashed back and forth, left and right, trying to get her off.

They hadn't talked about money at all, though she knew Harry had to be pretty well off. And a little voice inside herself told her that she didn't need to get country music gigs. She didn't need to be looking for another job, something that she hadn't done for a while as she prepped for the concert tour, then played in that and then started organizing this meet-and-greet in Nashville. There hadn't been time for much else, and she had a little bit of savings from when she'd sold her house before going undercover. So far, it had gotten her by.

"I'll miss you while I'm gone," she said, and she could get her voice to say that.

"I miss you already," Harry said, and he kissed her again just as an alarm went off on her phone.

Harry, though tall and strong and with muscles as hard as rock, was a squishy, soft, sensitive man. And she'd known he'd want to say goodbye for as long as possible. He pulled away and said, "You better get going." He fell back a step and tucked his hands in his pocket.

Belle reached for the handle on her suitcase, realizing that the past five months between airplane trips for her had been filled with Harry, Harry, and more Harry.

"Love you, Belle," he said almost casually now.

Belle looked up at him again. She wanted to ask him how he knew that he loved her. He said he'd never been in love before, and Belle certainly hadn't. So how did he know?

This was why she needed to go to Oklahoma City and talk to her mom and dad alone. She had to tell them about Harry. She needed to be away from Harry to see how she felt when she was on her own. Not part of a couple. Not his plus one. His partner.

When she had to lay down on the couch by herself without him, how would she feel?

She also couldn't walk away from him without saying anything, but *I really like you, Harry* sounded stupid in her head.

So she reached for him and pressed her lips to his in another quick kiss.

"I am so close to knowing if I love you," she said.

"We've got plenty of time, sweetheart." Harry had been kind and patient with her for weeks. He didn't love her idea of a meet-and-greet in Nashville, but he'd agreed to go. He'd helped her plan it. He'd used all of his contacts in country music and so had his family. They'd just given them all to her freely, and her heart filled with tears at their kindness and generosity.

So while Belle didn't know some things, there were others in her life that she knew absolutely for certain. One, she did not want a country music career in the way that Harry had it. She did not want to be on the stage playing and singing and greeting crowds and dealing with photographers and reporters. She didn't want to do interviews.

Belle craved the life out of the spotlight, doing something she loved from inside a strong support network and a small-town community.

She turned and grabbed her bag again. As she walked away from Harry, she thought, *Like the Youngs.* It was one of the truer things she'd thought in a long time.

And Coral Canyon.

She did love Harry's family and the small town where they lived. She knew without a shadow of a doubt that she wanted to make that her life and her family.

Then you must love him, she thought as she entered the airport. Things got busy from there. She had to go through security, tow her bag everywhere, and get to her gate. She didn't have time to stew through all of her feelings, and that was never really Belle's style anyway.

She put her head down and got to work. And so, on the flight to Oklahoma City, she went over the meet-and-greet details one last time. She distracted herself by reading a romance novel. And when she landed in Oklahoma, she sent Harry a text that said, *I am alive and well. My daddy's already texted that he's here, and I'll send you a picture of us soon.*

Harry came back with three red hearts, and Belle smiled at her device then tucked her phone away. Again, she had to navigate through an airport. And since she hadn't checked her bag, it didn't take her long until she found her dad standing in the waiting area, holding up a sign that said, "Belle Graves" in all caps and her mom clapping her hands in a cheer.

Belle jogged the last few steps to them both and wrapped her arms around them simultaneously.

"Oh, it's so good to see you, Tinkerbell," her mom said, and Belle gripped her, though the nickname drove her mad. She wasn't a child. She'd lived on her own now for thirteen years, she'd gone undercover, she'd solved one of the biggest cases Wyoming and the western states had ever seen, and she was dating country music sensation Harry Young.

Belle was anything but a tiny fairy from one of her favorite childhood cartoons. The nickname almost felt demeaning to her, like her mom didn't trust her or didn't believe that she was old enough to take care of herself, though she'd never given any other indication as such.

Belle stepped back and sniffled, saying, "What's with the sign, Dad?"

"Oh, you know," he said in his Southern drawl. "You're a big star now." He chuckled and folded the manilla folder he'd written on in half, and Belle laughed too as she shook her head.

"I'm not a big star," she said.

Especially from far away, Belle felt like a pinprick of light, though she knew stars, in all their glory, were huge, like the sun. It depended on how close one got to them that determined how big and bright they shone.

"Are you starving?" her mom asked. "Because Daddy has a hankering for Saddleman's."

"Fish and chips," her father said.

"Absolutely famished," Belle said, grinning at her daddy. "You know what they don't have in Wyoming that they really need? Sweet pea salad." Her mouth watered just thinking about it. "I want that and some of their fried chicken."

Her dad slung his arm around her shoulders and said, "Well, let's go."

Belle grinned her way out of the airport because while she hadn't come to visit her parents for a while, having a family meant she could always ease right back into the spot that she'd left previously. She hadn't felt like that at the Sheriff's Department, and that told her that she didn't belong there. She'd already left, but it was a nice confirmation from God Himself.

"So tell us," Momma said the moment they got in the car. "How did you meet Harry Young?"

Oh, the stories Belle could tell, and they'd be good, something that brought a smile to her face and a skip to her heartbeat, something where she didn't have to talk about dank apartments, dirty carpet, and the loud chimes of slot machines in a casino.

"I met him on a case," she said. And she let everything she'd experienced and done and felt with Harry pour out of her mouth as her daddy drove them to Saddleman's. By the time they got their food, Belle's stomach clamored for it.

"One more question," her mom said.

Belle had just forked up a bite of sweet pea salad. "All right, Momma, one more question."

They hadn't talked about her job or the meet-and-greet in Nashville yet, so surely her mother would have more questions. It was something Southern mommas were really good at—needling their children to death with questions.

"Sounds like you and Harry are very serious," she said.

"That's not a question," Belle said, putting her coveted salad in her mouth.

"Do you love him?" Momma asked, going straight for the jugular. "Are you going to marry him and stay in Wyoming?"

In that moment, Belle realized that perhaps her mom had been thinking she'd come back to Oklahoma someday. Belle's mind blitzed through all the memories of the past dozen years. Had she ever given her parents an indication that she would come back to Oklahoma? She couldn't think of a single thing, so she chewed and swallowed and looked her mom straight in the face and grinned.

"Yeah," she said. "That's the goal. Finish falling in love with Harry, marry him, and raise our family in Wyoming."

"Well, then we have to meet him," her momma said, almost with a touch of coolness in her voice.

"I can't wait to meet him anyway," Daddy said, always the more easygoing one. "We watched your live stream from the Yellowstone Café." He picked up another piece of fish. "It was fantastic. The man's real talented on a guitar."

"He sure is," Belle said, dropping her chin and studying her food.

"So are you," Daddy said, without missing a beat. "Just incredible, Belle."

She raised her eyes to his again. "Really, Daddy? You think so?"

"Absolutely," he said. "Those fools in Nashville." He chuckled. "I bet they're really kicking themselves they let you go ten years ago."

Belle saw the door open for the next conversation she needed to have with her family, and feeling brave and bold and strong and courageous the way Harry did everything, she said, "They are, as a matter of fact. I'm going there right after we finish our visit here."

LATER THAT EVENING, BELLE SIGHED AND PUT DOWN her phone. She'd been texting Harry about the places she'd eaten that day, and all her parents had said.

She smiled just thinking about him, and she peeled back the comforter and sheet and slid to the floor. A mighty sigh slipped from her lips as Belle knelt beside her bed, folded her hands, and bowed her head.

"Dear God," she whispered. Emotions stormed her then, and Belle's throat closed around them.

Seeing her parents had been healing for her in a way she hadn't anticipated and couldn't describe. She did love Oklahoma, but "It's not home," she said aloud, sure God could keep up with her thoughts, the things in her heart, and what came out of her mouth.

Oklahoma wasn't home.

Wyoming was.

"Harry is," she murmured, and she breathed in and found her center. "Thank You for Your constant guidance in my life."

She could thank the Lord for His hand in ensuring her safety, for orchestrating it so she and Harry had been in the Jackson Hole airport at the same time, for all the performances she'd had the opportunity to do.

But most of all, she needed to thank Him for Harry.

"Thank You for reminding me that I'm amazing on my own, but also for showing me that Harry and I belong together. Please help me to navigate this next step in my life, to find the courage and strength to pursue my dreams—but don't let me do anything that will cost me Harry, okay?"

She knew better than most that country music couldn't replace true love, and as she knelt next to her childhood bed, she let her feelings flow over her the way a waterfall rushed over cliffs.

And she knew without a shadow of a doubt that she now

knew what love felt like, and that she was falling, falling, falling the way that water did when it went over the cliff.

She was in love with Harry Young.

She stayed still for a few more moments, feeling the peace settle over her, before climbing into bed. She sent Harry a quick text: *Can't wait until we're in Nashville together.*

Belle lay back on the pillows, a sense of calm washing over her. She was ready for whatever Nashville had in store for her, knowing that she wouldn't be alone here, there, in Jackson...or Coral Canyon.

45

"**R**eady, bud?" Harry asked as he looked down at OJ, who'd pulled open the door at Uncle Otis's house.

"Ready!" OJ reached over and grabbed his black cowboy hat from the table and smashed it on his head. "I'm leaving, Momma!" And with that, he jumped outside and continued down the steps.

Harry stood there watching him and then turned back to the house, as Georgia hadn't confirmed that she'd even heard OJ yell.

"Come on, Harry," OJ called from the sidewalk.

Harry grinned at the exuberant ten-year-old. "Are you sure you can just leave like that?" he asked. "You didn't even close the door." He stepped back up into the house just as Georgia appeared at the end of the hall.

"Oh, there you are, Harry," she said.

"Yeah, I'm taking him," Harry said.

"All right." She smiled and continued to wipe her hands on a towel as he pulled the front door closed and moved to follow OJ.

Harry didn't have to help OJ get in the passenger seat of his truck because Uncle Otis drove just as big of one as he did.

"Who are you going to ride today?" OJ asked as Harry started the truck and backed out of the driveway.

"I usually ride Senora," OJ said. "Who are you going to ride?"

"Oh, whoever Bryce tells me," Harry said nonchalantly.

"Can you believe he got those two new dogs?" OJ asked, perched on the edge of the seat now, his eyes wide. "I mean, I guess they're Codi's, but still."

OJ loved animals, and Harry chuckled. "I didn't know they got new dogs," he drawled.

Bryce had played in every show on Harry's tour. And Harry could admit that on this first night with Belle gone, he didn't want to sleep in his own house. Maybe it was childish, maybe immature. Or maybe he was just really in love with her. Either way, he'd asked Bryce and Codi if he could stay at their house, and they'd said yes. This afternoon horseback riding before the sleepover was simply the icing on the cake.

"One's a bulldog," OJ said, and he kept chattering about everything he knew about the breed. Harry simply let him talk because then he didn't have to. And before he knew it, they pulled onto the Rising Sun Ranch in Dog Valley, about a half-hour north of Coral Canyon.

OJ unbuckled and jumped down from the truck. He

went left out onto the farm instead of right and toward the house. Harry felt extraordinarily slow and old compared to the boy, but he followed, his cowboy boots crunching over the immaculate dirt on Bryce's ranch.

He loved his cousin with his whole heart, because Bryce had done some very difficult things in his life. He'd come back from some terrible mistakes, and he'd run toward what he wanted instead of running away from what he didn't.

He'd given up his country music career to buy this ranch with his best friend and move back to Wyoming. Harry had been looking up to his cousin for a great many years now, and he didn't see himself stopping anytime soon.

He saw Codi first, leading Dragon out of the stable. OJ circled around them the way sharks did fresh meat, but Codi simply laughed and chatted with him. She was so good and so kind, and Harry couldn't wait to meet their baby—a boy, they'd put on the family text string last night.

She glanced down the road toward him, threw the rope over the tethering post, and raised her hand. Harry waved back and called, "Howdy."

"Who do you want to ride today?" she called.

"Whoever needs to work," he said as he approached.

She scanned him from boots to hat and said, "Harry, I think you've gotten taller." She tipped up onto her toes and hugged him. "I'm gonna get you one of our new browns. He's real big, and he needs to be ridden by a big man."

"Bryce is big," Harry said as he pulled back. "And I'm not entirely sure you're not making a fat joke."

She laughed and shook her head, her white hair covered

by a brown cowboy hat. "Foxtrot is new, but I think you can handle him."

"I'm a soft cowboy," Harry called after her as she headed back to the stable. "I play a guitar for a living, Codi. I don't wrangle horses."

She just waved over her shoulder and kept going.

Bryce came out a couple of seconds later, a white horse with paint-flecked spots all over it following him.

"You've got a lot of new horses here," Harry said. He hadn't been out to the ranch during the tour, but in the months since it had concluded, he came out plenty.

"Yeah, we got six or seven new ones," Bryce said. "A farm over in West Yellowstone was closing down. Kassie and Reggie went to check it out." He threw the rope over the tethering post and then drew Harry into a hug. "How're you doing?"

"Just fine," Harry said.

"Belle left today, didn't she?"

"Yep." Harry wasn't sure why it felt like someone was carving out his heart one teaspoon at a time, but it did.

"How long is she going to be gone?" Bryce asked.

"All week," Harry said. "Adam and I fly out on Saturday to meet her in Nashville."

"Meet-and-greet's on Tuesday?" Bryce asked.

"Meet-and-greet's on Tuesday." Harry gave him a glare, because he obviously knew all of this already.

Bryce chuckled. "Lord, he's real salty today already. Bless us to have a good time."

"Bless us to have a good time!" OJ yelled. Bryce laughed

and swooped over to him. While the boy was growing up tall, he sure was skinny, so Bryce could still lift him up easily, which he did.

OJ laughed and held on to his biological daddy's shoulders. Harry marveled at their relationship, and he just knew Bryce would be the best daddy in the world to his own baby.

Belle had texted a couple of hours ago, saying she'd landed safely in Oklahoma City. Harry wanted to text her or call her right now. He even pulled out his phone to do it. Then he shoved it away as Codi came out with his horse, and he went to saddle the dark brown beast and focus on his time with his family.

Maybe they could drive the beautiful Belle from his mind. Maybe he wouldn't feel like he was missing her too much if he kept busy. Maybe he wouldn't wonder what she needed to know before she could tell him that she loved him if he didn't sit idle for too long.

"Kassie and Reggie are going to meet us in a few minutes," Codi said. "She texted saying they're on their way."

"We better get these guys saddled then," Bryce said. He put OJ down and swooped over to Codi. He kissed her and said, "Thanks for getting the horses out, baby." He put one hand on her belly, which bumped out plenty, as she only had a few months to go before she would deliver their baby. "Can't wait to meet you too, baby." Bryce grinned and then headed back into the stable to get the tack.

"I'll help him," Harry grumbled. He went not because he wasn't happy for Codi and Bryce—of course he was—but because he still wasn't sure if he and Belle were on the same page. They seemed to be reading the same book, but something still felt a little bit off between them.

He'd thought about asking her to marry him in Nashville after the meet-and-greet, but he'd quickly decided against the idea. He knew how he felt about her. He knew what he wanted. He was ready to take that next step.

But Belle had had a whole bunch of doors open to her, and it seemed like she was still trying to pick which one to walk through. And a couple of them didn't have Harry on the other side.

So as he saddled his horse and then mounted it, he tipped his head back into the glorious August sunshine, and he let God carry his burdens. He moved out when everyone else did, and he caught both Codi and Bryce looking over at him, but neither of them asked a question. For Codi, that was nothing new, but for Bryce, that meant the man had employed some serious restraint.

Harry wasn't going to volunteer any information though. He just wanted to spend the afternoon with loved ones and pray that God would take care of the rest.

A FEW DAYS LATER, HE LAY ON THE COUCH WITH KERI, Clay, and Avery, a pillow close to his chest. Daddy and Ev had gone to the grocery store, something they both claimed was far easier if they didn't have to take the kids with them. And Harry had said he'd love to come over and play with them in the backyard if he could get a free meal out of it. Daddy had immediately offered to grill hamburgers and steak.

A kid's cartoon currently blared on the TV in front of him. The world felt slow and small here in this house where he'd grown up, where he'd finished growing up in Coral Canyon. But it wasn't the same without Belle.

Keri got up and wandered into the kitchen. Harry barely paid attention. Clay did the same, and even Avery scooted to the edge of the couch and toddled away.

"Are you alive?" his dad leaned over the back of the couch and looked at him.

Harry flinched and looked up. "Yeah."

"I called your name at least four times," Daddy said.

Ev appeared at his side, her blue eyes seeing so much as she said, "Oh, this is bad. This is so bad."

"This is bad?"

"Look at him, Trace," she said, and Harry wondered what she saw.

He didn't make any move to sit up and instead clutched the pillow tighter and watched the ridiculous animation on screen across the room.

Ev came around the couch and held out her hand. "Give me the pillow, Harry."

"I don't want to," he said in a grouchy, sassy voice.

She sighed and knelt down in front of him. "You don't look good, Harry," she said calmly, quietly, and somehow kindly. "I know exactly what you're feeling, because I lived through this after Avery was born."

Hearing that made his eyes focus on her. He knew that she'd suffered from postpartum depression.

"You think I need to go to the doctor?" he asked, very aware of his father still hovering on the other side of the couch.

"I think you need to figure out why you've hit this low," she said. "You've always been a high-low, high-low kind of guy, but the past month or so has been particularly bad."

Harry had told his daddy that he really liked Belle, but he hadn't told him that he loved her. Part of him felt like he'd gone too fast, like maybe he'd rushed through things when he'd promised he wouldn't.

So he sighed and gave Ev the pillow. She took his hand and helped him sit up. He pushed his fingers through his hair, pressing it flat again from where it had been pushed up as he lay on the couch.

"Is it Belle?" she asked. "Are you still together?"

"Yeah." He sighed heavily afterward. "She's just so focused on Nashville right now," he said. "And I told her I loved her weeks ago and she never said it back." His throat clogged, his voice caught, and he couldn't make himself continue.

He looked down at his hands, which had once felt so capable of doing such great things—dishes, playing tennis, strumming the guitar, writing songs, tying a tie, brushing his teeth, holding Belle's hand.

"I miss her."

Ev looked up to Daddy, and he came around the couch

too. He settled right next to Harry and asked, "You told her you loved her?"

Harry nodded miserably. "And I do, Dad. And I don't know if it's too fast for her or if I'm just not what she wants."

"She hasn't said that, has she?" Daddy asked. Harry shook his head again.

"Well, then don't put words in her mouth," Ev said.

Harry became aware of her trying to communicate with Dad without saying anything, which he found almost comical. He watched them for a moment, and then Ev's bright blue eyes came back to his.

"Why don't you just say it?" Harry asked. "Daddy's clearly not getting it." He grinned at her, and she gave him a soft maternal smile back. She had taken very, very good care of him for the past twelve years, and Harry loved her for it.

"I was just trying to get your father to admit that you Youngs are a little bit intense," she said. "In the very best of ways." She spoke quickly now. "But sometimes it can be a lot."

"Can it?" Harry asked.

"It definitely can," Daddy said with some resignation in his voice. "And Harry, you're not just a Young, you're not just part of this giant family that can overwhelm and smother people in a moment. But you're a country music star too. Maybe she just needs more time."

"Maybe the timing isn't right," he said. "We've been through that before."

"Yeah, and look at you now," Ev said. "Your Daddy and

I had to try a few times too. There's nothing wrong with that."

"And you're far younger than me," Daddy said.

Harry nodded again. Drew in a deep breath and then blew it all out. "I think the kids are still alive at least." He grinned at Ev. "Sorry, I'm...like this?" he questioned. "I'm not really sure how not to be."

"You're going to Nashville in a couple of days," Ev said. "You'll see her, and she'll get through whatever she's doing for the meet and greet." She put both hands on his knees and peered at him. "Remember, Harry, she's still her. Even when she's passionate about something. You're allowed to be passionate about *your* country music, aren't you?"

"Yeah," he said.

"Then she can be about this, too."

"I know," he said.

"Have you let her be passionate about this?" Daddy asked.

"I've supported her every step of the way," Harry growled at him. "I've gone over every paper with her, gave her every contact I have. Heck, I even booked her tickets. Yes, I've been right there supporting her."

And he had been, which also only baffled him as to why she didn't seem to feel as strongly about him as he did her.

"Maybe I am smothering her," he grumbled. No matter what, Belle's main focus didn't seem to be on him, and self-ishly, Harry wanted it to be. He got to his feet and said, "Let me help with dinner."

"Oh, you don't need to do that, baby," Ev said as she got up.

"I need to stay busy," he said. "I'll feel better if I have something to do."

"All right," she said. "Then I'm gonna have you cut up the watermelon." She exchanged a glance with Daddy, who watched Harry in the irritating way he had where he acted like he could see everything Harry thought and felt just by looking.

"You can't stare at me all night or I'm leaving," Harry said as he picked up the big chef's knife that Ev had put on the counter for him.

"All right," Daddy said. "I won't stare at you all night."

"Harry, are you sleeping over?" Keri asked.

"No," Clay said. "He's not sleeping over here. We're sleeping over at his place." He looked up at Harry. "Right?"

Harry ruffled the six-year-old's hair. "That's right, Clay. Y'all are coming with me tonight."

"Not Avery," Ev said. "She gets up way too early for you." She grinned at Harry, and he chuckled because, in the words of Bryce, that was one-hundred percent true.

Two more days, he thought as he cut the watermelon in half. *You just have to make it two more days, and then you'll see Belle again, and everything will be fine.*

46

Belle sat in the Nashville airport, her legs crossed and her foot bouncing, with her baggage standing guard beside her. She'd arrived forty minutes ahead of Harry, and she'd been people-watching to pass the time. She didn't need to go over her notes for the meet-and-greet again. In fact, if she did, she'd want to rip them to shreds.

She'd enjoyed her visit in Oklahoma with her parents, and they seemed happier for her next stage of life than anything else she'd done. She supposed she couldn't ask for more than that, and yet she found herself begging the Lord that the next two days until the meet-and-greet would be some of her sharpest and that the actual event on Tuesday afternoon would be the single best day of her life.

She lifted her hand to her mouth once again and chewed on one of her nails. He should be here any minute, and he'd already texted when he and Adam touched down. Then they just had to deplane and make their way to baggage claim. Harry never carried a bag with him bigger than a backpack, so he'd have checked his bag and both of their guitars. He had taken a picture of himself with them in Jackson Hole this morning, so she knew he'd had them at the gate.

Her phone chimed, and she glanced at it to find a message from Harry: *At the gate.*

She dove onto her phone then and picked it up. *I can't wait to see you,* she said.

She'd never been an overly emotional or sentimental person, but if going undercover had taught her one thing, it was that she did feel things deeply and she did want people around her that she could trust and love.

She had missed her cats terribly when she first returned, and now she had Simba, who brought her such joy. She needed something where she could contribute. She needed something where she could pay her bills. Even though her momma had told her that if she married Harry, why did it matter if she sold a bunch of songs to other artists or not?

It was a good question, one that had been plaguing Belle for several days now. And the truth was: She wanted to matter too. She wanted the bad things and the negative things and the hard things that she'd experienced in her life to be bled out through songs, through writing.

That was what songwriting had always done for her—it had been a form of therapy, and Belle hadn't even realized it until recently.

She couldn't wait to talk to Harry about it. She fixed her gaze on the security exit that all passengers came through when they arrived in Nashville. The baggage claim spread in front of her from there. She was fairly certain she'd see Harry before he saw her.

She knew he was coming, because the flow of people trickled to nothing, almost like he was the last one off the plane instead of seated in row two, first class. That testified of Adam, who cleared the area around Harry wherever he went, especially in crowded places like the airport.

Someone sat down next to Belle just when she thought the opaque glass door would open and Harry would walk through.

"You're Belle Graves," the woman said, and Belle turned her eyes from the security exit to look at her. She'd been sitting here for forty-five minutes, and not a single person had even looked at her strangely.

"Yes," she said, putting a smile on her face.

"I watched four of the live streams that Harry did from Jackson Hole just to see you play *These Empty Halls*. I downloaded it, and I listen to it on repeat when I'm having a bad day." Her face crumbled only for a moment, but Belle saw it.

She reached over and took the woman's hand in hers. "I'm so sorry," she said, for she knew she'd lost someone important to her. She didn't know who or when. But *These Empty Halls* spoke about an amazing love that lingered long after whatever or whoever had gone. It testified to the enduring power of love, and this woman had clearly had it.

"My husband was taken home too soon," she said. "And when I play your song, I can still feel him in our house." She smiled through her tears, and Belle leaned forward and kissed her cheek.

"Bless you," she said. "I'm so glad this song helps."

"I'll leave you alone," the woman said. "I just saw you and wanted to thank you."

"It was my pleasure," Belle said. "Thank *you.*"

The woman got up, quickly wiped her eyes, and walked away, where she met a couple of other women close to her age. They looked like her sisters, and they continued toward the security line entrance. Belle glanced over to the exit again and found more and more people coming through, which meant Harry had already arrived.

She stood and glanced down the row of baggage claim belts, but she didn't see him. Of course she wouldn't. Harry didn't wait for his own baggage. Adam would get it, or security would get it, and they would bring it to wherever he was. Her phone chimed again, and she looked down at it in her hand.

Walking toward you, Harry said. *You okay?*

She looked up again. She still didn't see him. People came and went, hustling and bustling, pulling their luggage behind them, wrangling their kids, and dashing to and fro. They parted, and there stood Harry. He wore a backpack and carried nothing but his glorious smile and a great big cowboy hat.

Belle's heart practically burst within her chest. She hurried toward him and grabbed onto him as he did the same to her. He laughed as he lifted her right up off her feet, but she actually felt like crying—something she rarely did. She sniffled as he set her down, and he bent closer, creating an intimate space between them with his cowboy hat.

"Are you all right?" he asked. "I saw that woman talking to you. What did she say?" He looked around like he'd hunt her down right now and give her a piece of his mind.

"It was good," Belle said. "This is happy emotion."

Harry searched her face. She didn't want to tell him she loved him in the Nashville airport. How lame was that? They had three hotel rooms for the next few days, and she wasn't sure that that was a good place either. She wished she'd have been brave enough to tell him before she left Coral Canyon, but she hadn't been.

"Is Adam getting the luggage?" she asked.

"Yeah, he's waiting with security over there. He figured I'd be okay with you." He grinned at her. "I don't know what that says about me or you, but I'm pretty sure it's not something good." He chuckled, and Belle's happiness doubled.

He tucked her against his side, and they walked back toward where she'd been sitting. Her bag still stood next to the chair, and he sat down next to her where the woman had been, and Belle took his hand in both of hers.

"Harry," she said, her voice and courage suddenly failing her. She looked at the way their fingers fit together, his much larger and longer but still created for the same purpose. She looked up at him, and he looked at her, pure questions, curiosity, and concern in his eyes.

"I'm in love with you," she said simply. "And I know

it's totally lame to tell you in the Nashville airport, but that's how I feel. I figured there's not a better time or place, and you've been waiting a long time for me to say it anyway."

Harry's smile spread slowly across his face, and he leaned closer and closer and closer, and with the brim of his cowboy hat touching her hairline, he said, "I would wait a thousand lifetimes to hear you say you love me. And I will love you for that long as well."

Tears streamed down her face now, and she brushed angrily at them but couldn't get rid of them fast enough. She scoffed, then laughed, and then looked at him.

"You sounded like you were writing a song right then," she said.

He did not laugh or scoff, and his smile had faded. "I mean it," he said. "I've been feeling like maybe we're not on the same page. Maybe God's pulling us into two different timelines again. And I've told Him every day that you've been gone that I will do whatever I have to do, and be wherever I have to be, and say whatever I have to say, to be on the same page as you.

"Because I love you. Because you're it for me. You're everything I want, and being loved by you makes me a better man."

"Are we ready?" Adam asked crisply.

Belle ducked her head further away from him, Harry's lovely words filling her ears, her head, her heart, her very soul.

"You made her cry in the first ten minutes of seeing

her?" Adam griped to Harry. "You are unbelievable. I told you to stay over by me."

Harry burst out laughing, and he stood and moved in front of Belle to shield her and give her some privacy while she composed herself.

"They're happy tears," Harry said. "We need another couple of minutes." He pulled out his wallet and handed it to Adam. "In fact, why don't you go buy us some sodas? I hear it's quite the drive to the hotel, and I'm thirsty."

"You're *thirsty?*" Adam said, his voice incredulous. "I'm buying ten bags of Muddy Buddies," he called as he walked away, leaving the luggage and guitars with Harry and Belle.

Harry sat back down and simply laced his fingers through Belle's. She managed to stop crying; she wiped her face. Her breathing continued to hitch a little bit like it did in a toddler who'd really had a temper tantrum, but she managed to hide it so that anyone walking by surely didn't think that she'd been sobbing.

"When do you want to get married?" he asked softly.

"Is this a proposal?" she whispered back.

"Hardly." He scoffed, then his fingers around hers tightened. "I know I'm intense," he said. "I know I may have moved faster than you in this second part of our relationship, and I'm willing to go slow. Especially if you want to get married in the summer, we've got loads of time to keep dating before I buy a ring."

"I don't believe for a single second that you didn't buy a ring this week," she said, and Harry brought his hand to his chest.

"Miss Belle," he said as if she'd wounded him greatly. "I did no such thing." He grinned at her, and Belle wasn't sure if he was kidding or not.

"We don't have to talk about it right now," he said, the left side of his smile lowering faster than the right. "These next few days are about the meet-and-greet and the meet-and-greet only. But I would like to know."

"Do people get married in the winter in Wyoming?" she asked.

"It's not recommended," Harry said dryly. "But my uncle Luke did it, and he and Sterling didn't die. Indoor wedding, though."

Belle grinned at him and laid her head against his shoulder. "I love you, Harry Young," she said. "I'd marry you tomorrow. So whenever you ask me, we'll just pick a date and get it done."

He laid his head against hers. While he'd already said the most amazing things, there was nothing quite as magical as hearing the cowboy she loved say, "I'd marry you tomorrow too, my Belle."

47

arry opened his hotel room door and found Adam standing there in one of his crisp black suits. He had spent yesterday morning interviewing with other people, which had put Harry in a bad mood and sent him into a tailspin for the evening.

This afternoon though, he was ready to take Belle over to the Motown building for their meet-and-greet. Adam looked at Harry, his eyes traveling down the length of his body to his shiny cowboy boots.

"Wow, sir," he said. "You look amazing."

Harry grinned at him. "So do you, brother."

He reached to shake Adam's hand and then pulled him into a hug. He wanted to tell him he'd miss him, and he was real sorry that he didn't want to keep being a country music star. But he and Adam had hashed through it a couple of times already, and Harry just wanted to enjoy the rest of their time together. Adam wasn't quite gone yet, and Harry would have him through the end of September.

"You go get Belle," Adam said. "I'll meet you guys in the lobby."

Belle's room sat three doors down from Harry's, and Adam continued past it to the elevator so that Harry could pick her up alone. Belle had bought her dress online, and he couldn't wait to see her in it.

She'd been nervous yesterday too, which had contributed to his anxiety and bad mood. Harry told himself that everything would work out. No matter what happened this afternoon, he had Belle, he loved her, and she loved him. They'd return to Wyoming together, and they'd build their life there.

He knocked on her door, and she yelled, "Coming!" from inside. He'd gotten them suites, so they had sitting areas as well as beds, but it still only took about five seconds to make it to the door and open it. She moved her hand up the door and gripped it, cocking her hip out and putting her hand on it. Everything about her glittered, and Harry felt like someone had poured sparkles into his bloodstream.

"Wow." He blinked as his eyes slid down from her eyes. "Wow, wow, wow," he said as he drank in the form-fitting ballgown. It looked like she was going to the Country Music Awards as Artist of the Year, not a meet-and-greet on a Tuesday afternoon in September.

The dress bore the color of royalty—deep purple—and had multicolored gems that seemed to put off a rainbow effect from the shoulder straps to the skirt that barely brushed the floor. She wore black heels and dark burgundy lipstick, and her hair pulled back out of the way—professional, sophisticated, classy.

And while it wasn't a Sheriff's vest, the dress still made Harry's blood run hotter through his veins.

"Are you my date?" she asked coyly.

Harry grinned at her and said, "I sure am."

She glanced left and right. "Where's Adam?"

"Waiting for us in the lobby."

"Okay, let me grab my purse." She moved out of the doorway, and the door started to swing closed. Harry barely managed to get his boot in it so it wouldn't slam shut in his face.

Belle returned with a small, black, quilted purse with a gold chain she looped around her wrist. "I've got my phone and my thread wallet." When she looked at him, pure nerves lived in her eyes.

"It's going to be fine," he said. "These are people we know."

"These are people *you* know," she said. "I've never met any of them."

"Sure you have." He put his hand on her hip and guided her down the hall. "I believe one of the execs from your old label is going to be there."

"Don't say stuff like that, Harry," she said. "I don't want to think about it."

He chuckled and turned to press the button for the elevator. But of course, Adam stood there, not down in the lobby, and he pressed the button when he saw Harry and Belle.

"You look amazing," Adam said, his smile professional and charming.

"So do you." Belle returned his smile. "Thank you so much for all the work you've done on this, Adam." She stepped into him and swept her lips across his cheek without leaving a single smudge of lipstick.

"He gets a kiss, and I don't?" Harry griped good-naturedly.

Belle turned to him, her eyes wide. "I can't kiss you now," she said. "Then you'll have lipstick all over that beautiful mouth of yours." She grinned at him and fell back to his side. She took his hand, and Harry liked that she led in some things and claimed him, making him feel wanted and desired.

Adam had a car waiting at the curb, and they made their way to the Motown building quickly. The party didn't start for another forty-five minutes, but Belle wanted to go around and talk to everyone—the waitstaff, the kitchen, and the manager of the restaurant—to let them know how much she appreciated them hosting her event.

Harry did the same, and they both signed albums, cards, and even T-shirts. He didn't mind, because he did like talking to people, especially about his music. And he heard more than one person tell Belle that *These Empty Halls* really meant something to them.

She glowed as if someone had sprayed her with iridescent chemicals and then shone a black light on her. She radiated waves of fuchsia, hot pink, and turquoise, and Harry basked in the sound of her laugh, the vibrancy of her smile, and the way she truly cared about people.

Adam came and got them and said, "We're five minutes out. People are lining up outside, and the manager wants to know if he should let them in early."

"Yes," Belle said, her face a bit flushed. "Let's go, Harry."

Their guitars waited for them in the corner, as they would be playing three songs today—all of them Belle's. Everyone knew of Harry's songwriting ability, and he didn't mind turning the spotlight on her.

He'd have no problem selling songs in the country music industry, and he wanted the same for Belle. As he went with her, he could just see his name and hers lined up in the credits of an album: *Written by Harry and Belle Young.*

The thought made his heart grow ten sizes.

Adam nodded to the manager, who opened the doors and said, "Welcome to Tumbleweeds," and people began to stream into the building.

Harry and Belle stood back a little bit, and he had his rockstar smile on to match her movie star one.

"Welcome," Belle said as she stepped forward to shake hands. "I'm Belle Graves. So great to meet you."

The woman who got there first was a talent scout, and they continued to welcome managers, agents, and music executives for the next thirty minutes. Belle's invitation had been very clear: it was not an open house. The event would run from four to six-thirty, where they would do a half-hour of welcome, then she and Harry would present and play, and then they would be around for a Q&A session, visiting, and well, a meet-and-greet. The event would be done by six-thirty so everyone could attend other things that evening if they wanted or needed to.

She glanced over to Harry, and for the first time in the past couple of hours, since he picked her up from her hotel room, he saw a tell of her nerves. "You ready?" she asked.

"Sweetheart, we were born ready for this." He grinned at her, and they made their way over to the small stage that had been set up specifically for this event. They did poetry readings here too, as well as other one-man concerts, usually someone on the piano or guitar.

Tonight, Belle lifted the hem of her skirt and stepped up on the stage. Harry handed over her guitar, and then he took his from Adam and joined her. Everyone had gathered around the chest-high tables closest to the stage, holding drinks and noshing on mini appetizers.

The waitstaff faded away, and all eyes came to Belle, even Harry's. She looked like she might pass out, or throw up, or both, and Harry fell in love with her all over again in that moment.

He wanted to ask her to be his wife that evening, but he didn't have the diamond ring with him. No, he truly wanted to ask her to be his in Coral Canyon, the place where they would build their life together. Not Nashville, the first chapter of his life that he was turning the page on.

"Welcome, everyone," Belle said again. She reached up and touched her chest right above the neckline of her dress.

"I'm Belle Graves, and I'm from Oklahoma City, Oklahoma. I've been living for the past, oh, eight or nine years." She glanced over to Harry and gave him a winning smile before she focused on the crowd again. "In Jackson Hole, Wyoming. I'm a missing persons investigator for the Teton County Sheriff's Department, and I've done one stint of undercover work. And let me tell you, that is a far cry from where I stand today."

Several people laughed and twittered, but all Harry felt was pure pride. His beautiful Belle standing in front of everyone and talking about these hard things that had plagued her for so long—unbelievable.

She'd made great strides in therapy, but truly, Harry had seen the biggest difference when she started to play with him on tour. Her music *healed* her, and Harry heard the Lord yelling at him as he stood on that tiny stage in Nashville.

The world got very, very small—so small that it was just Belle. Harry wasn't even there. He floated away somewhere else, and he knew that Belle would need to have songwriting and music in her life to be whole and complete—to bleed out the bad, to erase the hurt, and to calm the stormy seas.

He blinked, and everything zoomed in again. He stood on the stage with her, and she'd continued by saying, "Beside me is a country music legend. Most of you probably know Harry Young." She beamed over at him, and he gave her a smile back before he turned his charms on the crowd.

"He just finished his third album for Rebel Records, and he's decided that he wants a slower pace of life in Wyoming with his family, a girlfriend with a cat, and maybe an adopted dog that he hasn't committed to yet."

More chuckling came from the music executives, as well as Harry himself. As far as he knew, Belle had not written a script. She was just good with people, and while it looked like she might fall apart right up until the moment she opened her mouth, once she did, she was in complete control, dialed in, ready to nail it.

"We've prepared three songs for you today," she said. "I wrote all three of them in a time before I met Harry Young, which is a pretty good story. And if you want to hear it, we're going to be around for a couple of hours after this—but I'm sure we'll have two different versions."

Harry had not said a word yet, and he wasn't going to. Belle lifted her guitar into position, two fingers on the strings.

"I'm a sucker at heart," Belle said. "And I love love songs. So this first song is called *Fields of Forever*. Then we're going to play one called *Tangled Up in Tennessee*, and then *Under the Southern Sky*."

She looked over at Harry. "Harry is much more of a showboat than I am, and he could probably be persuaded to play something for you of his own, if you'd like. I'll leave that up to him after we do these three songs." She nodded at him, and Harry only wanted to lean closer and kiss her despite their guitars between them.

She looked down at her strings, stepped closer to the mic, and started to play. Pure beauty came from Belle when she played the guitar, and Harry wasn't even sure she knew it. He knew it, though. He could see it—almost a tangible energy that came from her and flowed out in gentle waves, entrancing everyone who heard the beautiful, glorious music she could produce with her fingers and the strings of her guitar.

He blinked when Belle looked over at him, something urgent in her eyes, and he realized he'd missed his cue to come in. He was supposed to sing the first verse, and he'd blown it, because he was staring at his gorgeous girlfriend.

He cleared his throat, and she plucked through the notes again, leading him where he needed to go. He hoped she always would.

At the right time this time, he leaned into the mic and started to sing. *"In the quiet of the morning*
With the mountain dew on the ground,
I walk through the fields not making a sound.
I feel your hand in mine,
Your heartbeat echoing strong,
Your love is the rhythm, and your kiss is the rhyme."

Belle stopped playing, and she leaned forward and said, "We're going to go ahead and start this one over, folks. Harry just sang beautifully, but he forgot that he's supposed to play the guitar too."

She giggled into the microphone, and pure embarrassment filled Harry. He still hovered only an inch or two away from his mic, and he said, "If your girlfriend was this pretty and this incredible, you'd forget too."

That caused laughter to echo through the restaurant, and Harry met Adam's eyes. The man smiled from way in the back, near where he stood with the manager and the waitstaff.

Belle said, "We're just going to go ahead and try this one again. I swear we've practiced."

"My fault," Harry said. "I won't mess up this time." He played a riff on his guitar just to prove that he could. Belle started again, and this time Harry came in in the right place with the vocals *and* the instrument. They played the song, those four minutes some of the most beautiful four minutes of Harry's life.

One of the music executives wiped her eyes at the end, and they all cheered and clapped like they had just been privileged to witness one of the greatest concerts of their life. The evening was far from over, but Harry wouldn't make another mistake. He'd had so many revelations in the past hour, and he needed some time to himself to go over them. Maybe journal them out. Maybe write some songs about them.

But most of all, he couldn't wait to get back to Belle's room, curl up with her in a pair of sweats and a T-shirt, put something on the TV, and hold her as they lay on the couch together.

They'd talk through everything that had happened tonight and everything Belle wanted to happen in the future. But the world would narrow to just the two of them —something small and meaningful and beautiful.

When they finished the third song to more raucous applause and cheering, Harry slid his guitar around his back, took Belle in his arms, and kissed her. That caused the whooping to turn to a different kind, and catcalls and whistles filled the air.

Belle pushed against his chest, and Harry stepped back. Then he lifted her hand in the air as if they had just won a wrestling match, and then they went out to talk to everyone.

48

Belle sat on the front steps of Harry's house, her knees pulled up to her chest as she watched the sleepy neighborhood beyond. Fall had definitely arrived in Wyoming, with the aspens boasting their glorious, fiery leaves in every shade of yellow and orange known to mankind. She loved the white-barked trees, and Harry owned a clump of them that stood proudly in the corner of his front yard.

A sneeze behind her made her turn as the front door opened, and Harry and Adam's voices filled the air.

"She's just sitting out here on the steps," Adam said. "I'm sorry, Miss Belle, I didn't mean to make you sit outside."

"You didn't," she said as she twisted to look over her shoulder at him. "I knew you guys had stuff to talk about."

"How long have you been out here?" Harry asked as he settled beside her.

She smiled at him and kissed him quickly. "I don't know, twenty or thirty minutes."

Adam sighed and settled on Belle's other side.

"So," she asked. "What's the news?" For she knew they'd have news. In fact, big things were going down in Coral Canyon with the Young family.

Kassie and Reggie would have their baby before Christmas, with Bryce's and Codi's coming before Thanksgiving.

That alone had caused a huge stir in the family. Harry had quit his country music career, and just last week, Morris had announced that his house would be finished before Halloween, and he'd need all the help he could get to move.

But that wasn't really the noteworthy news coming out of the Morris branch of the Young family tree. What was? The fact that he would like to retire from being Country Quad's manager.

That news had stunned all the Youngs into silence, even the babies, and Belle smiled just thinking about when he'd said it at a family dinner only a single Sabbath Day ago.

"Do you want to tell her?" Adam asked.

"It's not my news to tell," Harry said, and he did sound a bit grumpy.

She reached over and took his hand. "We're still going out to your uncle's recording studio right after this, right?"

"Yeah," he said. "They're expecting us."

The meet-and-greet in Nashville had gone quite well.

They'd only been home for a couple of weeks, but they'd both gotten a lot of interest in their songs. Belle received emails and calls every day, and she'd started working on a deal for one of the songs she and Harry had performed at Tumbleweeds.

She wanted to be able to produce more demos, and Harry had said they could go look at the white-barn-recording-studio that stood behind Tex and Abby Young's home on the northeast side of Coral Canyon.

Belle turned her attention to Adam now, raising her eyebrows, because if Harry didn't have news, then Adam must.

"Country Quad has asked me to be their manager," he said.

A smile burst onto Belle's face, but Adam looked like he'd swallowed an entire bushel of lemons.

"Don't be so happy about it," Harry said from her other side. "He's not happy about it."

"I *am* happy about it," Adam argued back. "I love Coral Canyon."

Belle felt whipped between the two of them like she was watching a tennis match in 3D. She glanced to Harry and then back to Adam. "What's the problem then?"

"I have another offer," Adam said.

Of course he did, because Adam possessed talent in spades. Belle had never met anyone who could do what he did, and he had a lot of contacts in security at airports, restaurants, and more.

"Who is it?" she asked.

"Yeah," Harry echoed. "Who is it?"

"You don't know?" Belle turned her attention back to him. Left to Adam. Right to Harry. Left, right, left, right.

"He won't tell me," Harry said.

"I don't have to tell you who I'm working for next," Adam said. "My last day with you is six days from now. And then you don't get to know anything."

"We're *friends*," Harry said, all the bluster in Adam going out, and Belle watched the last of it as she turned back to Harry.

"My *best* friend," Adam said. "I'm sorry, Harry, but I've signed an NDA that I would not disclose who I interviewed with in Nashville, and if that was you, you would expect me not to say."

"You're right," Harry grumbled.

"Are you going to take the job in Nashville?" Belle asked, truly surprised. "You can't do that. You've got to stay here."

"I do?" Adam asked acidly.

"*We're* here," Belle said as she linked her arm through his. "We want you here. Is Country Quad not paying well?"

"They're paying plenty," Harry said.

"As if you know," Adam fired back. He softened again as he looked at Belle. "Yes, they're paying well."

"Well enough for Wyoming," she said with a grin.

And Adam finally smiled. "Well enough for Wyoming."

All three of them seemed to breathe out at the same time, a collective sigh that influenced the breeze. It picked up, rustling the leaves in the trees. Then Adam put his palms on his knees and stood.

He exhaled heavily again and said, "I'd better get going."

"See you later, Adam," Belle called, but Harry simply glared him down the stairs and then the sidewalk.

"You are seriously so grumpy," Belle complained to him.

He lifted his arm and put it around her. "Do we have to go to the recording studio tonight? I just want to lay on the couch with you."

"Yes, we have to go to the recording studio first," she said. "Besides, I heard they have a couch in the lobby there where you used to do your homework after school."

He turned his glare on her. "We're not cuddling on the couch in the recording studio."

"Fine," she said as she got to her feet. "*I'm* going to the recording studio. If you're in such a bad mood that you can't come and be pleasant, then just stay here."

He looked up at her, and for half a second, she thought he really was too grumpy to come. But then he said, "I'm sorry, Belle," and pulled her back to the steps. "Forgive me?"

She searched his face. "You're going to miss him terribly."

"I already do," he whispered. She didn't want to tease him, because Harry hadn't needed help with his grocery shopping and getting dinner reservations. He needed to ensure his safety, and Adam had done that flawlessly.

"Maybe he'll stay," she said quietly.

Harry shook his head sadly. "You never know with Adam."

"He's a real go-getter," Belle said as Adam drove away from the house in the sleepy suburb of Coral Canyon. "Small town life might not be for him."

"Might not be," Harry said. He took a breath and let it all out too. "Come on. Let's go. I told Uncle Tex we'd be there around six, and we're already going to be late."

Belle let him stand first, and then he pulled her to her feet as well. He drove them twenty-five minutes from his house in the middle of Coral Canyon to the outer edge of town where the bigger farms and ranches sprawled.

"How much land does your uncle have?" Belle asked as Harry pulled into the driveway. A cute farmhouse sat there with a patch of lawn that looked like it had some parts where the sprinkler system didn't quite reach.

"Two hundred acres," Harry said. "Abby's brother lives right next door. He's got that much too. They work hard."

"Uncle Tex works the ranch?" she asked.

"I think he's got a couple men who come to help, but Tex takes care of it, yeah."

Belle nodded, and for some reason, she couldn't get out of the truck. Harry stayed in his seat too, both of them just looking out the windshield, with the farmhouse on the left and a barn straight back past the garage.

"Why am I nervous?" Belle asked.

"I don't know," Harry said. "It's just a recording studio."

"I've been in one before," Belle said.

"Maybe you don't have good memories of it?" He finally tore his attention away from whatever he'd been studying on the horizon and looked at her.

"Maybe," she said. "We'll go in together, right?"

"Yeah, we're gonna go together." He got out of the truck and then came around to open her door.

They started past the steps that went up to the second-floor entrance on the side of the house, and Belle asked, "Do we need to go get your uncle?"

"Nope," Harry said. "He said it would be open."

Around the back of the house, Belle found a big deck shading a patio, more manicured lawn, and a white sidewalk that led diagonally through it to the most perfect white barn she'd ever seen in her life.

"This is really nice," she said, awed.

The barn had no windows and only one door in the front, and a nervous flutter wove through her bloodstream with every step she took.

"Oh," she said, her feet faltering. "I left my guitar in the truck."

"They'll have plenty out there," Harry said.

"But I want mine," Belle said.

"All right," he said easily. "Go grab it. I'll wait here." He waved her on, and Belle turned to hurry back to the truck. He hadn't brought his guitar, probably because he had one here, though he'd never said that. Either way, Belle wanted hers, and she grabbed her case from the backseat and started back toward the barn. The door opened by the entrance, and Melissa came out.

"Hey, Belle," she called, and Belle stopped, though she wanted to get back to Harry as fast as possible.

"Hey, Melissa," she said.

"Are you gonna play in the barn?" the girl asked.

"Yeah," she said. "Your daddy said it was okay."

"Yeah, it's fine," Melissa said. "My mama wanted to invite you and Harry to dinner after."

"I think we're counting on it," Belle said, because Abby had already invited them for dinner.

"She made pizza pockets. And they're *so* good."

"Okay," Belle said. "I don't think we're going to be long. We're just doing a tour and a little soundcheck."

Abby poked her head out of the house behind Melissa. "Take all the time you want, Belle," she said. "The pizza pockets keep warm forever." She grinned too, and then she guided her daughter back into the house.

Belle went between the steps and the garage again and started up the sidewalk before she realized that Harry wasn't standing there anymore. He'd been complaining about the heat this summer, and while it was almost October and definitely not hot, she would never describe Harry as outdoorsy.

He liked horses and horseback riding, but he'd never taken her hiking or camping. He never even *mentioned* doing those things.

She figured she could open a door and walk into a recording studio by herself. She simply didn't want to. As she approached, her fingers tightened around the handle of her guitar case, and she slowed. God seemed to know that she couldn't do this on her own, because the door opened and Harry came out.

"There you are," he said brightly. "Got it?" He reached

for her guitar and took it from her, then raised his eyes to hers again. "Come on, baby. It's just a couple more steps, and then you'll be inside."

She swallowed and nodded as he took her hand and guided her into the recording studio. They entered a lobby, the door in the middle of it. The couch Harry where had done his homework sat on to the right, with only empty space on the left.

In front of her, a wall of glass separated this entryway from the recording studio, and Belle realized the genius in such design. This way, someone could come into the recording studio without interrupting the actual recording. So the band could finish their song and still have guests.

She saw all the typical equipment—the huge panels with knobs and sliders and buttons—and then the studio beyond with its soundproofing materials. The weird way the ceilings and walls echoed the sound back to the band. There were indeed many guitars, a drum set, and microphones everywhere.

"They don't use it much anymore," Harry said. "It's kind of a mess right now."

"Making music is kind of messy," Belle murmured. She hadn't written since she'd been home from Nashville, but she could definitely feel something buzzing and burning inside of her. A new song would come out soon enough.

"This is incredible," she said.

"Right?" Harry chuckled. "For a barn out in the middle of Wyoming."

She met his eyes. "Can we play?"

"Yeah, let's go play." He led the way in, and he took her guitar out of its case for her, then selected one from a stand in the corner.

"This is my dad's," he said. "I think I can probably play it."

"Yeah, I think you probably can," she said dryly.

He started to pluck through some chords, but Belle didn't have her strap on yet. The guitar Harry had chosen did. His fingers moved as expertly as ever as he looked up at her and said, "My dad and I wrote this song for Ev when they were dating."

Then he moved straight into singing.

The first time Belle heard a song, she paid attention to her emotions and how she felt. It was hard to hear every word and capture the exact meaning of lines that were short and stanzas that had to be put together to complete thoughts. But her heart and soul had been born of music, and it didn't take her long to realize that this was a love song.

Harry only sang one verse and one chorus, and she started to clap, her smile absolutely huge on her face. She surely looked like a magic clown. Harry didn't return the gesture. He looked down at his hands, the notes and rhythm automatically changing to something else. She hadn't heard this song before. When Harry looked up at her, his eyes burned with dark fire.

"In a small-town Wyoming world where big dreams fly,
A country music star finds love in your eyes,
We'll build a home with laughter, cats, and song,
A missing heart found, with you lying here in my arms."

Tears burned in Belle's eyes, for he'd written her a song about their love story.

"Through every song and every tear we've shared,

Even when we were apart, I've always cared,

Two stars collided, found rest in each other's arms,

Will you marry me, and make me the happiest man on this farm?"

Then he performed the classic Harry move and swung his guitar around to his back. With the phenomenal acoustics of the recording studio, the last chord he played still hung in the air, reverberating around from corner to corner and floor to ceiling as he dropped to both knees in front of her.

He stuck his hand in his pocket and pulled out a ring and held it up. "Every moment with you has been a blessing, and I wish I could've met you sooner simply so I could love you longer."

Belle sighed, because what a perfect line.

"I know I'm an impatient man," Harry said, lifting his eyes from the glinting gem to Belle's. "But I want to be with you right now and forever. We had to wait to get where we are, and I don't want to wait anymore. Will you marry me?"

"Yes," Belle gasped out.

Harry grinned at her, all of his grumpiness gone, and said, "Well, get over here then."

She practically threw her guitar in her haste to get closer to him. Thankfully, she didn't, and she managed to set it in a stand and get close enough for him to slip the diamond onto her ring finger.

She pulled in a breath and stared at it. "Harry, this is a really big diamond."

He got to his feet and gathered her close, sending warm shivers through her veins. He gazed down at her and said, "You are my ultimate happiness. I'm so glad that our timeline has finally come to this."

He leaned down and kissed her. Belle had never felt as loved or as cherished as she did in that moment, kissing the man she loved, who loved her, and who would become her husband.

After several seconds, she pulled away. "When did you write that song?"

He chuckled and swayed with her. "I wrote it this morning, so it's still rough. But, since I've had the ring since we got back from Nashville, I figured now might be as good a time as any to ask you."

"It was perfect," she said.

He slid his lips down the side of her neck and kissed her there. "A winter wedding?" he whispered.

"It's almost October already," she said, her skin smoking and sizzling where he touched it.

"January then?"

"That's only four months."

He lifted his head and looked at her with such hope that Belle couldn't deny him. She also had no idea why she wouldn't be able to get married in four months. And even though something in the back of her mind needled at her, whispering, *This is* the *Harry Young*, and surely *he* would need longer than four months, she nodded and said, "I'd love to marry you in January."

Read on for a sneak peek at **JOEY**, the next book in the Young Brothers series. Can she make a relationship with Adam work while figuring out her life too?

Scan the QR code below to preorder JOEY now!

Sneak Peek! Joey Chapter One:

J oelle Young carried a clear plastic tote up the wide steps at Uncle Morris's house. "Keep going, Ana," she said to her younger sister, who carried two grocery sacks. One had a loaf of bread and a bag of hot dog buns in it, and the other had two bags of chips.

The girl had just turned eight years old, and she exuded spunk and sass. She loved ponies, coloring, and hula hooping, and Joey loved her with her whole heart.

"In the kitchen," she said to her sister as she crossed the threshold of the house. The tote she carried had been labeled "office," and Joey detoured to the left just off the foyer of this great big mansion that Uncle Morris and Aunt Lee had built for their family.

It sat on the northern highway of Coral Canyon, just inside the city limits, and had taken them almost a year and a half to get to today—moving day. Everyone in the Young family had been recruited to help move five children and two adults, as well as a pet lizard, a *secret* pet snake—that Uncle Morris and Aunt Lee had found out about and steadfastly refused to move from their other house—and a hot tub.

Joey barely weighed a hundred pounds, but she'd tied back her white-blond hair and was determined to help her aunt and uncle however she could. She usually ended up doing something with the kids to keep them out of the way, and she didn't mind that.

Today, she went back and forth with OJ and Ana, each of them carrying something light that someone had set in a pile for movers just like them. *Many hands make light work,* as Grams said, but sometimes it could also put a lot of bodies in a small space, and that didn't help anybody.

Joey had moved back to Coral Canyon after her first and only year at the Culinary Institute in New York City, and she had been working two jobs and living with her grandparents since. She told herself she was only twenty-two years old and she didn't need to have every step of her life mapped out.

She liked working at the bakery and had graduated from being a roller-skating runner of orders to a baker. That meant she had to be awake, dressed, and alert by four a.m. so she could have pastries ready to be bought and picked up when Cake Bites opened at six.

Her boss, a woman named Miriam, was a smart businesswoman. She had built and opened her bakery right next to a coffee shop. Aunt Michelle owned Daily Grind, and the two ladies often ran specials for each other's shops. Aunt

Michelle had stopped her own in-house baking and simply purchased from the bakery next door.

Joey's new baker position meant she had to quit at Michelle's coffee shop. She didn't mind working in the food service industry; she loved to cook, after all.

To fill her evenings, she had gotten a job with Ev's brother, Shawn. He owned a catering company called Pork & Beans and had expanded it to a single restaurant in Coral Canyon. Joey worked on the catering side, which meant she didn't have to interact with people very often, and she got to cook—something she loved.

When she wasn't working in either of those places, she tested recipes in her granny's kitchen, fed her grandparents, and kept them company while spending afternoons with her tablet, taking them for walks, or lying in bed watching crime documentaries.

She wondered if her life would simply be baking cupcakes in the morning and smoking meat in the afternoon. *It wouldn't be a bad life*, she told herself as a commotion broke out in the kitchen.

"I told you now wasn't a good time to do this egg experiment," Aunt Leigh said, handing Eric a roll of paper towels. "Clean them up and get out of here." She sounded stressed, and Joey wanted to help.

She waited while Eric muttered his apology and started cleaning up the broken eggs that had fallen to the floor— their brand new, pristine tile floor.

She met Aunt Leigh's eyes. "Can I take the kids somewhere where we could help you unpack?" she asked.

Aunt Leigh ran her hands through her hair, pushing her bangs back as she sighed. "Yes. Why don't you take the girls into the sewing room? Rachelle helped me pack it up, and she'll be able to help you guys get everything put away."

Joey nodded and glanced over to Eric, a gangly fifteen-year-old who'd been making messes since he was a little boy.

"Eric's going to go outside with all of Luke's kids and Uncle Gabe. They're working on setting up the shed out there." Aunt Leigh gave her son a severe glare, and he tossed the ruined paper towels in the trash and stalked out.

"All right," Joey called. "Rosie, you're with me. Corinne, Rachelle, Liesl, Grace, Celeste, Melissa, Carter, Pippa, Keri, and Clay. Let's go unpack the sewing room."

That was basically every child between the ages of five and twelve in the Young family, and Joey led the way down the hall to the room where Aunt Leigh had put all of her sewing things. Joey had underestimated how many boxes there would be, and she and all the kids could barely fit in the room with them.

"Okay," Rosie said, whipping a pocketknife out of her back pocket. Joey simply blinked and stared at her. She wasn't even sure if she'd ever *held* a pocketknife before, but in Rosie's hand, it looked like a natural extension. Rosie was all wild cowgirl, while Joey was more of a stay-indoors-and-read type of girl.

Rosie had started riding horses by age four, following her daddy, her cousin Cash, and her brother into the rodeo. She'd just started training to ride the barrels, and Joey actually couldn't wait to see her do it at next summer's rodeo.

"Rachelle, you get up here and help," Joey said. She turned and found the wall to her right completely full of built-in shelves. "What do you think your mama wants to put over here?"

"Her fabrics will go there," Rachelle said.

Rosie lifted out patterns, set the box down so that smaller hands than hers could take the things out of them, and sliced open another box.

"Okay, everyone," Joey said. "You're going to take something out of the box, bring it to me or Rachelle, and we'll decide where to put it. Okay?"

Several *okay's* chorused back to her, and Joey had been part of the Young family long enough to be used to this sort of chaos. Her family hadn't moved since Daddy had married Georgia when Joey was only eight years old. Joey herself had moved to Jackson Hole to go to college and then to New York City to go to the Culinary Institute, and then back.

Always back home.

Where will you move next? she thought as she established one of the shelves for Aunt Lee's patterns.

Rosie broke down the boxes as they went through them, which created more room. Joey opened the cupboards built into the other wall to reveal more storage, more shelves, more places to put things.

She thought of Bryce and Codi and Kassie and Reggie about to become parents. She thought about Belle and Harry and their recent engagement. Joey wondered if she'd ever meet that just-right man for her. She had dated a lot in high school and even had a couple of boyfriends in college.

No one in New York City, as the enormity of that place had scared her more than she thought it would.

And no one here in Coral Canyon, though she knew some cowboys who hadn't left town after they'd graduated from high school. No one seemed interested, and Joey wasn't really looking for a boyfriend anyway.

She had just turned to tell Grace, Liesl, and Celeste to go put a sewing basket on the lowest shelf by the door, when OJ asked, "What about this, Joey?"

Joey turned and came face-to-face with a cupboard door that had not been opened a moment ago, and she rammed it with her face. She cried out, and her hands flew up to cover her nose. She tasted blood on the back of her tongue, and tears flooded her eyes. Pain smarted through her sinuses and down her cheekbones, but Joey was more startled and embarrassed than anything.

She cried when her emotions got the best of her, and so it wasn't surprising to her that tears streamed down her face.

"I'm sorry," OJ said, and he really meant it. He was a sweet kid that wouldn't hurt a spider, but instead carried it outside so it could be free.

"It's not your fault," Rosie said as she closed the door. "We just gotta be careful, guys."

"It's fine," Joey said, her voice nasally and pinched. "I just need to go to the bathroom." She rushed out of the sewing room.

Behind her, she heard Rosie start to lecture Ana for opening the cupboard door when Joey had been standing right there. Her nose stung and her heartbeat flopped in her chest for some reason.

She ducked into the bathroom, but her nose wasn't bleeding too badly. Thankfully, as she didn't handle the sight of her own blood very well. To her great relief, the bleeding stopped within a few seconds, but she couldn't stop sniffling.

"This is so stupid," she whispered as she tossed the tissue away so she didn't have to see the blood. She wasn't even sure why she had completely lost control of her emotions.

Her uncles kept bustling by the bathroom with bigger boxes and items of furniture as they had to go past her to get to the stairs that led to the second floor where a lot of the children's bedrooms waited. Down the hall, she heard crying, which had to be Lee and Morris's twins who had just turned two.

Suddenly, everything felt too big, too chaotic, and too fast. Joey rushed out of the bathroom, kept her head low as she ducked around the corner, and then went out the back door.

In the corner of the yard to her right, Uncle Gabe, Uncle Morris, and several of the older teen boys still wrestled with garden tools, a lawn mower, a wheelbarrow, several rakes and shovels, and other larger equipment waiting outside the shed for its proper placement.

Joey ducked to the left, away from them. Her chest hitched with every step, and she held a new tissue to her nose to check if it was bleeding. It wasn't. Aunt Lee and

Uncle Morris had built a large house, and it seemed to take forever to gain the corner and duck around it.

The side yard over here wasn't very big, maybe only fifteen feet between the house and the fence beside it, and shade covered everything here. Joey pressed her back into the house and slid down until she reached the ground, her knees folded to her chest. She put her head against them and cried, hoping that this tsunami of emotions and this deluge of tears would subside, and she could get back and continue being helpful.

Several trees had been left on the property, giving Aunt Lee and Uncle Morris a maturely landscaped yard. As Joey quieted, she listened to the wind rustle through the tall trees. The leaves had already started to fall, and in fact, most were gone as Halloween lingered only ten days away now.

She sniffled, but thankfully she wasn't outright sobbing anymore. She'd just checked to make sure her nose wasn't bleeding again when someone came around the front corner of the house, saying in a clipped voice, "I can't help that, Delaney. It's not my job to find you an assistant."

Adam Harmon. Glorious, gorgeous Adam Harmon.

The blond god of a man took two steps and then turned as he paced back the way he'd come. Clearly, he hadn't seen Joey. Her breathing turned shallow, because she didn't want him to find her there, pressed against the side of the house, bleeding and crying.

You're not bleeding, a voice whispered in her head. But she may as well have been, and Joey simply felt stitched together wrong right now.

Adam, however, had been cut from one of God's choicest cloths. He had hair the color of the warmest sandy beach Joey could imagine, and those broad shoulders.... Joey dreamt about them at night.

He wore a suit coat as well as he did a polo, and Joey hadn't realized he'd be there to help Uncle Morris move. In fact, Joey thought Adam had left Coral Canyon at the beginning of the month to start a new job with a new country music star in Nashville.

Her heartbeat thundered like a herd of stampeding mustangs as she heard his voice fill her ears. She couldn't even tell what he said, but he certainly didn't seem happy. She wondered who Delaney was.

Probably his girlfriend, she thought. Adam had to be a decade older than her, and she had no right to be crushing on the man at all. He'd helped her several months ago when a rude customer at Cake Bites had launched into her, that was all.

She'd fallen and skinned her knees, and oh, Joey couldn't handle the sight of her own blood, and she'd nearly fainted in Adam's car. He'd doctored her up and taken care of her, and she couldn't help but wish he'd come around the corner of the house to do the same thing again today.

He'd sit down on the ground beside her, put his arm around her, pull her close, and say, *Tell me why you're crying, Roo.* And she would, and he wouldn't judge her, and he wouldn't make her try to spell out why she felt the way she did.

He turned around again and started along the length of the house, and Joey held very, very still.

"I did not violate any contracts," he said. "I did not sign a contract, and as Mister Young has said, you're free to hire someone else. I followed everything to the letter of the law, and I never signed an employment contract. In fact, I *told you* eight days prior to the agreed-upon signing day that I would *not* be signing and that you would need to find someone else."

Joey's nose started to itch, and it felt like it might leak a trickle of blood at any moment. She lifted her hand as slowly as she could to press the tissue there.

Adam's eyes zoomed to her. He froze, suddenly silent and unmoving, his phone stuck in his ear and his mouth partway open still. Then he barked, "I have to go. If you need to contact me again, please call my lawyer." He lowered the phone and stabbed at the button. Then he marched toward her.

So maybe Delaney wasn't his girlfriend.

She almost flinched away from the angry storm of emotions preceding him. Then he softened right before her eyes—the muscles in his face, the set of his shoulders, the way he swung his arms, the anger in his step—it all melted away until he sighed as he sank onto the ground next to her.

"Are you okay?" he asked in a voice one-hundred-and-eighty-degrees different than the one he just used with Delaney on the phone.

To her horror, Joey sniffled, and that only triggered a

new floodgate of emotions to open. She managed to shake her head as tears flowed down her face once more.

543

Sneak Peek! Joey Chapter Two:

Adam just wanted to go home. The problem was, he didn't have anywhere in Coral Canyon that truly felt like his. The rental he'd been living in since he'd moved here six months ago had been a blank canvas when he'd rented it, and it still held white walls, beige carpet, and zero personality.

Now that he'd be staying in Coral Canyon for the foreseeable future, he'd be buying something. But he hadn't had time to look yet.

He hated the sight of Joelle Young crumbled against the side of the house, sobbing. And he'd be an astronomical fool and a total tool if he didn't do something to comfort her. Therefore, he found himself doing the most natural thing in the world: he lifted his arm and pulled the weeping woman into his side.

He wasn't sure what had happened. She held a tissue,

but she didn't seem to be bleeding anywhere. This could be emotional trauma from something someone had said, or physical pain from stubbing her toe against any number of piles of boxes in the house.

No matter what, the fiercely protective and possessive streak inside him reared up. He would do anything to protect her and make sure that she didn't have to feel like this again. He hushed her and whispered, "You're okay. I've got you."

And he stroked her soft, silky hair over her shoulder, his heart screaming at him that it had been far too long since he'd held a woman like this. Years since he'd had a girlfriend for any length of time.

Morris's parents had just arrived at the house when Delaney Alabaster had called him, and he'd ducked out of the way. But Morris wanted to make the announcement that he would be retiring at the end of the year as Country Quad's manager...and Adam would be taking over. They'd work together for the next couple of months as Morris brought him up to speed on everything Country Quad had been doing for the past dozen years. And then Adam would be on his own to field all the concert requests, the emails, the interview calls, and social media.

The four Young brothers, still mega country music stars in their own right, needed a manager, and Morris wanted to be a father. Harry had decided to manage his own career, which was just as large as Country Quad, but Adam had never really done business things for Harry. He'd handled Harry's personal affairs, and the young man simply didn't need him to run to the ATM, find him some reading glasses, or go pick up his take-out any longer.

All of the Country Quad brothers, plus Morris, knew of Adam's new job, but no one else did.

He felt like he'd swallowed a freight train that was trying to chug its way up a hill. The taste of metal and grease and smoke seemed to constantly be in his mouth, no matter how much he drank or how he tried to swallow it away.

He couldn't wait until this announcement was out, and he could find a house with a home office and get started in this new phase of his career. Band management wasn't quite the same as personal assisting, though his meticulous eye for detail and his excellent networking skills would certainly come in handy. Plus, he knew a lot of people in the country music industry because of his work with Harry for the past year and a half.

He tipped his head back and looked up into the sliver of sky that he could see between the rooftop and the tree branches and whispered, "Dear Lord, help me." Not only with his new job and the Young family, but specifically with Joey. He tilted his head down to look at her and she looked up at him.

Her pale blue eyes became the most beautiful thing Adam had seen in a long, long time. He'd had no idea that robin's egg blue was his favorite color, but oh, it was. It so was.

She blinked, and he swore the blue in her eyes darkened. It mirrored that of a lake now, and Adam wanted to dive into that crystalline-blue water. He'd even be okay if he drowned there.

His pulse bobbed in his neck, telling him that he wanted something with this woman. What, he wasn't sure, but he could start with something simple like coffee. He licked his lips and reached out to wipe the tears away from her left cheek. "You okay?"

"I don't know," she said.

"Did someone say something?" Because he would seriously find them and lay into them until *they* were the one crying out of sight on the side of the house.

She shook her head and wiped the other side of her face. "No, it was stupid. I just ran into a cupboard door."

"You're not stupid," he whispered.

"I just...." She trailed off and didn't continue. Adam didn't know her at all, so he couldn't presume to figure out why running into a cupboard had prompted her to hide from her family and sob into her knees.

"I didn't mean to hear your phone call," she said. "You came around the corner really fast, and you didn't see me at first."

"It's fine," he said. "It doesn't matter." He heard the hardness in his voice come back and he swallowed to get it to go away.

His phone chimed. Since he never let it get very far away from him, he heard it loud and clear. The weight of his device sometimes pounded him into the ground by noon, but he couldn't just leave it behind. He worked with celebrities, and they expected him to be on call twenty-four-seven. In fact, they *paid* him very well to be available at all hours.

As a band manager, it would be far easier because this was *retired* band management, and Adam might be able to get an hour away from his phone to go on a date, or get a massage, or simply go running up the canyon.

His life had definitely been a little bit out of control, though Harry had been one of his least demanding clients.

"Do you still work in that cupcake place?" he asked.

"Yeah," she said. "They promoted me to a baker." A hint of brightness entered her expression, and Adam smiled at her. Her eyes dropped to his mouth and quickly rebounded to his and then flitted away. Adam had seen other women look at him like this, and his heart grew a size and then sprouted wings.

Could Joey be interested in him too?

He shook the thought away, not sure what to do with it. His phone chimed again, and then again. Then it rang. He sighed the mother of all sighs and looked at it. Morris's name sat there, and reality came rushing back at Adam.

He had no idea what time it was, but it didn't matter. Morris had said he wanted to make the announcement when his parents arrived, and he'd likely gathered everybody into the main living room of the house to do exactly that.

With his right arm around Joey, he was slower picking up his phone and swiping to answer the call. He'd moved too slow, and the call ended before he could tap it on.

He swore under his breath, and with his left hand, tried

to dial Morris back, but he wasn't as ambidextrous as he'd like to be. He couldn't quite do it before his phone started ringing again. This time Tex's name shone on the screen, and Adam managed to swipe on the call and say, "I'm on my way in."

"Yeah, we lost you, bro. Where'd you go?"

Adam looked at Joey, and she brought her gaze back to his.

"I got a phone call," he said. "I need a minute."

"All right," Tex said good-naturedly. "We're all in here waiting for you."

Adam could only imagine what Tex would look like when he walked in the house with Joey—probably ready to take a weed whacker and give him a haircut with it. He let Tex hang up, put his phone back down on the ground next to him, and said, "I've got to go in, sweetheart."

He swore someone else controlled his body as he reached up, took her ponytail in his hand, and ran his fingers down the length of it, letting the hair slide through. She looked at him, and he gazed back at her, an invitation for coffee sitting right there on the tip of his tongue. He couldn't quite get the words to go out, and she sat up and leaned away from him.

"What did they want?" she asked.

Adam's brain misfired because he'd forgotten that she didn't know that he was going to be Country Quad's manager—*her daddy's manager*, he thought. Adam felt sick to his stomach.

No wonder God hadn't let him speak a dinner invitation

and make a complete fool of himself. He scooted away from Joey and got to his feet, then extended his hand to her. "Your uncle has an announcement," he said, donning his professional skin again.

He'd hidden feelings for women before. He could do it again. He and Joey's paths didn't cross that often, and she didn't even live at home. Besides, once he had a house and a home office, he'd call Country Quad to him. He wouldn't go to them.

She dusted off her backside, then turned and went around the back of the house where Adam had come from the front. He glanced back that way, then followed her instead. The backyard sat empty, the big lot extending out diagonally from the back of the house to include at least an acre of lawn. There were some apple trees back here, and a shed over against the fence where the cement pad ended. Tools and small yard machines still sat out in front of the shed, and Adam hated moving with everything inside him.

Of course, he didn't have a wife and five children, and a solitary move was far easier than what Morris and Leigh had to accomplish.

Joey slid open the sliding glass door about the time Adam realized that they'd be walking in and facing the entire Young family together, as if they were together as a couple. Before he could say anything, she stepped inside, and she'd barely moved out of the way before Adam did too.

He managed to stop then, but he'd already committed himself to the lion's den. Every eye came to him or Joey, and he felt the weight of their stares like gravity pushing, push-ing, pushing him down into the ground.

"Well," Trace said in his homicidal cowboy tone. "Where have you two been?"

Thankfully, he didn't speak too loud, and Morris, who held a mic, said, "All right, now that everyone's here, we have an announcement to make." He nodded around the room and said, "Can I get Tex, Trace, Otis, and Luke over here?"

"What is going on?" someone demanded from Adam's left. Murmurs ran through the family, and Adam side-stepped behind a couple of teenagers, hoping to disappear completely from Joey's side.

She'd moved too, and he found her standing with Harry and Belle, which was the worst place possible for Adam. He wasn't sure how Harry would feel about him taking a job with his uncles and daddy, and Adam once again questioned the decision he'd made.

He hadn't felt like he'd made it irrationally or impul-sively. Morris had approached him the moment he'd returned from Belle's meet-and-greet in Nashville. He'd said several of his contacts had told him how amazing the meet-and-greet was and how much they enjoyed meeting Adam specifically.

He'd outlined his desire to retire, be a full-time dad so he didn't miss his kids growing up, and Morris had offered Adam a contract with Country Quad as their manager. Everyone had already signed off on it, even Harry's daddy, though they hadn't told anyone.

It was a million dollars a year to live in small-town Wyoming and manage a retired band of four country music stars.

A million dollars.

Adam had had a few interviews in Nashville, only one of which had produced a job offer from an up-and-coming female country music star who'd landed a three-album deal. It would have been like working with Harry from the beginning, but she was spoiled and demanding, and Adam had not truly enjoyed their first interaction.

But he needed a job.

Rather, he needed something to do. Because in truth, Harry had paid him very well, as had some of his previous celebrity clients, and Adam had plenty of money in the bank. He simply wasn't an idle man. He wouldn't know what to do with himself if all twenty-four of his hours every day truly belonged to him.

"All right," Morris bellowed into the microphone. "Everyone settle down."

Luke said, "Dude, you're holding a mic. You don't need to yell."

That caused some in the crowd to laugh, and Adam told himself he better be happy. He better put on his professional celebrity skin. He better be ready to shake hands and hug and give explanations.

He paused at the end of the island where he could see Morris and the rest of Country Quad.

"Right, right," Morris said. "Sorry, but everyone just keeps talking."

"That's why you have the mic." Tex grinned out to everyone.

Morris ignored him and kept going. "We wanted to make a quick announcement. First, thank you so much for coming to help Leigh and I move today. We've ordered food from our favorite place, Pork and Beans. It'll be here in half an hour, so make sure you stick around long enough to get fed. Shawn's going to set up a tent out in the driveway, since it's kind of chaotic in the house."

"Yes, thank you!" Leigh yelled without a mic, and plenty of people heard her.

Morris grinned down the line of his brothers. "Country Quad is retired, but I didn't retire with them. I've still been working on managing their appearances, their requests, and their social media. They still get paid all the time. Someone has to manage that, and there's plenty that goes on residually even after someone retires." He paused and took a big breath, his dark eyes taking on a heaviness they hadn't had a moment ago.

"So they need a new band manager, because I'm going to retire at the end of the year."

Murmurs moved through the Young family crowd, and they definitely constituted *a crowd*. People started to chatter over each other, and Morris said, "Don't make me yell into this thing again," in kind of a yell.

Adam grinned at him and folded his arms.

"So, the five of us are all real happy to say we've brought on Adam Harmon as the new band manager for Country Quad."

The words sat there, echoing through the house from the amplification of the microphone.

Then someone shrieked, several people gasped, and Harry himself said, "You have got to be kidding me," in a voice definitely loud enough for everyone to hear without a mic.

"Come on up, Adam," Morris said, and Adam moved through the crowd of teens, adults, and children until he stood next to Morris. He smiled out at everyone and raised his hand as if they didn't know who he was. Of course they did.

"Good, yeah," Morris said, "Harry, make yourself useful and take our picture so we can announce our staffing change on our social media." Adam stood next to Morris with Tex and Trace pressing in on his right side and Otis and Luke pressing in on his left.

Morris lowered the mic, and Harry's wasn't the only camera held high taking pictures. Adam only looked at his, though, and when he lowered it, he met his best friend's eyes. Harry didn't seem like he'd commit murder in the next ten seconds, and Adam's gaze automatically fell to those who had been close to him, Belle and then Joey.

Now, *she* definitely looked like she was about to go postal and commit some sort of homicide here in this room.

She glared back at him, her arms folded, and one skinny hip cocked out, and he knew then that she wasn't going to commit homicide. She wanted to commit Adam-icide. She scoffed loud enough for him to hear, then turned and stomped out of the house.

Adam watched her go, noting that he wasn't the only one. In fact, her daddy said, "What's wrong with Joey?" which sent a tremor of fear right down to his heels that rebounded up to the top of his head.

Then he got swarmed by other members of the Young family congratulating him, and he came face to face with Harry, who said, "You dirty dog. You did not say a word," before he grabbed onto him and hauled him into a hug. As he clapped him on the back, he said, "I'm so glad you get to stay in Coral Canyon."

Adam was too, or he had been until he'd seen that murderous look on Joey's face. He should just leave well enough alone. But he knew he wouldn't. He'd have to find her and ask her why him being the manager of Country Quad had upset her so much.

And maybe, just maybe, they could discuss it over coffee and cupcakes.

I WANT SOME COFFEE AND CUPCAKES WITH ADAM! Preorder JOEY by scanning the QR code with your phone.

Mav (Book 0): Meet Maverik Young, the cowboy country music star ready to hang up his guitar strings in favor of being a father.

Oh, and he'd like a good woman to settle down with in Coral Canyon too, please. :)

Tex (Book 1): He's back in town after a successful country music career. She owns a bordering farm to the family land he wants to buy...and she outbids him at the auction. Can Tex and Abigail rekindle their old flame, or will the issue of land ownership come between them?

Otis (Book 2): He's finished with his last album and looking for a soft place to fall after a devastating break-up. She runs the small town bookshop in Coral Canyon and needs a new boyfriend to get her old one out of her life for good. Can Georgia convince Otis to take another shot at real love when their first kiss was fake?

Morris (Book 3): Morris Young is just settling into his new life as the manager of Country Quad when he attends a wedding. He sees his ex-wife there—apparently Leighann is back in Coral Canyon—along with a little boy who can't be more or less than five years old... Could he be Morris's? And why is his heart hoping for that, and for a reconciliation with the woman who left him because he traveled too much?

Trace (Book 4): He's been accused of only dating celebrities. She's a simple line dance instructor in small town Coral Canyon, with a soft spot for kids...and cowboys. Trace could use some dance lessons to go along with his love lessons... Can he and Everly fall in love with the beat, or will she dance her way right out of his arms?

Blaze (Book 5): He's dark as night, a single dad, and a retired bull riding champion. With all his money, his rugged good looks, and his ability to say all the right things, Faith has no chance against Blaze Young's charms. But she's his complete opposite, and she just doesn't see how they can be together...

...so she ends things with him.

Gabe (Book 6): He's a father's rights advocate lawyer with a sweet little girl. She's fighting for her own daughter. Can Gabe and Hilde find happily-ever-after when they're at such odds with one another?

Jem (Book 7): He's still healing from his vices, and Jem has dedicated everything he has to his two kids. At least he's not mourning his divorce anymore, and in fact, he might be ready to move on. She's his former best friend, and once he breaks his wrist, his nurse. Can Sunny somehow rope this cowboy's heart?

Luke (Book 8): He swore off women when his ex told him he might not be their daughter's father. But a paternity test confirmed he is, and Luke Young has dedicated his life to his little girl and his brothers' band. There hasn't been time for a girlfriend anyway. He's tried here and there, and the women in small-town Coral Canyon are certainly interested in him.

But he's been thinking about his massage therapist for a while now. Can he ask Sterling out when all they've ever been is professional? Oh, and there's the fact that she's seen practically every inch of his body... Awkward, right?

Bryce (Book 9): Bryce Young has been broken and drifting for years. After giving up his son for adoption, he left Coral Canyon and hasn't returned...until now.

Harry (Book 1o): He's looking to make a change from his country music stardom, but the woman who's caught his eye isn't convinced he's permanent enough for her... Can Harry and Belle work out their differences to find a happily-ever-after?

Joey (Book 11): He's a renowned celebrity assistant, now taking over as manager for Country Quad, the legendary band of Young Brothers. She's a young cowgirl trying to find her place in life and her family. Can Joey take a leap of faith and land safely in Adam's arms? Or will small town gossip and expectations crush them both?

About Liz

Liz Isaacson writes inspirational romance, usually set in Texas, or Wyoming, or anywhere else horses and cowboys exist. She lives in Utah, where she writes full-time, takes her two dogs to the park everyday, and eats a lot of veggies while writing. Find her on her website at www.feelgoodfiction-books.com.

9 781638 763802